this side
that side
the middle

By

Chris Travis

W & B Publishers
USA

W & B Publishers

For information:
W & B Publishers
Post Office Box 193
Colfax, NC 27235
www.a-argusbooks.com

ISBN: 978-1-94298104-6
ISBN: 1-94298104-X

Book Cover designed by Dubya
Printed in the United States of America

Chapter 1

El Lobo Maldito

J.J. Martinez, born Jose Jesus Martinez, a.k.a. The Wolf, or El Lobo Maldito, was not evil by nature. Some considered him unscrupulous and perhaps he was, for he was not governed by the same laws as ordinary men. El Lobo followed no rules save for the few his employer Globe Hood demanded, but those were hardly exacting. The universe of his existence included the ten-thousand hectare farm that served as Hood's main agricultural production and distribution facility. Dirt roads, glorified wagon trails that now carried pick-ups criss-crossed the property separating furrowed fields planted to soy, corn, strawberry, peas, carrots, potatoes, onions and on and on. As Hood's omnipresent foreman and solver of all problems big and small the laws that governed El Lobo were more the esoteric concerns of precipitation, the mundane of turned soil, logistical nightmare of produce delivery and immediacy of fungal pathogen.

The slaughter house was perched on the far edge of the property, keeping the blood and guts as far from the other products as possible. Behind the slaughter house sat the squat, fat butcher shop that catered exclusively to Hood and his wealthy friends. Personal meat storage, beautifully tiled space with drains in the floor and muscled men making clean precise cuts. El Lobo had done some carving in there a few times himself. Sometimes Hood's enemies needed to learn. Another responsibility that fell under the umbrella of his job title.

The greenhouse complex in the approximate center was impressive and one of El Lobo's favorite structures. The A-frame design repeated hundreds of times running E-W and N-S such that from above the complex looked like a giant glass letter-X, X marks the spot. A large tank abutted the northern limit of the greenhouses, a gray water storage tank, used by Hood and El Lobo, his foreman in all things, to irrigate greenhouse and field crops with recycled water, full of nutrients, made the plants happy.

A kilometer distant a towering fifteen-story geodesic dome stood like a glittering glass sphere, the symbolic heart of the farm and the research and development center. Within the giant glass bauble Hood employed lab coat-wearing scientists to experiment with genes, chemicals and anything that could maximize profit.

Surrounding the greenhouses, the farm undulated; a patchwork quilt of green and brown agricultural prosperity, stitched together by the red-dirt roads that provided safe passage for illegal farm worker. The field hands usually kept bandanas over their mouths to protect them from inhaled fertilizer or pesticide, repeated a thousand times. Fallow fields here and there, El Lobo was schooled and educated, he knew enough to keep almost a dozen large fields fallow every year; rotate, rotate. There was one field that he would never plant again, never let anyone work again—no one noticed. He allowed wood lot and patches of secondary successional tree and shrub to grow between active fields, thick with juniper, maples, holly, pine. Hood forever lamented the loss of arable land, El Lobo ignored him. Healthy forest and wind rows decreased runoff and erosion, kept the black gold that was soil on their fields, kept healthy flora and fauna to pollinate, interact and make the farm more resilient.

Row after row after row, drive by, bounce and jostle, strobe-like view down each row, flicker, flicker, illegals bent double, handkerchiefs, bandanas on face after face. Thick black eyebrows, black eyes peered at him like a thousand bandits lying in wait, ready to spring their trap. Too bad they were the ones trapped. Head west along a dirt road fifteen feet wide, not at all level, squeal and squeak of his truck's suspension, click of his teeth, almost bite his tongue off with all the damn bouncing. Pull out half smoked cigar, chew on something.

Red-brown soil caked into rills and ruts where grooved wheels left tracks the last time the road was wet. Tufts of Kentucky-blue grass, plantain, ragweed flanked the road, spikes waved in the gentle breeze. Hedgerow of cedar and hawthorn planted close to the north side of the road separated the adjacent field of soy from the road he bounced along in rusted out pickup. The trunks of the cedars were about eight inches in diameter, and their canopies stretched to fifteen feet tall. The hawthorns, about the same diameter at the trunk, were ten feet tall. To the south was an untouched piece of forest that separated Hood's property from the barrio.

He left the woods for the workers, for the wildlife, for the kids to party in. A diverse array of pine, maple, some hemlock, oak, the occasional birch and hickory made up the large tract. The dirt road undulated up and down. Workers passed to and fro across and along the road, some waved, but most kept their eyes down. The building in the distance slowly marched up the horizon as he crested over and descended the last hill. A red rectangular barn, converted to apartments for illegals, tucked next to the woods and the barrio, edge of Hood's property. El Lobo had chores to take care of, illegals to handle, plants to harvest, farm to run, money to make. After that, alcohol to drink, pain to numb.

Such mischievous behavior trended to and fro, farm field and greenhouse, cantina and pub, ale and whiskey. Borrowed time from shadowy meander, hazed and confused. El Lobo stumbled through the darkness of lost memory. The passageways of his mind riddled like halls of Swiss-cheese. Missing pieces here and there, gaping holes of lost time, put down somewhere, circle shaped moments that couldn't be found for the life of him. Glimpse here, remembrance there, like peeking through mini-blinds, or hidden behind a curtain. A smile here a song there, lost to him, though he was unsure if lost forever. One such lost moment returned recently. He felt the urge to check with the witness to see if her Swiss-cheese matched his forgotten hole.

El Lobo wasn't sure if she sat on his lap or if he lay on her chest, but the memory was his face on her chest. Pressed against the sweet smell of shadow, fragrant hair tumbled over his face and tickled his cheeks. Breath of sunshine, silk of the soul. Words tumbled from his mouth though ears could not hear the ramblings of retrieved memory. She was who..., he couldn't say.

The death of an innocent during the dark moments of lost time, not his innocence, that was long dead. The remnant of deed, like a taste in his mouth. The idea of the act and the mystery of provocation left him filled with wonder. Had there been a fool's part to play? To whom had the role been assigned? He'd been a court jester once, not a horrible gig, all that buffooning grew old, as did the sound of jingling bells and that nasal whine. The guitar's strum and drunken voices echoed through the cantina those nights, and through his skull.

The simplified cobweb, straightened and examined is alarming in its beauty, awe inspiring in its promise of death. The nice becomes the naughty. A plain looking demeanor and comely gait present a labyrinth of wonderment. Lost, he wandered through corners so dark sound was muted. He skated home through said darkness, right past the den of inequity that passed as a police station. On the edge of the barrio, perched so it leaned over the poor, ready to strike, ready to mind, ready to incarcerate. The pulse of wine hammered through veins swollen with revelry. Memories lost forever, or for a time yet to be determined. Would they wash upon the shores of his mind? Messages in bottles thrown out to the sea in desperate hope for rescue. Rescue from the darkness.

Follow the white rabbit, they told him, The Wolf talked to himself. Lay on his back, made snow angels on the lawn, despite the lack of snow. Through the looking glass and over the bridge, into the woods to grandmother's house we go. He had forgotten he would never be the helpful hunter, but always the Wolf, come to eat them all. But what wolf would forget his intention, his nightmares, his ravenous appetite? Music soothes the savage beast, lest the nightmare become part of the waking world, crossing from the wisps of psyche to the flesh of earth. Auntie night sheathed deeds in obscurity and shrouded the moments of realization with mayhem. Only night knows. Lights out, cheese wheels and Swiss-cheese, forgotten dreams and remembered realities, left the Wolf wondering which was which.

The texture and nuance of thought echoed down the halls of his mind. What went on in the arc of each synapse? Nostalgia evoked, the smell of summer grass, longing pangs, the smell of her hair in his face, chest and head, heart and loins, heat and doubt. Cascading ions of charge, transmitters arrived with keys to the locks of his mind. Ions opened doors to dark and poorly lit rooms, full of shadows, cobwebs and thoughts better left un-thought. Beware those, lest one should act and give wing to denizens of shadowy places; darkness moved with those thoughts, blotted out the light, his little secret. El Lobo rolled through the darkness in search of the darkest shadow, the darkest of the lot. That one please, the better to see you with my dear. Oh Little Red, his canines were sharp and the shadows were deep into which he would drag her. Feast on her flesh, so supple and sweet, his tongue would lick the freckles right off her skin. Salty tears to season her cheeks, scented so lovely with auburn locks.

"Do not struggle little Riding Hood," he would say to her. "The more you struggle more it will hurt, I aim to swallow you whole."

He stumbled home, wondered who really knew what they bumped into in the dark. Oh sure, he bumped into a table leg, stubbed his toe, a child's toy stabbed his sole, made him cry and swear. Those were the easy notions to grasp. But what of the bump in the night that came with a flutter of movement in the corner of the eye just as you opened them? What of the shadows that huddled in the corner of the room, even when the lights are on? Was he the only one that saw them? What of the void, the silence that waited when he woke in the morning? For one reason or another he could never quite put his finger on the why of those in-betweens.

Could it be all the molecules and atoms assuming the position as it were? The position defined by his perception, a place for everything and everything in its place. Did the molecules go about their business whilst his brain ceased its tyranny over their roles each night while he slept? He stumbled into the other him that night. Shuffling down the hallway, half-awake, there he was. Scruffy shuffle to the bathroom, his mirror image answered nature's call. El Lobo had forgotten about his other, the domesticated boring him, the one he wanted to be, shoved in the garage of his mind with all his tools. In the empty space between thought and recognition the other Lobo smiled, waved, punched him in the face.

Morning's arrival, tip-toed quietly, almost missed her coming in. Rise to greet his Mrs. Wolf, Isabella returned from a night at the cantina they owned. Her goodnight was his rise and shine, off to work he went. Strolled through the cloud that still slept in the back yard, nestled next to the creek and willow. The absurdity of it all, trapped and released by the necessities of survival. The field and a full day's work, keep the mind occupied, take something home to Mrs. Wolf. Forest path wound here and there, early morning meander and loli-gag. Thin line through the brush, worn by the wanderings of misguided doe or buck it joined with the larger trail delineated by wheel ruts.

The Wolf caught a flash of movement in his peripheral vision, his being sharper than most. The flicker of red crested the hill in the distance, the Red Hood moved toward him, El Lobo loped in the opposite direction, picked up his pace. He should've taken the truck but he liked the dying days of summer too much, the sweet smell of morning, the slow burn of rising sun. On to check the field and greenhouses, warehouses and main office, keep an eye on the workers.

Wheels and ruts, grooves and spokes. Clay becomes dust for want of water. The path was well worn from decades of wheels hauling people and things to and fro across the sprawling plantation that counted as the holdings of a Mr. Globe Hood. Reputedly of good stock and noble forefathers, Mr. Hood had strayed somewhat from the family credo of robbing the rich and giving to the poor. His personal philosophy and zest stemmed from ideals more in line with those of a certain Sheriff and false prince his forefather purportedly thwarted centuries past. As such, his concern for his workers was genuine, in the way a carpenter guards his blades, the forester his ax.

Like said instruments he went to great lengths to ensure their efficiency, sharpness, ergonomic function, and comfort. But should one of these tools break; repair was more costly, less efficient than replacement. Broken tools were disposed of, a tool becomes obsolete, non-functional in many ways. Rust and corrosion, the merciless hand of time robbed keenness from the edge, awareness from the mind, joints became feeble, work left undone. A tool became outdated, full of function, but unable to perform same old tasks with new hoops, hurdles or prerequisites. Stumbling blocks to a job well done meant goodbye. Poor dejected tool, ignorance is never bliss.

One section of the forest was mostly hemlock, smelled bitter of decaying needles, fresh humus and moisture of the creek that bubbled past. Amanita scurried here and there, flanked by the shyer boletes and numerous others. Fungi silently breaking the world; bring out your dead and they will live again. His claws scraped roots, exposed purple wooden flesh masked beneath gray flaking bark. Nettles sting the skin if they can penetrate the coat. Pish-posh silly grouse, beat not till he hath past. Crawdads filter beneath limestone rock, crystal cool bath of a domicile, how lovely for them. Padded feet splash through clear refreshing stream. Clean enough for a drink for the daring.

El Lobo Maldito dared. Pink tongue flashed, water is life, smooth, cleansed mouth, throat, chest, gut, good. He kept company with ground cedar, wintergreen, goldenseal, Indian cucumber root, blueberry, ironwood, hemlock, hickory, oak, the gallery of plant life. Forest flows over flesh and ears to eyes, nose, settled on the tongue with the taste of a place. Cascade of Earth Mother's fine handy-work sent synapses aflutter with the here. A Hare, a Hawk, ha Frog, ha Snake. Circles intertwine, bound who and what, why and where. Trot-on, trot-on, friend Wolf, touch-me-not, hate-me-not, honeysuckle, snap dragon. The Wolf worked because he must, heave and scurry, search and hurry. Follow orders if he had to, but much better to do than to follow.

And so it was that she had drawn very near before he noticed her. She was close enough he smelled the sweet sweat on her neck. Insolent lass she was, though El Lobo worried not, his business was none of such low import to be waylaid by boss's daughter. He felt it in passing. Felt the slightest tickle, her finger stroked the tip of his hair, the in-between ethereal nothingness of oxygen, nitrogen, and carbon molecules that separated her hand from his coat. Ever so slight, light as a breeze, she smiled or smelled of laughter rather. He couldn't see her face. Little Red, next time Mr. Wolf thought, he might ask her name, her true name.

The next day Miss Katherine Hood, a.k.a Capucha Roja or Little Red Hood, found him on his way home, again. Whether she knew his route through the woods to the barrio or happenstance once again lay a trap for the pad-footed predator was never clear. She slipped up next to him, red rain boots and red cloak, didn't say a word, only held his hand. Little Red held his hand all the way there, she leading him, it wasn't at all the way people told the story years later. She held his hand and undressed like a woman, without batting an eye yet managed to keep the sweet look on her face. She folded into him and he felt the heat of her sigh on his neck. Her soft breasts warmed his chest, sputtering embers burst into blazing inferno.

There in the deepest, darkest, moss-covered hollow she could find he lay with her. The girl and the monster collide, the beauty and the beast intertwine, Red Hood and Big Bad ride to ecstasy, to infinity, to nothingness. He smashed into her and she into him, lock and key. Opening, glowing, humming, vibrating goodness. Overflowed through, in, around, over, above, below, within, without, onto the here, there and everywhere. Whilst then, when, never, now and forever. Before they knew it they had burned, blazed, branded into their flesh, seared into their memory of forever, that night of soil-stained bliss. A precious momentary flash, resound, remembered, evoke, tear, fear, joy, sorrow. The crush of Lobo and Red resonated through the two, through groin and pelvis, teeth and jaw, into the earth, out to the heavens. He savored the moment of devouring, the supple flesh so candied, lightly flecked with freckles and all beautiful, all delicious. Fine and delicate, precious and nourishing did give life and love unto they. Neither he nor she would have it any other way.

There in the dark hollow of the wood on a bed of moss and fern, her red cloak for a blanket, she was his. With flowers in her hair, she opened herself, and he devoured her luscious flesh, savored every drop of sweet nectar; candied lips, muscles tight, flavor pearled on the tongue, toes curled into soil, neck and mouth, chest and gut, goodness gracious, in and out, please never, never stop, danced all night. Pulled hair, scratched skin, bit again, and again. Her legs, his teeth, little fists, hand-full of fur, please, yes, please, nails, thighs, obliques, ribs, breasts, neck, mouth, eternity, infinity, wings, rebirth, death, heaven, hell, ash, ember, clouds, sun, sky...dance all night.

It's true; El Lobo Maldito left her there, in the hollow beneath the hummock in a bed of moss and fern, with flowers in her hair. If you asked Red, she would've stayed forever in said sepulcher. The collision of two celestial bodies is not easily extinguished, as the meteor burns, large and small, smash and crash. Atmosphere or no, burn and burn, ash and dust. Stand back, Carbon, Nitrogen, Potassium, Sodium, Phosphorus, the rest. Molecules, time, space. Wolf, Red Hood, humus, fern, moss, love, loss. Padding footsteps of away, till gone. Alone she lay for but a moment, light of day crept like infant over the edge of yonder ridge.

Red Hood coasted home, warmth spread through chest and ha-ha, what a lovely day. Sunrise, rays skip through onto the next day. To Gloria's house she went, hummed a lovely song of flowers, moss, fur and fern.

After devouring the Red Hood, El Lobo fell ill. Not in the physical sense of viral contagion or bacterial infection. The chest cavity in which his heart beat felt inflamed, as if Red left a piece of herself lodged within his breast. The wound festered for the better part of a month before he was able to breathe crisp morning air without the weight of a peck of stones on his chest. Fresh air, mental exercise and physical exhaustion were the best remedy, the only remedy. He mulled and meditated for hours, trying to detour thoughts skidding headlong toward the inflamed, infirm heart. Still, drips and drops slipped through. Sweet nectar of her flower, drip, drops across thighs, glistening, trapped in whisker and chin. Tongue darted to savor and taste. Claw and scrape, away, away, from the iron-maiden that pierced viscera, mesentery, artery, muscle, brain and blood. Crimson pools of life blood is slick on tile, muddy in the forest. Claw, scrape, away, away.

He took great care to avoid the prize specimen. Miss Hood and her red cloak were easy enough to spot, though he quickly learned not to depend on her clothing to recognize her. He could smell her now, more than ever, even when she was absent he smelled her. El Lobo retreated, to cantina, garage, bedroom, greenhouse. The alpha male distracted in alcohol anesthetic, the mock smoke and mirrors of male endeavor. Cathartic or otherwise the bottom of a mug of beer helped. He managed to avoid her, only just, but her voice still caught him at times. Around the corner of a building, at the end of a corn row, in the office supply closet, he couldn't escape that torturous voice.

His desire to devour her again was so great he wept the first time her voice caught him unawares. Since, he fled from her with all the speed he could muster. Still she found him, one night in the cantina, his cantina, in his shadow. The back booth, red vinyl, red lights, seats cracked, frayed threads and foam cushion exposed to stale bar smoke, swears, ash and asses. What a proper thing like she could possibly be up to in a squalid, fetid, irreconcilable place was beyond all the wisdom El Lobo had in his whiskers. Isabella, his wife, watched from the bar.

They did itch mightily, his whiskers, they twitched madly at the sight of Katherine Hood. When he approached, moth to flame, butterfly to guano, beast to beauty, she did not recoil. She did not snatch her hand away, nor did she shirk his touch. Instead greeted his Wolfish grin with her own knowing smile. He was too drunk to care.

Tortured voices chased El Lobo through the landscape of his dreams. Not the sonic waves generated by a singular set of vocal chords or tremendous wind of contracting diaphragm, but the tossing, turning, panicked screams of hope and angst. The pitter-patter of ogre feet on the fortitude of his will. Draws he, draws he; draws the soul. The siren's song undermined intention, tossed by the wayside when the ogre kicked the windows out. Try to try, may just stumble onto that for which he searched. Magic is everywhere, hidden within the frailty of the inconsequential, the strength in the smallest particle, sparkling eyes, smiling lips, the beauty of the female form.

The want, the grasping need was so powerful it nearly drove him mad. Time helped. A month after feasting on Little

Red he emerged from his stupor. To the relief of Mrs. Wolf, who suspected her mate was seriously ill. He picked flowers from the forest and placed them in a vase on the table. She assumed they were for her, but something in the way he stroked their petals.

Each time El Lobo scraped the lass from under his nails, exfoliated all trace of her touch and scent from his skin, she found a way, a way to restore her mark. A glove left by a dirt path, a lock of her hair in his pocket. Whimsical nothings she left for him to find. Convinced himself it was happenstance for a while. She was flighty and prone to fancy, just the type to lose a shoe by the side of the path. Especially should she see some flower or butterfly to chase. Locket of her hair in his pocket, not so easily explained away, but he did somehow. Why would she put her finger on his nerve anyway? A fool is man, and at times so is wolf. Uncanny divination or perhaps unseen vibration strummed and thrummed with the thumb. She knew where to touch him, each and every time, for good or bad.

She touched him so easily and try as he might he was unable to penetrate her defenses. In the fields surrounded by goats, sheep, the oxen-like foreman, she ignored him. He may well have not existed for all the attention she paid him and his shaggy coat, piercing eyes, or lolling tongue. Woe is wolf, searching forever and a day. Days and days they stayed away, he from she and she from he. It was impossible to avoid each other indefinitely; her father owned the place after all. She trotted by on her beautiful horse every day, far in the distance, on the edge of the next field, or the next, or not at all. El Lobo was a Wolf when she stayed away. He would admit the truth to none, that his intestines, his guts begged for a leash each time she came too close. It is a strong sensation for a Wolf, sacrilege even, to want a collar.

Magic lived in-between the ordinary of their lives, her name on his lips every morning. Mundane monotony ruled the diurnal cycles of life and labor. Mundane, esoteric, hum-drum, drum-hum, how now brown cow. Fickle beast is man, slightly less so is Wolf. Dainty and ephemeral were the tangled webs and overlapping trails of her life, crossed his padded paw prints. He chased ghosts, wisps of her scent. He was guilty as sin, even more than. He should have kept his head down, picked fruit, put it in the basket, clone plants, hide in the greenhouse. Shuffle papers, glass conservatory for an office, smell the tomatoes. Miss Hood is not to be looked at that way. He peeked in windows, ducked around corners, and sighed in the shadows. None the wiser, save he. Followed her through the woods, she hummed along on silent feet.

He preferred to stalk her as prey, but refrained, instead watched from afar, content with glimpses from a distance, her scent on a breeze. Keep tabs if he could, though not a luxury afforded a laborer, even one with as much authority as he. There were times he was not sure if he pursued she or she he. The treats she left for him became a game, a given, their little secret. A bone she left for him to chew on, found next to the forest path, same spot as her shoe. She knew he followed her sometimes, as she followed him. He spied her deep in the forest, hunting for flowers again. Milky white blossoms, star-shaped yellows, pink slippers too.

Flowers he could tell her stories about, stories of his father, grandfather, and back through the branch and crotch of family tree. Tickle her cheek, tickle her thigh, petal softer than silk. He woke in the still, deafening, dead of night, cold sweat trickled down neck, sheets soaked through, tears from dammed eyes. Phantom lips, firm and floral scented, crushing him beneath her fervor, ardor burning in her loins, scalding his phallus with her desire. Howl in the night. Mrs. Wolf not at home, howl at the moon, blue like he. Remembrance of fern and flower, her hunger seemed sated, but his not a bit, not a whit; so who ate whom?

Skeletons. Bourgeoisie, royal, and destitute families have few things in common. Skeletons and closets however are two characteristics both share. Regardless of economic or social-class every family has skeletons shoved to the back of a metaphorical closet, guarded jealously by patriarch, matriarch, or the entire clan. There are times when gravity, severity, or plain phenomenal nature of a family skeleton is too much to remain a secret. There are ways secrets will free themselves from the shadowy depths of a closet, squirm and slither, find their way into the light of disclosure.

Such was the nature of the skeleton that inhabited the closet of the Hood family. The twin of which hung like a decorative calavera on the door of El Lobo's bedroom closet. Isabella Anna Martinez, a.k.a Mrs. Wolf or La Bruja, knew something was odd with her man, but couldn't quite put her finger on it. When she asked, he told her; bad news all around. Foul enough and precipitous enough to keep her hands full, mad dash to the cantina, warn who she could. He was calling ICE, tonight. Globe Hood wanted the meddlesome gone, the upstarts, those who organized. The minions of the invisible hand would arrive tonight, in the dead of. Tell who you can while you can he said, sent her running around the barrio with her skirts hiked up, keep the hem out of the muddy ruts. Still, her mind churned, trollop after trollop considered and discarded, she knew misdirection when she smelled it, her Wolf nose fairly twitched. With which of the little whores had her man become entangled? The only woman she'd seen talking to him in the cantina was Katherine, and only while she was waiting to speak with Isabella, heart skipped a beat.

Chapter 2

Ramon Malquiades Mondragon

The living room was full of workers. Work clothes on some, no time to go home and change. A few were squeaky clean, but not many. Many of the workers brought food with them to the unionization meeting. The kitchen table was over-loaded with tamales, flautas, burritos, rice and beans, diced tomatoes with cilantro, cucumber and habanero, and on and on. More food than Ramon had seen on his table since last Thanksgiving.

His mother and father sat in the circle of chairs with the rest of the workers. Heated debate echoed off the tightly spaced walls of the house. Half the neighborhood was there, screaming in English and Spanish, men and women, young and old, clean and dirty, all screaming. No kids though, odd for a meeting of the farm community. On a normal night the place would have been overflowing with kids, wonderful din, barely hear himself think. Not today, this meeting was too important for distrac-tions, left the children at home. Even Ramon, a child no longer, was tolerated more than encouraged to participate. If the meet-ing hadn't been at his house he doubted they would've let him stay. They didn't know he had his own plans to make.

Granted, a baker's dozen of hyperactive, laughing, cry-ing, snot-nosed, skirt-tugging children were not conducive to a constructive meeting. There was one huge negative to leaving the kids at home. Children were always the best sentries. Their adventures, the getting lost, getting found, hide and go seek, fall down and get hurt, made them the best sources of infor-mation. Lacking the pitter-patter of children's little feet, the tag you're it, hide in the yard and go seek up the driveway, inevita-ble outdoor banishment, no one saw the strangers pulling up the drive. The adults inside didn't have to scream over kids, just each other. They didn't hear the crunch of gravel, the snapping of twigs, the hushed whispers of anxious men. Ramon nearly missed it too, sitting on the porch smoking a joint, spacing out thinking about Katherine's breasts.

He didn't notice the lights until they were across the front yard. He stood and screamed.

"La Migra!" And summarily bashed in the face with a shotgun butt, went to sleep.

Unconscious Ramon missed the raid. Black-clad agents wearing full swat gear, goggles, helmets, assault rifles, bullet-proof vests, boots for stomping etc. Armed to the teeth in case the organizing members of the Illegal Farmworker Association decided to fight back with raised machetes, refused to be taken alive. That was not the case. A lot of screaming male and female voices, English and Spanish flying from mouths and teeth begged to surrender. Blood spilled, skulls cracked, broken arms. Get on the ground, if you don't they'll put you there, forcibly. Break an arm, break a leg. Hobble and limp, weeping fools loaded into the ICE van. Snot and blood, beg for release, beg for a phone call.

They didn't take Ramon, or even try to. Like they knew he was legal. Didn't stop them from kicking his unconscious body, cracked a rib, sub-dermal bruise, purple and green in a few days. Invasion. Haunted house come to life. Slaughter of the innocents, or the guilty, depending on who was talking. Round-up, herd 'em up, rope 'em up, throw them into the black bus, barred windows, insulated walls, kept out the screams.

Ramon woke, splitting headache, felt half-dead, dragged himself to his feet. Broken plates, coffee cups, salsa on the floor, chips, rice, a woman's shoe. Some poor woman was weeping her way toward the holding center with only one shoe; it wasn't his mother's, thank goodness. Poor woman. Ramon zombie shuffled through the house, checked every closet, under every bed, in the attic, the crawlspace beneath the house, nothing. Of course not. Back in the kitchen he teeter-tottered a tower of broken plates and cups. Started washing.

"Ramon?" Katherine's voice. Turned, room spun, there she was. Blood Red cloak pulled around her, cowl pulled back, "What happened?"

"ICE." He felt the frown on his face, hot tears in his eyes, frog in his throat.

She crossed the space, two graceful steps, did her feet even touch the ground? She was on him, filled his senses, her head on his chest, floral scent invaded his soul. Muscled velvet, her arms wrapped around him, squeezed the air out of him. Her weeping sobs joined his own.

She directed him to the worn, multicolored, multi-generational sofa, sat him, stroked his head and gasped in shock.

"Oh my God Ramon! Your head!" He hadn't forgotten, or maybe he had, he felt very slow, ponderous.

"Rifle butt." All he could manage. She ran into the bath-room, reappeared with first-aid accoutrement. Got to work dabbing his skull, he saw stars, screamed.

"You need stitches Ramon, come on, let's go." She pulled him to his feet, arm around his waist, walked him to the door, out to her car.

Flash of lights, flicker, flash, high beams, and the wind in his face. Her voice in the background, talking, talking, her white face, red hair shades of gray in the dark, come to life when light hit it. Thin fingers and slender arms gripped the wheel, rubbed his leg, stroked his face at red lights. Her hands were rough, cool, reassuring, heavenly. White blouse looked like cotton, comfortable, open necked, peak at her breasts when she leaned toward him. Confined and constricted beneath black bra, peaks of the mounds like fresh cream. Ramon crushed the guilt that had been bothering him all day, a sentiment flying about his ears like a lamenting mosquito, getting on his food like a green-eyed fly, in his drink like the drunken yellow-jacket. He crushed it into a little black pill and swallowed it down where it was burnt to a cinder by the churning bile roil-ing therein. He would not feel sorrow for the actions he had taken against Hood, the man had it coming.

"I know you're in there somewhere, you perv." Light kiss on the lips, she wanted to keep him engaged, dangle her sex, she knew he was a sucker for her sex. They'd both returned, Degrees in hand. Hers in horticulture, his plant pathology, how genial.

Gone but not forgotten, their high school love affair, budding romance, or awkward teenage experiment. Their shared past lurked in the background like a funny uncle; they were overdue a roll in the hay. Back for months, loose strings of their own, tie them up, get to work on the farm. Time flies. They hadn't spent more than five minutes together, certainly hadn't done any catching up, throb of his skull. She pulled up in front of the hospital, walked him inside.

Several hours, a dozen stitches and thousands of insured dollars later, good benefits being a scientist for Hood, or a legal employee anyway, of which Ramon was one. She took him home. Her home, or apartment rather. Above the corner market she ran in the Barrio, left to her by her mother. Katherine worked in the greenhouse on her days off, experiments of her own. El Lobo let her use the greenhouse and field space she wanted for her trials. The Research Supervisor of the Dome gave her the go-ahead as well. She wasn't on Hood's payroll, only the boss's daughter. Made her money from the Bodega, sold her products there, purchased from Hood at a rock bottom discount, especially if she dealt with El Lobo.

Her apartment was large, same square footage as the store below. On the corner of the block, two of the walls were more window that not. A balcony outside was big enough to accommodate an iron bistro table and chairs. Newspaper forgotten, open pages turned on wind's fingers, back and forth. Sitting area nestled against French doors of the two walls merge into one large lounge, thick red rugs, plush deep cushions. Kitchen and counter space along one of the walls. Marble-topped island across from the stove, shelves and drawers beneath, on wheels, it rolled. She knelt by a cabinet and put a blue tea kettle on to boil, served him hawthorn and rose-hip tea a few minutes later.

Perhaps it was his numbed skull, or numb brain, but it felt like a few minutes later she had him naked in her bed, her naked skin hot against him. She kissed him gently, nibble at his lips, harder then, harder, rough instead. She took the initiative, mounted and rode him, took his member into her, circled her hips, mixed his phallus with her concentric gyrations. Kissed him deeply, she was ravenous, taking from him, searching for something, digging for treasure, find something buried. She placed his hands on her body, moved them here, there, told him to squeeze, bit his lip, apologized when he yelped. Nebula, fog, dust-storm, clear the fog from his brain it didn't.

He told her he was coming, with her panting breath she said she was too, she didn't move. He ejaculated, she mewed into his mouth, contracted muscled of her own, lay panting on his chest. His head was fine after all. She cleaned them up, peck on the lips, climbed into bed next to him.

"I'm not sorry for what I've done." He stared at the far away ceiling, the grooved ridges of the commercial roof faintly visible.

"I'm not sorry either, Ramon. I think we both knew this was going to happen." She stroked his face, lie on her back. Held his hand.

"No, I mean for all the things I've done in the past, and the things I want to do in the future, even if some people get hurt."

"What did you do, Ramon?" His veiled subterfuge was useless on her, always had been.

"You'll see." He played with the red strands of hair splayed across his arm.

"What did you do, Ramon?" Yawn, it had been a long night, sky turning purple in the east.

"You'll see." He left it at that and she didn't force the issue, she lay back with a sigh. He was asleep in seconds. She wasn't in bed when he woke, clock said eleven. His head felt better, called into work, they already knew what happened, of course they understood. Lay back in her bed. He'd never imagined the absurdity of the grand cosmic joke that was his life. In the bed, in the arms of the woman of his dreams, and he a hollowed out wrenching blackness of anger and despair. He'd never been so miserable in his life. Globe Hood would pay.

Chapter 3

Globe Hood

Globe Hood was a son of a bitch. At least to his employees. The shareholders and investors thought otherwise. To them he was a golden boy that could do no wrong, as evidenced by ever increasing profits. In all reality he didn't care one iota what the workers thought, as long as they showed up on time and did as they were told; they could think whatever they wanted. The shareholders were another story. He was not overly fond of any of them, but he did not harbor the same distaste for them as he did for the workers. The investors were at least after the same goal as he, money. Maximize profits and minimize costs, music to his ears.

Papers crowded his over-sized desk, invoices and expense reports he'd poured over the night before. Gathered in a neat pile he placed them in a desk drawer to review once again that evening, just to be sure. Crunching gravel outside and squeaking breaks marked the arrival his foreman. Rusty door protested loudly on opening, minor key squeak close, slam. Globe Hood leaned back in the leather high-backed chair and waited. Jose Jesus Martinez, El Lobo Maldito as the workers referred to him, slipped into the large office, not a sound gave away his arrival. Hard to imagine, the gruff, well-built, chiseled jaw, boot wearing foreman moved so quietly, but quiet he was, and discreet. A characteristic Globe valued beyond words, a necessity for the "other" work related tasks he charged the man with.

Jose Jesus Martinez stopped in front of the large walnut desk. Of all Hood's employees El Lobo held no fear of Hood, an issue that bothered Hood but the price of his necessary evil and well worth it. El Lobo was not cheap, fifteen legal salaried workers would live happily with his pay.

"ICE did their work last night," El Lobo spoke matter-of-factly, "75 workers picked up, the ones we wanted, and Rosalinda." Black eyes under bushy black eyebrows drilled down into Hood's own.

"Rosalinda?" Globe was on his feet, pounding the desk, "Shit! My house will never be clean again, Katherine will never forgive me." A vein throbbed in his neck.

"Collateral damage, Hood. One illegal is the same as the rest to ICE. Doesn't matter if Miss Kate bounced on her knee or not. Perhaps if you make a phone call it is not too late."

El Lobo raised one eyebrow, lowered it again almost immediately.

"I thought not." El Lobo stood, pulled a cigar butt from his breast pocket, threw it between full lips, turned and strode from the room. He left the dark wooden door wide open. Globe Hood snarled at the void space in front of his desk. He wanted to chew something and throw papers on the floor. Instead he stood and walked to the window. The beaten pickup ambled down the rutted dirt road toward the fields and greenhouses kicked up plumes of dust in its wake.

El Lobo intimidated Hood but Hood was just fine with the arrangement as it stood. El Lobo served as spy, enforcer, supervisor, overseer and frequently general contractor. The man would be within his rights to ask triple what he was paid, which would make him a millionaire, and then some. El Lobo was probably already a millionaire, what with the humble adobe house he and the Mrs. shared on the southern edge of the grounds. Shaded and quiet under a lovely large willow and a dry creek that filled when it rained. Globe liked riding his horse by that creek as a boy. The funny thing was, no matter what the man asked Globe would have paid it, he just didn't want the damn Lobo finding out. Fleece him for sure.

He mused silently to himself, wondering how realistic it would be to get some Chinese in here, INS would never deport Chinese, we owed them too much money. He sighed mightily, more illegals would be easy to come by, always were. The flow of illegals had slowed somewhat in the last few years, but he could replace 75 workers in 20 minutes, the Lobo could do it in 5. Goddamn seething masses. Better to be rid of those few upstarts and old-timers. Many of those had been supervisors and now production would be slowed considerably; the price to pay he supposed. Smart men rose to smart positions, too bad they weren't all pliable with threat and compensation.

He hadn't purged such a large group in years, but the downturn, decreasing remittances being sent home and the whisper of an amnesty sent ripples like wildfire through his masses. When El Lobo told him of the whisper of a unionization meeting, that was all he needed to hear, he placed a call. Washed his hands of the whole mess.

If only he could get his hands on some good employees that weren't after benefits or a living wage. How was he supposed to keep this enterprise profitable? Federal subsidies were on the chopping block, god damn liberals, farm bill dammed up forever. He was already branding a quarter of his products as all natural. Of course they were all natural, they were produce, don't worry about the pesticides, herbicides, fertilizers, that was his business. A rather pressing business, according to El Lobo, they were missing a pallet of fertilizer. The thought sent shivers down his spine, he dared not alert anyone, El Lobo could handle it. Hopefully the culprits were now exiled with his phone call and the missing Nitrogenous compound would appear post haste. God-damn immigrant scum.

At any rate the brown bastards needed to get over themselves. His forefathers had done the heavy lifting when they immigrated from Ireland. Grandpa Hood went on and on before he finally died, bless his heart. They had done it, lowly outcasts on coffin ships, now established business family, damn near a legacy. If he could get his Katherine in line. She was difficult since her mother's passing and near intractable since University. Damn liberals. Returned and infected with knowledge she treated him like kryptonite, not that she was superwoman, or he Lex Luthor, but she practically loathed him. Nevertheless she was on his mind. She was to inherit this legacy, and now more knowledgeable than he, at least with the plants, she contributed less than ever. Damn the liberal worms that writhed their way into her head. She came home preaching about huge compost rows, field cuttings and manure she said. He could buy better at .50 cent a gallon. The price was going up lately. Damn Arabs.

Globe Hood respected J.J. Martinez, the God-damned Wolf. No nonsense and all that. Scary fellow, though he wouldn't admit that to a soul. El Lobo winked in his mind's eye and snickered. He knew so goddamned much. Globe shrugged off the specter, only to have it replaced by images of his red-haired daughter. So beautiful, so much like her mother. He hoped not as sexual as her mother, a nightmare for any father. Slither and writhe, bend over baby, he missed her mother.

Shaking the nonsense out of his head, Globe pushed on, he had payrolls to check, inventories to double-check, phone calls to make. The Wolf would take care of the new hires, no problem there.

Set about his business, the morning and remainder of the day passed with ever increasing speed. Phone calls with petroleum interests, natural gas boom underway and the damn liberals in his state were dragging their feet. No matter, he was already waist deep in wells the next state over. A new gas platform, his second, off the east coast. Lucrative that, though the decreasing price of natural gas, damn glut, was hurting the bottom line. He was actually keeping several wells off-line until the prices started to increase again. The feds better let him export some of his gas or there would be hell to pay.

Checked the rent checks from his apartments. An investment started years ago, he and the Lobo retrofit an old barn, forgotten by Globe's father and left to rot. They built dormitory style rooms for the single men and women and a few apartments for Rosalinda, the Lobo and a few other families that had children. That had been almost twenty years ago now. The Lobo had barely been twenty and he Globe barely thirty. Simpler times those. Now his daughter was almost thirty, no longer the ten-year old that helped with hammers and lemonade, but she still visited the apartments sometimes. She had so many friends there. He stopped retrofitting barns after the third one. Too expensive by far. It was far more economical to buy run-down dwellings in the slums that circled the farm. Those houses he didn't need to sink a dime into and provided housing for his workers, two birds, one stone. Thus the money he paid them for their labor came back to him, full circle, God Bless America.

Now the three barns, fifty houses with at least two apartments per house and four apartment buildings were his property holdings. Little or no maintenance budget was necessary, save for those homes the Fed paid the rent for. Those he had to at least give the facade of decency. Goes around, comes around. The three gas stations and five convenience stores were all within walking distance of the properties he owned. Keep his money in his pockets so to speak. All the better to provide his workers with the products they needed, at a small mark up of course. Money makes the world go round. Hey if they didn't like it maybe they would teach their kids to get a better job and they could escape the working class in a generation or two, or five. He chuckled under his breath.

His family did it after all, shipped from Britain to Ireland and from Ireland to the East Coast of the United States. He tried to keep the damn workers from growing their own vegetables in the beginning, he razed two community gardens before El Lobo told him if he did it again he would lose all his workers and wouldn't be able to get more anytime soon. So let it be said Globe Hood made concessions. He let the workers grow their own tomatoes and squash and corn etc. El Lobo pointed out to him the benefit, in fact many of the pests that plagued the large field crops were now localized to the fields that belonged to the workers. How convenient.

He spent the day rifling through report after report. Not good for the digestion the reports El Lobo left for him. The man was systematic down to the last detail, the reports were categorized, organized and concise for ease of use. He could wish for as good from his corporate stiffs. Expense on fertilizers and pesticides led to projected crop yields per field and totals with eye bulging reports that detailed losses to insects, damn bugs, fungus, damn mold, drought, damn drought, E.coli, damn fertilizer. Shit, he couldn't help but pour himself a scotch. Was it noon yet? No matter. He sat back with the food contamination report and promptly sprayed liquor all over his desk.

The report detailed the deaths of several individuals. Reports were as yet unclear but all individuals had been eating mixed salad greens. The question being, was it a Globe industry product? According to some random samples El Lobo had taken in the field and in the processing plant, it could have been. The last report in the bunch, buried under the stack, detailed the seventy-some odd illegals deported that morning. They were ripped from their beds, pajamas and hard-ons, rollers and crotchless panties, in the middle of union meeting, packed onto a cold bus to lock-up. It detailed the budding union movement spearheaded by the employees at Ramon's house and how they made up the command hierarchy and impetus for the movement among the workers.

Hood couldn't bring himself to get through the thing. How could he care? Those fools were gone. E.coli and death were around the corner. Down the street as it were. Damn the luck. Bleeding heart liberals and Government beady eyed inspectors creeping all over his business was the last thing he wanted. He paid a lot of good money to get this place up to snuff, in all the right places. He didn't need a fed's nose in the wrong place, surely tax him and take his hard earned money. He tossed the report to the corner, it teetered and fell off the desk. He didn't care.

He should've finished the report. He would remember Ramon, his daughter's childhood friend and Rosalinda's grandson. He would've read that he deported Ramon's grandmother, mother, and father, leaving Ramon with only his Aunt and cousins. Ramon was a citizen, as were his cousins. Ramon had been born in the states and was approaching thirty, like his Katherine, fresh from grad school with his Masters in Plant Pathology. Seeds of the rebellion? Maybe, El Lobo said it was possible, heard a rumor in the barrio Ramon was getting people together, even before the ICE raid. Keep an eye on that one. Could food poisoning be the sabotage? He should have read the report. As it was Globe drank scotch and looked up news reports on food related deaths.

Cats and mice, wolf and rabbits. He'd sick the Wolf on them if need be. Kids or not. E.coli and dollars flying from his pockets clouded his mind. He imagined short, stubby, rounded ends of bacteria microscopic capsules, covering his money and crops. Bacterial infestation would cost him dearly because some nincompoop was too much a fool to wash his food before eating. Damn fools. Probably some illegal at a fruit stand, they didn't wash anything.

He summoned Gloria his secretary half way into his second glass of scotch.

"Gloria, cancel all my appointments today and tomorrow. Please occupy yourself with damage control, come up with some mumbo jumbo about food contamination, throw some numbers at them. Maybe keep the bastards off our backs for a little while. Make sure it sounds pretty, then release it to the press. I don't need to see it. Don't disturb me for the rest of the night."

He ushered her out and slammed the door, spent the rest of the night ruminating in his large leather chair, watched three large televisions positioned throughout his office for signs of disaster. He finished the bottle of scotch. Forgot about dinner. Between Gloria and El Lobo he was confident damage control was already well under way.

El Lobo would clean any contamination detected during his inspection. The more apt question being, did he take the steps to ensure the contamination would not occur again. If the Wolf had a failing it was that. Sometimes he would "fix" a problem over and over. Damn Wolf.

Crunch some numbers, do some math. Lawyer Little Jon on the phone, soothing words. Little more scotch with his soda. Get some sleep the lawyer coos, call you in the morning. Good idea that. One eyed shuffle to his private bathroom. Forget the damn report, maybe it was a bad dream. Steam, shower, towel dry. When he emerged, neat and clean, pink and rosy, there it was on his desk again. Damn Lobo, a newspaper next to the clean white paper. Someone somewhere was dead due to food poisoning, Eschera coli or some such nonsense, and this article was hot off the press.

Globe saw his business named in the third paragraph with several others. Globe's blood ran cold, his daughter walked in, screamed.

"Daddy, oh my God! What's wrong?" Panic morphed her features, soft beautiful lines, jagged and sharp with worry. Globe stood, towel forgotten, modesty forgotten, penis and daughter forgotten. The face in the wall sized mirror was whiter than white, death and destruction on his head. Trembling fingers, trembling knees, she pulled the towel tight around him and tucked it snug.

"Go lie down Daddy." Her voice scolded, if he could have heard. Globe stumbled into the back. The simple room at the back of the office with a clean single bed and spare clothes had a nice view of the fields too. He lay down and watched the world spin. Muffled voices in the office. Katherine and El Lobo, damage control, come clean, press release, recall. He thought he might swallow his tongue, damn   immigrants, someone was responsible for this. Someone would pay.

Lawyer Little Jon woke him with his cane in the morning. Not as ceremoniously as a man of Globe's wealth deserved. Little Jon may have struck him several times rather hard, Globe couldn't be sure. Fog and haze of scotch cleared. Sour tongue, stale eyes. Retire to the bathroom again.

"Give me twenty minutes you damn snake!!" Globe bellowed his way into the bathroom and blearily scrubbed his way to decency. Little Jon sat on a chair near the door talking the whole time.

He never stopped or asked if Globe was listening. That wasn't his job. His job was to tell Globe of his legal liability. Globe paid whether listening or vomiting, and sounded as if he was doing the latter. Little Jon did pause for the retching.

An hour and a half later they were in a SUV headed for the heli-pad on the far side of the property. The farms were Globe's favorite business, but really just the foundation on which his house rested. He had other holdings. Heli-pad to helicopter to Gas platform off the coast of Louisiana. Whir of helicopter blades cut the air. Chop-chop, whir-whir. Drown out the necessity for conversation. Lawyer Little Jon kept quiet for the duration, even though all of the headsets had microphones. The helicopter shot through the sky, thanks to the industry of man, of many men.

The oil platform rose from the water, metallic waterbug, skating nowhere on skyscraper legs, round and red, rode the waves. Proboscis drilling into earthen crust, extract the gas, extract the petroleum. Globe generally enjoyed his visits to the platform, far south from his farming Mecca, the tropical Gulf waters were inviting and crystalline, the sun fairly sizzled. Shirtsleeves were a must, damn polyester pants felt like hell. The rig itself was a gorgeous sight. All metal scaffolding, support beams, piping, drill housings, grease and steam on a scale ten times that of typical industrial setting. The clang of industry always lifted his spirits. Music to his ears.

A firestorm of controversy on-shore, off-shore hydraulic fracturing was going gangbusters, and Globe couldn't have been happier. At least until yesterday. The helicopter landed and he and Little Jon were escorted by a grimy foreman to the offices. The man was clean compared to the rest of the crew, he was the captain or some such, barely a half dozen grease smudges marked his clothes. The rest of the men seemed to be wearing grease atop their clothing. Globe couldn't have guessed the original color of a single garment he saw. They wound through a large control room full of screens manned by clean-cut, polo shirt wearing engineers, past the dials and lights, through a tight, organized office with almost as many screens as the control room, the captain's he supposed. The man stopped in front of the large oak door at the back.

Globe knew the man had a key, it would be foolish otherwise, too many documents and cameras in there. Globe waved the man onward, he unlocked the door, proceeded inside and poured a glass of scotch after placing ice in the crystal rocks glass.

"Sir." He handed Globe the glass and left. The captain was a competent man, he knew Globe was not on the rig to discuss gas, Globe frequently escaped to the rig for solitude and peace of mind.

The suite was stocked with supplies for a year at least. Salmon, snacks, scotch, beer, cigars and all the assorted necessities for a man of his stature. Globe and Little Jon settled in. The room was decorated with dark wood, brown leather and brushed chrome fixtures. Home away from home. Bathroom, sauna, exercise room, kitchen, bedroom, even on a micro scale perhaps a bit ostentatious but so was Globe. The leather required special protection, he had the furniture reupholstered each year and kept the skins covered with plastic. Salty sea air was unkind to the leather no matter how carefully he cared for it. The foreman surely prepared the room for his arrival as soon as Globe left the farm. Sound dampening design muffled the hum and whir, clang of metal barely reached into his inner sanctum. The room furthest to the rear, his office, let out onto a balcony where he liked to sit and take it all in. Sit there drinking and smoking to the soothing sounds of human endeavor and venting steam, with the ocean's waves crashing three hundred feet below. Heavenly.

Katherine's mother Lily hated the place. Granted the platform had been less accommodating way back when, hardly a floating box on stilts with a helicopter pad. No private room then, rubbed shoulders with the sweaty grease monkeys. The whine and whir of metal strained her nerves and agitated her spirit. She faded so quickly, so unexpectedly they had all been in shock. A bad stomach, a burning fever, and inside the span of two months she passed, faded before his eyes. Money was never an issue for Globe Hood when it came to his honey and he had thrown all he had at the problem to no avail. He kept her pumped full of morphine, there would be no pain for his baby, no pain. She died on a Monday. Full of fever and morphine she convulsed, spasmed, bit through her tongue, broke her teeth, foamed at the mouth. She died, strength and life slipped away in the early hours of the morning.

There was no lucid moment at the end, no last words. Just sweat and tears and the sour stink of infirmity. No closure, just memories and anger at God the world and all the rest. The sun rose just after, flooded their ample bedroom with clear light, illuminated her pale and faded face.

Globe cried over her body the entire day. It was El Lobo Maldito that pulled him away. The room filled with workers dressed in their very best to escort the body. The workers loved Lily, she knew them all by name, their families and countries of origin. Never as openly insubordinate as her daughter, she found ways to help the workers without his knowing. The first market on the farm, for the workers, free at the time, full of produce that would never make the cut in American stores. Spots marred wilted leaves, bruises and discolorations served as price tags, free. The food would only end up in a dumpster somewhere behind a restaurant or supermarket. Waste-not want-not was all she said when he berated her about it. She opened two more after his outburst, one more on the farm, opposite end of the sprawling hundreds of hectares, then a third in the barrio of the workers. Greatly discounted and openly second hand, the store was an enormous success and quickly took on a life of its own. Lily managed it all. She never told him anything about the store, business wise that is, she always deflected his verbal barrages with long-winded, anecdotal stories. The moral of which would eventually wriggle its way through a torturously tangential tale to land with a thud at his feet like a smoking hot turd. Globe seldom had the patience for such, as he suspected was her intent.

The funeral was on a Saturday, every worker Hood had on his farm showed up. Only about three-hundred workers back then, dressed in their best or what passed for such. Death is the great equalizer, words of his father echoed in his head. The man had been too soft with his workers, why he had so much difficulty. The cemetery was aflood with his workers. He thought about telling them to stay back, keep away, the service was supposed to be for family only. He suggested as much to El Lobo. The man stared at him with those deep black eyes and shook his head in the negative, he would do no such thing. So it was multi-millionaires, a few billionaires and illegal farm workers stood with bowed heads and damp cheeks murmuring the Lord's Prayer. The procession took the whole day.

Globe was convinced he heard his wife chortling on the wind. A naughty throaty laugh she reserved for him and him alone in their more indecent undertakings. She would have goaded him into a fury and laughed at his red face if she were there. Pat him on the cheek and pinch his bum. Loved that woman.

Katherine did not take the loss well and in all honesty, if Globe could be so with himself, neither did he. Seeing the girl reminded him of Lily, such that he thought he would weep. Katherine must have suspected as much because she stopped hugging him and in the end she shipped herself off to private school. Globe wrapped himself in business and money. Cash money flowed like water after Lily's death. Thanks in no small part to his iron fist and tightened restrictions, maximize profits and minimize overhead. Hood industries lost many senior and dependable employees in the days after Lily's death, legal and illegal alike. Many couldn't handle the draconian capitalism inspired changes Globe enacted. A core of loyal workers remained, muscled through the changing times, used Wolf as their intermediary. They feared the man, but so did Hood, somehow that made negotiations possible and concessions palatable.

They were gone now. The last remnants of those loyalists deported, thanks to a well-timed call to ICE. Now Katherine appeared, spouting tree-hugging best management practices. Full circle, the cycle repeats. He drained his scotch on the rocks. Little Jon was perched on a bar stool sipping his own drink, watched the news on a television across the room. Globe thought the man may have been speaking to him but had given up. The news ticker scrolled across the bottom of the screen, five deaths linked to contaminated food. Damn it all to Hell.

El Lobo Maldito confirmed what Globe suspected, but didn't want to admit to himself, not even the slightest. Pesticide and herbicide application upwind of Lily's tea house, prevailing winds, twenty years worth, chronic exposure had taken its toll. She had tumor the size of a golf ball in her brain when she died. The very same "poison" as she called it, made them millionaires. Not just using the stuff, but making it too. The power of petroleum products. God Bless America.

Not that he cared when his workers fell ill. Lily went to their bedsides, paid medical expenses, nagged him about worker protection and attended their funerals. The stares at the wake and funeral made perfect sense the more he thought about it, he was a damn fool. He had been blind to all the accusatory glances, pity and shame. Wallowing in his grief and misery he wept into miserable oblivion.

The funeral and mourning lasted nearly a week. The day of the funeral and burial nothing got done. All of his employees were at the cemetery or funeral home so how could it. The festivities ran long into the night, the next day, the next. Hood had no part in it, but it seemed he was the only one. El Lobo made sure work got done, but only just. It was nearly ten days before he stopped receiving tamales, burritos, empanadas, and so on.

The mourning or merriment, he was not sure which, filled the evenings with the smell of roasted pig, sulfur smell of fireworks, and the incessant horns and drumming of their music.

He razed her tea house at the end of the week, built the heli-pad, the workers stood and stared. Accusatory stares all over again. What did those fools know? He wasn't going to stop applying pesticides, that was for damn sure. But he couldn't risk Katherine or any other of his dependents using the Tea house. They were lucky he didn't build more worker dormitories there. Let their women and children inhale the poison. He would have done so, out of spite, he was consumed by rage back then, El Lobo and Little Jon convinced him otherwise. Little Jon especially. Illegals or not, prior knowledge, negligence and poor management practices would end up costing him dearly.

"This is not good, Globe." Little Jon was done letting him daydream. "It would seem several of the cases of E.coli have been linked to you. This is bad, very bad." His cell phone rang, grimace and assent, he hung up.

"Like I said. Gloria and my secretary have both received notifications from our people in Washington. I smell a Senate inquiry, Globe. Not good for business that."

Globe would've hurled his rocks glass across the room but his initial rage was spent. His mind was already churning into his assets and how to isolate them from this insidious probe.

Damn them all to Hell. Globe's office phone rang. Seldom used save for conversations he did not want traceable. El Lobo Maldito, no nonsense on the other end. He could hear the stubble on the man's cheek rubbing rough against the phone.

"We have a problem, Globe," Globe hated for anyone to call him by name, least of all his employees, and Juan Jesus Martinez knew as much.

"What else? I already have DC climbing up my ass!"

"It would seem our food contamination issue is an inside job." Long pause. He continued when Globe said nothing. "I have a few suspects, though we shipped several of them away thanks to ICE." Now Globe swore up a storm, spittle and oaths spewed from his round white face.

"Just keeping you in the loop, I'm on it." El Lobo hung up, left Globe panting to a fast busy tone. He slammed down the receiver and sat back in a large leather chair, leather creaked, stretched under his weight. Some illegal bastard was going to pay. Globe Hood's innovation and hard work had grown his father's failing farm into a multi-million dollar a year business. He was responsible for food contracts, distribution monopolies and secondary investment like fertilizer production, which was a gold mine in itself. It had always been his butt on the line, applying for credit and loans, selling his soul to the damn bankers that used to smile at him like he was on the wrong end of an inside joke. They were the very same lily-white assholes with their pointy noses and thin little fingers that fawned over him at parties. The same bank CEOs that offered him money, threw it at him now.

They knew he was the best kind of investment. Hard work and years of attention to detail earned him his position and no wet-backed bleeding heart was going to bring him down. Quite the contrary. He'd send them up the river if he could get his hands on them, better yet sic El Lobo Maldito on them, get the job done right. Blood and guts, eviscerate them, blood teaches quicker than words. Teach a lesson to the rest of the upstarts, nip this in the bud. Serve the fools right. Warm Gulf breeze brushed aside curtains and brought salt and sea smells to his office. Little Jon on the balcony, workers nowhere in sight, Globe wasn't sure whether it was quitting time or not, but he trusted his foreman.

The man knew what he was about. He called the chopper back for the following morning. He and Little Jon would spend the night on his metal fortress, battle plans to be made. Chef from the galley paid them a visit and whipped up salmon and green beans, Gruyere cheese, French bread and sliced tomato, fuel for the all night think. Little Jon barely managed to get a word in edgewise, not before three in the morning anyway.

Chapter 4

Auspicious circumstances

Globe didn't know how El Lobo did it but the bastard always knew when Hood called him for a hit. Cowboy hat pulled low, almost hid dead blackness of those eyes. Smoke bellowed, tendrils writhed from the corners of his mouth and nose. A dragon, forget the wolf. Smoking token of death. Bronzed skin as dark as the best Cherry, muscled forearms like steel cables, choke the life out of the bastards. Handsome face, chiseled stone, scruff of black beard flecked with white. Globe didn't know how the man did it. Smoke snaked into his eyes, crawled under the brim of his hat and trickled skyward. Ephemeral strands of reaper's breath, burn you to a cinder.

God damn it. Globe wanted the man to die, just as instinctively he knew it would never happen. Why was it those one wanted to die never did, and those one wanted to keep had to die.

"Hierba mala nunca muere." Damn saying of Lily's flowing through his head, 'bad herb never dies.' First things first, sparkle and shine, glimmer and glint of golden yellow rays off the greenhouses that pressed close along the ground. Huddled and ridged like accordion bellows, A-frame roof repeated a hundred times, more than 50 hectares under glass. The open space, well lit from above, automated hydroponic water and nutrient solutions at specific intervals. The air constantly moving, fans in the roof moved air for the plants, kept it moving. Stale stagnant air led to pests and disease. A nice breeze and low humidity were the desired conditions. The helicopter shot over the property, slowed and turned, prepared to land.

The greenhouse was a sight to behold, a maze of greenery and plumbing ingenuity. Plenty of time for that later, during the tour. The helicopter hovered over the landing pad and landed gently, back on the farm again. Globe slid from the cream brown leather of the chopper to the multicolored display of the blossoming farm. Jasmine blossom on the breeze, Lily's fingers in his hair. The phone in his pocket vibrated as a black SUV crunched to stop at the edge of the helicopter pad.

Gloria scurried from the vehicle, smart, tan suit fit her 40-something body like a glove. Strawberry blond hair beginning to gray over the last few years, she was still beautiful, if exasperated. Her skin was smooth and unwrinkled, eyes gray and sharp. She had time for none save Globe Hood. The effect was ruined by her falling at the edge of the platform. She crumpled onto all fours, heel caught in the hard packed soil at the edge of the pavement, a cracked, dry plate of soil grabbed for the stiletto, refused to return it. Her white blouse, thin fabric, almost shear, gathered soil noticeably. She bent double, removed her foot and yanked the shoe fee, hair strands freed from ponytail.

Gusting breeze blew hair in her eyes, she replaced the shoe and stepped in front of Hood. The man seemed to have no intention of stopping, or asking after her well being. He kept walking, nearly bowling her over.

"Mr. Hood!" She screamed "The Chinese investors are HERE!" Through gritted teeth she delivered her news. "They arrived about 30 minutes ago, they are having tea and biscuits while they wait. El Lobo is seeing to them." She turned on her battered stiletto heels and led him back to the SUV. Damn Chinese, he hadn't expected them until tomorrow, though he was forewarned. Both Gloria and El Lobo had been machine gunning text messages at him for the last hour of his helicopter flight.

They bumped several miles down the pock-marked dirt road to his office. He made a mental note to have El Lobo fix the road immediately, at least the one from the helicopter pad to the offices. Lobo should've known better. In reality El Lobo told him to pave the most heavily used roads on the farm, suggestions which Globe conveniently forgot. The rutted, grooved clay transects cut from here to there across the farm. As long as the vehicles could pass from one end to the other, what of it?

He wished his rutted and uneven trails were evenly paved or graveled, at least the one from the helipad to the offices.

The white farm house that served as the farm offices came into view, white fence paralleled the road to the house for the last kilometer. When Lily was alive he kept horses. Dappled Palominos and Suffolk Reds, she loved them all. Lily knew what was what, he could barely tell them apart. Race them home some days, mud splatter or sun shining, a couple would chase the car up the drive every time, only when Lily was with him. Never, not even once, not even a colt when he was alone.

He sold them when she died, they looked as lost as he felt. A Chinese gentleman stood on the front porch of the white farmhouse. Hands on his hips, a large smile splayed across his face. He was tall, as tall as Hood if not a bit taller. A cluster of what Hood took for lackeys clustered close behind the man. Globe tamped the end of a cigar on his fat thumb, passed it to Gloria, she cut off the end, lit the cigar for him, handed it back. She would've poured him a scotch but he waved her offer away.

Summoning his business persona, large and in charge, Hood exited the SUV shrouded in blue smoke like a well done ham.

"Mr. Chen, Welcome to the farm. My apologies for keeping you waiting. Shall we lunch then?"

"Mr. Hood, how good to see you again, we only just arrived. Food after, tour first." He stepped down from the porch, shook Hood's hand.

"My kind of man. Business first, play later." Globe patted his shoulder and pointed to a second SUV that pulled up behind his own. The finely dressed man, pleated suit, shiny shoes and entourage piled into the SUV, Globe piled into his own. Crunch of gravel as they made their way towards the acres of greenhouse. Gloria rattled details and reports as they went, Globe half listened. The Chinese investors were a big deal. The greenhouses beckoned. Blinding sunshine reflected through lenses, stung the eyes. Clomp and shuffle, Globe and Gloria ushered the guests through the front office, ne'er a twitch of the eye nor request for documents.

Mr. Chen wanted to see the operation. Very well, in they went. Wall of humidity and heat, where was El Lobo? He wanted this handled correctly. The air was thick with the scent of green plants and shit, natural shit and chemical shit. Globe could tell the difference after all the years. He ushered them down the first row, walls of climbing tomatoes to either side. Hydroponically grown each plant twined up a black bar, a vertical rooting medium penetrated by roots up the length. Misting water floated over the plants, nozzles ensconced inside the black rooting medium, spewed a nutrient laden mist at regular intervals.

They reached the end of the row. A long glass table with a black wrought iron frame sat waiting surrounded by chrome high-backed chairs. Hood had the thing brought in for just for such occasions. Hot steamy air pushed past, currents picked up and the breeze became constant. Somewhere, a timer turned on the fans. Giant industrial things, too far away to bother conversation, but at least the air was moving. No cooler, but the breeze helped.

Mr. Chen's lackey's clustered around their leader, whispers lost in the breeze. Globe thought the whispering wasn't necessary; he didn't speak Chinese, not yet anyway. He'd have to soon though, follow the money and all. Mr. Chen nodded in the affirmative, stepped forward, the lackeys fell back, parted like a curtain for his approach.

"This is a gorgeous meeting table and very fancy." His English was perfect, probably better than Globe's. "I understand there is a glass office further down," he gestured randomly, some unspecified space behind, except the gesture was in the correct direction. Not to be underestimated this one. Globe wondered what the Chinese spy apparatus was like, and did they, like many governments, use private citizens as informants.

"I would like to see this glass office, Mr. Hood. We will discuss particulars there. No?" Hood waited, definitely a man accustomed to power. Very well.

"Well alright. Not a bad idea that, let me send someone ahead to clean up my paperwork." Not his, but El Lobo's. The Lobo appropriated the office, Hood hadn't used it anyway. He preferred the cooler climate controlled farm-house office. Globe pressed thick white fingers, smooth red palms against the muscled small of Gloria's back. The woman was like steel, his turn to whisper in her ear.

"Be a dear would you?" Not really a question. "Find that damn Lobo." The top two buttons of her white dress shirt undone, sweat glistened on her bosom, Globe eyed her breasts pressed close as she was he saw right down her shirt, he looked up into her eyes, she was not surprised. Her hair twisted in a bun, silver pin holding it all in place, a gift from the Chinese on their last visit.

Gloria turned, and strode down the aisle in the direction of the office. Pants suit snug against her firm bottom, her crisp white blouse nearly transparent in the humidity of the greenhouse, Gloria was beautiful and good at what she did. This was not her first rodeo. She set off at a brisk walk, pretty slipper-like shoes in brown earth tones silent on the concrete floor, she changed out of the heels in the truck. She hurried without appearing to. Her near perfect posterior tugged at Hood's eyes .

Wide aisles between rows of twining tendrils that climbed skyward toward sunlight had been designed wide enough to maneuver forklifts up and down as necessary. Mr. Chen was not satisfied with the ornately worked wrought-iron table. Globe pushed chrome chair back under the table and gestured down the aisle after Gloria. A tree in the distance looked small, like a shrubbery, 200 meters distant the orange tree, obovate glossy leaves with smooth margins and pointed tips. Heavenly scented flowers when time. The tree stood at the crossroads of the N-S and E-W greenhouse complexes. The E-W greenhouse stretched further but the N-S complex was equally productive and important. Hectares worth of important. Rich black soil decorated the nsdr of the orange tree, fed delving and divining roots. Globe loved the blackness of it. Even as they approached some minutes later he longed to grab a handful, play the granules between his fingers, soft to the touch.

He had golf carts to shuttle him to and fro, Lobo had his own, bells and whistles, literally. Not for this investor though, they would all walk today. They passed the orange tree, at least 10 meters high and easily as wide. Grey bark darkened with moisture. Just beyond the orange sat a glass building at the southwest corner of the junction, which housed the suite of offices to which intention directed their steps. A small square conservatory, like a glass schoolhouse, whitewashed panes obscured some sections from prying eyes. Large glass panes 2 meters by 1 meter made up the walls, small horizontal panes open outward, shiny metal handles.

Two ceiling fans pushed air about the space, hot humid air summoned sweat. The floor a smooth concrete slab, drains in the center, spaced 3 meters apart. The sunlight, bent and reflected, passed through numerous panes before reaching the interior of the office, pierced motes of dust kicked up by shuffling feet. Warm rays lacked intensity or burn. Globe held open one of the double doors and waved Mr. Chen and his entourage through.

El Lobo Maldito stood in the outer room. Wooden chairs, leather couch and low walnut table the only décor besides a large leather recliner placed strategically facing the doorway with its back to the white washed wall of windows that lead to El Lobo's inner offices. Hood was grateful for the man's intimidating appearance at such moments. No suit and tie for him, no pleated pants, Hard worn jeans, hard worn skin, bleached and bronzed by the sun. Crossed arms a toothy grin caused Mr. Chen to hesitate, barely perceptible. His entourage stopped with a gasp, those in the rear bumping into those in front. Good show Lobo, good show. Globe sighed with relief.

"Welcome, Mr. Chen." El Lobo stepped forward, shook the man's hand. With his other hand he directed Mr. Chen to a wooden chair, a comfortable high-backed wooden chair, fine craftsmanship, made of ash. Globe sat in the large leather recliner, excellent flair for the dramatic, damn wolf. Mr. Chen hesitated, he could sit in the wooden chair, on the red sofa with his lackeys, or stand.

The choice would tell Globe a lot, damn El Lobo was sharp. Mr. Chen took the wooden chair, crossed his legs and smiled cool silky confidence. No ruffles, commendable. El Lobo remained standing. Shuffle of feet, creak of leather, Globe repositioned himself in the leather chair, Mr. Chen waited patiently on the wooden chair. The lackeys arranged themselves in a semi-circle behind Mr. Chen, sofa vacated. Eyes darted to and fro, tried to see everything. Globe wondered how many of them were recording the visit, he surely was. More than one if he knew his investors correctly. Globe could only just make out the geodesic glass dome in the distance. A large greenhouse as well the dome was more for publicity than function. The shape was novel and inspiring, even shut the tree-huggers up for a while. He used the space for research projects and lab coats.

The dome was impressive, a good investment at the time it came with media exposure, research money and increased name recognition. He never pretended to run a chemical free farm but the dome suggested he cared and maybe he did. As long as the bottom line increased all was well.

Rumble in the distance. Crackle and squelch behind white-washed office door called for El Lobo. Garbled urgency, repeat, repeat, repeat, gone. Globe hoped nothing was amiss, but no way to be sure without making a scene. The Wolf stood head cocked to the side, like he heard something.

"I'm sorry gentlemen we need to go, Now." Globe turned to El Lobo, ready to chastise but the man didn't give any of them time.

"Now, I mean NOW!" He had Mr. Chen out of the chair, nearly over his shoulder. Globe heard something thud against the glass, water sloshed against the bottom pane. A loose flower pot bumped into the window. Water crept into the room, under the doors, under the walls, trickled down the drains in the middle of the room. Slurp and gurgle.

"What the Hell?" Dead words on the tongue of a dead man, if it hadn't been for El Lobo who saved Hood's sorry ass.

Unbelievable, frothed white capped waves of gray water sluiced down the aisle, slammed into the glass office. A migrant body carried along past the windows, still alive, the man clawed at the glass. Tumbled end over end and was swept away, thud of boots on glass. El Lobo had them both by the scruff of the neck, shoving Hood and Mr. Chen toward his back offices unceremoniously. Was there refuge there? An inverse aquarium. Time slowed, seconds to minutes, minutes to hours, slurp of water down the drain, louder than raging river. Water surrounded them, engulfing the glass offices in gray murky water. The men inside froze, trapped like fish in a tank, nowhere to go. Crack, and splinter, the grating sound of failure of glass panes, spider webbing cracks sent goose bumps crawling up the spine. Explosion of water, the men were knocked from their feet with the cresting crash of water used to feed the plants. Rapids swallowed them, exploding all windows, all normalcy, all hope, ejected men in no particular order, two a time.

Globe paddled, tried to swim with the current, tried his damnedest not to die impaled, skewered, decapitated, so many ways to die in the torrent. Globe tumbled, flotsam in the tide, water rumbled around him, clanging metal, muted screams, shattering glass.

He couldn't tell up from down, left from right, his head broke the surface, screams and din, madness. His own voice howled with the rest. Twining tomato stems rose upward through the water like pond millweed. Floating green tomatoes ripped from the stems bobbed along side. End over end until a hand on the scruff of his neck pulled him toward the surface, the glass ceiling only a few feet from his head. Large metal cables parted the water and split anyone unlucky enough to hit them. The water divided in a white V behind each cable. Hood screamed for mercy.

Alarms screamed, chaos layer-cake of sound, a cacophony of chaos. Globe's feet brushed the ground, knees dragged along the concrete, and finally all the water was fading to a trickle, drains slurping the water away. Globe was face down on the cement floor, far from the greenhouse offices.

He lay three quarters of the way back to the glass table, or what should've been the table. The wrought iron frame was intact but mangled. Distorted and bent, the thing was twisted like a pretzel, glass top shattered into a million pieces and swept away. A worker downstream lay in the middle of the aisle, dead, a glass shard stuck through his chest. Hood wanted to wretch, did wretch, gallon of water. Damn.

Moaning, movement, Mr. Chen next to Globe, unconscious, but the man's back rose and fell with breath. Behind them El Lobo was already on his feet, hat gone, goggles on his forehead. Where had the man grabbed goggles? And when? He glanced at Hood and Chen, turned and ran back to the offices. Globe didn't see any of the lackeys, wondered if they survived. Globe struggled to rise, accomplishing the task after some huffing and puffing. The orange tree still stood, though more than half the canopy was gone. He wiped his thighs, wiped off dirt that wasn't there. His suit needed to be wrung out.

Mr. Chen stirred, Globe knelt and helped the man sit up. He sat and stared, nothing to say, shock for sure. El Lobo came back, dead run, four of the lackeys at his heels, shoes optional, clothing too. Once lackey was missing his shirt and one sock. The Wolf stopped in front of Hood, eyed Chen who looked to still be collecting his thoughts. The lackeys ran to their master, except the one that was bleeding.

"The other two are dead," El Lobo grabbed Hood's eyes, "one in the greenhouse, caught on a broken window, run right through. The other," he paused, grabbed Hood's elbow, "I don't even know how something like this could happen, never seen anything like it. Cut right in half, lengthwise. I've got someone on it. The gray water tanks were sabotaged, Hood, punctured inside the greenhouse where they meet the greenhouse in the northern complex. The water did what bombs, bulldozers and hoodlums could do together." He stopped, gave Globe a moment to take it in, continued.

"If you were wondering, Globe, Gloria wasn't in the building, I sent her home. Be glad I did." El Lobo turned and walked away. He still had his boots on, Hood looked down, both of his shoes were gone. Mr. Chen stirred, his four lackeys helped him to his feet. Globe Hood commenced treading water for the second time in less than an hour.

Chapter 5

Senate Hearing

The death count was five, three of his people and two employees of the Chinese investors. Shit. Three weeks later, cleanup complete, Hood was hemorrhaging money. Subpoena on his desk, summons to House hearing, date to be grilled by politicos, perform political theater, waste of his time. Not something that could be ignored, of that Little Jon assured him. He knew it to be true. Globe could ignore phone calls, emails, polite requests, but not summonses. The greenhouses were almost repaired, a few million dollars later. Little Jon had people on the insurance company, they were slippery pigs on a normal day, getting them to pay for the greenhouse sabotage was going to be a headache.

El Lobo appeared in his office, smoke, grease and soil, surely up to his elbows in the how and why of greenhouse repair. Damn cigar in his mouth. Cowboy hat too, damn Lobo.

"Someone used fertilizer in the explosive that ruptured the water tank. Now we know what happened to the missing fertilizer." The man stood there hands on his hips. Globe breathed into his scotch, he wanted to rage, wanted to smash his desk into a thousand pieces. Some piece of scum was working from the inside. The insolent peasant fools, he would crush them like insects. Damn them all.

"It's time." Hood waved El Lobo over to his desk, opened a mahogany box, felt purple interior. Cuban cigars, almost full. He gave one to the other man, threw the other in his mouth. Neither of them spoke, puffing and huffing they filled the room with smoke.

"You know what to do. Damn them all the Hell." Not exactly explicit, but clear as crystal to El Lobo.

"Alright, Globe, I will give you a report next week." No need to discuss particulars, those had been worked out years in advance.

The man exited Hood's office, trailed undulous smoke tendrils behind him. As El Lobo went out Gloria came in, hired hit-man held the door for his co-worker, she didn't thank him.

"We need to get you to the helicopter sir, your hearing begins in four hours." She peered over rimless glasses.

"This may be your first subpoena sir, but I fear it may not be your last. If the Chinese were not scared off by the 'incident' and are still willing to invest I can almost guarantee another summons. The Chinese do not have a stellar record when it comes to food contamination. Given our current situation I would expect the utmost scrutiny on the part of the community and more Department of Agriculture inspections than you can imagine." Hood nodded, she was right, as usual, and two steps ahead of him. Little Jon had suggested as much but was focusing his efforts on the food contamination debacle. Globe harrumphed, pushed himself out of the chair and motioned to Gloria. Resting his plump hands on her shoulders, he spoke.

"Gloria, you are the best, I couldn't do this without you. Thank you." Shock registered on her face, nanosecond, then gone, a master of self control she was. He pulled her close breathing in her beauty peppered with scent of female perspiration and grabbed a handful of ass cheek. Her lips tightened, face went pale, she was not about to faint, that was her angry face. Tightened lips and white as a sheet. She pried herself loose, rubbed her bosom against his for her efforts. She stormed from his office, slammed the door on her way out. Globe chuckled; he would get her into bed yet. Sooner than later, he hoped.

The chopper ride to D.C. was muted. Gloria wouldn't speak to Globe and when she did it was through Little Jon. The two briefed him as if he were an infant, all the better, he couldn't pay attention anyway. His mind was still underwater, flooded with rage that someone on his farm had the audacity to fuck with Globe Hood. He nodded in all the right places and repeated what they told him to repeat. Before long they were exiting the limousine, climbing the capitol steps and being led into an already full hearing room.

He didn't notice the icy tendrils creeping up his spine. Dancing a jig on his grave, someone was. The icy fingers elicited goosebumps, tightening skin, reached up and under his scalp and into his brain.

Wood paneled walls, pink faced politicians sat on a raised dais behind an absurdly long table. Microphones for those that wanted or needed them, white tablecloth, several pitchers of water along its length. His head spun, more underwater than ever, what was wrong with him?

Ice cold fingers reached down from his brain and into his torso, down to his balls and ass. His sphincter tightened, like the runs were knocking. Maybe it was nerves. He sat at a table by himself, Little Jon and Gloria a few feet behind in the first row of the gallery. They faded from his mind as soon as he sat, as did the rest of the world. Wild cackle in his brain and his entire body felt wooden. Panic in his head.

Someone banged something, pasty white man in a gray suit talking to the room at large and finally addressed Globe Hood directly.

"We are here to address the food contamination of your products, Mr. Hood, so that we may get to the bottom of this horrible occurrence. We will start this hearing with a statement by Mr. Globe Hood. Mr. Hood please, you have the floor."

Globe cleared his throat, arranged the papers in front of him and opened his mouth to speak, but couldn't. Swollen tongue, chills throughout his body, gurgling bowels, he had no control over his body, panic to terror.

"I am here today to represent the downtrodden and the exploited. I am here to confess my sins as an exploiter and capitalist pig in the first degree. I take advantage of illegal labor at every opportunity and flout the law with the utmost contempt for you political puppets. I farm from an office and spray my people indiscriminately with pesticides and herbicides. I don't give one iota about the repercussions because there are none. The system is rigged and I, thankfully, am seated at the top." Swollen tongue, swollen testicles, something animal in the back of his brain screamed over and over.

"You people must understand our economy is composed of many sectors, one very important sector being food." he pointed to his chest, continued, " Information, infrastructure, clothing, health care, finance, education, recreation, in no particular order, are vital to our success as an economy regardless of how large or small our economy may be. We must support each of these sectors as needed and neglect leads to a hamstrung economy. These are proven facts gentlemen. I have citations if you need them." And in fact he did, thank you daughter dearest.

"Our current economy is hamstrung. All sectors of our once great nation are neglected in favor of one sector. Not military, no, the financial sector as much as I hate to say it, is out of control." Gasps sounded through the hearing room, click of cameras. A lily white man sitting above opened his mouth, but Globe drove on. It was true, he did hate to say it and in truth was trying his damnedest to stop, but couldn't. True those banking frauds had wrecked half his worker barrio, he lost customers and workers. The cost of new employees was negligible, though not insignificant. And he did want someone to pay, he knew no matter how much he wanted it, no banker would pay a dime. He was at least going to get his.

"The financial sector is so coddled that not a single soul has been held accountable for the debacle of the great recession. I'm a greedy bastard, but those white collar criminals have got us all beat." More gasps, more plowing forward. Hood wanted to swallow his own tongue, what the hell was he saying? Heat gripped his loins, his guts, his lips continued to move, he couldn't stop them.

"Roads and bridges fall into disrepair, our rail system is a joke, our kids are idiots compared to other first world nations," air quotes with his fingers, "even many third world ones." He paused for the shuffling papers and murmurous tide, ebb and flow, flash of cameras.

"Now, not all of the sectors of our economy are hamstrung. Food processing is doing well, though my subsidies have decreased, it is to be expected. At least I don't have to sell tomatoes at 10 dollars a pound and meat at 50. That would be the reality if we priced food at true value."

"In fact it would cost more to be honest. I don't think I'd last very long." The truth even if they were not his words. Globe tried to force his mouth into a snarl, a scream, anything. He only harrumphed and continued.

"Look, the mistakes made on my farm were made by an underpaid, under-appreciated migrant worker, illegal if you will." More gasps. Tears would've streamed down his cheeks if he could have controlled himself. "The fault is mine as owner and operator." Choke on his tongue. If he could only will himself to die, heart attack or stroke, end it all. He screamed somewhere deep in his soul.

Cameras flashed behind him.

"Poor management practices are merely the symptom of an infirmity reflected by the larger economy. I should pay workers a decent wage, I should provide them with benefits. But it is far easier to hire migrant illegals and more important-ly, cheaper. If you really want to make me pay, make me hire citizens, pay a fare wage and fine me for hiring illegals. I cut corners, ask for more government money than I need, hide as-sets and I bet you I'm not the only one. Not just in my sector, but in the other "healthy" sectors as well. My wrongs pale in comparison to those committed by the financial sector, howev-er premeditated them may have been. I believe you may have had senate inquiries about that as well. No?" Globe's mouth finally stopped working, whomever was speaking for him had finally gone dry. His throat was parched, yet he couldn't lift a finger to drink the water right in front of him.

"Your errors cost people their lives, Mr. Hood. While the banks acted in an unethical manner no one lost their life as a consequence." Older pink gentleman. Hood thought he knew the man's name. Couldn't remember.

"Really, don't you think? Maybe not directly, a matter of semantics if you ask me. You are a fool if you think the loss of a home didn't cause pain, suffering, grief, humiliation, stress and a great deal of loss very akin to the loss of a loved one. And you would be an even greater fool if you didn't realize, someone, somewhere out there in this great nation of ours went homeless, as a result of this great misfortune and disgrace. You would be a great fool to not to realize stress, illness, or assault as a result of being homeless can kill. Such was the nature of the debacle this senate governed over and failed us all." Hood slammed his right hand down on the table. Damn them all and whomever was controlling him.

"As you will Mr. Hood, your efforts to deflect have been noted, as well as your significant opinions. But continuing with the matter at hand let us assume you are at fault as owner and operator of your farms. I believe that was the most important part of your testimony." Damn Mexican-American senator from God knew where. Shit, she had him by the balls, she?

"Yes senator, I agree. I, Globe Hood, am responsible for the deaths of those individuals. However as an addendum let me add that the entire agricultural sector needs close scrutiny. Let my earlier words not be forgotten." The last words exited his mouth like a knife being pulled from his chest. Globe fell to his knees, foam in his mouth, dripped down his chin. Throat constricted, head like an inflated balloon. He heard his own gurgling, screams and shouts in the Senate hall. Flashes in his eyes, click of shutters captured the moment. Red face, surely he was going to die, at long last, darkness.

***

The white buttoned shirt she wore was so sheer the rising sun pierced thin cotton, illuminated round breasts and bronze bottom. The shirt came just to the bottom of her rounded ass, firm and naked. She leaned over the kitchen table as Hood let himself into her shack. On tip-toe, placing fresh-cut flowers in a white porcelain vase in the middle of the table; her bottom was bare of imperfections and smooth like caramel. A shock of black pubis drew his eyes, flooded his phallus with blood. His erection climbed down his pant leg, pressed snug against the denim of his jeans. He imagined he could smell her sex in the air.

In fact she had just fucked her husband and sent him off to work, pat on the ass, nibble on his ear. Isabella Martinez was beyond beautiful. Quintessential, archetypal, take a picture and frame it beautiful. Jet black hair and Native American genetics undeniable in her high cheek bones, smooth hairless body and rounded calves. Globe tried to approach quietly but new boots gave him away. Scuff the floor, creak of wooden plank. She turned slowly, sultry eyes, half lidded and naughty, expecting her man no doubt. Eyes widened in shock, cheeks blush crimson. She pulled at the front of the shirt, legs scissoring closed, eyes to the floor.

"Mr. Hood, I thought you were Jose."

Hood couldn't speak, blood rushed in his ears drowned out sound, throbbing phallus robbed rational thought. Little immigrant whore, so sweet. He pushed himself against her, squeezed her between his mass and the table. Felt her smooth skin, firm little breasts beneath her cotton shirt, fabric was so worn it was almost non-existent. Hard penis pushed against her, she pushed on his chest. Violent inhale, she turned, presented rounded golden buttocks, displayed and presented for Hood. He thought she surely meant for him to take her from behind, until she smashed the vase across his head, his belt buckle already unfastened.

Stars and spots danced across the kitchen, blood in his mouth. She dashed for the door, almost free. He grabbed her by the hair, back of the head, pulled her close and back-handed her so hard she fell on the floor with a thump, mewing in pain and fear. Hood dropped his trousers, boots still on, thrust his fat dick into her moist privates, still hot and wet from her morning exercise. She writhed beneath him, half conscious, titillating him even further. Fat pink hand over her mouth, fuck her.

He came with a moan, she bit his hand, ripped his testicles down hard. Hood thought his head would explode, pain shot up his balls and into his stomach, he left a bloody handprint on her cheek when he slapped her. Hood disengaged, pulling his weapon from her sheath, checked his balls. Still there but all of his hair was in her left hand, blood trickled from the corner of her mouth, a dangerous coiled snake. He hobbled to the door, fell over, pants around his ankles. He pulled them up in a hurry, still hoped to make a quick getaway, fool man. He was the boss, he took what he wanted, a small tithe of flesh was peanuts for payment for the opportunity he was providing her and her husband with. They would be rich, like him. He didn't feel guilty in the least, in fact he felt justified. Her ass belonged to him anyway, and now she knew it. Hood scurried up the drive, eager to be gone before others saw him there.

He suddenly had pressing needs elsewhere. Time to investigate capital investments off the coast. They said there was oil out there, if they drilled deep enough. Hood may have been concerned if he knew Isabella's history. A mother called a witch by the people of their small coastal Mexican town. Voodoo dolls for playthings Isabella grew up immersed in rituals and magic. He may have been more concerned had he seen her collect all of his let blood calmly with a cotton swab and eye dropper, drop it in a glass jar. A plastic bag for the hair and then she squatted, legs wide and pushed.

Milky white ejaculate dripped from her vagina like latex sap of rubber tree. Semen collected in another glass jar. All three samples she placed in an old wooden box behind the shrine they had in the corner of the living room. The Virgin bowed in prayer in the center the shrine received the offering in mute approval. Isabella would have use for Hood's bodily fluids one day. Globe would have been worried if he believed in such things. As it was, he didn't. He left town and stayed away for a week and a day.

***

Globe sat up panting. Sweat soaked sheets clung to his chest and torso. A television across the room flickered bright images his brain was unable to process. Flicker and flash, no sound. A memory banished to the dungeons of his soul, surfaced to drag him under or drive him insane.

Now he remembered why he hated that woman. Why he feared the Wolf. He thought for sure El Lobo would kill him after. The catalyst that began the metamorphosis of a competent intelligent Veterinarian into the cold-blood enforcer Globe knew. If Hood suspected the man wanted to kill him, he was right. Lily had her part in it of course. His best and worst projects always did. She told him she'd handle it. He arrived at the house with blood all over his shirt, trousers undone, balls broken. He told Lily everything, always did. She fixed it, a bit too tidy, as usual.

Gloria materialized at his side. Dabbed his brow, smoothed his hair. Muted tones and wooden furniture coming slowly into focus, home then. He remembered the last, a most unpleasant memory.

"You're home, sir." She read his mind, or the searching nature of his eyes. Globe relaxed.

"I don't think you garnered much sympathy with your episode, your diarrhea of the mouth or your fit. Dr. says you're fine, can't explain your episode or the fainting, what's going on, Globe?" Gloria never called him Globe, he checked his body, made sure he wasn't dead, or almost. Still there.

"I don't know, Gloria, never had anything like it before. Couldn't control myself or what I was saying. Like someone's puppet." Looked around the room, he could barely move, sore everywhere. "I will never repeat this to anyone, Gloria. You are it. Had me by the balls, Gloria, someone did."

Chapter 6

The Angry Goat Army

The screaming voices of children, shrill laughter; clomp and patter of little feet. Smelled like corn tortillas and sizzling meats. Blasting ranchero music floated through the air, threaded the days together with the scent of summer. Ramon could remember a thousand Sundays identical to that one. Easily replace one for the other, no one would notice, only the cast of characters would change, the rest the same. Ramon had been one of those clomping kids once, tag you're it.

Kate had been there too. The 'huera,' they called her. The blond/white one. Treated no different than the rest of the children, one of the reasons she loved them all so much. No special treatment here. She was scolded just as the rest when she stepped out of line, at times even worse, she was ignorant of things the other kids took for granted. Don't interrupt adult conversations, don't snatch food and on and on.

Ramon sighed into his cold beer. She was fine, he had a more important task afoot than courting the Boss's daughter, as much as he wanted to sing her a song. His people were scattered throughout. The ranchero music provided the backstop for his screaming ideas, coming in hot and fast. His Aunt and the portly butcher played cards and smoked cigars, tequila half gone on that table. His comrades played horse-shoes, soccer, drank in the corner, watched kids on the playground, they were everywhere.

Shortly after Ramon returned from University he put rubber to the road, started having meetings in living rooms, no need for cover. He was well practiced at such meetings, having exercised the very same need years before with Katherine, though theirs had been much more clandestine. The very first meeting as far as Ramon was concerned occurred in his closet when he was thirteen. Ramon had hidden in the back of his closet. Heard his bedroom door bang open, she ghosted through his room, stopped in front of the door, two pillars of shadow moved in front of the bar of light under closet door. She opened the door, ignored his protests, pulled the door closed behind her.

She crouched on the floor next to him and kissed him. He wiped his tears away after she was done. He yelled at her once the tears were gone. Her father was a bastard; she agreed.

Her father was a thankless son of a bitch who got off humiliating the powerless and he deserved to die a painful death. She agreed. Soft, smooth fingers, so delicate, scented like nectar, brushed the hair from his face, kissed him some more. She teased him for crying. The first time he touched her legs, slid his hand up her leg while she kissed him. He stopped just short of her panties, too timid to proceed. He'd seen his father do the same to his mother enough times, their passionate kissing in the kitchen, the only quiet moments in the little home. His father's hand disappeared up the hem of his mother's dress, taking the pleats with it. Exposing her bronzed, muscled thighs. Her blush and giggle, slap at his hand, she'd turn and get back to cooking or washing, or to lead him to their bedroom. Not so quiet that. Good time to sit outside on the porch, swing in the hammock or take a walk.

Katherine opened her mouth and they practiced French-kissing, tongue and mouth, teeth and saliva. When the screen door creaked on the front porch they scurried to his bed and the cartoons already playing to an empty room. Ramon's mother eyed them quizzically when she stuck her head into the room. She was no fool, red cheeks, red lips and mussed hair didn't escape her sharp eyes. She shooed them into the living room using the pretense of snacks, kept an eye on them. Ramon was no fool either. After snacks he and Kate talked the day away, through dinner, and into the night. They spoke about how to make Globe Hood pay. As far as Ramon was concerned that had been the first meeting of The Army of Angry Goats.

Old man Hood would have and apoplexy had he known Katherine was a founding member of the organization that worked to undermine his business empire. Incipient angry adolescents met in tree-houses, basements and tool sheds, they kept up their meetings though high school. They never did anything and for weeks at a time only he and Kate would show. They practiced a lot of French-kissing. After, some left for school, others stayed on the farm, now they were all back. The economy being shit and all. Ramon had every intention of picking up where they left off. Katherine was angry with him; she refused to participate in any of the group's meetings or actions. The food contamination issue decided it for her. She knew who the biologist among them was and she remembered what he said while still concussed and told him so. An act of terrorism she called it. His act of terror killed innocents, but also lay waste to all their righteous indignation, however justified, undermined their legitimacy and turned people against the cause. She even called him a terrorist, when they were alone. Glorified bandits and that was that, she refused calls to meetings, everything. She still came to picnics in the Barrio, ran her bodega. She was angry with Hood, enough to refuse his money or help but not enough to commit terrorism, her words.

Ramon's secret love for the daughter of the Don was not so secret. Everyone in the barrio knew about it, Katherine knew, Hood knew, Gloria knew, everyone knew. Closet kisses and teenage awkwardness dashed with a torrent of throbbing hormones, perfect stew for sexual discovery. The summer between Jr and Sr year in high school they discovered each other. Gangly, skinny, all care and consideration, she allowed him into her inner sanctum, secret garden, soft underbelly. She allowed it a few more times before they both went off to school. Once he came back even his girlfriends from the barrio teased him, said he would drop them once she came back. They were right. She wasn't returning his calls.

Ramon chug a lugged the rest of his beer, caught the eye of one of his soldiers. Ramon signed for the man to round up the thirteen. The man turned and walked away. Ramon snagged the arm of a little girl running by, her pink flip-flops a few sizes too large. Ramon asked her to get her daddy, she nodded and ran off. In five minutes twelve other people sat with him at the picnic table. Together with Ramon they made up the Thirteen. Three Captains, in charge of platoons of thirty-odd people each, Nine Lieutenants below them, each in charge of a squad of nine to twelve. Ramon was the Commander, in charge of them all. The Thirteen or Trece as they were more commonly referred to, were the command structure for The Army of Angry Goats. If Ramon felt ineffectual a few months ago, he did no longer, they were firing on all cylinders now. His Captains, two men and one woman. All three were supervisors, one in the greenhouses, one in the fields and the third in the lab with Ramon. All three older than he and legal; they were not afraid of ICE.

The nine Lieutenants s consisted of six men and three women, most of them were of age with Ramon. Six of them were illegal. They all worked in various functions on or near the farm. They assigned animal code names initially for communication purposes, the names became call-signs among their revolutionary bands, denoted squad or platoon assignment. The men were trained well enough to keep their mouths shut when necessary.

His Captains, the Badger was a burly man with black eyes and muscled hairy arms who worked as a greenhouse supervisor. The Deer, a scientist that worked with Ramon in the lab, she had large eyes and managed to look perpetually startled, her mind was very shrewd. The Hawk, a wiry lithe man, a supervisor in the fields. He had a hooked nose over a bushy mustache, sharp brown eyes beneath bushy eyebrows. The Nine Lieutenants; the Swan, because she glided when she walked. The Hedgehog because of his spiky hair. The Monkey because he could never be serious, or sit still. The Mare because she was sexy and desirable. The Coyote because he was one. The Crow had dark unkempt hair and her black eyes stared right through you. The Dove was a peace-loving quiet type, no one suspected her. The Bull, a barrel-chested hard worker, looked like he could crush the life of someone with those arms. The Pig was a butcher by trade but also a glutton and a lecher to boot, he brought food to all of the meetings and to their families too if needed.

None of them knew anything about the E. coli. That was Ramon's baby. The Doe suspected, not surprising, she worked with him in the lab and she knew the nasties they had access to.

Katherine confronted him outright, told him he was a criminal. Ramon's animal was the Goat. The irony not lost on him. The scapegoat took the blame when things went wrong, fitting for the leader to fall for his men.

The greenhouse was their first collective action; sabotage was a good starting point, protests and strikes still in the works, months away but Ramon knew they were coming. After the success of the greenhouse action a sense of tempered excitement charged them. Their group lost three members, all under the command of the Bull, a foreman in the greenhouse; and he under the command of the Badger. All three men lost were directly involved in the action, caught up in the watery surge.

If not for those losses the Thirteen would have been hooting and hollering, Ramon was sure of it. Maybe he blew the load too early after all. They had proven to Hood that they could disrupt production in unexpected and expensive ways. Ramon knew what he wanted to strike next but thought it better to meet with the Thirteen so as to distribute labor, hammer out the details, preside over the meeting. He contributed little, moderated less. The age and experience of the members negated the necessity to demonstrably guide the session. Production vulnerability exposed, Hood was burning through money. They knew the target points; research dome, loading docks and storage warehouse, the roads in and out of the farm, computer system, irrigation systems and chemical storage.

Now that irrigation capacity on the farm was considerably diminished, the consensus at the table suggested the warehouse was next. Which meant the loading docks, warehouses and access roads. Ramon agreed and told them as much. As a group they managed to avoid the most difficult conversation for most of the meeting, but ultimately the topic was unavoidable.

"Do we know anything about El Lobo?" The Pig's jowls shook, gelatin inside a sack of skin.

No need to expand on the question, they all knew Hood's jack of all trades, his enforcer, El Lobo Maldito, the Wolf.

"We know he'll be on our asses soon, if not already and we can be sure he is not going to warn us or play nice." Ramon spoke first, he knew the man relatively well. Isabella used to take care of Ramon years ago, Katherine too. He still spoke to Isabella, his parents had as well, until they were deported anyway. Of all those at the table he had the best grasp of what the man was capable of with the exception of the Badger who worked with him. The man didn't add anything.

"We expect him to figure something out soon, we're organized but we need to take great care to keep our identities hidden, the man is not above using our families to threaten us." Nods all around, they knew it to be true.

"Someone needs to speak to Katherine Hood." Caution moderated the Swan's tone. Like Ramon she was a childhood friend of Katherine's, they still talked, if they did she certainly knew there was no way Ramon could do it.

"She and the Wolf have something going on....," The woman tried hard not to look at Ramon, so hard she may as well have been speaking to him alone. Eyes widened around the room, shuffling feet under the table, none would look at him. Not a secret then. Everyone knew but him. Boil and seethe, his heart in a vice, burned to a cinder by the boiling acid in his constricted stomach. He wanted to vomit.

"Well Swan, that's your homework then, add it to your list." Metallic lifeless voice, his voice, they all breathed a collective sigh but no one relaxed. They were well trained after all.

Hours later the plan was complete. Ceramic plates piled high with bones, used napkins, leftover rice and beans scattered over the table. Lovely orange-red plates, red like the clay they were fired from. The Thirteen sat in satisfied repose, enjoyed the after dinner glow, the picnic growing quiet, families drifting home, no mess to cleanup, beautiful.

Each of the Thirteen had assignments; even those not directly involved in the next action, things always needed doing. The Captains and Lieutenants would disseminate the message to their people. Different squads for this action; give the Badger's people a rest, Hawk and Doe on this one, better that way, maintain efficiency and surprise. They had people everywhere, the warehouse included. The threshold of blue-collar and administration, the Hawk commanded warehouse workers and drivers, the Doe administrative personnel and custodians.

Perfect. Disrupting the roads had been the one point of contention in all their planning. Not the if, but the how. Explosives or blockades, split among the group, down the middle, six on each side Ramon decided it, blockades, flaming blockades. His plan was to sabotage the trucks already in route, cause destruction and delay. Which would allow the two squads to strike the warehouses. Dead of night would be the best, Hood shipped produce and products twenty-four hours a day from the warehouse. Five of the nine squads to be in action, the remaining four assigned secondary and tertiary jobs. All eyes would be trained and strained to cry Wolf at the first sight of the hairy toothed harbinger of death.

Ramon went looking for Katherine as soon as the meeting adjourned. The Thirteen disappeared like smoke into the neighborhood, el barrio, back to their lives. Ramon headed for the bodega, expected to find the object of his affection. The plump cashier working was his cousin. She sent him to the cantina, said Katherine went with Dona Isabella, El Lobo's wife. Oh great. He slid through the abandoned cantina. Dark inside, chairs upside down on the tables, floor swept and clean. Voices from the back. Through a door behind the bar and another, he entered a room dimly lit by tall glass candles with the Virgin printed on the side. The room flickered with ten candle feet of faint light that struggled to pierce the smoke hanging in the air like a haze. Palo Santo was strong in the air, twined up the nostrils with incense and charred paper.

Hard to breathe for Ramon, he coughed fitfully until someone shushed him from a shadowy corner. After several minutes his eyes adjusted to the gloom, dilate iris, dilate. Peered through tearing eyes, made out a large circle drawn on the floor in chalk, inside the circle a triangle. At each point of the triangle, where it intersected the circle, sat a small bowl with a different colored liquid, one red, another white and the third bowl seemed clear. A woman sat in the center, a small effigy in her lap, gems and stones adorned her forehead, wrists and neck. She chanted in a low voice, sounded like Spanish mixed with Native American.

Sweat trickled down Ramon's back and down his chest. Goosebumps and a chill crawled up his spine, the hair on his head stood on end. The woman in the center of the circle was Isabella Martinez, Lady Wolf, Dona Lobo, La Bruja. Ramon couldn't see her clearly. A shawl draped over her head fell over her eyes, down to her nose, cherry red lips moved in chant. Though her body was hidden within voluminous clothing and undulating shadows that reached out to caress her, Isabella Martinez was unmistakable. Her beauty plain to see. Ramon wondered if she knew about Katherine and El Lobo. The woman opened one eye to look at him, pointed to a dark corner. Shadows twitched and reached toward him, enveloped Ramon, sat him in his corner.

Eyes fully adjusted he made out the other two individuals in the room. Katherine sat across from him in the opposite corner. To his right sat Senora Hernandez, mother of the other cantina employee, Gino the bartender. A no-nonsense business woman in her own right, she kept her husband and boys in line, all five of them. They all worked for her at the churrasceria, a Mexican grill. One of her boys was a Coyote on the side and her husband was Hood's slaughterhouse supervisor and a movement member, the Pig in fact. Better able to see, Ramon inspected the circle. Double lines formed the outline, runes and markings marching around the edge. Markings Ramon knew nothing about. A repeating pattern, nothing he could make out but the pattern repeated four times around the perimeter. The points of the triangle were smaller circles, the bowls placed neatly within, rays extending inward to a point beneath Isabella Martinez. The candles scattered haphazardly around the room lacked order entirely, cast more shadow than light. Cicadas. A shadowy twitch in the darkness. The fourth corner occupied by a statue of the Virgin, many more bowls, assorted sacred objects and the shrine. Plump purple pillows worn thin by use usually covered the floor in front of the Virgin. A black cat with a large cicada in its mouth glided past a tall candle, stopped to stare at Ramon. Twitched his tail, disappeared behind the shrine. Ramon could only just make out Katherine in the corner opposite. Her red cloak gave her away was much as her milky white skin peaking out here and there. Her mouth worked though Ramon could not hear her voice. The old woman nearest him was audible, creaking shrill voice hard to ignore, not that he understood a word.

Cicadas. The click and whir of cicadas anew, not one but thousands. Ramon couldn't stop himself from scanning the walls. The room should have been teeming with them. He slapped his hands to his ears, ineffectual, the buzz filled the room, rattled his teeth. Candle flames erupted to twice the height, filled the room with flickering light, accentuated the creases and hollows in Isabella's face. Eyes dark pools under the shawl. Her words were not intelligible and whispered. She went on about farming, pesticides, exploitation of immigrants. The speech sounded prepared and Ramon realized, Isabella was screaming, only sounded whispered beneath the drone of the cicadas, in truth her voice echoed around the room. Sound of sand falling. Cascading soil, reminded Ramon of the field hands unloading a dump truck worth of sand, the smell of silica dust filled his nostrils but nothing to see. The old woman in the corner laughed hysterically, her loud cackle sounded maniacal. Katherine reached a hand toward Isabella, placed her hand palm down on the floor, atop a radial line connecting the circle she sat within to the larger circle Isabella sat within. Blood tipped each of her fingers, pin pricks, bleeding all, five points and her palm.

Ramon looked at the ceiling, no longer trying to feign aloofness, his eyes wanted to roll into the back of his head. His heart hammered, terror clawed at his throat, urged him to scream and run. Another circle on the ceiling mirrored the one underfoot, identical if a bit larger. The old woman in the corner kept laughing, clawing at her head. Sent shivers up Ramon's spine. Noise grew, fires grew, crescendo of sound. The laughter froze his bones, Isabella threw her head back and screamed. Katherine too, the old woman kept laughing.

Thunderclap deafened in the small smoky space. Deathly quiet, maybe he was deaf. The sound of water drops. A large drop formed on the ceiling, covered the entire circle. Milky white, blood-red and brown streaks ran through the drop like veins on an enlarged phallus, glowing light within. The drop grew in size, became a perfect silver color, like a bead of mercury. The whole ceiling was covered by the drop, pulled by gravity it hung down, lower and lower. Silver droplet touched the crown of Isabella's head, lowered, engulfed her, five seconds, ten, sixty. Ramon almost stood up, with a loud ker-plunk of a water drop hitting a liquid the droplet was sucked up into the ceiling. Ceiling rippled like it was water. Silence.

Silence stretched into infinity, pushed Ramon to the brink of sanity. His mouth worked but no sound. He screamed at Kate, at Isabella, no sound. The old woman was till laughing, eyes crazy with delight. Was he deaf? Not so lucky. Sound returned in an explosion, second clap of thunder, rocked his tympanum, puncture the drum. Felt like his ears burst, crushing sound of crested wave crashed over his head. Sound enough to prove to Ramon he was not deaf.

Breeze blew through the room, stiff and wet like he stood at the edge of a waterfall, mist and spray soaked his face and clothes. Silence. The candles were extinguished, tendrils of smoke to the ceiling. All three women, one man and one cat were panting. Their clothing was dry, though Ramon swore he saw a puddle in the corner near the shrine, wet one instant, dry the next. Ramon stood on trembling legs, newborn lamb, caught Kate's eye and ran. Scorn, derision, dislike flitted across her face. The last and final, pity, was too much for him. Escape from that look was all he could do. Had he seen his own face in a mirror he may have understood. Wide-eyed and pale as a ghost, Ramon's hair was standing on end. Scared stiff was an understatement.

Chapter 7

The Warehouse

Dust motes rose to meet shuffling feet. Dry the throat, tickle the nose, try not to sneeze. Ramon adjusted his position, yet again. Stiff muscles and creaking joints demanded stretching sooner than later. Crouched in a forgotten loft of the farm's largest warehouse the space looked to have been an office or love nook. A working kitchen, bathroom, bedroom with an airy cross breeze, big windows and forgotten twin size bed. Perfect space for hard working overnights or illicit trysts. He waited patiently, crouched between forgotten sofa and wall, waited for the second shift to end. Let the innocents leave, get home to their husbands and wives. Then he and the rest would get started, round about midnight, crickets on the brain.

Ramon minimized his involvement in direct action until now. He needed physical exertion, mental strain, run until he puked, fear to his bones. It all served to keep him from the Red Hood and cricket chirp plague out of his mind. Keep himself busy, that is what this really was. The group moved people from squad to squad as necessary. Two of Hawk's people and one of Doe's were transferred to the new greenhouse complex, replaced the three men the Bull lost in their first action. Ramon was filling in for the man the Doe gave up. Functioned to keep his skills sharp and his mind occupied. Occupied it was. He couldn't stop wondering who used the hidden suite tucked into the back of the loft. Hood? El Lobo? Everyone knew El Lobo's office was in the greenhouse, another reason they selected the growing complex as their first direct action.

Bang of a metal door below, second shift workers began to leave. The plan was to give them an hour to clear out while he and members of the movement readied the place for action. The fun was set to kick off at 12 midnight, zero hour. Movement members took care of the third shift; they wouldn't be showing up tonight. Called earlier in the day, all were told the warehouse was closed for 'maintenance' that night. A few had questions, but not many. A paid day off sounded good to all.

Hood didn't pay enough for loyalty. The truckers would still make their runs. Most of the drivers were members anyway, they knew what was going down, and were necessary for the action. Only two others on premises would need to be handled before the action commenced. Ramon sniffed through his nose, regretted it immediately as he sneezed fitfully, trying his best to stay quiet. Twin beams appeared below, security walking the warehouse floor. The lights wandered to and fro, between the long rows of shelves cloaked in shadow. The topmost level of those shelves stood even with Ramon, other side of the catwalk railing. The shelves were piled high with crates of produce or packaged dried goods, all from the farm. No dust on those shelves, the crates were never long on any one shelf, fork lifted away before dust had time to settle. He watched the twin beams bob up and down next to the far wall on the opposite end of the warehouse. Ramon knew stairs there led to a catwalk, which led to the loft he crouched in. Damn.

One of the security guards worked for the cause, but the other was a bit of a loose cannon. The security guard working for the cause knew his role and the importance to the action. His first task was to deal with the real security guard without being found out. The twin lights bobbed their way up the stairs, divided on the catwalk. One went left, the other right. They would meet ten meters in front of Ramon, he wondered if they knew about the suite. Probably, it was part of their rounds. Ramon hefted the bag at his side, swung it over his shoulder and stood. Mad dash for the edge of the catwalk, he'd jump the gap and hide behind a pallet of what looked like grapes in the non-existent light.

Ramon took one step and the ground rose to meet him with a loud thud, magnified by the vibrating metal of the catwalk, a loud groan escaped his lips. One tennis ball must have rolled free from his bag, an escapee underfoot, he hadn't seen the ball in the darkness and stepped right on it, sent him sprawling. He heard muffled swears in the wings and the clanging of boots running toward him. Ramon shuffled to the railing, slung the bag over, it landed on the grapes without a sound, the top of his bag, tied tight, did not spill any more balls. He jumped the gap, fully expecting the tall shelving unit to creak and sway under his weight, but thanks to its sturdy construction he made not a sound.

The flashlights reached the spot of his failure, searching back and forth. He crouched behind a pallet of what indeed were grapes, sure smelled like grapes, held his breath.

Muffled questions and curses, they knew someone was there. One light trained on the ground.

Ramon was sure his footprints in the dust showed a trail to the catwalk, thankfully the catwalk did not collect dust. One of the shadows, the one training the light on the ground, bent down and picked something up. In the light it was revealed, a yellow tennis ball with a cork stuck in one side. Shit. The owner of the light moved back through the kitchen and into the bathroom of the loft, Ramon took a chance. He hopped the gap, sprung to the metal railing of the catwalk, quiet as a cat.

He crossed the catwalk, brushed the security guard he suspected worked for the cause and whispered, "Aqui." Ramon hugged the wall adjacent to the alcove. The voice of the other security guard spoke out, talking to his partner no doubt.

"Just a tennis ball, pero tiene heucos y huele como gasolina and there's liquid sloshing around inside." The man's back was to Ramon as he exited the suite onto the catwalk. Ramon stepped close, the other security guard pretended not to see him. Just in time for Ramon to pistol whip the man into unconsciousness. The security guard crumpled to. The fellow movement member turned off his flashlight before the other man hit the ground.

"Good job." Ramon uttered and jumped the gap to retrieve his bag of balls. The key to his fiery blockade, he needed his gasoline and orange juice concentrate filled balls. The two of them stood in the dark for a few minutes until their eyes adjusted again. The man spoke to Ramon.

"Jesus Maria, hombre, think you made enough noise? I thought we were going to knock him out sin todo tu bulla. I might say something to your Lieutenant." Ramon cringed inwardly.

He had come off as a klutz. The subterfuge and necessarily complex uncoupling of the soldiers from the Captains was evident. Knowledge on a need to know basis and thankfully the man did not know who Ramon was. Disjointed and disconnected out of necessity, each man knew the chain of command within his or her own squad and within their platoon. Should the Captain or Lieutenant of his squad or platoon go down, every man in that platoon knew who was next in command. The knowledge stopped there. Captains and Lieutenants knew the command hierarchy and Ramon's identity.

Individual soldiers did not. Sure they met at picnics in the park, but so did half the barrio, if not the entire barrio. Lts. required their squad members to play something. Three of the Nine Lts. fielded football teams, real football, the one with the feet. One had a baseball team. All of the squad leaders did some sort of team building exercise. The fact that they tried qualified them as Lieutenants. Besides, there were two dozen other groups or clubs in the barrio, a meeting of thirteen people in the park could've been the traditional food and culture preservation society. There was one.

"Do what you want, huevon, but let's do this so I can get in my grapes." So it was that Ramon would lie in the pallet of grapes. A small space cleared in the center. He would ride to the first road block, set the truck on fire with his tennis balls, run back to the second and third roadblocks, helping as necessary, melt into the darkness. He knelt and bound the unconscious guard, he didn't need light to tie those knots. He blindfolded the man last.

"Don't want this fool seeing your face." A legitimate concern. Of everyone involved in the action the security guard was the only one of them not wearing an animal mask. All of the men and women involved wore the masks of their Lieutenant. In this case the Coyote squad was out there helping. Six truck drivers, four fork lift operators, and two driving front-end loaders. Half of Coyote squad was in this warehouse, the other half would be working at the other warehouse.

Coyote squad was tasked with clearing the loading-docks, the roads in and out, setting up the roadblocks and loading the "cargo" onto the trucks. The Hedgehog squad handled this warehouse, the Crow squad the other. Ramon wore a hedgehog mask, as he was a member of their squad today. The twelve member Hedgehog squad was tasked with clearing the warehouse. Their members were all custodians, office workers and security guards, made the task that much easier. Easier said than done, the building was massive, they would spend an hour, from 11 to 12 clearing the building, checking and double checking that the space was clear. The Monkey squad was working both warehouses as well, half here, the other half there. They were in charge of video surveillance, digital recordings, and computer systems, they were the IT squad, they were to erase any and all evidence.

"Oye, help me carry him outside and into the bushes, we don't want to leave him here." Ramon pointed at the man's legs. The other man nodded and they lugged the unconscious man down the stairs and outside. Ramon stopped them on the loading-docks. Another two men were carrying a struggling man toward the bushes. The fork-lift operator, tho only other non-movement personnel that showed up to work. The two coyote masked men carrying him were supposed to knock him out with ether.

"I don't want that man seeing you, those fools were supposed to knock him out. They waited for the pair to disappear into the night. They eased into the dark beyond the reach of loading dock floodlights, deposited the guard under a bush and returned to the warehouse to make sure it was clear.

Forty-two minutes later Ramon and his partner, both wearing hedgehog masks by now, stopped on the loading docks listening. Radios crackled, cell phones chirped, men in animal masks stopped in their tracks, hands to their heads, cocked, listening to ear pieces they all wore. The all clear. 12 AM on the money. Ramon was already sweating like a pig, and the night promised to get much hotter. The Crow squad was ready, Coyote squad ready, Monkey squad ready. The other warehouse was identical to this one, if a tad smaller.

Men and women wearing Crow, Monkey, Hedgehog and Coyote masks were ready to get the party started. The first truck rolled into the loading area, beeped its way backward to the loading dock, ready for product. While the truck drivers were complicit in the plan, best to make them look like victims as well, confuse Hood and the Wolf as long as possible. Ramon ran up the catwalk and leapt into the pallet full of boxed grapes. His bag of gasoline filled tennis balls lay waiting. A pint bottle full of gasoline to soak the outside of the balls before he lit them. He crouched low and waited. The rumbling sound of the large loading dock doors being pushed open, followed by the creak or truck container doors and the whine and beep of a forklift moving from the loading dock to the warehouse interior. The trucks were to be loaded with fruit and vegetables and an odd assortment of Hood's perfumes and specialty items.

Mostly celery, lettuce, greens, blueberries, melons etc. Not the most flammable of items, but the inside of the trucks were all wood, well vented, but with plenty of incendiary materials. He waited.

The beep and whir drew closer, the sound stopped just below and he was being lifted into the air and down to the floor. He hugged the bottom of the crate. While everyone worked for the cause, their action was supposed to look clandestine. The only way the truck drivers and warehouse employees could claim ignorance, he hoped. He sat tight, dropped into the truck container he listened for the sound of the latch securing the truck's trailer door closed. He never heard it, which was good, if the latch were closed he'd be locked in. The truck bounced and bounded its way for five minutes to what Ramon imagined must have been the edge of the farm property. He bounced with the fruit as the truck came to a hard stop. Time to get the party started.

Fire…time to summon fiery flame to lick everything. Ramon lit the first tennis ball as soon as the truck stopped. Dousing the ball in gasoline, some of which sloshed onto his lap, he lit it with his lighter. Roll little fire ball, roll. He sent it rolling down the length of the container.

Lost from sight save for the faint glow it gave off, disappeared beneath a crate of melons. He lit another and another,

another, lit fifteen in total, time to exit, left the last ten for just in case. Fire popped, snapped, exploded balls in a corner. Ramon shielded his head reflexively. The mask was hot, he pulled it up onto the top of his head. Gewy flaming entrails exploded from a tennis ball, spewed fire, ignited everything. The effect was not lost on Ramon. Fiery balls danced across the floor, exploded under crates, destroyed melons in fiery fury like lava filled cantaloupe. Fire climbed the burning walls. Heat blinded him. Sweat and tears rolled down his face in waves. Fire dripped from ceiling, balls popped, exploded glowing fiery death. The truck was set.

Kick open the door, nearly fell out of the container, wheezed and gasped. Smoke billowed into the night sky. Air so fresh, Ramon shook the smoke from his brain and coughed for the trouble. He ran to the cabin, exchanged grunts with a frightened coyote. He walked the man into the field that flanked the road on the passenger side and bound him, far enough away to be safe.

Once the man was tied up Ramon started running, it was a mile to the next truck. It took him seven minutes, his lungs ached, couldn't get enough air. Worse than he thought. Cricket chirp in the night, just the one, it was summer.

Large concrete blocks, easily thirty cubic meters of concrete, weighed tons. Hence the use of front-end loaders and back hoes. The stones were too heavy for one or the other, or so he imagined. The truck beyond the blocks smoldered, a few minutes of burning behind his own. A quick glance over his shoulder, he could see the orange glow, smoke and towering flames where the truck he ignited burned. He imagined the fuel tank would go soon. The coyote member was bound, though gagged and somewhat closer to the truck than Ramon would've liked. The man screamed into his gag, mask thrown back into the smoldering truck. Ramon bent over him, lowered the gag.

"El Lobo, El Lobo maldito is here hombre, hurry! I think he got the next truck.

Suddenly the night was ice cold. The blood in Ramon's veins froze, heart hammered to pump the molasses his blood had become. Thunder in his ears. The third truck, another mile away. It seemed to be in position, he couldn't tell in the dark but it seemed to be smoldering ahead. Too far to see in the dark.

Feet and heart hammered in time as Ramon tried to sprint the mile to the next truck. He pulled his mask back down, just in case. Mentally he fingered the balls in the bag that jostled at his side. Switched the radio back on, listened. He turned it off while working s

o he could hear if anyone approached. The surprise was of a different nature tonight. The chatter on the radio seemed normal. Hedgehogs one through six were lighting fires, six thought twelve on watch. They didn't use names, only squad assignment and number rankings. He listened while he ran.

Hedgehog members on watch, no signs of alarm. Checkpoints were clear, no movement detected. Two hedgehogs missing. Ramon's hair stood on end. Two of the members on watch were down for some reason, obviously radio silence was necessary at times, seeing as Ramon just turned his back on. Recon and sentry assignments were required to maintain constant radio contact. Run faster. From the chatter both contingents of saboteurs were wrapping up. The hedgehog squad had all three trucks lit, the third just beginning to smolder, Ramon could see it now. He must be in the trees, Ramon thought, off to one side of the road. Ramon looked back to the truck, watch was right. The truck was burning in earnest, still small in the distance, licking tongues of flame were plenty visible, tasting the cool night air, filled it with their red-orange glow. Maybe the Wolf was out in the field to Ramon's left. Greater visibility for greater distance, perhaps the man lay there watching and listening.

Crow squad was similarly wrapping up at the other warehouse. Like clockwork they were all in the final stage of the action, light the warehouse. A hedgehog sentry finally noticed one of the watch was not checking in. From the sound of it they found him stuck to a tree. Mierda, carajo. Hedgehog eleven, waiting just beyond the loading docks, crouched in the bushes should have reported to Hedgehog captain, three and four igniting the warehouse. He should've been waiting for them to emerge from the warehouse and sound the end action signal. Tightness in the voices, no panic, this had been rehearsed too many times, they were indoctrinated and trained but the strain was undeniable.

Ramon thundered down the drive, squelched the radio, listened for all he was worth. Shit. Mierda. The Lobo was out there, somewhere, lurking in the darkness. He contemplated sounding the alarm, decided against it. Better to finish up and get everyone out, fill them in later. Barely ten minutes until the end of the action by his estimate. He reached the third truck, flames licked from the destroyed roof, popping melons inside showered the walls with fruity shrapnel. Ramon ran around the truck, no driver. No hedgehog. They should've been there to meet him, the hedgehog member at least. The driver should've been bound like the rest. They were to rendezvous in groups of two, head for the cantina, then home.

He wrapped his hand in his shirtsleeve and opened the container door. It was latched from the outside, alarm bells sounded in his head and in the warehouse he heard the fire alarm sound. Fire engines would begin arriving soon. Inside the container lay two heaps unmoving on the container floor.

They were pressed close to the door, bloody fingers all the evidence of their attempts to claw the doors open. Smoke bellowed out, hack and choke. Ramon wheezed. Blackness billowed in his face. Adrenaline surge, surprised there was any left in his veins. Ramon grabbed the first prone form, the driver, a burly heavy man. Ramon heaved, pulled the man to the edge and over. The man fell to the ground in a pile, unconscious and burned. Ramon grabbed the second form. Dressed all in black the body was significantly lighter. Hedgehog two then, second in command of the hedgehog squad. Slight, athletic and pretty, Ramon knew who she was, a secretary in the warehouse.

She had the skills necessary to be a squad captain, in fact they were grooming her for just that. She liked to drink and party, chase the boys around, but what twenty-something didn't. Her body, considerably lighter, moved with a fraction of the effort needed for the fat trucker. Ramon pulled at her black skin-tight clothing, muscles charged with adrenaline and ended up throwing her out of the container, lifeless limbs flailing as she rolled to a stop. Quick check, they were both breathing and they were both burned. Her arm looked broken, Ramon winced, his doing. *Jeezus*. The night sky exploded in thunderous noise, fire licked the heavens with a towering column. The second truck, a mile back exploded, flames reached gas tank. The truck Ramon stood panting next to wouldn't be long. He dragged the two of them as far from the truck as he could, out into the open field. There he found, only because he fell over, the body of Hedgehog Eight, knife through his shoulder, unconscious. The sentry for the third truck, sentry against attack, explained why the two he found in the container were surprised. Blood pooled in the grass, black stain in the black night. Ramon watched as the warehouse filled with flames forked tongues licking the sky. This was bad.

Ramon was on the radio immediately. From the glow in the sky on the other end of the farm both actions had been successful. He sent the success signal and the man down code with it, four times. Allow them to temper their fiery success with the cold water bath of failure. How many lost to the Lobo Maldito? He hoped he could get the wounded out before the cops showed. One problem at a time.

Chapter 8

El Lobo bites

Isabella was a bitch in the morning. Not all mornings, just the ones when she was awake. El Lobo likened it to a hat filled with creepy crawling spiders that invaded her head, tickled the brain in the worry wart, forget-me-not, diarrhea of the mouth lobe. Every thought that filled her pretty head came out of her mouth sans filter. Not pleasant. It was easy to leave her those mornings, slipped out into the yard with as little noise as possible, left her banging things in the kitchen, talking to herself. Bellyache and moan, no one ever helped her with anything. He knew it wasn't true, as did she but her mouth and brain couldn't let it be.

He preferred peace and quiet in the morning. A slow rise from the numbing, obscuring fog that burned off as the sun rose into the sky. He had the misfortune of standing in the kitchen drinking coffee that morning when the dragon rose, smoke and fire poured from her mouth. She threw a rolled cigarette in her mouth, how dare he leave squash on the table. The kitchen was full of dust, even more since the bastards he sent over were putting in a new door and window, couldn't he do it? Her panties in a bunch, quite literally, jammed up her crack revealing so much beautiful, bronzed muscled thigh. She was irritated as much because strange men would be standing in her kitchen in a few hours as she was at being awake. He brought the squash from the fields the night before. She had mentioned something about grilled vegetables, so he brought the squash, zucchini, onions and tomatoes. How dare he leave dust and dirt from said vegetables scattered across the kitchen table. What was he thinking? She demanded to know. Waterfall of complaints, how her brain could contain such goings on, like a bowl of worms, writhing with worry, ideas and problems, was beyond him. He would go mad if he allowed his head full of worry to wriggle and writhe, mad indeed. Out in the yard, grass damp with dew, wet tips of his boots changed from tan to brown. He heard the back door slam.

She finally realized he was no longer in the kitchen. No longer withstanding the barrage of complaints and wrong-doings, his fault of course. Injustices visited upon her, perhaps he should have gotten her a maid, someone to help. Even if she said it would be too pretentious.

Not so hard to imagine leaving her on the bad days, screams and slamming doors all the goodbye necessary. Leave this place and never come back. Disappear with the fog, fade away, gone by mid-day, never to return. That would be nice. Set himself up on a Caribbean island or on the coast. Let some other man deal with her anger. She was so angry and had been for a long time. Maybe another man could help her, make her happy instead of angry. Katherine flitted through his thoughts, spicy and sweet, naughty and naked rubbed her body against his.

Maybe Isabella could tell. She had always been very in tune with his moods. She knew when he was thinking of other women, he wasn't sure if it was conscious or not, but she knew. A good Latina wife, she made sure to fuck him good and feed him well but what wife didn't give her husband a piece of her mind. So exhausting, better to get to work. So he did, strolled toward the greenhouses and his office, heard something break back in the house. Smash, bang.

Honeysuckle and Euonymus, Magnolia and Azalea, Rhododendron and Holly. El Lobo Maldito spent the evening with Isabella after an uneventful day of work. She was agitated and annoyed with him, picked up where they left off. She was drunk when he walked in the door. No dinner, no nothing. She went to bed an hour after he arrived. No matter, he had some-thing to take care of. The buzz among the illegals was that something was going down tonight. Headed into the night, wandered the grounds. Good thing he did. Two hours and sev-eral miles later, darkness wrapped in shadow and there he was, surrounded by shrubbery, the warehouse was dark, but people moved to and fro. Something was amiss. He suspected as much, just not something so organized. He'd imagined one or two individuals behind the problems. The situation was otherwise.

Coordinated groups of men and women, assigned tasks, the saboteurs were many. One of them crouched not far from where the Wolf stood, still as a stone. El Lobo was late to the party, from the movement he suspected whatever was happening had already begun. Slide through shadow, time to act.

The fool had an ear piece in, volume way up, though he was smart enough to keep his head on a swivel. El Lobo watched him for five minutes, the man had his back to a scraggly pine tree, facing the loading docks and parking area behind the warehouse. His ear piece faced the darkness and El Lobo, the real mistake the sentry made was facing the action.

The sentry should have been facing the darkness with his ear piece turned low or off, checked as specific intervals, better to hear El Lobo's approach. Shadow embraced by darkness. El Lobo materialized on top of the sentry before the man knew what was happening. One fluid motion, El Lobo ripped the radio from the man's belt, ear piece came with it, knife to the fool's throat.

"Stand up." Hedgehog mask shook, the man was frightened, whimpers and shrieks made him sound like a rodent. El Lobo shoved the man hard against the scraggly pine, demanded answers. Hedgehog was giving none, only gurgle and whimper, blood dripped across his knife blade. Pulled off the mask and discovered grim rectus of pain, the man unconscious. Damn. Jagged pine limb, sharpened to a point, pierced the shoulder and clavicle. Blood poured in rivulets down the end of the wooden spike. No answers from this one, not anytime soon anyway. El Lobo Maldito ran into the darkness, followed the trucks, left the fool on the tree. He would've donned the hedgehog mask if it hadn't been full of blood. He stuck to the trees, moved quickly and quietly.

Hustle past the first truck six minutes later, the vehicle pulled up short, screeching tires, swearing driver. El Lobo kept on, running in the dark, through the woods, he loped like his namesake. Chatter on the radio echoed their actions. He arrived at the next truck, seven minutes later, the container already smoking in earnest. A dark shape sprinted back down the road. The driver was loosely bound in the woods. Foolish person left him obscured from the road and the sentries laying out in the field. The Wolf punched the man in the face then gagged him correctly. Left him close enough to the truck to get burned. Serve him right.

Turn, melt into the shadows, back to the first truck. He'd bet by the glow in the sky and the chatter on the wire that they had one more, lit first, surely about to explode. He might still catch one of them back at the first roadblock. He took care of the fool on watch in the field first.

Pretty little thing just finishing up in the container as he approached. Lobo floated in the shadows until she came around front. He caught her with her mouth open, calling for the driver to get out of the truck. Smashed her in the head with backhand fist and she crumpled. Heft and drag, El Lobo threw her unconscious body into the truck, did the same for the driver. He kept their masks, one Hedgehog and one Coyote mask. Let them burn, burn baby burn. El Lobo addressed the warehouse. No flames visible, flashlights though. Trotted around the side of the loading docks, no one around. El Lobo Maldito strode into the dark interior, wondered if he'd have to kill anyone else. Wasn't necessary. Shadows caressed his face, penetrated the darkness, find the interlopers.

A flaming ball flew out of the darkness, arcing high out of the black, bounced in front of him, then soaring over his head. Bounce, bounce toward a cluster of fifty gallon barrels tight against the far wall. Bounce, bounce, flames from the ball propagated along the floor, a flowing wave of flame exploded outward. Whoosh of oxygen consumed, flames running along the walls, to the other side of the warehouse, behind him. Hundreds of meters distant, the same setup, shit, no time. El Lobo ran from the warehouse, slipped into the darkness, loped for home, damage done. He had some ideas now. The warehouse exploded behind him.

Chapter 9

Sweet and Sour

Little Jon sipped at edge of rocks glass. Neat was how he liked his Brandy, his work area too. Untidy mountainous heaps of papers teetered on the edge of collapse all around him, drove him to distraction quite visibly. His eyes, fixed on the insurance report in front of him were drawn repeatedly and with increasing frequency to the swaying, poorly constructed piles. Hood had half a mind to walk over and knock the whole thing over just so the man would get on with it. Instead he waited. No sense in yelling at Little Jon. A millionaire several times over, his obsessive compulsive nature was generally a good thing.

The pile slated for shredding and disposal consisted of internal memos and reports acknowledging the risks of the gray-water system in the greenhouses, the potential for failure and the results of such failure. Not exactly compromising material but he wanted any proof that might give the insurance companies more reason to resist and drag out their payments destroyed. Great lengths to prove this greenhouse disaster was not an inside job, sabotage. That would've had him locked up in litigation for years, never see his money. Even though it was an inside job, they didn't need to know that. He needed all the contacts and resources at his disposal after the Capitol hill debacle. Some banks still wouldn't speak to him.

He would never admit it to anyone, maybe Gloria, but he suspected Isabella was behind his "fit". Never prove it though. He knew the Feds would descend on his farm sooner or later, hopefully later. Political theater was nothing if not long and drawn out. Gloria coasted through the office. Pants suit a deep burgundy, blouse a smooth mustard color. Like blossoming Foxglove he saw in her yard earlier in the year. She tended a beautiful garden. He'd gifted her a small house, in reality a small mansion on the edge of the farm property, same side as the bodega.

The woods surrounding her house were untouched, a full five acres to herself back there. Gloria teeter-tottered the unstable towers one by one into a big gray recycling bin she pulled along behind her. Bound for the shredder and then the incinerator, better safe than sorry. Her bottom was particularly enticing but Hood refrained. His cheek still stung from the slap she delivered earlier. Gloria finally had enough and told him as much and as was her nature did so thoroughly. She left no room for doubt. She told him with words and actions and he respected her for it. He was fairly certain she hated him. Chuckle under his breath.

"Gloria, could you send the girls in here please?" By the girls he meant two twenty-somethings he pulled from the custodial pool and turned into his private secretaries. They were un-ambitious under achievers that knew an opportunity when they saw one. They were his toys and he their sugar daddy.

The girls knew what to wear and more importantly what not to wear. Gloria rolled her eyes and left. Little Jon raised his eyebrows. Relief plain on his face now that the leaning towers of paper no longer frayed his nerves. Hood liked the girls. Tight backsides and willingness to please. He hadn't even needed pharmaceutical assistance. The girls didn't mind his round hairy stomach, fat pink prick or stink of scotch and cigar. They fucked him anyway. What he paid them for, after all. They were completely useless as secretaries, Gloria didn't even make an effort to train them, nor would she. That, she made perfectly clear when she set him straight.

"Gloria hates you for that, you know." Little Jon spoke, still staring at the empty space where the papers had been.

"I know." Hood sighed loudly. He'd rather fuck Gloria than the little whores she was less than interested. "Her loss, I offered, she declined. I think I deserve to enjoy myself, I've earned it."

"So you say," Little Jon's eyebrows had yet to come down from their perch next to his hairline, "but are you sure now is the best time? We've got the insurance company on the ropes, cutting checks, finally. Now our two distribution ware-houses go up in flames. I'm sure I don't need to tell you, they are going to be all over us, especially considering that every-thing about it screams inside job." Little Jon the ever prudent.

"All the more reason to have a twenty-year old rub her sweaty, greased up body all over my fat, you dolt. I can think about that unpleasantness later. The Wolf will be here post haste with a report. So in the interim I am going to enjoy the firm backside of this little Mexican whore. You should have some, I can order more."

"They aren't chattel, Globe." Little Jon chastised Hood, stared into the bottom of empty rocks glass.

"Aren't they, Jon? They will be fine grade A for another five years, maybe ten, after that they'll be knocked up with saggy tits and a fat ass. No thanks."

"As delightful as that sounds, Hood, I think I'll pass."

"Your loss."

The girls filed in, feigning demure expressions until Glo-ria left. Once the door closed behind her blouses unbuttoned, and bouncing bosoms blossomed, barely contained under bikini strings.

They were in Hood's lap before the clothing was com-pletely off, rubbed legs and chest, groin and head. Called him Papi all the while.

"Well Jon, you can stay if you like but this is going to get explicit." Hood pushed himself to his feet, one of the girls unbuckled his belt, pants fell to the floor. The other pressed her breasts against his chest, rubbed them from side to side, the other hand stroked the hole in his boxers, stroked his fat pink prick to excitement.

"I'll go, call me if you need me." Jon wasn't embarrassed but kept his eyes on the floor all the way to the door. Hood caught him getting an eye full of bronzed ass as he pulled the door closed. Hood chuckled. Warm mouth and lips closed around his member, the girls pushed him back into his chair, one worked on his penis, the other had her full tits in his mouth. It was nice to be rich, these little bitches were his, bought and paid for, time for them to earn their money.

***

El Lobo heard the fat man grunting before he opened the door. Gloria went home early, he was sure. Didn't knock, he just went in. Small of sex, pussy, balls and sweat. Like musty fish left in the sun. Neither girl stopped, Hood had them trained, they stopped when he told them to.

El Lobo sauntered closer to the action; one of the girls was bouncing up and down on the fat man's lap. The other was leaning over him from behind, pushing erect brown nipples into his mouth, the fat man sucked on the pendulous tits. He tried to speak with his mouth full, only mumbled.

El Lobo cleared his throat. The girls turned to look but did not stop. Hood removed luscious brown nipple from between teeth.

"Ready?"

"Yes."

Hood smacked the bouncing girl on the ass, sent her on her way, his pink tongue snaked down her throat his manner of goodbye. Grabbed the other girl's breast, pulled her around front and bit her between the breasts. His fat, stubby prick, erect and throbbing, leaked on the fine leather, no condom then. Hood smacked the girl on the ass, she found her clothes, bent over double in front of the man, backed up so he could see it up close. Hood buried his face between the glistening ass cheeks, slurping and gobbling loudly to her apparent delight. She shook rounded sculpted ass back and forth, helped him and his tongue dig deeper, she leaned into his face. Hood finally pulled his face away, mouth and nose glistened, shit-eating grin on his face, pun intended, laughed all the while. Slapped the ass, sent her on her way, for real this time.

"What is it Wolf, more bad news, better have names this time."

"Seems bad news is what I do and all I have to offer." The Wolf's boots were mute, he stepped from carpet to carpet across the office, opened a window, fresh air rushed in. El Lobo knew the two girls. Watched them grow from pig-tailed, gap toothed teens to the buxom beauties, bounced and jiggled their way out. Their mothers were so proud the two girls were hired as secretaries. White collar pathway to real money. If only they knew.

"God, those immigrant whores are so tasty." Licked his chops, rubbed his naked tummy. His deflated penis retreated to safety beneath the overhang of copious belly, the fat man stuffed himself and deflated phallus into tan pants. Lobo mused, both girls were born in the barrio, under his nose and dominion, damn lecherous fool.

"I see Gloria left early." Hood was too dense to know the how or why of Gloria.

"She hates me these days, but what is a man to do?" Fat bastard almost sounded sorry.

"She hates herself, you ass, she hates herself for loving you" Wolf waited.

"Loves me? Are you mad man?"

"Only call it like I see it. She's loved you since the one and only time you showed your humanity." It took Hood a while to answer.

"When Lily died." It wasn't a question, they both knew.

"Yes." A full decade lost to the oblivious fool. Hood paused for a long time.

"Oh well. I'll talk to her at the dinner party next week." Dry washed his hands, back to business. Wolf wasn't done yet.

"You know those girls aren't as dumb as you think."

"I don't know that, but thank you my old grizzled friend. To think you have a soft spot for women." He clicked his tongue, whimsical look dancing across his face."Now, why have my warehouses and trucks been burned to the ground and by whom?"

Slid masks across the table, Lobo had them tucked under his arm until then. Coyote and Hedgehog, vacant eye holes stared at the ceiling.

"What the hell is this?" Globe picked them up, turned them over, fingered singed edge of the Hedgehog mask. The one the girl wore.

"These are disguises worn by the groups of men and women that sabotaged your operation."

"Groups? Men and women? I thought we were dealing with Ramon and a few of his cronies from back in the day."

Apparently Hood remembered Ramon, as they all did, always underfoot, always at Kate's beck and call.

"We are and we aren't. I'm certain Ramon is involved, just don't have the goods on him yet. Apparently one group were hedgehogs, the other coyotes. The hedgehogs were lighting fires and keeping watch. The coyotes drove trucks and construction equipment, I suspect they put the barriers in the road. All the drivers were bound and gagged, meant to look like victims but I'm not buying it.

"Maybe one or two were clueless but not likely. This was a well-organized, well-coordinated inside job. There is no surveillance footage from either warehouse. Just this." He slid monkey and crow masks across the desk.

"More?" Hood was on his feet turning the paper masks over and over. A vein bulged in his neck.

"Don't pay them. Every one of those illegal bastards, the whole lot of them. Not a single one of them gets paid. Let's see how that sits with them. Tell them all, even the ones we know have nothing to do with this. Their pay is being used to reconstruct the warehouses and buy new trucks." Face so red El Lobo thought it might burst.

"OK, that is one solution." Lobo chewed on a cigar butt retrieved from shirt pocket. "Of course that will serve to escalate the hostilities you realize? They have you off balance and out of sorts." True statement.

"I don't give a shit about those illegal, wet-back, river-crossing scum!" Globe's pressure was rising. Evidenced by the bright red hue of his face and neck. Fat fists pounded on desktop. "I want them all dead, every last one! Damn those ungrateful pieces of shit. They dare to mess with me? I will crush them all and their families too! That's right, the barrio, I will call in all the property I own and evict every last one of them!" The temper he was so well known for began to rise to the surface.

"All right, Hood, I agree with the wage freeze but if you act to evict them all now you will be undermining my investigation as well as the productivity of your business. One threat at a time. We'll use the eviction threat to leverage some of the more easily intimidated ones." Hood was huffing and puffing, veins throbbed on neck and forehead.

"Damn you, cursed wolf, always make my blood boil. Fine, hold their wages, let them keep their precious barrio, for now." Wolf thought a change of subject might be in order.

"Have you and Little Jon addressed the insurance company and police investigation?" El Lobo didn't mind handling workers and neighbors, corporate goons or cartel members but he left the cops to Hood and Little Jon. He had too much blood on his hands.

"We're dealing with them currently which was why I had my face buried in that little brown ass. About the only thing making me feel halfway decent today."

"I see, here." Crisp white paper, list of twenty names in a neat hand, two were crossed out. "That is my first list. The people I think are in the hedgehog and coyote groups. I'll nose around the other warehouse, ferret out crow and monkey, cross reference with the greenhouse etc."

"And these crossed out names?" Fat fingers pointed to the black lines through black letters.

"They are no longer members of the Guerrilla movement, nor your employees." Long stare, Hood nodded. He understood.

"Good work, Wolf; if we're done send the girls back in on your way out. I'm upset all over again." El Lobo did as ordered, sent the girls back in on his way out.

They sat half naked in the lounge, bare skin on the tanned, stretched, stitched skin of some long dead cow. White blouses remained unbuttoned, gum smacking lips popped bubbles while they waited. El Lobo heard them fussing over Globe as soon as they ran back in the room, scolded him for becoming upset. The door slammed.

Chapter 10

Party

Cat and mouse, dog and cat, predator and prey, El Lobo wasn't sure which he felt more affinity for come the night of the dinner party. Globe invited the usual assortment of fat cats and big wigs. Fewer bankers showed than usual, he could tell by the lack of shit-eating laughter, those bastards were always laughing. Their absence was not a surprise given Globe's tom foolery at the Senate hearing, but more than one banker was too many in the Wolf's estimation.

Lawyers, doctors, real-estate magnates, oil tycoons, politicos and the like on the short list. Globe encouraged his farm supervisors to attend as well, provided they could clean up to respectable degree. Most important attendees were Katherine and her date, Mrs. Wolf on his arm and Gloria trying to stay in the kitchen with a bottle of red. He needed to speak with each of the ladies. More specifically he wanted to speak with Katherine; head, loins, and chest pulled him toward her. Sixth and seventh senses going haywire. He was ordered to speak with Gloria at Hood's behest and was avoiding speaking with his wife lest she make him squirm. His hackles on end, shook smooth doughy hand of Katherine's date. Hunter something, how very well to do of him with a name like Hunter. College friend, his familiarity with Katherine evidenced by his hand on the small of her back, said enough. Bared teeth, toothy grin, grimace or smile for the boy. Smart button-up shirt, close fitting with vertical blue stripes, no tie, khaki slacks, brown deck shoes, sun bronzed skin. The boy looked like he belonged on a boat. El Lobo wanted to crush the man's hand when he shook it. Katherine refused to look at him, her eyes darted to his shoes, his belt buckle, Isabella's face. She avoided his eyes with such dedication he wanted to shake her or maybe bite something. A touch on the elbow, a whispered word. El Lobo left Isabella chatting with some banker of import, Globe meeting and greeting near the foyer, cigar and scotch strangely absent.

Old habits, ingrained in his fibers, the Lobo went out in the darkness, recon around Gloria's mansion, chosen site for the festivities. Through Rose garden, thorns grab for khaki dress pants, kitchen garden, silly by some accounts.

She had all the produce she could ever need, never need to ask, did her shopping at Katherine's grocery anyway. Gloria liked to get her hands dirty, something he admired about her. Her garden was untended, not usual for Gloria, over-sized squash and zucchini lay rotting, barely visible between the weeds. Kentucky Blue, invader plantain, errant Shepherd's-purse, volunteer St. John's-wart. Was she depressed? Some old-timers believed the weeds that grew in a person's garden were the plants the person needed. She'd been too busy to weed from the look of things. Poked around the garage, checked on the van brought by the kitchen staff, both hers and Hood's. Within that van they ferried carafes, trays, burners and all the makings for a feast this size.

A red Jeep Wrangler with the top off, mud splattered like decals on large tires and sides. Gloria had been off-road in the woods or somewhere. He returned to the party through the back door, it led through the mud room, cleaned the mud from his shoes, into the kitchen. Gloria leaned against the center island, large cup of red wine in her hand. Glum expression and far away eyes told El Lobo all he needed to know. She was no more thrilled to be hosting the party than he was to be attending it. He couldn't help but wonder if every person in the place was attending under duress. Globe needed to cultivate the friends he still had, the wait staff had to work or they'd be fired, Katherine and Gloria did it for Globe. And he, like it or not, was an employee after all, show up to work or don't show up at all. He grabbed a glass for himself, filled it half-way, filled another for Isabella. The kitchen buzzed with frenetic activity, women in white aprons dashed to and fro, here and there. Spanish, cumin, English, cilantro, Spanglish, serrano and anaheim chilis, spices in the air. He stopped in front of Gloria on his way back to the party.

"Perk up, beautiful. We'll get through this together. Let Hood do the heavy lifting today. You look run down and worn out, you'll be no good for kissing tight puckered ass. Let that old windbag blow some of that hot air he's so full of. Isabella and I are always here for you." She looked up at him. Tired eyes failed in their effort at a smile, he would've hugged her but too many eyes. Walls could talk and they did.

"Thank you Jose, I'll need the help." She shook herself, semblance of life returned to her face. She pushed through egg-shell colored kitchen door, lead him into the parlor and library, tables arranged around the room, manned by men and women of Latino heritage, farm employees actually, dressed in smart red vests and black slacks. Plush cushioned couches and thick rugs atop a bamboo floor, every square foot occupied by fancy dressed types. Kept an eye out for the weak and wounded. Circled the group, waited for blood to spill.

***

Globe was so pissed he wanted to spit. That damn Wolf, practically scaring the shit out of the guests. Looked like blood on his lips, red wine in his glass. He exited the kitchen behind Gloria, licking those blood red lips. Like he just dined on her flesh or someone's flesh. Drip, drip, blood, sanguine and crimson coated orifice of Death's messenger, Death's handmaiden with grizzled jaw, crimson lips, black eyes of provenance.

The man coasted around the party like a god-damned Wolf. Blood-red morsels well in hand. He observed the prey, waited for one to fall. And fall they would. The drinks flowed, music played, husbands and wives crept out back for a smoke. Isabella was already loose, done charming the pants off some banker, the man looked dazed and dumbstruck, unsure if he was in love or if he should check his pockets for his wallet. She coasted away, alternated between that tinkle of a laugh and the throaty witch cackle that was her calling card.

She avoided Globe as usual, and julienned him with her customary dirty looks. She hated him, always would. Ask no questions, hear no lies. She found Gloria shortly after El Lobo brought her a cup of wine and the two had their heads together ever since, no help for Globe there.

***

El Lobo hadn't seen Gloria drink in years. She used to come to the weekend B-B-Q's in the barrio, that was ten years ago perhaps, when she was fresh and new. Before Hood's us and them speech, the one he gave all his executives eventually.

Now she and Isabella hunkered together in a corner, hocus-pocus, glasses of red and white disappeared down their throats. They hadn't spoken in years, not since they were been best friends actually. Fickle creature is woman, one day they're friends, the next they don't speak for five years. Gloria knew Isabella hated Globe if not the why.

Her bubbling hatred had risen to the surface, coated her with a caustic shield, acidic, acrid stink of sulfur. El Lobo smelled hatred and rage wafting from the two of them and had to stop from wrinkling his nose. Of course he didn't smell of burning fire, the fire had been weeks ago and those clothes were disposed of properly. Gloria and Isabella were on the same page apparently, as far as Hood was concerned anyway.

Leave them to it, heads pressed close. Whisper, murmur, jab and point. Globe needed to watch out, if Gloria turned on him Shit Creek would be a pleasant glide down a lazy river compared to the shit storm she'd bring down from the heavens. Very like if El Lobo were to turn on the man. They'd both go down, but down they'd go. He decided to wander the house in search of prey. Katherine must've slipped away when he was distracted, checked the cheese and wine, her favorite, not there.

Flicker of red hair, flash of pink and black skirt, linen white blouse, more transparent than opaque. Tight body, no need to use his imagination, he knew. Turned his head, pursued her scent, Wolf with his nose to the air, and she was gone. Her home, or nearly so.

She stayed with Gloria after Lily's death, before Hood sent her away to private school. When she finished her graduate studies in horticulture she moved in with Gloria until she got her apartment in the barrio fixed up. El Lobo knew for a fact Gloria wished she had stayed on. Always saying the mansion was too big for one woman, especially one without a family. He had heard her argue with Katherine on the phone in

Hood's office, when the sweet young thing told her she'd be moving to the barrio. As a result, Katherine felt more at home at Gloria's house than in her father's. That being said she knew the ins and outs of the place. Absurd to think his plodding, adult ramble through the house could compare with the clandestine forays of the once adolescent heir.

Long ago she mastered pantry passageways, crawl spaces and fake walls. Seemed like she was using every rabbit-hole and hidden path to avoid him. Growl in his chest before he knew it. And just like that she was there, come to attend to her duties. He was still unable to reign her in.

She moved to and fro, saw to the needs of her father's guests. Never a harsh word for any of the workers. In fact they loved her, as did everyone that worked for Hood. A glow about her, wine spilled from his mouth. Jealousy seethed, tamped down beneath the weight of reality, burden of lust. Perhaps he'd drawn too close, like a moth to a flame, he would be burned to a cinder. Damn fool is man, Wolf too. Change of tactics in order, worked for her, would work for him too, perhaps he could corner her before the night was done. El Lobo worked the room, bounced from Mr. Hood to his Oxen-like foreman, to Badger the greenhouse foreman and his wife. Keep your distance, he scolded himself, who let the Coyote in? Wonder if Hood noticed. He kept Kate across the room, within eyesight and earshot, but too far to touch. He could tell Isabella suspected something but not much more than a tickle in her brain, a wonder why that was driven away like a buzzing fly. A woman's intuition, who let the Pig in? With the Coyote probably.

Tasted blood, avoided chestnut eyes like hot branding iron. Marked the flesh, marked the beast, the soul, the spirit, already bore her mark. Perhaps that was the glint, the glimmer Isabella saw; something shiny in the corner of her eye, the Hood crook mark on El Lobo's zip-adee-doo-da; gleamed in his mischievous eyes, then gone.

The gleam, the glint did shine the spring in his step and the smile on his face. Strange that the brand backfired all over him, what a mess. The brand burned into El Lobo's flesh, a shepherd's crook, arrowheads and fletchings, an unstrung bow.

By hook or crook avoid the shore and those treacherous rocks. Ride the tide of here and now, to and fro. Obstacle avoided, for the time being, another day, another time. Here, now, there, then, when, every, all, to know. He knew she knew, the crystals in the chandelier knew. His, theirs, ours, mother of pearl handles on the silver. Probably the second set for the guests. Globe Hood's bald head gleamed, picked up the glare of the chandelier far above.

Crystal teardrops hung above the tables, pendant shards split light into its component wavelengths. Tinkle and jingle in unseen wind, through upstairs window sneaks. The tables set, places assigned. She managed to touch him once, from whence she came, he knew not, but suddenly she was there at his elbow, laughing at the foul joke he told her father. Inappropriate discourse for her pretty young ears, about marriage and jail, had Mr. Hood guffawing much too loudly. A jolt, a shock, a spark, a burn. Her touch set her mark, the brand on his soul, afire. He nearly howled then and there, moon or no. Shatter crystal tears hanging above. Drunken monk, rocks the boat, howls at the moon. Ganesh loves, the maintainer, and destroyer, rock that boat Buddha boy.

Isabella noticed something was amiss and deftly pulled words from the unsuspecting mouth of her prey. Red Hood, one of her favorites, had information she wanted. El Lobo followed the young thing a bit too voraciously with his eyes. Something was off with him and his relations toward Isabella in every way had cooled.

His affections were no longer a tumultuous embrace with him devouring her like a starving beast and her a morsel of food, he drinking her in like a man crossed a desert and she the oasis of life and love. They gyrated to brink of ecstasy, which hung like a white hot burning ball of fire, just out of reach, the climax to burn her to a cinder, but they couldn't quite get there. Something was amiss.

Little Red lingered, never touching, or even looking at El Lobo, but linger she did. Isabella could smell her must. She was wet for Big Bad. El Lobo practically stank of quivering desire and the acrid odor of frustration. Deny the flesh all they wanted, their smells mingled and flared every time they passed, she was no fool. Big Bad never acknowledged Isa's gentle inquiries, probing delicately for threads of truth. Dumbfounded he assured her he knew of no such feelings stirring within his loins or little Red's. Isabella knew better, she played dumb. Yes my dear, I've heard of the movement, why certainly we can talk about it my dear, and so on and so forth.

Free to ride on the ebb and flow of life. El Lobo resigned himself to the currents of karmic dogma. Maybe they would pull her to him, swim against the tide will exhaust and cost your life. Currents push and pull, far too strong for a mere mortal. Still she swam in his veins, blood and plasma, heart and mind. Australian crawl, backstroke, butterfly, scissor kicked her way through his veins and arteries. Like a leaf in a stream El Lobo gave himself to the current of karmic fortune. A willow in the breeze, he bent in the strong gusts of life, desire, wont and ignorance, did not break. Pearl of wisdom, the jewel of truth, his to discover. If only he could pan enough grit and misery from the stream of life. The miner turned over cobble and boulder, gravel and sandbag. The leaf floated away, carried by current, to rest where the current lays. Ganesh and his trunk. Wisdom and obstacle, letter and intellect, road block, damned stream. Flow is impeded, the ten-thousand things within and without. Block of stone, rush of water. Obstacles literal, obstacles metaphorical. A love of letters and intellect tantalizes, tickle the trunk of Ganesh. Happy birthday elephant god.

El Lobo asked the universe for guidance, for wisdom, he knew not who, but he asked, implored the heaven, the earth. He lacked the wisdom to navigate his dharma dilemma. Lacked the fortitude to wrestle with psycho-spiritual longing, the base nature of man and apparently wolf as well. A truth Big Bad had to admit to himself. His psyche, his spirit, longed for her. Deny, deny, deny, come to terms. Terms to grip.

The obstacle to his dharma, karmic roadblock, built brick by brick, he, she, life, wife..., scurry to and fro. He aimed to embrace the obstruction, come to terms with the impassable today, will be the fluid of tomorrow, or the next day or the next... drunken monk spills wine over lips and scruff. Wooden boat adrift, streams of time, the 10,000 things, within, without. Adrift on the currents of life, pushed by the flow of time. A slightly buzzed Lobo found himself eating cheese and wine across from Miss Hood. The wisdom he begged for urged El Lobo to keep his jaws shut and his paws to himself. She was as beautiful as ever. Her hair tied up in a bun. Blaze of strawberry when it caught the light just right. The birthmark above her lip, he licked it last time. Drunken monk adrift in wooden dingy, rock not the boat, rapids and white water, surely drown if he fought the currents. She had gained some weight. Not in her hips or bottom he noted earlier as she glided by, running to fetch scotch for her father.

A bell sounded three times. Dinner is served. Globe asked for many tables at this dinner party, as many as necessary. Round tables like those of bat-mitzvah, wedding, prom and the like. Eight to ten at a table, Gloria arranged the seating, so of course they were not with Globe. Isabella, Wolf, Gloria, two old matrons both of their husbands and a son rounded out their table. Globe, Katherine, her friend and three banker type baboons sat at the head table. Globe usually asked Gloria to address the formalities at these functions. However, correctly sensing she was uncooperative, he did the explaining of the menu, the where and the why.

They would be dining on food grown entirely on the farm, with a few exceptions but only a few. Hood was proud of this fact, his pride was genuine if not deserved. Opening the meal they would find appetizing Blue Corn and shrimp tamales with a mole dipping sauce for those that dared. The shrimp were not grown on the farm obviously but the corn was, chilies too. Soup to follow, a homely Posole; pork shoulders hand picked by our supervisor of the slaughterhouse providing a divine flavor, thank you Mr. Emilio Hernandez. Hood gestured toward an undetermined table somewhere near the back. Please note the smokey Anaheim chile, delicate, savory and nowhere near as fiery as its smaller relatives, but fantastically flavorful.

The main course, continuing with the homely, comforting theme, Chicken cooked in a clay pot; the earthy tones imparted by the clay pot are seductively sumptuous and intertwined with the Serrano chile flavor. Where one flavor stops and the other begins is up to the diner to decide. Chicken is served with cheesy rice, a regional favorite for many of the workers on the farm, merely white rice sprinkled with fresh mozzarella and scallions as it comes off the stove. Confessed they didn't grow the rice, but the zucchini and yellow squash in tomato sauce accompaniment were. Lastly dessert was the choice of the diner, they could choose between Pastel Tres Leches, a smooth spongy cake, or Meringue with mangos and soft custard, as decadent as it sounded. With that Hood took his seat to a polite smattering of applause, as if he had cooked the meal himself or even selected the menu.

Music resumed from somewhere, light and classical, murmuring voices and the clattering of utensils on fine dinnerware commenced. El Lobo had to admit, the old codger could still deliver when he had too, even if he swayed while he spoke and gestured with his scotch glass as if conducting a symphony. Globe and the young Hunter lad sat to either side of Katherine. Wine dripped from the corner of her mouth, ran crimson over lip, chin. She wiped her chin with the back of porcelain white hand.

Skin so soft, hands so dry belied the hours of manual labor she put in the fields, machine shop, stables, corn rows. He licked his lips, to catch his own escaped drops of wine, Chianti, hints of woody places, forgotten grottoes, pangs of her in him. Drunken monk rides the tide, wine spills down the chin.

Witty and charming the Wolf turned it on. Whatever It was, a hodgepodge of anecdote, sardonic commentary, woven with wit and the tragedy of the human condition. Of prose and poems to glorious epoch. Escaped her gentle eyes, the caress of her brown chestnuts, roan or otherwise. Her cheeks looked plump, something about her face, a glow, a shine, a sheen. Chunky monkey...certainly not.

Isabella pounced on El Lobo while she had him at the table, she was concerned. She always said the cooler he got, the more likely things were going bad, getting messy, intestinal display on terracotta tiles. Well he was real cool, skating on a momentary lapse of reason. Head and gut screamed mutiny, heart all aflutter, cheered in drunken wonder. He didn't buy it, the icy bit, but it was her theory. She boxed him in him, during the chicken course.

"You aren't here on work are you?" Raised eyebrow adds depth and danger to her beauty.

"No, baby, I do have to speak to a certain someone though." Held her eyes.

"Would it be Katherine whom you've been trailing like a dog in heat all night? Or Gloria?" Her raised eyebrow dared him to say something. He didn't.

"Of course that fat bastard would sic you on Gloria. His closest confidant, his most loyal employee. That's what these swollen egos and swollen bellies do with their problems. They have someone to handle it." She fairly snarled at him. "That man needs to talk to her rather than send you to scare her. She's hurt and ashamed and very, very angry. I know you understand that, Jose." Dead-pan stare, heart flutters against rib cage. Wow, long time since that. She did look an appealing morsel glaring at him like he was a problem that needed fixing. Ripe for the plucking.

The white noise of chatter, guests and hosts, hazy and happy, stumble and shimmy. From here to there, table to hearth, sitting chair to mantle. Tobacco smoke filled the large den Mr. Hood presided over, post-repast. Spoke emphatically with the Hunter lad, beat the boy on the back over and over. Wolf and Little Red did not speak a word the entire night. He spoke next to her, across from her, with her father, with the young Hunter but never directly to her or her chestnut eyes. Wine trickled from the corner of her plump lips. Loins contracted, growl in his chest. He needed to depart ASAP, before the cresting wave of emotional tsunami arrived. Gone dry was the shore, the tide had receded far out to sea, the surge cometh. Swallow him whole, bury him in mud and debris, cut the heart right out of him. Business to take care of first.

***

Hood trundled up the stairs, repast complete, digestion underway, para-sympathetic nervous system firing up smooth muscle, digestive juices, cracked jaw muscles with mighty yawns, increased oxygen intake. Trundle up, climb the pale stairs, strong ash, smooth as a Louisville Slugger. Even though this was Gloria's home, Hood had no qualms retreating upstairs into her study, cigar and scotch, give his throat a rest. He hadn't schmoozed so much since he was trying to get this place off the ground.

Her study was pleasantly floral, smelled lovely like Gloria though the study felt masculine, whatever that meant. Pale wood, more ash, no pastels, a box of Cubans and a crystal bottle of scotch. He could've meandered outside with his guests, smoking was well underway on Gloria's back patio, but his throat begged for mercy. Terracotta tile, Adirondack chairs and comfortable wooden benches made for a pleasant outdoor sitting area. Smoke rose to the heavens, laden with thoughts and hopes, dreams and dreads of the lot contentedly exhaling one story below. Hood peered around the study, closed the door behind him.

Serve Gloria and the Wolf right if they had to handle the party even a little. He'd seen them all night, and both failed to complete their assigned tasks. Gloria failed to schmooze, left Globe to do it all himself. The Wolf engaged but half the time he was distracted, the rest of the time he was scaring the guests half to death. Globe was content to learn he still had game, he had been masterful in his day and still was. Only the oxidation of his jaw required grease and frontal cortex required some time to reboot. He had a lot of explaining to do, one catastrophe after another, acts of god, these are depressed times, people will do anything. Is it any surprise the disenfranchised, the outcast, the unable and the shiftless would strike an such a cache of bounty as a food warehouse and its cargo? He lost two good men to what Globe suspected, and asserted in loud accusatory tones; there were police present after all, were no more than common thieves, if rather skilled ones. Surely unsavory immigrants from a dark and undeveloped way-station of poverty, insert country here. An hour or two into the gathering he had it all in hand, though he'd forgotten how little a host gets to eat and drink, what with attending to the damn guests.

Three hours of running around were plenty, they'd all be just fine even if he was up here smoking a cigar for half-an-hour. He'd descend in time to send them on their way. More light ash, floor, walls and furniture of the beautiful wood. Hood exhaled into the large sofa against the wall, safe in shadow.

"Glad you made it, Globe" Gloria sat in her large leather chair behind the desk, smoking on an unlit Cuban cigar. Had she known? How had he missed her?

"Of course I knew, you old fat windbag, I know your rhythms better than you it seems." Old windbag? She pointed to the deep leather seat in front of the desk, pointed at the box of cigars, slid the lighter next to the box. As he sat, she rose, moved to the windows overlooking the garden and garage. The flood-light poured into the backyard so folks downstairs could navigate the garden without injury.

As she had all night she stared defiantly at him, stopped directly in front of the window, surveyed what lie beyond. The rays of light pierced the soft linen dress that clung to her skin as close as beaded sweat. She had no panties on, the rounded hills of her bottom perfectly curved. The inside of her thighs looked taut, the silhouette crisp clean lines. He thought he could just make out a bit of pubis.

"You know, Globe, you really are an ass. I go around defending you all day, every day. They say you're out of touch with the real world, living in a fantasy of wealth and power." Still she faced the window.

"I'm bailing water on this sinking ship of yours and you pretend to be oblivious to it all. How did it go tonight?" She turned on him, wine stained lips, the other theme of this party. Her tragic smirk meant she knew. "I saw you working for once, putting out your own fires, hot work isn't it?" A rhetorical, but it was a good one so he answered.

"It went OK but damn-it Gloria you owe me some answers." To which she snorted, very un-ladylike for Gloria.

"Don't try to pull that bravado bull-shit on me, Globe, it won't work." She was so close, standing over him so he could smell the perfume and tobacco clinging to her. She bent over, looked him in the eye, light peck on the lips. Serpentine lightning, her left hand flashed behind his head, fist full of what hair remained, tilted his head back.

"If you ever touch me like I'm one of your little whores again, I'll leave your ass, make a stop at the USDA, ICE, EPA offices on my way out of town. How's that sound?" Hood heard his own involuntary gasp, she pushed his face and open mouth into her pelvis, feel the soft tuft of her fair pubic mound under barely there linen dress. Another deep inhale, at least he managed not to fight against her, breathed in her musk, coriander and cardamom, frying in a pan, sweet savory scent. Slowly he brought his hands up to cup her ass beneath the dress. She moaned a little.

Lighting flash, she pushed him back in the deep leather seat, she kissed him again, harder. Damn snake of a hand strikes again, wrapping around his stiff phallus and tightening balls.

"Remember what I said Hood. I've got the goods on you and the paper trail to match, disgruntled employee or not. Touch me again and I'm gone. You'll not be fucking those bimbos in my office again either, keep your shit in your own yard." Released her grip, he exhaled the sweet smell of her pussy. His penis loved it. She patted him on the cheek and left the room. Globe wasn't sure if he was angry or turned on; or a jumble of both in his brain and balls.

Alone in her light and airy office with an erection that just wouldn't quit. Jeezus, that woman. How dare she threaten him, he'd given her wealth, she was a millionaire thanks to his business. Granted her finger prints were all over every deal and every dollar he made over the last two decades. No matter, she owed him thanks not anger. His penis hardened even more, so hard it hurt. Fumbled in his pocket, no cell phone, damn. He lit the cigar she'd clipped and placed facing him, the scotch on the rocks he didn't see her pour. Her glass, cream colored lip stick matched her translucent dress, kissing the rim. Place his lips atop hers, cock hardened more. So hard, steel rod hard, iron re bar hard. He hoped the erection would dissipate, that blood filled capillaries would empty, send blood to more important tasks. Over the course of his smoke and drink he hoped and waited, waited and hoped. Thirty minutes later his cigar was ash, drink empty. Globe hunched in the corner tossing ice cubes down his pants in a vain effort to scare his erection away, assault it with ice. No luck. He heard pleasantries and farewells being exchanged below in the garden. That was his cue, seemed he too would fail in his duties as host tonight. Eventually Katherine coasted out into the drive and handled the good-byes.

***

El Lobo Maldito let himself into the study, eyed Globe quzically. Globe returned with an exasperated look of his own, secretly grateful for the man's uncanny ability to show up when needed.

"Your guests are leaving, Globe, Gloria would too if this wasn't her house and if she wasn't loaded."

"Damn it, man, look at me!" Globe gestured toward his crotch, big top tent of his zipper, forced upward by his painfully erect member.

"They say you should call a doctor if you experience an erection lasting longer than four hours, or pain." The man couldn't stop the grin creeping across his face.

"This isn't funny, you son of a bitch." Spittle in the corners of his mouth, jettisoned with desperate ferocity, if Hood wasn't careful he might descend into the black basement of apoplectic fit, again.

"She did this to me! Gloria did this to me!"

"Isn't that a good thing? Haven't you wanted to defile her in horrible nasty ways? If she's finally on board I'm sure she'd oblige, especially in her current state."

"No, you asshole! She grabbed me by the balls, she made me smell her pussy, planted some seed of desire in my head and now I can't get rid of this thing!!" Desperation crept around the edges, hysteria cometh.

"I still fail to see the problem; sounds like you have a good jump on the rest of us who have to wait till we get home. I could send in Gloria or summon your little toys from the barrio."

"Neither, just go have the talk with Gloria you were supposed to have and tell her if she threatens me again she'll end up digesting in a waste water treatment plant or out in the Caribbean with the sharks. Make sure she gets the message, Wolf." He re lit the cigar, what remained of the butt.

"All right, I'll speak to her." The Wolf let himself out, leaving Globe alone with his painful affliction. He briefly con-

- 95 -

sidered allowing the Wolf to summon the girls from the barrio but decided against it, he was certain there was no pleasure to be had in this hard-on from hell. Poured himself another scotch, listened to the fine people slur their words and sway their thanks to the valets retrieving cars.

***

El Lobo had no trouble tracking Gloria down. She had ceded the responsibilities of guest services to Katherine and Isabella, who were trying their best to wrap up the festivities in a gracious and tactful manner though Isabella looked pressed not to throw everyone out and be done with it. All those years of managing the cantina allowed little patience for wandering drunks, wealthy or poor, BMW or burro, cultured or ignorant. In the end she did yell at some of the bankers and real-estate types that had no intention of going anywhere as long as there was sauce to be had. Said they had yet to be excused by the great and powerful Mr. Hood. What a load, Katherine shooed them away once she heard the ruckus.

Gloria was in her bedroom. Stood by the window, or rather swayed, watching guests leave. She turned to face him when he closed the door.

"I knew it. As soon as I saw that bastard squirm, saw the fear in his eyes I knew you'd be on me in a twinkle. Well, have at it, you damned Wolf, thanks for the advice by the way it felt good. Never seen that bastard work so hard."

"Take your clothes off Gloria." She didn't move. He proceeded methodically, pulled off his belt and placed it on the table, folded double, he watched her.

"I'm waiting, Gloria." She acquiesced, slow motion movements. She shook visibly. He hated himself for this nonsense. Hood really was a bastard to believe Gloria had anything to do with sabotage. Gloria couldn't betray Hood if she wanted, she had been in love with him since forever. The fool man, she'd surely get over her love after a night like this. Taking off her clothes only required that she drop one shoulder and slip her arm through the thin strap, then the other, the soft linen piled on the floor soundlessly. Gloria really was beautiful. Her firm unsuckled B-cups tightened in the air, goose flesh stood thin blond arm hairs on end. Flat belly rippled with more mus-cle than fat, not a wrinkle to be seen. She was no longer shak-ing, stared back at him with a blank expression.

He crossed the space between, heartbeat, hers not his, see her blink in surprise, nostrils flared, pupils dilated, his breath on the nape of her neck.

"What did you do to Hood, Gloria?" He let the question hang in her ear, soft spoken bangle, dangling on the lobe.

"I told him the truth, I told him to leave me alone and no fucking in the office." She spoke quietly, his ears alone. He pushed it. Place hand on the small of her back, pushed her na-kedness into his business casual dinner wear. She was panting at his shoulder.

"What about the warehouse, Gloria? Do you know? Do you know it was an inside job?" Her breath caught, she looked up into his face, pushed him away roughly.

"What?" She demanded. "Is that what this is about? I thought this was about Globe's wounded pride, and you my punishment. Damn fool Gloria, here I was, I was... leave me alone, Lobo!"

"I take that as a no."

"No, damn you, no! I didn't know a thing." She buried her head in her hands, naked and crying, too beautiful by far. He touched her again, shoulder, reassuring gesture.

"I had to ask, as it turns out a bunch of secretaries were part of the inside group that sabotaged the warehouse, men and women you interviewed. Of course security guards and drivers were in on it too and I interviewed some of them." Sobbing slowed, her racing heart too.

"Yes, well, Hood is nothing if not thorough. I remember the secretaries that work in the warehouses, perhaps not all by name but I remember them all to be competent well-adjusted types." It was odd hearing such professional analysis from a woman with tear-stained cheeks and taut areola standing in her dark bedroom.

"I'm sorry, Gloria." She sighed into his chest and sobbed the rest away. Door creaked open, light pushed against the dark. Twin silhouettes in the doorway.

He barely registered the two women before they were upon him in flurry of skirts and shoves, pried Gloria from him. Katherine stopped to slap him on the way out. Isabella shook her head and shot a look promising him a sleepless night until he unwound this yarn in painful detail and it better explain how a naked Gloria ended up in his arms, a weeping, sobbing mess.

Chapter 11

Mondragon's Manifesto

Ramon saw red, god-damn the fucking Baby-Boomers. So sick of hearing Baby-Boomer demand, rotten melons and crying brats. The whole generation behaved like a bunch of spoiled babies, temper tantrum, stomping feet, water works and an angry voice, give me what I want, I want it now. As far as he was concerned the convenience store, cop and a doughnut on every corner, I want a burger now culture was entirely the fault of the Baby-Boomers.

Boomers were just the next batch of idealistic fools that believed their shit was new, different, golden, Midas touch to happily ever after. Of course they continued the shit storm started by their brainwashed parents, the children of the great depression and their parents before them, children of the civil war. But the boomers were the hypocrites. They claimed liberation, freedom of choice, burn a bra, snort a line, dance fever, as their battle cries. If Boomers were so realized why didn't they spit in the face of their brainwashed Greatest Generation parents? Damn. They Greatest had an excuse at least. Brainwashed, propagandized and under-educated were as American as apple pie back then. We were fighting a war, saving the free world and all that. But that is exactly what saved those war-torn bastards and hardworking Rita the Riveters from the truly harsh judgment by the critical minds of history. The bending of their shoulders, the grinding of steel, the sacrifice of flesh, the last drop of toothpaste in a tube, save it anyway, scrape it again, mete and measure of the Greatest Generation left them insulated from the harsh judgment cast on their progeny.

The hungry mouths of the clamoring Boomers reinforced their dogma, their illusion, the me first principle. New plastic wrapped, processed everything, disposable everything, was, is and everything must be. How on god's green Earth had an entire country, an entire planet deluded themselves into believing this is the way things always would and should be. Incremental paralysis of political process proved problematic, proves pathetic. Damn infuriating actually. The Boomer's politics was like their world view, Boomercentric. They were the end all, be all, center of the universe, my way or the highway. Temper tantrum, stomp those feet.

God bless Styrofoam and the mini-mart, microwave ovens and high-fructose corn syrup. God bless the feed lot, god bless the immigrants crossing the desert to work for a pittance. God damn Secretary of Agriculture Earl L Butz. May he burn in hell in a puddle of ethanol or suffocated for an eternity in a grain hopper. Happy as a pig in shit no doubt, his mission was a smashing success. America was the land of corn, corn and more corn. Gone so big all the little guys were bankrupt and migrated to the suburbs. Corn from fence row to fence row so we could all choke on it, pesticide and herbicide turn the waterways into undrinkable quagmires. Eutrophication, algae bloom, cyanobacteria, death. Don't swim in the water. Drive away the poor whites, blacks and browns. Make them walk in their loose shoes all the way to the city, good riddance. Let them shit inside the house, better than they were used to those black and brown bastards. Give them a whore's pussy to keep them quiet. The Butz method for subverting the American Dream, ship the blacks and browns to the cities where they can be controlled and corralled. Industrialize our food. White flight to the heaven of endless corn, cash and packaged convenience. God bless America, fuck Butz.

God bless antibiotic enema, thank you big pharma, thank you industrial agriculture. Tell the Boomers what spoiled brats they are and watch the condescension pour down, over and out of the haughtily raised noses. Stomp you in the tantrum, dive for cover. Things have always been this way they'll say, Boomers lost and deluded by the illusion of a generational long hallucinatory experience. Let their disgusting, narcissistic, rapidly failing cerebral efforts fade into Alzheimer's already. Dementia, cancerous tumor that was this extended trip of hubris and audacity, mainlining petroleum eight-ball of entitlement, stock and bond chaser.

Mass produced media, tell them what to think, monoculture corn, a million rows. Whore to the world's needy, of course the corn's not free, pay up please. Ministers of multinational monopoly, scales of justice and barbwire fence, cavity check because you look suspicious. Sir, place you hands against the wall. If you don't conform we'll burn you, shun you, turn you into a bum, ruin your credit. Imaginary measure of your worth, determine your value, you aren't worth a loan, more imaginary value in that piece of paper than in your entire life. Get away from me you toothless bum, no I don't want to pay for your welfare, your health care, your public schools, go back where you came from. But could you please let the dog out first, serve some eggs, drop off the kids, clean the shit off my ass and lock the door on your way out. Give me a call on Saturday, I might need you.

What happened to Boomers and burning bras, righteous waves of indignation. Gone sedentary and soon senile was the here and now. How to shake their foundations, the whole paradigm on which the whole mechanism was built? Off to a rocky start for sure, but maybe Ramon could still right his ship and move some people. It wasn't supposed to be this way, the rural landscape should have been dotted with hundreds of family farms, growing community and feeding people in them. Instead they were surrounded by one contiguous mono-culture nightmare. Country homes and country gardens should be the heart and soul of the land of the free, instead what exists is the asphalt rat maze, no bell, no exit, no cheese, no scientists watching. Because we built the thing. Grind and grind, down to the nub, until nothing is left. Throw it away. Throw it all away.

And the house crashed down around their ears, again, thank you Great Recession. Let the banks lead the way they said and the Earth trembled. At least the monetized world, a full three billion people were completely unaware of any financial crisis beyond the panic stricken faces of patrons, passengers, clients, Jons or victims. Golden towers, Ivory towers, Glass towers, endeavors of man ironically idealistic, tragically mythical.

And they'd scoff at him from on high, pelt him with sta-plers, folders, computers, printers, all signs of economic pro-gress and production. Keep the numbers up. If things get really bad they defenestrate, pull the cord on golden parachute, float home, happily ever after. Monkeys on high throw refuse on us all. Aged and infirm, afraid to die, try to live forever, invest in medicine pray to the gilded altars and glittering skyscrapers. Give it a rest. Feed the world, better than starving. The arro-gance, the lies, corporate chainsaw fed big agriculture, big pharmaceutical, big petroleum. This social experiment was never about the poor, the downtrodden, the needy.

Let the Boomers choke on their pride, let it get stuck in their throat. Can't remember the Heimlich maneuver guess they'll die. Hexa, hepta, octogenarian Baby Boomers presided over the insidiously insipid, the mind-numbing carnival of lights that stomped on the American psyche. Told the same lies for so long they now believe their own lines, no longer can they pierce the veil to look beyond the end of their nose to the world at large and the inevitable crumbling of farcical faux communi-ties. Like an extending main street of Disney, not populated with soft, squishy lovable creatures but fat cats, sharks, wolves and greedy pigs herding the foolish and ignorant with electric prods into homes and buildings. Blend them up, money, pow-er, ours. Crumbled around their ears, social experiment a fail-ure, too bad the damn Boomers won't be here to clean up their mess, just like a Boomer, fuck shit up, leave it that way, don't worry, cleaning is someone's job. And whoever it is will be glad to have the work, minimum wage is better than no wage.

God bless globalization, god-bless container ships, pre-fab houses, suburban cul-de-sac, mowed lawn. Why would an-yone want to grow tomatoes in their front yard? We have farm-ers in the mid-west, in the country, in China, feeding the world. Feed corn and soy to cattle, to feed the world. Corn and soy, soy and corn. Feed the poor on corn, feed them soy, its more nutritious.

Fattened the poor with corn on the feed lots of America, would you like the value meal you lazy slob, get out of your car and take a walk, ride a bike. None of us are entitled to shit, slovenly, lazy generation. No he won't read their bible, it is all a crock of shit anyway. What made their god more real, more important, more sacred than his god? Or his pantheon of pagan, naturalistic gods, sprites, deities, demigods. God tread more frequently, more fervently and more fantastically through an old growth forest, a desert landscape, an adobe dwelling, arctic tundra, heart of darkness. Their churches, synagogues, mosques and everyone in them could go the Hell, since they believed in that nonsense, they could have it. Called the native cultures and sacred rites those of heathens, called all the brown people of the world devil worshiping animals. The blood of the innocents stained the hands of righteous zealots, martyrs and conquerors.

Of course the 'civilized' countries have wealth; they robbed, cheated and stole for centuries. Of course the same countries have the power, they have everything. The have-nots, the victims of civilization's greatest larceny, victims of the greatest fraud, lost and forgotten, beggars on the corner of our soul. Stay away from me you dirty bum. Why do you think the wealthy hate the poor? Like a personal insult to the dignity of the white man, if only they knew where grandpa's grandpa got it from.

Wealthy, white, northern countries made, learn, invented for themselves a fanciful tale of renaissance and revolution. The luxury, wealth, the resources that overflowed their cups allowed for leisure, time to ponder, philosophize and consider great thoughts, invent, rediscover science, build it on the backs of the broken. Browns and blacks, raped and plagued across the epochs, used by the Romans, the Greeks before them the Egyptians before them. At least they knew the slaves were responsible for their wealth. I am Sparticus!! Ramon wondered if he could undermine the entire food distribution network of the country?

He crossed the threshold into the barrio cantina. Controlled chaos ruled in the bar. Smoke filled the place, summoned by tobacco, old candles, deep fryer in the back. Voices hummed, auditory comforter with which one could wrap himself. Let the drone sooth, sound all around but nothing to listen to. Meaningless noise. Table in the back, private dining room that was rarely used, large and long, separated by a threshold and glass doors that were perpetually open. The table was full. Twelve people sat around it, most yelling, a few just drinking.

Someone threw food, such was the descent into the emotional quagmire. Blue corn tamale crumbs, pink shrimp splattered on the table. Blue corn tamales with shrimp, leftovers from the hob-nob farce put on by Hood and his cronies. Ramon would've sent a whole parcel of hogs through the affair, let the swine dine with their ilk. Pesticide bomb had been his first choice, though pigs through the party were a close second; his Captains struck the idea down a week ago. He suspected all the members that attended the party did so to ensure he didn't act precipitously and release the pesticide bomb anyway.

As such, the current argument stirring this pot of curses and accusations was exactly that, an emotional bomb exploding in an enclosed space, very dangerous. The guerrilla tactics they used were yielding results, just not the desired results. Many of them had been denied pay, all of them that were illegal anyway. To whom Globe Hood argued he owed no pay on account of their involvement with the sabotage. Not a statement he made to the workers himself but delivered through the mouthpiece of El Lobo. As each supervisor communicated, worker alarm and anger at the lack of pay grew and was directed squarely at members of the movement.

"Well they're illegals, while Globe has no obligation to pay them, he is and will continue to withhold his money until such time as they deem it appropriate to settle their debts with him. We understand none of your workers has all the information, nor can one single worker compensate for the damage incurred by the sabotage. But each and every one that comes forward with information, he or she, will begin receiving pay again and at a considerable increase too." Such was the speech El Lobo gave to each supervisor. Made Ramon's blood run cold.

Ramon seriously hoped the Wolf had no takers. The first week he was sure the members would stay strong. Two weeks later with no pay and some of the members had haunted eyes. Chased by the invisible burden of family and food, he knew some of them were only getting by thanks to the support network of friends, family and movement members. But the barrio was in a tizzy and those that knew of the movement, there weren't many, had nothing nice to say.

No wonder food was flying. The decibels decreased when he entered but not the arguing or name-calling, quite a mess. Tamales flew, what a waste. Rosalinda's daughter, Carmen, the new head chef for Globe's enterprises both business and personal would've been displeased and vocally so. Unlike her mother Carmen was legal, born in the barrio, a fluent English speaker and professionally trained at some fancy-schmancy culinary school. She was not afraid of Hood, and she definitely didn't clean. She was a cook, not a domestic and she'd shout down the whole lot of them for wasting her food. Food was sacred to everyone in the room, the fact that food was flying spoke of exposed raw nerve, panic and fear. Smack, a shrimp on his cheek. The room fell quiet. Giggle of laughter eased the tension, just a little.

Ramon circled the room, took an empty chair, red lights and haze obscured the details of most of their faces, but the general sentiment was understood. Unrest in the ranks was not a good thing. Heads pressed close and whispering spoke volumes to a commander. No sense in putting it off, best to grab the bull by the horns, figuratively and literally in this case. Bull squad Lieutenant was one of those chomping at the bit to give Ramon a piece of his mind. He'd also attended the party last night to keep an eye on the Coyote and El Lobo, make sure Ramon didn't cause any trouble.

"Well let's hear it." Words barely cleared his teeth, vocal chords still vibrating, and the large man was on his feet yelling and pointing at Ramon.

"Enough is enough Ramon. Four of us in the hospital, two skewered like kabobs, two burnt to chicharron, all of us lucky to be alive." It was common knowledge among the commanders that Bull Lieutenant was the lover of Hedgehog's second in command, burnt to a crisp as she was. Not an issue in the movement as long as it didn't interfere with their work. "On top of that we're broke Ramon. Every one of us that is illegal has nothing, we're hungry, scared and angry Ramon!" The man kept saying his name, it was unnerving.

"I understand but don't be angry with me. It is Hood that is responsible for withholding your wages and El Lobo Maldito is his man, he's the one responsible for the deaths in the greenhouses and the near miss at the warehouses."

"Is he Ramon?" As I recall we lost three people in the greenhouse action because you blew the charge early." He slammed a meaty fist on the table, those were his men, his greenhouse.

"In every war there are casualties." The room exploded in yelling, everyone at once. It took five minutes to calm them all down again. The numbers were against Ramon, all the Captains were of a similar mind. A few Lieutenants were defending him, not with conviction though. What did these fools think? Hand-picked or not, the mutinous tenor of the conversation was troublesome.

"This is just our first battle, it may be a long campaign but we have Hood by the balls. You were all so scared I'd do something you stuffed the entire party with our people, every waiter, valet, half the kitchen staff." Not so many in reality. They dared not mess with Rosalinda's daughter Carmen, Ramon's Tia, Hood's chef. She was not to be trifled with. No one argued the point. Ramon continued.

"This idea of the pesticide bomb is what they deserve, especially Hood. He's been poisoning us and our loved ones for years, one dose may be what he deserves. My uncle died, right around the time his wife did, pesticide exposure. He didn't get a grand funeral, he didn't get a fancy coffin, just a wooden box and wooden cross." Huffing and puffing didn't blow them down. Many of the eyes held sympathy, some pity.

"Ramon, most people think Hood suffered enough, got what he deserved and all that. He fixed the pesticide exposure problem after Lily died. You know how strict the rules are to even touch those chemicals. His punishment was the death of his wife. Dios manda Ramon." The Doe spoke, her quiet voice hushing the crowd. Nods and murmurs of assent echoed her last words. She didn't mention the field hands were still exposed daily but they all knew it.

"Can't you see, Ramon, tu Tia estaba alli, anoche (your Aunt was there last night). You could've killed her too. This

isn't a war Ramon, not like that and even in wartime mass killing of innocents is terrorism." She let the statement hang in the
air, jukebox dead, since when? The place was empty, Isabella
behind the bar drying a pint glass over and over. Her keen eyes
and sharp tongue sent everyone out as soon as Ramon sat
down. Ramon wondered, complete nonsense, why every single
one of them knew she would never say a word to El Lobo and
he wouldn't ask. Strange those two.

"We aren't at war, we just want to negotiate the terms of
our employment. Por el amor de Dios Ramon, tenemos cuerpos
en la morgue(we have bodies in the morgue)! Three funerals
are enough Ramon." Had they all agreed to say his name as
many times as possible?

"Hood has to pay, El Lobo too." The wind from his sails,
gone like the music, flying hopes of a different sort now. Ramon's voice didn't convince anyone, least of all himself.

"We have a contact, Ramon, we're going to start negotiations with Hood." Doe handled him with familiarity, professional work tone, one scientist to another.

"What?! Who? El Maldito Lobo? Hijo de la gran puta!
Que mierda estan pensando hermanos?" His intention had been
not to scream. Failed miserably.

"Not El Lobo," pause, big brown eyes, deer caught in
headlights, about to cry or give him a pink slip, he couldn't tell.

Clang of tin cow bells, jostle against the door, light
sneaks in, frolicked and streaked through the bank of smoke,
pink slip then. Katherine Hood, she spoke a few words with
Isabella then joined them. And one makes fourteen, though not
really, she was his replacement.

"So you've come to save the day." Drip of acid in his
tone, sizzle on the floor.

"Hello Ramon, not to save the day exactly, but to help."
She kept her eyes down at first, peeked up at him as if to determine if he were a bright light or angry maniac.

"You know your father will never negotiate with us, he
won't give us the time of day." She was so naive. How did they
think she could help with this mess?

"He will." She didn't elaborate, short and sweet, like her
stature. Ramon had about enough, the whole thing was a farce.

"Mira Katarina, I don't know what you're trying to pull but this is my cause and I will take your father down, all of them down! That hijo de puta va a pagar!" Spittle flew from his mouth.

"We all had family deported, Ramon," Crow or Swan, other end of the table, "but this isn't the way. There are detectives nosing around the barrio Ramon, we don't want to go to prison."

Litany of Si's all around, chorus rising. Ramon stood, hands raised.

"Fine, bueno, lo que quieren, but I will not stay here and listen to this farce, this purse full of false hope." He looked each of them in the face, all thirteen of them, ended on Katherine.

"I hope it works out for you." He left, Isabella wasn't at the bar. Heard Katherine speaking, not the words, just the sound of her voice.

Chapter 12

Goat Shed

Ramon was sulking. He knew it, but it couldn't be helped. Usurped and chastised, his revolutionary movement wrenched from his hands by that little pain in the ass Katherine. Love her as he did, he'd already forgiven her, blamed the feeble-minded Captains and Lieutenants. Forever pandering to the American Dream, forever hoping, maybe this time there will be amnesty, immigration bill, immigrant rights inserted into the farm bill. Globe and all those of his ilk deserved to be punished. Fat-cat spoiled capitalists that pushed paper and people around. Ramon would've bet his last three paychecks Globe wouldn't be able to work in his own field, pick berries for five minutes. The man would faint, die of a coronary, curse all the damn fat he carried like a status symbol.

Old forgotten shipping container, he ignored the bittersweet irony of his being there. His old haunt. Clubhouse and base of operations for the movement back in the day, during the inception, just he and Katherine, hating Globe together, fire of teenage angst. They hatched plans to take over the farm, to be together forever. Clubhouse, fort and love nook. The container became their rainy day hideaway, sixteen, seventeen, exploding hormones, lips, legs, sex. Ramon fixed it up nice back when, bean-bag chair, patched the holes in the roof, kept his baby dry. A pile of blankets, a mattress he stole from somewhere, new he promised her.

Virginity given, hymen ruptured, swollen phallus blessed with her secretion, anointed red with her blood, awkward and jerky. Elbows and knees, teeth and nose, watch out, only hurts the first time she says. It was her idea after all, they've always been her ideas, he just followed along so he could be close to her. The container sat on the edge of an old forgotten farm field, the transition zone between forest and meadow. Pine and holly pressed close to the back side, he knew a fire pit was there, nice ring of stones, couple of logs. They used to cook out there, on the backside to keep the fire from prying eyes. Which meant El Lobo and Hood. The container was dingy on the outside, peeling paint, vacant rivet holes. Successive generations of farming kids left their marks, mostly graffiti and beer cans, not many though.

The mattress was gone, in its place a small wooden table, two folding chairs and a candle on the table. Ramon's doing. He reclaimed the fort when he started working with the movement, when it was merely an idea and he just returned from school. No mattress anymore but he'd pitched a two-man tent in the back corner, obscured by some pallets and an empty burn barrel. It provided protection from the cooler nights and the damp air when the rains came. When he stayed, which was more and more lately, he had his sleeping bag, mat and a reading light tucked in the tent. He slept well in there, grabbed a beer from the cooler under the table. He cracked the can and took a long swig. Damn those fools.

The rain increased in intensity, pitter-patter staccato on the roof. Doors to the container ripped of who knows when, weren't necessary or wanted. Planted nearly two decades ago by his industrious little hands and hers of course. Boston ivy and Virginia creeper twined and twisted, strangled their way up a haphazard trellis deemed fine craftsmanship when they were 15. Acceptable, passable, satisfactory, whichever; the dense vines served as screen, portico and secret doorway. Now, fifteen years later the vines climbed up and over the entire container, served as exceptional camouflage. They planted both sides the same way back then and the result was hidden in plain sight. Though well and truly not plain sight, the container was on an old unused field, hundreds of meters from the nearest rutted, hard packed truck trail.

Gloom gathered, especially on days like this. Great for teenage delinquency, drink and smoke, stay out of sight and out of mind. His impotence like a infected sore, usurpers and fools to blame, was inflamed, salt in the wound of, lemon on top of that, wounded pride and melancholy pout. Nothing to do but tie one on. Pulled a cigarette from a pack he left in the container, old habits, light with a box of matches. Turned on the fluorescent camp lamp, long thin tube and a forearm sized light that lasted forever and rarely needed new batteries. He had some extras stashed in the tent anyway. He only lacked a few things in the container and he could move in outright. His mother would love that, her son with the Masters degree in Plant Science a squatter on Hood's property.

Hood wouldn't find him but El Lobo would. He caught Katherine and Ramon once when they were newly christened sexual beings, drunk and half naked. Ramon still unsure what to do with his dick, Katherine giggled her head off. She giggled all the way home, once she put her clothes on. El Lobo didn't say a word, only that he found them drinking by the loading docks. Ramon had almost forgotten about that. The container only needed a shower and some running water. Enough dry goods in the warehouses and in the barrio eliminated the need for a refrigerator, would've been nice though, maybe another window too, awful dark in the container, especially on days like this.

Rustle of leaves, secret knock on the side. Shave and a haircut, starting with the haircut. No need to look up from the plans he'd placed on the table under the swatch of light cast by a glass candle, Maria looked down, considered his plans with him. Katherine was the only person other than Ramon that knocked like that; it was their knock, invented of necessity in their youth. Homework at Ramon's, then to Gloria's, hide and seek in the barrio with the other kids. The knock was theirs and theirs alone.

She slipped through the vines, held them aside, strands of red hair grabbed by dry brown leaf, welcome back, we missed you.

"I thought you might be here." Her navy-blue cloak, beads of rain freckled the surface, glistened, translucent, glinted like her eyes.

"I thought you were having a meeting." Drip sardonic solvents, dissolve the bond between them, if only.

"Too much to talk about in one night, I've arranged to meet with them squad by squad. Your people are well organized and they know what they're doing."

"Not my people anymore, they're yours now." She could choke on them for all he cared.

"Ramon, you know what I'm saying makes sense. I should be able to help them. Not only do I have sway with my father, but they trust me enough to let me help them." Beautifully imploring eyes.

"What can you do Katherine? Unless the incremental political process, perennially known as the American Congress passes amnesty, all those illegals will stay illegal and in that case you can do nothing." Waved his hands in her general direction.

She sat at the table across from him, lit a few matches, watched them burn. She lit another candle, opened a beer for herself, passed him another, exhaled loudly.

"I don't know Ramon, I'm obviously limited by their illegal status but I have to do something. I agree my father deserves to be on the hook too, for hiring them and giving them reasons to be here." He knew she was right about that, but even the man's nervous breakdown at his senate hearing, bold faced confession, hadn't brought the punishment Hood deserved. Not even a slap on the wrist. He tried not to think of the how and the why of its happening. Cicadas in his brain. Ramon secretly hoped the federales would show up, take Hood away. Fat chance that. There had been senators at that dinner party.

"But most importantly Ramon I want to protect them from the increasing scrutiny of the police, which we know is all the excuse overzealous conservative officials need to call in ICE on them. The Feds too, your little food poisoning scare has repercussions, the fire and greenhouse disasters not as much surprisingly, but I'd bet my piggy bank you've raised some red flags on someone's radar, the question is whose."

"You know Katherine, El Lobo nearly killed some of us." He stared her down, were the rumors true? Did she have a thing for the Wolf, dry washed her face.

"As I suspected, father says the wounded were attacked by other workers. Let's not forget you are not innocent of murder Ramon, so don't throw stones, glass houses and all that nonsense. You are not one to point fingers." Unexpected vehemence, maybe she did like the Wolf.

"So it's true, you do have a thing for him."

"No Ramon. I'm familiar and friendly with him, he's my father's right hand. Beyond that nothing." She picked at peeling table top, hand crossed the table squeezed his. "We may not know what tomorrow brings Ramon, but we know what yesterday left for us and I hope the affection between us will remain a constant." She squeezed, he squeezed back, caress her face, she didn't pull away.

She kissed him, quite a surprise that. They talked of this and that, finished the six-pack, smoked some cigarettes, she let him kiss her some more. She wasn't wearing a bra, her perky B-cups were hard, even under her warm sweater, nothing on under. Just a college sweater and rain cloak, no wonder her nipples could cut glass. Beautiful nipples he'd put in his mouth on more than one occasion. Soft kisses of remembrance escalated to passionate embrace and panting, lip smacking skin sucking frenzy. At some point Ramon disengaged and asked,

"Are you sure you want to do this?" He should have known better.

"Ramon, are you sure you want to ask me that question? You know what a fickle creature is woman, too much time to think about it and I might change my mind, come to my senses and all." A look that dared him to ask again. Grabbed her hand, pulled her toward the tent, it was dark outside, still raining, a good night for a roll in the hay.

He left one candle burning in the center of the table, faint glow, warm colors, warm bodies slipped into the sleeping bag. It was cold in the sleeping bag, even with her little body kicking off heat, she understood his body and warmed his manhood with gentile stroking, kissed his mouth and nibbled his neck. He was at attention before he had his socks all the way off, slid into her, mouth and labia. Pity-fuck, not the act itself, that was not pitiful, perhaps a bit frenzied. Ramon was all over the place, kissed her neck, sucked her breasts, chewed her shoulders. He'd slept with her since they both returned from school, the night ICE raided his house but just the once, felt like ages past. She cut him off and had barely been able to look at him since the food contamination issue.

If anything he was a bit rough on her. His pride still smarted, his loss, the movement taken, he thrust into her, punished her for her insolence, do gooder. His good was greater than hers. Fucked her hard, tried to wipe the pity from her face, he knew she was spreading her legs to sooth his wounded ego. She pushed the small of his back when she felt the waves of ejaculation tighten his ass.

"It's OK." She whispered and didn't allow him to pull out, wrapped her legs around him. He filled her with his pitiful frantic clawing tongue and genetic donation. Madness.

It was the middle of the night when he woke, she was gone. Just like last time.

Chapter 13

Mojados

It was raining. No torrential downpour, not washing out the roads, not blowing out the levies or washing away his crop but a non-stop, no sign of letting up soaking. Felt like he needed to squeegee his eyeballs, which was why he had his polarized lenses on even in the black as pitch, lights out of a night. Nothing to see yet anyway. Headlights bobbed in the distance, rutted roads, muddy puddle, trailer full of cargo. A fresh batch of illegals ferried in by the coyotes.

The Wolf and the Coyote, the Wolf was the acquaintance of several Coyotes. Each less desirable than the last. Perpetually mottled coats and hungry eyes suited their constant nomadic search for ways and means. The worst were from south of the border. Closer to jackals in their lack of compassion, they routinely shut their country-men in what were to become tombs. This particular Coyote drove a truck for Hood, but knew the when, where and how of illegals. El Lobo didn't mind using the man, he was careful not to kill any of the merchandise. Most coyotes with whom he'd dealt in the past were the uncaring, callous, spit on the illegal hope and dreams Coyotes, this one at least took care. The coyotes he'd killed were dead for not caring, for killing cargo, wasting his time, slaughter of innocents, the principle of the thing. They deserved the death he doled out. Locked in their own trucks, last hours on Earth spent with the rapidly decomposing corpses of the poor bastards unlucky enough. Die slow and steady, cooked alive, taste the medicine. `

Rain drip-drop, run down the brim of his hat, run down jawline, onto lips and cigar. Work of futility, self-delusional to think semblance of spark, fire, ember could maintain thermal combustion on a night like this. Cuban cigar in his mouth, Hood's supply, sopping wet, no matter. He was chewing on it more than smoking, wished he hadn't brought a fresh cigar to this dance. Hood huddled in the car with the Tweedles, Tweedle-dee and Tweedle-dum, drinking, smoking and fornicating to be sure.

El Lobo was having difficulty getting a bead on Hood. The man was as easy to read as Dr. Seuss, one fish, two fish, straight forward, eye-test at the DMV. The whore-monger, pussy chasing misogynist was in character but Hood's attention to detail, overbearing, micro-managing, look over your shoulder, shout at Gloria, leave the door open because the intercom is stupid, management style was lacking. Gloria noticed too. He stopped by her place that morning, but she'd gone into the office at some point during the night. Saturdays didn't matter, her dominion over the small farm building they used as the office was complete. The place was well lived in. The porch that wasn't quite level, the screen door that banged, the close quarters in the kitchen suited Gloria much more than her cavernous mansion. She frequently stayed overnight at the office, well and truly only five miles from her house, one side of the farm to the other.

He hadn't slept much, caught a little shut-eye after the all night marathon with Isabella. Usually she left his work alone, but this crossed some invisible line in her judgment and both Gloria and Katherine were off limits, taboo. So he had out with it. First time for that too, Isabella prying, the usually aloof wife demanded answers. Not in a bad way, so he told he told her about Ramon and the group, she was less than impressed, didn't lend any insight more than, "Ya se." I already know, the whole Barrio knows. Globe's orders, shake up Gloria, give her a good scare.

"You really are maldito." Her tone was fatalistic, "what about Katarina, are you going to come clean about her too? You're pussyfooting all over the place, I think your tongue is bleeding from trying not to say her name." The rhetorical question, ball of yarn, worm on a hook, den full of pit-vipers came in the wee hours, after explaining over and over that Globe had absolutely no reason to suspect Gloria's involvement in anything. If Gloria hadn't accosted Globe in the study El Lobo would've done nothing, but she had Globe in a tizzy, his balls in a bind, bruised balls and bruised ego needed something more than scotch.

So he delivered, El Lobo Maldito. No, nothing was going to happen the whole thing was sad. Gloria in her lost and frustrated state had much in common with members of the movement, save allegiance.

"What about Katherine?" He wasn't yawning now, red eyes pierced the darkness of their bedroom, her amber eyes gone red in the pre-dawn light. Candle flicker in the corner. "She is sweet on you, even with her camouflage boys, a woman can tell." Isabella didn't look or smell like she wanted confirmation, snarled lips, wrinkled nose. She pressed on.

"You've been like an oozing, puss filled wound of melancholy nonsense of late husband, perhaps she is why?" So loaded the question, so gentle her tone, maybe his tongue was bleeding, tasted metal in his mouth.

"If you fuck her, do you think that will be it?"Almost innocent question, he had only been unfaithful once before Katherine, as bad as they all said he was, he actually went home and fucked his wife for twenty years between unfaithful acts. Tasted blood. Kept his mouth shut.

"Already fucked her then? That would explain how she got so far under your skin, in your head, in my bed." Thankfully he was tired enough that rolling over seemed the best option, onto his stomach, look away from her, stared at the wooden floor, beautiful hand-woven rug, geometric squares, diamonds, lightning bolts.

"And if she's pregnant? She looks funny, I noticed last night, I don't think she knows yet." From a million other women he would've taken the comment as nonsense, a wives' tale. From Isabella it made his hair stand on end. He wanted to howl at the moon. He finally snapped at the bait.

"As I hear tell, young Miss Hood is rather promiscuous, Ramon being one of her lovers, she's half my age and my employer's daughter." No denial, no omission, no engagement. Shut up you fool. Roll back over. "She is your student after all, isn't she?" Couldn't help himself. Shit.

"You can't fool me you toothy grinning bastard!" Heated and panting. "So if she gives you what I can't, a baby, mi vas a dejar no?!" More accusation than question her desperation was plain, drove her voice toward shrill. He stayed on his side, faced away from the storm. Not for long, she jumped on him sobbing and pounding, blind rage, frustration and fury, blind because her eyes were closed.

His turn to strike. He grabbed her and pinned her to the bed, kiss, bite, she drew first blood. She busted his lip with an ear ringing slap, snapped his jaw, bit his lip, sucked his blood. Ran his nails down her thigh, start by the hip, around to the buttock, cut in a little too deep, left a mark, around the back, palmed her flower, kissed her deep. Ripped off her skirt, his shirt then hers. He paused, sat to remove his boots, gave her time to escape if she wanted, see if she changed her mind. Maybe she would pass out, pretend to be dead, run for the hills. He undid the laces, not a twitch. Naked in a flash, kissed her, mouth protested, half argued, half tongued him to bliss's heavenly door. She guided him into her, postponed the argument, temporary cease-fire, she wept, he begged for forgiveness. Pleasure loosend the tongue, admitted the longing, confessed the sins. She was beautiful, his wolf mate. Sleek lines and bronze skin, lithe arms and dextrous fingers. She diddled his ass, pulled his hair, scratched his chest, his blood on the sheets. Flipped him over and rode for daylight, rising sun warmed the room with light and their exhaled exaltations. Squeezed the breast, too hard, scratched her ass, hand full of hair and screamed at the ceiling. Howl at the moon. After, in the glow of post orgasmic cuddle he claimed it wasn't real, just the heat of the moment, nothing really to confess, just kidding sweetheart. He didn't say a word, tried not to ruin a good thing. Bit the tongue, definitely bleeding.

"They're here." Rain beaded on the second Coyote, the one who would deliver the new employees while the other returned the truck, which definitely wasn't Hood's. The man squelched and hunched, shifted from foot to foot, fools in a downpour, before acceptance, anger, denial or compromise. They hot footed like on hot coals, hunched inward, protected the core.

The Coyote stopped after a few minutes, inevitable chill seeping down his spine, a cold rivulet of acceptance, the ass crack of work to be done. The approaching truck squeaked to a halt, wipers on high. His asshole hurt. Figuratively with this new batch of illegals. A dozen wide-eyed, scared shitless new-bies and another dozen grizzled desert crossing fools, back and forth, by grace of God or Luck.

Twenty-four would do for now, replace some of the dead and deported. Time to send the flock to the barracks, or the barn as it were, the farm's contribution to illegal immigration, a place safe from prying eyes with facilitated ingress and egress. Highly illegal, shame on those Senators at the party last night, if they only knew, or cared.

"Take them to the Barn One by way of the Barrio, if any of them have money or people let them get some supplies." The Coyote nodded, eyes squinted into the rain.

"No recruiting these ones you Coyote bastard." The man blanched, stock still in the driving rain, paled visibly, Wolf wondered if he'd faint into the mud. At least the rain would wake him up if he did.

"Recrutando para que cosa?" Playing dumb for all he was worth, not very convincing. El Lobo patted him on the shoulder, a little too hard, shadow face, let the cigar grin talk for him.

"Para putas, drogas, ou llevadas a ver familia. Se como ustedes los Coyotes siempre trabajan." (For whores, drugs, or rides to see family. I know how you Coyotes are always work-ing.)The man was shaken enough, his reaction all the confirma-tion El Lobo needed. He could see the confession and beg for forgiveness on the man's mind, just as he suspected. The man deflated with a sigh, fight or flight postponed for now. A green Jeep crept out of the darkness, lights off

"Get out of here, this is for me." Backhand wave at the confessed Coyote, he was only too happy to oblige, his truck was full. Behind crates of corn and squash, twenty-four Hood employees crouched, waiting for the truck to pull away already. Disappeared into the night. The Jeep squelched to a stop, one meter from the Wolf, the window lowered.

El Lobo knew, of course he knew but to him this fool was worse than gang-bangers and convicts, all lost souls, but this one was angry at his culture. Damn fool.

"Where are they going?" Cocky arrogance, didn't even bother to get out of the car for this bit of dirty work.

"To the Barrio, got 'em fixed up with where's and why's. They're going to work tomorrow." Chew on cigar, spit on the ground. Bad taste soaked into his tongue. An envelope, dry, clean and crisp materialized in El Lobo's hand, no need to dilly dally, this fool didn't want to be seen and El Lobo didn't want to see him. Never mind Wolf knew where the man lived. He forked it over, get out of here you traitorous coward he thought.

Self-hating chicano de mierda. Instead he asked, "Asi cuando deportas los nadadores y vagos del desierto les hablas en espanol? (When you deport the swimmers and desert vaga-bonds do you speak to them in Spanish?)

"Why would I do that?" Robot voice, robot face, soft as a pencil pushing marshmallow.

"Just wondering." Turned and walked away, the trucks were long gone. Soon so was the Jeep.

His asshole hurt, literally. Isabella may have been a bit too enthusiastic diddling his derriere, not that he minded but her nails must've nicked something. Well not something, his sphincter, poop-shoot, end-knot, whatever. If he could dish it out, right? Mud sucked, slurp and swallow, all the way to the tinted SUV. He got in the driver's seat. Partition was down, usually a chauffeur for Hood's tinted wagon, usually El Lobo did this alone in his beat-up pickup. Tonight Hood wanted to come, desperate cry of his subconscious psyche, too bad his face and dick were buried in one of the tweedles. So El Lobo was chauffeur, handler, and facilitator all. Stink of tobacco, whiskey, pussy, balls, asshole. The girls were naked, all three were drunk and stupid, he was surprised they could put any-thing anywhere.

Puke in an ice bucket. One of the girls demonstrated how it was done, her friend still impaled by Hood, tried to hold her hair, ass on Hood's lap. Hood grabbed and chewed on her back, gyrated obscenely, didn't stop her from holding hair or moaning. He closed the partition to the sound of regurgitation.

Gloria agreed, Hood was in a bad way. Something was wrong and whatever it was it was getting worse. As much as Hood liked sweet young tail, this was absurd. Supposedly the man was interested in figuring this mess out. Neither Wolf or Gloria could get the man's attention and keep it. Only the Tweedles and their give-away bonanza, pussy on a string had the power to hold his attention for more than five minutes. El Lobo navigated through the rain, made a left, away from the barrio, along circuitous back roads, barely a truck trail, more like a forgotten lane, more grass than rutted soil. Two hundred meters back from the road in a dense thicket of Oak and Hickory rose the red barn. Typical barn on the outside, large doors on both ends, leading into bare dirt floor.

That was where the traditional barn stopped. The rest of the place was a huge dormitory for illegals. Horse stalls, cow stalls, pig stalls, all converted into small rooms with one, two or no cots and just blankets on the floor. The rooms were intended for one single illegal at a time. Maybe in the beginning. Now, lucky if one family per room. Bathrooms were communal, the women had their own at least. Installed after one of the newly arrived tried raping a thirteen year-old in the shower. The women refused to do anything, that is anything, until they had their own bathroom. Years ago now, but El Lobo remembered the power of the protest. Brought the farm to a standstill. The kitchens were common, though El Lobo had installed two extra stoves; an extra eight burners and two more ovens made a big difference. Counter space was non-existent, but some handy illegal took an old wood working table and married it to several others, antiques for sure, provided a semblance of prep space for the mothers, fathers, daughters, and grandmothers cooking.

Upstairs was identical, open hay loft converted into small stall-like rooms, small play area for kids, sitting area for adults in the center, overlooking the first floor. That was in the beginning, currently the space was occupied by wives, children, sleeping mats and hay beds, as was the common space on the first floor. Bursting at the seams if you will. One had to tread carefully when answering nature's call in the wee hours, as easily step on a sleeping child as a man or woman creating one.

The poor did like sex. Like alcohol and drugs, sex served to distract, numb and entertain. Forget poverty for a few minutes, hours, or days. Binges being what they are. The place wasn't a den of inequity, a brothel or a scene of sordid hedonism. Quite the contrary, family units, nuclear and extended were very tight, became even tighter in the dormitory collective style living space. One had to keep an eye on belongings lest they wander. Couples new and old recreated frequently, cards and remember when stories only served so long. Human interaction, messy, necessary and cheap. No one had money to go to the movies that's for sure. As likely to hear a male or female voice on the road to sexual fulfillment as you were to hear a baby crying in the open space, dark of night. Be fruitful and multiply, and they were. The place fit eighty people comfortably.

Currently the population hovered near two-hundred fifty. Almost half of that being children, most younger than five. By the time kids got big enough for school the parents were ready to move to the Barrio and so the cycle repeated. El Lobo wondered whether poverty negated humility and modesty, there were few reservations and certainly no one trying to keep the noise down, perhaps it was cultural.

Interesting that a culture perceived by many as socially conservative had produced so many men and women comfortable in their sexuality. Guess conservatism is not frigidity, put away the chastity belts. Keep the windows open when lover visits, let the neighbors hear. Maybe humility is shed by necessity. Because the poor live in favelas, shanty towns, trailer parks, row houses, wards and tenements. Because they were raised bathed in a tin tub in the front yard for all the world to see.

Cramped, small, crowded abode, nothing to own and own nothing, we all know, both men and women, the flesh cannot be denied indefinitely. Should not be. Living so close together negates the possibility of privacy, so why worry. Surprisingly few disagreements required his attention in this hidden barn or the other two. Fear tempered all humors. Coyotes came and went, frequently, the only ones trusted by the illegals. They used the Coyotes like taxis, one hundred dollars to the drug store, go in for them, buy some cough medicine for the baby. A week's worth of pay. El Lobo pulled up to the barn, didn't bother lowering the partition, he knew what he was missing. Headed out into the rain, into the barn.

The barn manager; a matronly, plump woman, a self-serving, get it while she can, definitely not in the movement, didn't give a shit about community type of person, ran the barn satisfactorily. She had an eye for misplaced items and what recourse did the immigrants have? She had an apartment next to the large barn doors. The apartment was ample, formal living room, kitchen, private bath, bedroom in the back. Her flat screen blared weekend variety show, announcer yelled in Spanish at the sofa in the living room. El Lobo told her new people were coming in, twenty-four of them, no families, all singles. Not his problem if she was running out of space, really it was.

He suggested she send some of the oldest residents to the barrio. At any rate let some of them know they need to go, that was her job or he could get someone else to do it. As simple as that, he turned and left. Sabado Gigante irritated him. The woman irritated him like a vulture feeding on the carcass of fallen wayfarers, cross the desert, huddle in the dark.

Outside, in the rain, squelch and splatter, usually he waited to make sure all of the new arrivals were inserted successfully, no problems from the old bag, she would shake them down if they let her. Hood liked to introduce himself in the barn to new arrivals, lord over the scared and disoriented, ogle the fresh female faces while they cowered at his opulence. Without checking he knew Hood was neck deep in sexual escapade or vomit. Gloria was right, she was the one that mentioned it actually. She'd looked haggard and disheveled, puffy eyes and tormented hair. He showed up at the office door at nine in the morning the day after the party. Sexual appetite sated, Isabella fucked and tucked in, he greeted her at the door. Gloria didn't look like she'd slept either.

Marathon domestic dispute kept him engaged, orally and phallically. Isabella's sexual appetite was ravenous, something she had in common with Katherine. Even more so now, he'd only just heard a foreman walking though the greenhouse mentioning sleeping with Hood's daughter and how good she was. Almost stopped in his tracks to rip out the man's jugular, the worker was a member of the movement. Instead he went to the office after finding Gloria's house empty, brought coffee from the Barrio, delicious.

She asked him in, shuffled into the country kitchen, turned on the stove, kettle on the fire, skillet too, even though she held a cardboard cup of hot coffee to her lips. Habit he supposed. Unconsidered previously, El Lobo warmed to the notion that he and Gloria were closer than he'd ever imagined. Years of orbiting each other, satellites in the gravitational divot, stuck in the bear-trap named Globe Hood. A Good morning here, goodnight there, listening to Globe berate the other, listening to the other give it right back. They knew the thick and thistle after two decades of breathing each other's air. Maybe she would've let him take her last night, maybe he would've taken her.

Best not to forget the reason for his visit.

"Globe is in trouble Gloria." he said after a sip of coffee, burned his tongue, removed the lid, poured into the mug she offered. "We both know he has been in trouble before, he has, just not like this. And to put the screws to it he seems like he is more interested in burying his head in the sand," for lack of a better term, "than confront these issues head on, which is what the man we know would do."

"I couldn't agree more." Her back to him. Naked buttocks pushed on silk nighty, smell her he could. Be still Wolf. She turned and placed two perfect Spanish omelets in front of them. He hadn't noticed her beating eggs, slicing peppers or cooking, more exhausted than he thought.

"Here Wolf, we both look like we haven't slept. Eat up." He did. Deliciously fresh ingredients, flavors popped in mouth, explosion of savory, sweet tomato salsa, spice of jalapeno, sharp cheddar.

"I've been ruminating on just this aspect of Globe's dysfunction and I can only come up with two things. Globe's finally lost it and really doesn't give a rat's ass and sooner or later you and I will be unemployed. Or two, Isabella has something to do with it." Stop. She stared at him, sipped her coffee, continued because he was chewing and not speaking. "I don't know the whole story, but I know there is no love lost between Hood and Isabella, no love lost, found or anything in between. In fact if he died tomorrow I think she would say 'about time'." El Lobo nodded, correct observation. "I won't pry, but I know in the Barrio they sometimes call her la Bruja or Curandera and I know people go to her for alternatives to western medicine." All true, he nodded more, pushed the plate away, she was done too. Water boiled, fresh pot of coffee. She continued after he served them both.

"After Globe's fit in front of the Senate hearing he confessed to me what happened. He said he had no control over his body, someone was controlling him like a puppet, that someone being Isabella. He didn't elaborate on the why or the how, just said that it was her. I didn't ask but it occurred to me last night. His behavior, while not as erratic as the Senate hearing, does echo of something similar, something strange. Even Globe's confusion and ignorance of his actions." His nodding stopped because his blood ran cold, tickle up his spine. Isabella did practice as a naturalistic sort of medicine woman. She dispensed herbal cures and she was very popular with residents of the Barrio. Isa's mother told her there was a plant for everything and he believed her.

"I wouldn't put it out of the realm of possibility." El Lobo started, not comfortable speaking of his home life, Isabella taught him better years ago.

"Look Jose, I'm not asking for the details, If I want them I'll ask her, we're close enough that I owe her that much. But I know something happened, something bad, before I started working here. Given Globe's character I can only imagine. The way you look at him, like you might kill him at any moment plus Isabella's attitude toward him..." She let the sentence die, sipped coffee with puckered lips.

"You're right Gloria, something bad did happen and since then none of us has been quite right." Back to topic before he wandered into personal territory. Expose himself to Gloria like she did the night before, only he doubted he could handle exposing raw emotion as well as she did. He had neither her character nor her grace.

"I'll mention it to her." Sincere tone, trouble meeting her eyes, he already felt naked.

"Thank you Jose." She came around, kissed him on the forehead. Quite an enigma was Gloria. He left her a short time later, finished the coffee, almost told her everything. Left before he could, new arrivals and all.

"What is taking so long?" Hood bellowed and banged on the partition, the truck of illegals arrived from the Barrio was ejecting passengers through the rainy night, into the barn. Wide silhouette of larcenous landlady filled the doorway, hear her yelling already. He took Hood and the Tweedles home, made sure they got inside before he pulled off, drunk idiots didn't even get dressed to go inside.

Chapter 14

Poison gas

Ramon was sick of it, sick of them, sick of Katherine, sick of El Lobo, sick of Hood. Dry heave, taste bile. He woke with the dawn, made his way through soaked meadows to the pesticide storage bunker on the rear side of the sprawling greenhouse complex. Locked behind heavy metal doors and cinder-block walls the ventilation fans hummed twenty-four hours a day. The rain finally ceased at some dead hour of the night, soaked the ground, fed the plants, fed the animals. Cooling temps chilled the air, soaked through sneakers, socks, between the toes. Unlocked the metal dead bolt with a loud click, jangle of keys. Master set of keys, perk of the job as movement leader, wondered if the Captains or Lieutenants realized he still had them. Probably not or they would've asked for them back, rather taken them back, no question about it. The air moved, currents, breeze through the hair. Blow as the fans might, they couldn't rid the place of the sour, volatile organic compound, carbon ring character stink of the place. When he had necessity to enter the bunker, which was rare if ever, he hustled in and out as quickly as he could. Today he wore a respirator, knew he'd be stuck in there for a while, it still hung around his neck.

Powder, liquid, skull and cross bones, just right for Hood. Ramon's plan was simple, get the pesticide into Hood's mansion, down to the basement and into the heating ducts. The arrival of cool night air prompted harvest, changing foliage and turning up the heat. He was willing to bet Hood had his heat on, nice and toasty, especially if he had the girls over. Dumb ass girls, in it for the money, had to be, because it was impossible to feel affection for Hood. He'd show Katherine what a pity fuck looked like. She'd see, he'd show her and all of them. Gas cylinder, compressed Nitrogen, Helium, Hydrogen. There was room for them in his plans too. Soon.

Metal cylinder, shoved out of the way. Usually chained to the wall, thick quarter inch links embedded in the cinderblock walls. Fifty gallon drums, cross bones to death for those that dared. He dared. She dared him to, her father dared him and El Lobo Maldito dared him. Loosened top of 50 gallon drum, pour spout, stuck in a rubber hose, siphoned off into plastic gasoline containers.

Turned his back, kept an ear to the glug-glug. High on top shelf, powered organophosphate to deposit in Hood's ducts, should do the job, maybe in his shampoo too. Creak of door.

"Oye! Que haces?" Greenhouse worker, not a member, coming to get his pack, powder and sprayer, must have breakout of insects somewhere. Damn.

Ramon slipped off the stool, sneakers still wet from rain soaked grass. His foot clipped a five gallon drum of something, toppled sideways, grabbed for anything. His hand landed on a rounded metal top, Nitrogen canister, Ramon fell through the air, hit concrete floor. His shoulder popped, teeth jarred, oxygen expelled. Metal canister hit the ground with a loud clang, top shot off, gas exploded from the neck in a white stream rocketed the canister across the bunker, knocked over the fifty gallon drum. Liquid, black, green molasses, syrupy death, puddled on the floor, soaked into Ramon, poured over his body, soaked into his clothes and skin.

Someone was screaming, several someones, a loud boom, a thud, cloud of dust filled the room. Damn. Whole lot of good the respirator was doing around his neck. Screams in Spanish, he couldn't move, shattered shoulder, cloud of mayhem, chemical contamination, no air to breathe. Shit. How would he get them to pay now? Only sorry he didn't get to see Hood suffer, writhe in pain, squeal like the pig he did. Alarm sounded, red lights flash, black shapes ran through the cloud of powder, dragged him towards the light, perhaps it was death taking him home, sickle reaps, clean the chaff. Be free.

Tinkle of chimes, darkness, blinding light. Waves of nausea, smell of vomit. Rumble of voices, stampeding elephants down a hallway, trumpeting and stomping. Ganesh the destroyer sent to crush him. Round and round the world spun, gray fog enveloped everything. Pulsing red flower glowed in the fog, smog, airborne particulate. A woman screamed, a man wept, begged forgiveness, asked for his mother. Soft flesh on his face, teat in his mouth. Telephone ring, sheep and goat bleat. Convulsing spasms, arched the back, snap him in half. Death come to break him like a twig, cast him into the current. Swept away, forgotten, lost in the foam, spray of nothingness. Katherine looked down on him, El Lobo held her, kissed her, laughed at him.

Katherine changed to Isabella tending Ramon's wounds while El Lobo fucked her from behind, laughing, howling. El Lobo in his face, snarling, drooling, bared teeth wrapped around Ramon's throat, doesn't squeeze. Ramon screamed and shouted, Isabella and Katherine appeared with movement members, camouflage and automatic weapons, come to spring him. Turned out they're turning him in, collected their reward from Katherine, Globe laughed maniacally behind, face turned into a pig's. Screaming, pain, retching wretched fools, stink of vomit, warm water on his naked body. Water in his mouth up his ass, coming out his eyes, water everywhere. He was tossed and turned by the currents of life, the water filled him, leaked from ears and nose. Closed his eyes to keep them from popping out. Stink of shit, chemical death, vomit. Clouds, fog, smog, mist, wall of white.

Glowing orbs burned through the wall of white. Pulsing crimson, pulsing golden, fog of cotton. Stuffed in his ears, eyes, mouth, ass. Chew on cotton, chew on clouds. Like batting from a pillow, cellulose lodged in his throat, hardly breathe. Choke and rasp, crab crawled down his throat, pincers out, mirepoix of the esophagus. Chop and slice, julienne and fillet, to scream if able, throat on fire. Napalm poured down his throat, let the air pass, cork in his throat gone, tasted oxygen.

Muffled voices, wall of white. Angelic tones, wind chimes on the breeze. They soothed, air passes. Raw and ragged, fog undulated with his breath. Scarlet orb glowed, pulsing flower suspended above, thorns dripped blood on the bed, onto his hand. Grab for it, too far away, tried again anyway. Show them what happens, scapegoat he was not, he was the Goat Commander. Scapegoat commander, he'd insist on a cape, seemed fitting. Flitting wind chimes, tinkle of bells. Angel's laughter, she sighed.

"You know Isabella, I just had this talk with Ramon, I'm getting some serious deja vu here. I agree my father needs to pay, but did you have to turn him into a lecherous fool. I can't even get him to listen to me and usually he always finds time for me. How am I supposed to make headway with members of the movement if I can't negotiate. You know that's why they really let me in, because I'm the boss's daughter."

"I know Katherine, I'm sorry. The spell of binding obsession. It cannot be undone if he remains with the girls. Your father must distance himself from them for a time. It will hurt." Floating timbers, falling trees, vibrating vocal chords. Long stretched ligaments, twining fibrils of muscle arced off into space, vibrated gold and silver, he reached up and up toward the crimson orb floating above.

"Whatever it takes, I'll tell him he needs to go away for a while. How long?" Caress her voice with his hands, reach for the sky, someone gently pushed his arms down. Did they? Was that real?

"Two to three weeks should be sufficient for all three of them." She didn't elaborate, but pregnant were the spaces between her words. Golden chords vibrated, silver too, filled the room with light.

"I hope so." A hand on his head.

"And Ramon? Do you love him?" Golden chords of Isabella.

"Of course I love him, we grew up together. I don't want to marry him but I want him in my life."

"And the father of the baby, do you love him?" Pregnant words were overloaded with implications, twisting turning black shadowy bumper car shapes coalesced between the vibrating chords. The black shadows careened and crashed here to there, they'd bust out the windows at this rate. He covered his head.

"Ramon is the father." Silver chords hum and glow, red orb on fire.

"Are you sure? You have a reputation..." Enough said. Someone sucked on her teeth.

"I'm sure." Fog burns off, ice storm screamed in his ears.

The red orb exploded, filled his vision, burned off the cottony obfuscation. Not above but beside him, he lay on his side naked save for a blue hospital gown, empty pail next to the bed. The glow came from Katherine's abdomen, wolf ears and all. Vomit into the bucket. Good thing they left that there.

Chapter 15

Madness for the Wicked

Globe woke to the bang, wooden thud, opening and closing of drawers. The slide of closet door, zip of zipper, up and down, back and forth. Cracked an eye, the girls were next to him, naked as the day they were born, though the day they burst forth into the world they were probably not covered in glitter, alcohol, flavored lube and human secretion. Human secretions yes, the others not so much. Flash of red hair, Katherine then. Picked something off the floor, threw it in a pile by the door. Burn pile or laundry?

"Wake up Globe." He feigned sleep, she wasn't fooled. "The chopper is fired up and waiting. You're needed on the gas platform, investors are coming, gas if flowing." She touched a button on the wall, "Gloria, could you come help please?" Poke, prod, punch his arm. She had her mother's temper.

Hood groaned to his feet, shuffled to the bathroom, penis recessed into a little pink nub, Gloria didn't need to see that. Bloodshot eyes, beard stubble, stink of unwashed bodies. How long had he been locked in here with the girls again? Commotion in the room, heard the girls protesting, firm tones of Katherine and Gloria. He showered quickly, shaved, dressed, return to the bedroom. The Tweedles sat on the edge of the bed, wearing the miniskirts they hadn't worn in days and teary eyed frowns. They were on him as soon as he opened the bathroom door. They stank as he had, sex and sweat. Flood in his brain, crashing waves in his chest.

"Why aren't the girls dressed? They're coming with me." Squeeze an ass cheek, one in each hand.

"No Globe, they aren't." Gloria stood in front of him, shoulder to shoulder with Katherine. "They are staying here, you have work to do and I'll not have you appearing like an unprofessional lecherous drunkard. Even if you are one." No nonsense Gloria then. Katherine took both girls by the hand, pulled them toward the door. Spoke softly in Spanish, go home to the Barrio she said, your families have been asking for you, tears of protest, Pappi help us they plead.

He would've gone to them but Gloria pinned him with those Hazel eyes, dared him to move. He was quite certain she was prepared to hit him. Katherine made it to the door. Shrieks from the girls, shriek in is soul.

"It's okay girls, Gloria and Katherine are right. I need to attend to some business, and I can't keep my hands off of you. I wouldn't be able to concentrate." Harder to say than he thought. Of course he wouldn't be able to concentrate, that was the point. Tongue tied, erection growing just thinking about them.

"No Papi, we'll be good, we'll stay in our room and only fuck you at night when you're done." Whining, pleading tone, not a bad idea, raised his hand to agree. Gloria stopped him.

"You old fool, you'll be back in a few days. I think you can keep your dick in you pants for three days can't you?" Not really a question. He heard a sigh of resignation. His then.

"It'll be okay girls. I'll call for you as soon as I am on my way back, that way you can be here waiting for me." Pouts return but at least a sullen "okay Papi" came with them. Katherine left with the girls after reminding Gloria the chopper was waiting. His chest hurt. Vice on his intestines. He felt the distance between the girls and himself increasing, like a GPS tracker on his libido. Twist and shout, writhe and pull at his hair. Sucking black hole devoured rationale, logic and reason, digested him in the bottomless abyss of desire.

The sensation was akin to dehydration, every cell in his body screamed for the Tweedles, he screamed for them to return. Gloria got him to his feet, plopped him on the edge of the bed Gloria's turn to press the intercom.

"Wolf, could you come in here please?" She looked at Globe like a bad dog, shook her head. Sweat beaded on his brow, sweat stained the crisp white shirt, he'd just donned. Was it hot? Three count and the man was through the door next to her.

A new thing that, the familiarity between the two, Wolf's hand on her back while he talked to her, soothing tones, kept his eyes on Hood the whole time. Black eyes of the reaper. Hood wasn't sure how he felt about the two of them becoming close. His right and left hands as it were.

Eye blink and El Lobo materialized next to him, how did the man do that? He had Hood by the elbow, gentle shove. Mechanical, robot walked him to the door. Legs so heavy, fat lard filled balloons attached to his pelvis. Seething serpents of need, slithered around his soul, writhed around intestines, constricted, crushed guts. Damn the man to Hell.

"Don't worry Hood, we're almost to the car." Hood groaned, thought out loud. Good thing the man had a thick skin. Hood wanted to crumple to the ground, die in agony. The SUV was too damn high, unable to step up he rolled into the backseat. Belly first, roll over until his legs followed. Little help from El Lobo, push a boulder up the hill. Whisk him away, no Gloria either then?

"No Globe, Gloria and I will manage the farm while you take care of business on the platform. Little Jon is already there." No Gloria didn't mean no Lobo. The man escorted him into the helicopter, same deal, rinse repeat. He drank water like he'd never had the stuff, spilled half of it on his front, change later. Whir of blades, thup, thup in his chest. Blackness closed around him, giggle of laughter in his brain. Woke to grizzled jaw, steely eyes. Moving mouth, what did he say?

"I said I don't want to carry you to the office, won't look good, don't know if I could either. Last little bit then you can rest." Yanked Hood upright, opened the helicopter door. Mechanical noise, clanging metals, screaming steam, banging of industrious labor, comforted Hood. Nerves soothed by the layers of human endeavor. Behind it all, the canvass on which the rest was painted, the salty spray of the ocean, deep dark blue of the Atlantic ocean. On the new rig off the Carolina coast, skeleton crew, no drilling allowed yet but he knew it was coming. His newest investment, not that it mattered, his office was identical, he'd seen to that.

Huff and puff, trundle along metal catwalks, no workers to be seen. The Wolf handled the few they saw, talked it up for him, blue collar camaraderie more genuine than Hood could have ever been. The Boss had a wicked hangover and a jealous lover, needed to hide out for a few days. Whistles and hoots, go get 'em Hood. Cogs and sprockets, worker bees, commodities was all they were to him. Weight on his chest, peck of sand replaced with cobble, heavier by the minute. Handrail all the way, Lobo at his shoulder, elbow in gentle vice grip. The man could be tactful and gentle when warranted.

Oak door reached, Wolf's attention ended, dropped Hood on the leather couch, black like oil. Little Jon in the corner at a small desk with a computer, papers piled neatly, square corners all around him. Five more binders worth in the leather chair he'd pulled close. He barely turned, only his head, spectacles catching the sun, wave of the hand.

"Alright Hood, you're here for the duration. Little Jon will be with you for as long as it takes." Porcupine quills to his chest, barb in his heart, as long as what takes?

"As long as it takes for you to come to your senses." El Lobo answered. "As long as it takes for you to get over the Tweedles, go through withdrawal, whatever this is. I'm giving it a week or two." He bent over, patted Hood on the shoulder, had a word with Little Jon, gone. Helicopter thup, thup, disappeared over the horizon, into the setting sun. Hood somersaulted, carouseled, whirlpooled down into numbing darkness of unconsciousness. Black snake of desire waited for him there. Coiled around him, squeezed him to explode, doused in sweat, fat beads rolled down forehead and neck, gone for a swim even. Scream for release, unhand me you whores! Must of them, filled his senses, pushed into them, smell her womanhood, drank it in. Muscles contracted, pool of sweat, hated them all, melted into puddled muscles. Screamed for the pain to end. Woke in the darkness, his scream dying in the air, wetness draped all around, wrapped tight like the constricting snake. The sheets. He'd soaked through the bedsheets, through the pillow, wet mass of fabric girdling him tight across the middle.

No wonder he dreamed of being crushed to death by that awful snake. To what circle of Hell had he descended? Afraid and alone in the dark he wept for the attention of stupid immigrant whores, not worth his spittle or semen. Then why would he sell the entire oil rig for a taste of their caramel sweat, the touch of their fingers on his neck, warming embrace of her legs wrapped around him? Why? Good for nothing but fornicating, gold-digging opportunists, ready and willing to ride his coat tails to the land of plenty. And why not? Their miserable impoverished, three people to a room, twenty people to a house living environment begged for a golden slipper. A ride in his chariot, a negotiation with values, a compromise of the flesh.

Sold her flesh to him, leased it to him for the life she'd always wanted. A win-win. Poor miserable illegals were the perfect cogs and perfect sprockets. They worked for a pittance, were largely ignorant, had no recourse for garnered wages, poor working conditions, extended hours, zero benefits. A dream come true for the American capitalist like himself. A fluid, easily replaced workforce that was unorganized and under informed; the gild on the Lily being the economic gangbusters of benefit he reaped from the truck driving, back whipping of illegals. Their labor saved him hundreds of millions of dollars. God Bless America.

Hell in a hand basket, the country became more socialist by the day, thanks to the uppity POTUS. Why else would Hood try so hard to keep his money out of the hands of the IRS, who in turn rained it down on the wretched refuse teeming to be free. Social conservatives that waved their U.S. flag behind the guise of fiscal conservatism were just fine with Hood. As long as they gave that liberal black bastard the hardest time possible. Make everything he did difficult, even the little things.

Waves of cold, waves of hot, dunk tank of icy-hot, bengay, mentholated chest rub, over and over. Head to toes, shook him physically, twitch and shiver, teeth chatter, moan in pain. His workers should be grateful they had it so well. He let them work normal shifts, gave them job security, had no language requirement, El Lobo as intermediary. Fetch them at the border, room and board for the new arrivals. Charged and taken from their wages of course. No free rides here, none deserved, everybody started with nothing. If they wanted it bad enough they could make the most of it.

Hood wasn't overly fond of politicians, his hearing in the Senate proof of that but any one of them that was willing to stymie the socialist agenda of that pseudo-American, first African-American president was OK in his book. Shut down the EPA, get them out of his hair, out of his mines, out of his waste stream, out of his emissions. If he was in luck the whole federal machine would shut down.

These days the federal teat was better than handouts, stand in a line, pot of gold at the end of the rainbow. They took the taxes he tried so hard not to pay, gave them to the poor and infirm, the lazy, the slovenly, the leeches of the human race.

They'd get none of his money, none of what was his if he had his way. The problem with the once great nation was the handing out support to the masses, clamoring milk the system. Fat mothers at the corner store buying crap and chips for her gaggle of kids. Feed them crap because she was too lazy to cook a decent meal. Thanks for buying his corn by the way.

Now this damn Health Care, at least it wasn't free yet, though he suspected that was next. Tell Little Jon to take his money out of medical devices or the whole industry for that matter. Keep pharmaceuticals though, they always found a way. In a way, the coming change to Health care would suit him nicely. Those that were legal and demanding benefits would no longer find traction for that argument. Send them to the exchanges, out of his hair. One less placard, one less chant at the rally. Never say that out loud, but it was the truth. The country was going to Hell in a hand basket, due in part to people like his two lovers. Browns and blacks were mixing with the rest, assuming power, telling hard-working, god-fearing, red-blooded Americans what to do with their money. Upstarts were everywhere, getting their fingers into everything. Damn shame.

Night into day, fitful dreams, the Tweedles at a protest, Katherine at a protest, Katherine with Ramon plotting in a corner. Black snake of desire, Tweedles in stockings, wrapped him with their legs, pushed his face into her crotch, Tweedle becomes Gloria. Her pointing finger in his chest becomes grinding auger drilling for oil, found only blood. Woke panting, sun creeps under black curtains. Wondered if the crew could hear him, no sound of machinery reached into his darkness. Embrace the rage. Burning ember of screaming ego. Burn the hand, distract from the breast, the smell of pussy.

The politicians, the ones fighting the good fight, caught in the craw of those liberal socialist Marxists. They were heroes, warriors for the right. Unconstitutional, illegal, convoluted, bastardization of the law process, health care system socialization in sheep's clothing. Subsidies for the poor, everyone is signed up, even congress, they also get a fat subsidy, Uncle Sam's bill. Next time he woke the television was on, talking heads, ticker across the bottom. Health care reform graphic, angry heads. Something must've come through his muddled madness, enough for Little Jon to turn on the television. He huddled, fetal position, held in the heat of the gently stoked ember, the fire of rage he had cooking, nurse the thing before he went mad, kept his mind off the girls. Or not. He ran around the suite naked, screamed, damn them, damn them, damn them. Assaulted Little Jon, knock over his books, his brandy. Bad idea, Jon was quite adept with that walking cane, more able than Hood with his check book. The lawyer beat him soundly.

Slapped and beaten, nursing bruised head and ass Jon escorted him back to the room. He wanted them, needed them, call for El Lobo, get those little bitches out here, how could they do this to him. Little Jon ignored him and left. Hood raged, nothing to break, nothing to throw, huddle next to the rage, warmed himself with the heat, to burn would be better. Weakness washed through him in waves, crashed from his skull to his feet, leached hope and consciousness with it. He floated in darkness. Snake emerged from the Tweedle babymaker, bit him on the prick. Scream for mercy.

He swam toward the heat, green flames licked the boundary of the blackness, he pulled them in, snake flicked its black tongue. Hate them, the very same cogs and sprockets that worked for him were the very same gumming up the works, casting too many votes. The legal ones anyway. Damn the liberal bastards giving hope to the masses. The very same politicians were not men of the people any longer, the talking heads agreed with him, floated through darkness. The American people wouldn't stand for the socialism of the blacks and browns, the American people would rise up. The white ones anyway. Only the House of Representative can control the purse strings, that's right, strangle the libs with it, great to watch. Cloak yourself in the constitution, answer to your constituents, the ones with money anyway, or two years from now the House will be full of new faces. Power of the purse is mighty, government overlord cometh, drones humming overhead, biometric every-thing, media propaganda warps the truth.

Lies from the top, lies from the bottom, lies from every mouthpiece everywhere. Tap your phones, tap your email communications, they'll hold you indefinitely, with just cause of course, potential terrorist. Talking head, two dimensional, stared down on him.

Hood on the floor beneath a man in a suit with a red tie. He clung to hate, grasped at anger, life raft to salvation. Back to Guantanamo, throw those girls in there too, all the fucking immigrants, send all the illegals to Cuba, let Castro choke on them, return the favor, remember the nineties? Strangle them with the constitution, flicker of panic through conservative community, never said out loud, but panicked shouting match-es over cigars and brandy were country club common.

Big government cometh, he might have to sell his hold-ings in the U.S., give Katherine whatever was left after. Shut the government down. Maybe it would be better if the Chinese took over. Tumble head over heels through darkness. Snake wrapped around him, mouth around his penis and balls, teeth digging into his ass, he couldn't rip it off, agony and pain. He swam through darkness. Toward green flickering rage, warmed him, filled him, drove out the lust. Snake head turned to Tweedle mouth, lips and tongue, amygdala became round ass-hole, puckered around his prick swallowed his ejaculate. Head exploded in pain, fire in his crotch. Focused on the hate, hate them, hate them. Whores. Isabella you bitch!

Floating raft of flickering flat screen, ferry through the darkness, cross the river Styx. Maybe meet Madison. Carry a big stick. Constitution not worth the paper it was written on in Hell, even less if the Liberals got their way. They would hold hands with the Ayatollah next, Palestine and North Korea shortly after. Countries with nothing to offer other than terror-ism and sand. Didn't even want their oil anymore. He had his own. Killers and thieves, left their camels and tents at home. Ah yes, the brilliance of the group think, the House knew all about it. Good for the conservative coalition putting screws to the establishment fools, who cow-towed to the money and lob-byists. Granted some of his most influential contacts were members of the old guard but let the fresh blood stir things up, piss into the wind, scream from the rooftops. Change was a good thing, right?

Conservatism is not an ideology, it is a way of life, drip drop electro-magentic buzz through his floating blackness. From his toes to his hair, conserve his money, conserve his rights, conserve power. He was all for it.

Conserve the water resources from his animal waste, sure, just don't let the EPA stick their nose in his business. Give it time, already made to look fools by the Russians and Irani-ans, the uppity leader of the free world was a fool. Negotiating with global evil entities before he was willing to negotiate with his own House of Representatives spoke of the man's inept, narcissistic, naivete. The country was the weakest ever, terror-ism striking on U.S. soil, what a shame.

Cascading waves of water, waterfall of black liquid tumbled down, landed with a thud. Americans felt more frightened than ever, masked terrorist lurked in the shadows, walked the halls of your schools. The blacks and browns drooled over the token black blessed with melanin. Shut the government down, Senators and Congressmen still got their paychecks of course. Shoe dropped on the American people, thank you socialism. Liars and cheats, Marx would've been proud. He needed to drill through the layers of lies and expose the truth to the American people. How would the poorest of the poor be able to pay for this onus, this yoke, and we the oxen? The POTUS isn't an American, he's a Muslim, not a citizen, no birth certificate.

He's a fake, just like global warming, cooked books by scientists, making it up as they go along. Stop to vomit. Cold sweats, he danced over the black leather couch in his under-wear and socks, chased the cold away. Curtsy and ballet step, play with Little Jon's head till the cane came out. Cold sweats, he crumpled to the floor, wallow and moan. Pissed himself. Damn them all. Who were they to tell him he couldn't remove a mountain top? Who were they to tell him he couldn't pump coal dust into the river or the soil, or the air? Who were they that played politics with the will of the American people, with the purse strings of the nation. Fine, as long as his money wasn't in the pot. Seniors, women and children, the minorities, let them all suffer. It would scare the shit our of everyone, they would all suffer with the government gone. Good. Let them suffer, they took too much of his money anyway. He embraced the hatred, moved toward the heat of the burning ember. Damn them all.

Light shattered his skull like a marauding invader. Clubbed him to death, threw him over the side. Blur of movement, grainy darkness covered the light, roll into the shadow.

El Lobo stood above him, fat cigar wrapping the man in blue smoke.

"Jeezus Hood." Grabbed him by the elbow, lead him into the suite, deposited him on the couch.

Pretty young Latina in the corner, medical supplies in hand. Little Jon and El Lobo talked behind him, pretty little thing took his blood pressure, checked him over, looked afraid.

"Has he been like this the whole time?" Incredulous, the Wolf barked at Little Jon.

"Yes. The entire time." Suffering in Jon's voice.

"Pissing and shitting on himself, tearing the place apart, why didn't you call me man?"

"What would you have done Wolf? There is nothing to be done until this has run its course, you know that as well as I." Little Jon explained patiently.

"I didn't think it was this bad. Has he been shouting like that the whole time too?" The Wolf sounded as if he were struggling to believe.

"Yes, his body and higher functions are those of an animal but he has focused, latched on to this ranting diatribe of conservative thought. I see it as a positive sign. Indignant rage at the liberal agenda has always been near and dear to Hood's heart." Little Jon waited. The Wolf returned to the couch and Hood, removed Hood's hand from the young nurse's leg, told her to gather her things.

"Alright Little Jon. Good luck, I hope he's better next week. Give me a call if you need something or if he changes." Flicker of eyes at Hood who had his penis out, pranced around the room with rapidly deflating erection, rant revving up again. "Do you want me to send someone in to clean up this...shit." Not an exaggeration.

"No, I clean it when he passes out. Humble work is fitting sometimes." Little Jon stared out the window at the ocean. White capped waves danced across the ocean like waving fans, undulous and blue. Hood pranced into his cave, pulled the shades, fell into the bed. Fall end over end swim with the sharks, swim with the snakes, play with pretty nurse. Swim toward the anger, piss on the wretched.

Chapter 16

Digging out

Thup, thup over mid-Atlantic, back to the farm. Hood was very nearly insane, El Lobo wasn't sure if he should congratulate Isabella or scold her. Little nurse sat in the corner, leather seat farthest away from him, drawn in on herself. That she was afraid of him was obvious. How couldn't she be? He hadn't elaborated when he fetched her from the farm infirmary, no more than a few words for her to meet him at the helipad. The rig was eerily creepy when it was idle and she'd been jumpy all the way to the office. Then the feces covered degenerate Hood rubbed all over her. Thank god Little Jon kept the windows open and the woman well paid. Tormented by her naked boss, fat hand working up her leg, the other working his junk. No surprise she was staying as far away from him as possible.

The screaming rants, conservative vitriol was as odd and alarming as the man's descent into perversion. El Lobo was familiar with the man's political leanings, no mercy for the liberal tree-hugger, sick the lawyers on 'em, scare them away tactics. Little Jon was right, it was as if Hood was adrift in a sea of insanity, swells of neurotransmitter and Isabella's curse rising and falling like the tides in response to the moon's gravity. Bizarre to be sure. Seagulls on the shore, almost hear their cries.

The farm was well in hand, delivery and production were back on track, all repairs to warehouses and greenhouses near completion. The well-oiled machine of Hood's production and distribution hummed along as intended. Not all crises had been averted. Ramon was in the infirmary, along with five other workers. One that had been in the bunker when the fool nearly blew himself up and four of the movement members recovering from the warehouse job. Rumors were correct, the chatter about Ramon's pesticide bomb had been vague, none said what he intended, only that Hood need to be careful. Dumb kid. An hour or so later he waited at the bottom of the helicopter stairs. Held the slim hand of pretty young Physician's Assistant. She ran to her small import car in the helipad parking lot. Peeled out, gravel shot across the cement pad, he doubted she'd make next week's trip.

Hopped in his own conveyance, rusted and dust filled, cigar stuffed ashtray, smell of soil. He'd rather ride a horse around the farm, check on his people. A bit antiquated but more his speed. He used to do it that way when Lily was alive. Hood's wife loved horses, gave him one in fact, said it was a gift, said the horse reminded her of Jose. Made him blush too. Beautiful palomino, sure-footed and smart, nip you in the ass if you ignored him, he missed that horse.

Jostle and bounce, left rutted dirt road onto paved, headed to the dome. The large geodesic dome sat near the center of Hood's farm, visible from the air and every other building on the property, the thing was fifteen stories high. A media stunt gimmick to gain some publicity when Hood started his green line, the dome was initially touted as revolutionary. Gone from the public mind and eye after a month or two Hood hadn't been sure what to do with the monstrosity. Lobo suggested its current use and made it happen, with careful direction from his scientists of course.

The dome consisted of multiple platforms spiraling up the sixty meter height of the construct. The platforms were large flat discs, open air offices or enclosed laboratories both, bathrooms, snack bar, locker room and showers, the whole deal. A total of twenty-six disc shaped platforms spiraled up the inside of the dome. Twelve platforms per spiraling helix shaped stairway, climbing the side of the dome, slow and steady grade. The double helix intersected on several levels, as well as the top and the bottom with a total of twenty-six platforms. The space was sublime, far surpassing his greenhouse for beauty and serenity. Inside but outside, divine. Birds flew from here to there, bright colors, not native.

Hood wasn't overly fond of the place, just because it involved so much walking. Like all of his buildings golf carts were charged and ready for the portly owner to ride up the arcing ramps, even installed a freight elevator so he could ride his cart up to the top floor real quick like. The elevators only stopped at the third, fifth, seventh, eleventh, thirteenth floors, plus the roof, thanks to the engineering of the place.

One would have to walk or ride a cart to get to the other floors, a sparrow shot by his face. That was local. He'd come to the seventh floor, the plant research lab, Ramon's old haunt. The boy wasn't much better off than Hood. Plagued by delirium, nausea, confusion, bouts of blindness and maybe even brain damage, Ramon was one step above a drooling, defecating animal. One step above Hood then.

Ramon's supervisor and co-worker had been named by one of his informants. Drunk fool at the bar, couldn't see straight most days. Remembered Ramon meeting with a lot of people in the cantina, couldn't remember a one of them, he remembered that Isabella kicked him out though. Jostled his memory once El Lobo put a bottle in his hand, gave up three names, Isabella of course, she owned the bar, the greenhouse manager, and the supervisor of plant developmental research. Which was why El Lobo stood on the landing of the seventh floor platform; he took the stairs, it was more pleasant that way.

Marxist revolutionaries might be a bit of a stretch for the movement members, but they were angry workers with an axe to grind, bone to pick, voices to raise. Behind him a bank of square shaped rooms were lit from within, natural light allowed entry through a glass ceiling, it conserved energy and allowed the lab coats natural light to work by. Bad enough squinting into a microscope all day, the least they could do was make the scientists comfortable. Everybody loved it. Except Hood. The expense had been quite substantial, though his research labs were making up the difference.

The woman known as the Doe or Venado, moved within the rooms. Large picture windows inserted in each wall allowed for observation of the scientist, like some strange zoo exhibit. Once a month the handlers let the white coated, glasses wearing hominids out of their cells, or not. The Doe coasted back and forth between two rooms, both observable through the large windows. She worked at a microscope, moved into a back room, opened what looked like a refrigerator, but EL Lobo knew was an incubator, used to grow bacteria and mold.

It took her several minutes to notice him standing outside her window, hands crossed behind his back. She paused for several minutes more with pursed lips as she debated whether she should exit the lab to speak to him. She did eventually, removed her lab coat, hung it on a peg by the door, exited the room and closed it behind her. She came out and stood at the railing next to him, not looking at him, instead stared off into the sun pierced void, expansive, radiant, candescent.

"Lobo." No fear in her voice, guarded curiosity, she knew him, his wife better.

Easy to see why they named her the Doe. Her big saucer-shaped eyes made her look startled but he knew better. Absent minded scientist was a more appropriate descriptor and a great shtick for her. He knew how shrewd she was, too many card games in the cantina to ignore the mental push-pull she had going for her.

"Doe." He used her movement name, see if he could really startle her. She didn't bite.

"How is Ramon?" She asked, genuine when it suited. El Lobo was one of four people allowed access to the fool boy since he nearly killed himself with the pesticide mishap.

"Alive, por suerte, sick as hell, confused, vomiting and blind half the time. But he should recover in a few weeks or not at all. As for the rest of you, you may not recover, ever, unless you cooperate with me." Play some cards of his own, not all bluff, she knew it too, watched him from the corner of her eye.

"The movement is dead Lobo, at least the first incarnation, we've fired Ramon, disbanded the group and are beginning negotiations with Hood." He laughed out loud, threw his head back and guffawed at the glass dome, scared birds sitting in the limbs of trees and scientists working with multicolored rabbits in the topiary labyrinth one floor below. They stared up at him and wondered, got back to work, these types didn't need to be prodded. The Doe tightened her grip on the railing, knuckles gone white. Once he stopped laughing he asked.

"And I should believe you why?" He knew nothing of negotiations, and the mere idea threatened to cramp him with laughter and undermine his professionalism.

Hood was in no condition to do anything of the sort.

"I have no reason to lie." She still refused to look at him.

"Saving your ass is reason enough." He thought about lighting a cigar, better not, the place was too fragrant, too pleasant. He considered hanging her over the railing, suspended eighty feet over the earth, blood rushing to her brain might work to shake something loose. Didn't seem necessary. She was smart enough to be a leader in the movement, she was smart enough to know she had nothing to gain from lying to him. Especially if they really had thrown Ramon out.

Perhaps they could negotiate their way out of the whole mess, no need to involve outsiders in what was an internal dispute. Perhaps depended on Hood's mood on any given day and El Lobo didn't see any given days in their future. Currently Hood's days were writhing, shitting, erection chasing madness. Needed to remedy that, like yesterday.

"Who is it then, your negotiator?"

"Ramon's lover. Or ex, I can't tell who she's with anymore. They say she's sleeping with everyone from the movement, men, women, any that are interested."

Swallow frog in throat, swallow boiling rage, maybe he would hang her over the edge until her head exploded, tie her there with his belt, very tempting. She finally looked at him, over-sized eyes, sly smirk on her mouth, she knew how to get to him or so she thought.

"Have you been?" Keep to the point, find out what was up.

"No, but I plan on seeing her tomorrow, not sure what I should wear, or what to expect." Shiny eyes. With an open hand slap he could send her over the edge. She was having a good time with him, he threw his head back and laughed again, how the tortilla flips, what fun. Scared the lab coats all over again, shouts from the lower disc, ignored easily. He didn't bite at the bait, her goading was too obvious, too scientific.

"She wants in on the movement, she's tired of her father's nonsense." The Doe spoke after his mirth was played out.

Veil and evade. Answers to questions, just not the answers he wanted. Hang her over the edge by her toes, or nails, or toenails. That sounded right.

"I imagine she is trying to bring this nonsense to a peaceful end." Frog and toads. Throat hurt.

"Yes, I agree." Shit eating grin now, little Doe stared up at him, batted long eyelashes. Turned and left. The Deer evades the Wolf.

The long and the short of it, El Lobo ached for the little Miss Hood. In fact the ebb and flow, his ride on the tide of the karmic push-pull felt like it had worn a hole in his heart. Heart and soul, hole and heel, worn a hole in his heart like the sole of a shoe, right in the heel.

Wallow if he could. Like a pig in a sty, El Lobo wallowed in self-pity. Suffocated under the muddy brown waters of despair and heartache. Miss Hood and her projects, she was up to something with the movement members, apparently negotiations, maybe pregnant. Probably Ramon's. Her laughter tinkled in her wake. The Wolf dared not approach, not yet, but he wanted to kill something. The pigs noticed. Large potbellied workers that ran the garbage at the depot and the slaughter house. When El Lobo showed up at the materials recovery depot to wallow with them they knew something was up. The Wolf didn't show unless something needed to be done or somebody killed. When no one was upbraided, disappeared or otherwise invalid, the pigs relaxed. Stomp on sorrow, return her from where she came, kiss her not, touch her not. He vowed to allow her to find happiness, burden her not with the trials and tribulations, the exhausting ego petting of fur covered pride.

Materials Recovery. Hollow shell of a warehouse, more like a hangar. Glorified tin walls and roof. Could stuff ten barns in there, it was like a stadium, a Coliseum of refuse. Gladiators the pigs circulating below, arms and necks thick as tree trunks, wielded plastic bag and toilet bowl, garbage can lid, fight to the death. King of the mountain, shit rolls downhill.

Vacuous space through which trucks, backhoes, front end loaders scurried in and out, loads full of waste. Like the insects working their way through the crannies of the soil, colloids, cleavages and clay. Pushing, pulling, digesting the dirt, worked it for them all. Hood required convincing to set the place up, though less than some would've thought. He was a farmer before he became the megalomaniac, richer than ninety-nine percent of the world, business man. Ultimately he recognized the value inherent in a pile of shit. One man's excrement was another man's guano, million dollar product left in a steaming pile, pushed from the bowels of some creepy crawly's asshole. Such lack of vision plagued most people, not Hood.

The facility handled the waste from the farm and the Barrio. No need taxing the local municipality beyond the services already provided. Best way to keep the nosy town councilmen, mayors and appointees out of his business.

Provided batch solar heaters, small wind-mill generators for the workers wanting to decrease their energy bills and keep the local utilities from asking questions about the increased draw in the neighborhood. The Barrio grew and grew, no sign of stopping.

The waste was separated as it came in, a wet and smelly job, one of the worst, separated by illegals into organic and inorganic. Organic referred to carbon based food waste, yard waste and the like. The separation was done just outside the hanger sized space, men and construction equipment seemed tiny inside the enormous space. Once separated, the organic waste was laid out in long undulating mounds, covered with soil and mixed, allowed to sit for three to six months until cured, then used as fertilizer. Another idea Hood balked at initially, stick in the mud scrooge that he was. When El Lobo wheeled in two greenhouse tomato plants, one with the soil fertilizer, the other without, there was little need to convince him further. Similar to so many of Hood's businesses, the garbage business was lucrative, manned by the same cheap labor and a benefit to Hood's bottom line. A little trouble kicked up when they first started, unionized mafioso stuff, they'd taken care of that.

Stuck to the barrio, no problems. Great place for the disposal of "things" that need to go. The place was set up to recycle the organic food-stuffs and yard waste into soil, while recycling the cans and bottles, send them to the county. Lastly they shipped the last bit of unusable material to the incinerator. Of course once they pulled out all the organic matter, cans, bottles and paper there wasn't a whole lot that needed to be shipped to the incinerator. He didn't see the pig squad's leader, he had an inkling that illegal son-of a bitch was probably up to his elbows in blood about now. He hopped in his truck, bumped his way to the slaughterhouse.

Blood and mud, grass and ass, squelch and splatter. Pools of blood and mud, swirling darkness, brown and black. Stink of shit and Poacea. Ruminants like cow, sheep, and goat, the pigs were a different story, a different building, their entrails smelled different, omniverous diet and all. The result was the same, they all let blood over the slaughterhouse floor, pockmarked, uneven concrete, damaged from decades of high pressure water blasts.

Water heated and mixed with disinfectant cablecade armed to kill, stupefy and wipe the nasties down the drain. Especially the ones that fed on blood and guts. Shoot the water, power enough to pit stone. The water remained after, still soapy pools and rivulets of blood and suds. Blood of the pig, the cow, blood of the bleating goat. Mud from worker's shoes, fork lift, truck, trailer, mud from the road daring to enter as far as the loading bay, carried by workers to the slaughterhouse floor. Much like the materials recovery hangar, in fact identical. This hanger had innards of metal, iron, copper, bone and blood.

Hooks and conveyor belts, ferry carcass, quarters, half, wholes. Lamenting of imminent death in the distant corner. The last holding pen of their husbanded lives. Baa, Moo, Oink. Conveyors rotated like at the dry cleaners, hit the button summon your clothes from the back somewhere, the fashions of the clients chug a lug by, plastic sheath protects the laundered garments. Only here the clank and clatter, the rattle and hum is industrious, machinery at work.

Carry carcass, hooks through chain links that bound legs, carry to another station for the butchering to begin. Sand on the floor, to be blasted clean, grinding the stone beneath to dust. High pressure wash away blood and mud, down the drain, take the nasties with it.

The smell of guts, bowels, death. Shit balls, like marbles vacate the anus of decapitated goat, still wagging tail, twitching hooves, draining blood. Crimson oxygen filled hemoglobin courses and puddles, tinkle down the drain. Shit rolls downhill. Migrant worker with chaps, apron, goggles and bandana, someone has to do it. The workers rotated through the different jobs. Killer, axe, saw, rifle depended on the animal. Butcher, run a miter saw, hacksaw, table-saw, slice the body, rough cuts only. Deliver to the store, the market, the whole seller. Let someone with a sharp knife do that work. Chainsaws buzzed, blades whined their way through bone. Sheep, goat, poultry on another piece of property down the road a ways. Only beef in this facility, tidy little time and money saver for Hood. Goats were primarily for the workers, some lamb too, the older muttony meat. Increasing popularity of goat was an unexpected blip in profits for the farm.

What started as a side project after El Lobo made Hood try some goat cheese the workers made for themselves, turned into an artsy-fartsy, paper-packaged product. Hood's attempt at artisan cheese exploded in popularity, then the glut. Every small-time farmer, retired executive, and dot-com naer-do well was suddenly making goat cheese in his or her backyard.

El Lobo let the immigrants keep the herd, feed the workers, make them feel appreciated. And they did. They worked the goats into the slaughterhouse seamlessly. Coming full circle, as these things always did, the goat meat was selling like hot cakes. Katherine said she could barely keep her freezer stocked. The Mexicans, the Guatemalans, El Salvadorians, Colombians, Caribbean's, all showed up for the goat meat. Muslims and Africans came to the Barrio for the meat too. They all came for the goat. Hood started pushing it again, not hard to do, fill up the ethnic groceries, he had contacts, cha-ching.

Flies in his face, shit in his mouth and on his sole. Scrape it on one of the pig's faces, get the message across if necessary. He collected one of the butchers on the first floor, in a freezer, frozen meat all around. Muscle armed fellow, weren't they all? Short and stocky, broad chest, Honduran probably. All the boys in the slaughterhouse had big arms. Swinging saws and meat was an all day work out, no need for the gym.

Still afraid of El Lobo though, this one at least. The man shuffled backward into the wall of the walk-in freezer. Hook still in his hand, drag and hang a quarter cow like nothing. Probably was nothing. Rubber galoshes slip in shit and blood, scared eyes, the fool had forgotten the hook in his hand and the Wolf has none.

"Donde esta tu Jefe?" (Where is your boss?) Dark eyes looked back at El Lobo, pondering, considering, perhaps the heft of that meat hook felt good.

Tensed muscles, coiled spring, El Lobo would crush his windpipe, break his jaw or remove his eye, all depended on the pig squad member's decision. El Lobo was sure the fool was a movement member, panic play acting was his stall, time to think.

"Don't worry you fool, I don't want to hurt anyone." Oops, meant to speak in Spanish, opened his mouth to repeat, the man opened and closed his hand on the hook.

"Su oficina." His office, good, no need to translate, smart choice Honduran pig.

"Gracias amigo." El Lobo turned and left, let the man get back to work.

Left the severed heads, broken backs, hanging legs, stretched entrails behind. They loved tripe, the rest of the organs too for that matter. Good little side business for the workers. Red sold some in her shop and at the farmer's market but most of the organ meat went into the pockets of the workers. Sold out of their kitchen and garage freezers. Everybody loves organ meat, braided intestines, blood sausage and churrasco here we come. Or perhaps a hardy stew, keep the cold away.

The tripe was the first thing to go in a soup pot, after a good rinsing, clean grass and shit and all incarnations in between from the gastro-intestinal jump rope evolved and designed for biological food process. Maybe add some feet if they were lucky, skin too, once the hair was burnt off. Good soup. Happy soup, it really did keep the cold away.

Around back then, he'd known as much. Sometimes it served to let people know you were coming, word travels fast, fart in the wind. Around back, several hundred meters distant was a modest one story building with large air-conditioning units on the roof and a drive way that wrapped around the side and down a sloped drive. Loading dock on the first sub-floor. The building had three sub-floors actually, El Lobo was intimate with the building having used the cooling capacity and inconspicuous location more than once. The building was far enough from the slaughter to escape the smell, sound and blood. Maybe not the blood, that got everywhere. Couldn't be helped.

Pig squad Lieutenant, a big burly man with tree-trunk arms like the rest, only bigger, plus the large belly and shiny greased mustache. El Lobo wondered if the man greased it with the fat he pulled off the hog. The man personally attended to Hood's orders, aged and cured as requested. Pig Lieutenant stood behind a lovely porcelain tile and stainless steel island. Space and hooks for thirty plus carcasses off to one side. Doors behind lead to five rooms full of smoked, aged, salted meats, special request items for Hood and his friends. As reported there he was, in his office, up to his elbows in blood, quite literally. Leather apron beneath white smock spoke of bone cutting, just in case thinking. The man was careful. The sleeves of his button up, business casual shirt rolled up, covered with blood like the rest. Wonder what his wife said when he brought that shit home. White apron stretched tight over a rotund mid-section looked ready to burst, was not really white but an abstract homage to the violation of purity covered with blood splatter, marrow, sinew.

The pig slowed his work when El Lobo crossed his threshold but did not stop. El Lobo gave the room a quick scan. Boss pig worked behind the largest island of wood, tile and stainless steel. There were work spaces for four others, identical to his but smaller, flanking the grated and contoured walkway that lead to the main cutting table, all the place needed was a glass display case. Mental note. The walkway was textured to provide grip when the water flowed, wash away the blood, grated so the water had somewhere to go. Single drains clogged too easily. They were alone. He wondered if the rest of the workers were crouched in the smokehouse, knives at the ready, more likely on their way home, done for the day. It was getting late.

Fat, sausage thick fingers, too hairy by far, worked with finesse and efficiency. Large carving knife made short work of the pig carcass in front of him. Who knows where the fat back was, piled on a back table, or a shelf below, refrigerated islands? The loin and shoulder butt sprang from the bone, glistening and scrumptious, cleanest cuts he'd ever seen. No meat on the bone, none. El Lobo made another mental note, never get in a knife fight with Pig squad Lieutenant, bring a gun to that party. Sirloin roast, butterfly chop, loin roast, Canadian bacon and tenderloins materializing with surgical precision from the man's dextrous fingers. El Lobo whistled, tip of the hat.

"Wow, Hombre, no sabia que erea asi." (Man I didn't know it was like that.)

"Como que?" Didn't stop working, twinkle in his eye, menace in his tone. El Lobo couldn't help but like the man. A little.

"Asi de professional, de efficiente, de espactulo, sos dotado, una placer para ver trabajar. Aunque no debo estar sorprendido, he comido tus cortes bastante." (So professional, efficient, a spectacle, you're gifted, a pleasure to see work. Although I shouldn't be surprised, I've eaten your cuts enough.) Pig squad captain almost laughed. El Lobo could tell the man swallowed a guffaw, bit his tongue, intent on his work.

"Podria decir lo mismo Senor Lobo." El Lobo did laugh at that one, it was decided. He liked the fat bastard, hoped he didn't have to kill him. Pig was illegal, therefore easy to disappear. Hope not, want not. Blade steaks, shoulder butt for smoking fell away from his fine blade.

"Good one, good one. Bueno, imagino que sabes porque estoy aqui." Got down to business, obviously they'd both appreciate it, end the pleasantries, they were a bit too sincere. Blood on the table, spray it down the drain, the pig did.

"You are also a professional Wolf, do not deny it. I can tell." He alluded to El Lobo's detective work ferreting him out.

"Surprising what a sharp knife on the throat can do for people, especially disaffected wives." El Lobo watched the color drain from the man's face, the knife finally stopped. Ham half separated from the carcass.

"That fat bitch would tell you anything Lobo, probably screw you too." He was angry, not scared, correct though, to the tee. "We're meeting with Katarina, she's working with us, part of the movement now, took Ramon's place since the fool blew himself up. She's got daddy issues, but you know that don't you?" Knife started working again, slicing heart, kidneys and tongue now, fine and thin, like sashimi, really amazing, smiled from ear to ear.

"I hear the movement is over, squashed. Done." Wide grin of his own. A passerby would surely think the two were exchanging jokes the way they were both smiling.

"Quisas, no se, tengo una cita con ella. Supuestamente en su casa, dicen que esta dormiendo con todos que quieren." (Perhaps, I don't know, I have a meeting with her, Supposedly in her house, they say she's sleeping with anyone that's interested) Heart sliced fine, kidney cubed, lungs too.

"She's sleeping with everyone? Somehow I find that hard to believe." True statement. According to his estimate that would be approximately one hundred and twenty people, men and women.

"I don't know Lobo, just what I've heard. I'm not a Captain, but you know that." He spun the large French knife in his hand, leather strap around the handle stained from brown to black with blood, provided grip even when blood soaked the thing. All the knives were wrapped so, butcher, pairing, French, all. Blood splattered on steel tabletop with a whack, fatty yellow deposit.

"She's gone now of course. One of the boys took her somewhere," licked his lips,"hope it wasn't somewhere dirty." Disgusting.

"Quien?" El Lobo felt spider webbing ache through chest, kicked himself, Hood was away, sick as a dog. Did Gloria know about this? Pig smiled, deep exhale, mission accomplished, seed of doubt planted, chuckled to himself. Resumed cutting the brains, when did he pull those out?

"I don't know Wolf, someone. Not one of us, some gringo." Licked his lips, pig's turn to laugh, belly shake. The man was a philanderer and his wife disaffected, she would've fucked El Lobo if he asked. Not that it was on the table, fat and portly like her husband she fairly stank of beer and cigarettes. She gave up her info willingly, trying to tempt him into her bed.

"Is that so?" Suddenly glad he left his gun in the truck, stay out of trouble, the man was a valued employee. " Bueno Cerdo, ya voy." (Very well Pig, I'm leaving)

"Bueno Lobo Maldito, gracias por venir." The knife spun in his hand, blade flipping over and over, sharp edge up then down, up, then down. Maybe he meant it. El Lobo left, smoke in the wind, bite it if he could.

El Lobo meditated daily, physical labor was the only way to clear Katherine from his mind, facilitated his letting go. She certainly was the root of his ache, crush it, stomp it, let her go. Maybe she'd be back, maybe not. Crush the pain. He pretended she'd gone, not from his psyche, nor the brand on his soul, but she left the barrio. A patch over the hole in his heart, a patch to cover the brand that flared red and molten. Let her go friend Wolf. Let her go.

He plead to the universe, take her... but please bring her back to he, somehow, someway. The lies the Wolf told himself, he didn't have to dig much to find out where she'd gone. She was hurt, thrown from her horse and the baby? Meditation, ignorance, pretending she didn't exist only helped so much. He lost her, gone she was, laughing at the jokes of another, telling another she loved him. Give it up fool, the cause is lost. What was it he said last week? Submit to the ebb and flow of life's eddies. Hope springs eternal. Wallow, wallow, returned to the sty and visited the pigs, the mud is cool and cakes nicely over the wounds.

Despair, despair, red-blond hair, so beautiful indeed, cry if you need. Meditate away the pain, block out her chestnut eyes. Cry fool, cry fool, cry bloody tears fool. She was not his, never was, didn't want to be, stupid Lobo. He was a perverted sorry, small, small wolf. Hope escaped from his foolish heart like oxygen rich blood. Longed to throw himself at her feet, ego strangled him to death, longing for her, desire to own her, his desire to let her go...forever. Longed for psycho-spiritual sexual enlightenment to consume them, disappear into the ether, never to be seen again.

Heartache and despair, his soul aflame for Little Red. Cut off his head already, maybe then he'd be able to deal with the pain. She the opaque one, he the beheaded. Mud and slop, wallow and sty, how did one justify longing from afar. Focus on his mind, fall into it as far as he could. To the bottom of whichever barrel it was he deemed fit to drown himself in. His heart felt weak. Wallow away, starve in stoicism, suffocated in self-pity, drowned in sadness. Poor he, poor we, poor she. What was she up to? And why couldn't it be he that she was up to?

"At least wait for me to die." Isabella said to him, jealousy and hurt plain as day on her face. She was no fool. Were they dead to each other? Seemed that way for years. He never really had Miss Hood for himself in the first place, scream, shout, wallow. He pulled over outside the Cantina, gravel lot full of run down jalopies.

Multi-color kaleidoscope on frosted glass panes, spider webbed glass older than some of the patrons inside. No ID check at this door, blasting Ranchero music, melancholy in a minor key. Popcorn kernels and peanut shells on the floor, crunch beneath booted soles. El Lobo sidled up to the bar, Isabella absent, helper Giovanni served in her place. Harvest moon hung low in the sky, waning, rising toward the cheshire's grin. Plum and dusty on the horizon it rose into the night sky, peeked over the treetops. Someone had taken the time to hang calaveras around the cantina. Decorative skeletons for the day of the dead, All Hallows Eve. Someone being Isabella of course, skeletons hung behind the bar, from window sills, the ceiling, the bathroom stall.

Halloween and day of the dead waited at the far end of the moon cycle. About that time next month the celestial orb would wax full, just in time for All Hallows Eve, Day of the Dead, a favorite and sacred holiday for Isabella. She'd spend the day dressed in black, a veil pulled over her face. For protection she said, like sunglasses, as the veil between the world of spirits and the world of the living was so permeable that day and she so sensitive. She kept it on all through Halloween and the Day of the Dead too.

She would spend the day in quiet meditation, starting in the backyard, sit under the willow tree as the day dawned, whisper sweet nothings into the wind, flower petals in her upturned palms. She'd whisper until they were all carried by the wind. Move inside to the kitchen and the sun that bathed the room in the morning, Coffee and cigarettes, consult the runes, cast the leaves, talk to herself all morning. She would lunch on raw vegetables, fruit and the like, no shortage as harvest just past. Retire to her shrine once the sun began to set, chant and meditate there all night, crawl to bed around four in the morning, repeat for the Day of the Dead, end the night in the cemetery. She'd take with her offerings of fruits, vegetables, wine and don't forget the cooked meats for the spirits. She didn't dress up for Halloween, though the children assumed she was a witch and he couldn't blame them.

She looked like a witch, sounded like a witch, throaty smoker's cackle and her manic swings of temperament; she certainly played the part well. At least she wouldn't chase them this year. She was a few weeks early with her decorations, skeleton bones clattered together. Calavera hanging on the Cantina's door danced and jiggled each time the door opened. Clatter like wood on wood. Most of these Calaveras were wooden or plastic replicas but El Lobo knew Isabella had a few skeletons in her closet, literally. Those stayed at home, decorated her shrine during this time of year, the equinoxes, the solstices. He would've suggested she leave them perched on either side of the shrine year round, they did lend an increased air of solemnity to her prayer space. He would have but they gave him the creeps, empty eye-holes knew something he didn't want anyone to know.

"Patron?" Giovanni handed El Lobo a beer without asking what he wanted. Isabella and El Lobo owned the Cantina, though she ran it, from stem to stern. The business was more hers than his and they both knew it. The employees knew it too, still called him patron, jefe or boss. They knew what beer he drank, what snacks he preferred, lunch and dinners he usually ordered, Isabella made sure of that. He ate there several times a week, good way to see Isabella, catch her before she was drunk at a table, sleeping in her office, tending bar or cooking in the back. Which was why Giovanni knew he hadn't come for food and wasn't looking for Isabella. El Lobo wandered to the pool table, hugged the wall.

A line of movement members sat in mismatched chairs against a far wall, a closed door that led into the back through a store room, though a large break area, to another storage room In there then? Four men around the pool table, dirty looks, dirty finger nails, field workers. Smoke and shadow, whispered words behind hands. Whether Katherine went to the Hospital or not was not evident, but that she was in the back was clear as day. The line of illegals cued up to pass into the dusty dark storeroom of the Cantina was all the evidence he needed. Tug on his elbow. Badger Captain, waved him toward the bar which was hewn from a long Oak board, El Lobo brought for Isabella.

They kept it polished and fine, even with all the traffic. Garish green walls reflected brown, purple, blue in the rainbow of lights flashing in the room. Once a bright green now muted, coated with decades of tobacco smoke and revelry, the color was like blue tidal pool coated with green slime of algae bloom. El Lobo followed. Badger worked with him in the greenhouses, his right hand man as it were and the movement's third Captain. He'd been surprised, but not really. They sat down, exchanged tobacco products, exhaled blue smoke.

"You're scaring the troops, Wolf in the hen house."

"Sigo dueno aqui." (I'm still an owner here.)

"I know, I know. I'm just saying, you might not like what you see here."

"And what is that Badger, what won't I like?" Felt the hackles raise, he'd give the fool a mouth full of broken teeth.

"Sex Lobo, sex. Katherine is back there fucking every one of us that wants to and as you can see this line is pretty long. She says it is to prove her loyalty to the cause and to us."

"And Isabella knows about this?" He gripped the bar, denied the urge to kick the door down, storm into the storage room.

"She's the one that put out the word, tonight is men, see the red light? Next week women. Same deal though. Naked, sweaty sex. They always say red-heads are whores. Guess it's true. What do you think Lobo?" The statement had so many layers of meaning he left it alone. Opened his mouth to snarl a response, storage room opened, thin pretty-boy emerged, clerical worker. His cheeks were flushed. The men waiting in chairs, the ones playing pool, everyone at the bar, Giovanni too, they all applauded, explosion of applause. Gol carajo!

"I can't say anything about that, I'm not here for her. I'm here for you." He knew the rumors said he and Little Red had something, but why had a long tail. Boiling rage, rip out their throats, all of them.

"Let's get to it Lobo, I want to get in line too, fuck the sweet ass white girl." El Lobo required significant willpower to stay on topic and save what remained of his beer.

"Talk to me about the movement Badger Captain, I haven't killed anyone yet but I'm seriously thinking about it. If Kate gets involved I'm sure I will kill someone and not because Hood ordered it." Growl indeed. Of course Badger wasn't intimidated, he worked with El Lobo every day, he had trouble swallowing his mouthful of beer however.

"You've come damn close maldito. One centimeter closer and my man would've bled to death on that field and Juan, a branch through his shoulder? Was that necessary?"

"Now we're talking." El Lobo sipped his new beer. "Hood doesn't want bloodshed, if you come to me with names and the guilty parties we can put this all behind us." Hollow words from Hood's henchman.

"Surprised you don't choke on lies like that Lobo. If you want names just look around, you can see who's here, write it down." Burly shoulders, hairy arms and head, the man was broad, all muscle, easy to see where his movement name came from. El Lobo knew, greenhouse manager, he was reliable, a good man, his right hand. Shit.

"Look Manuel." Real name, Badger Captain choked on his beer, saucer eyes.

"Wow, addressed by name. I'm flattered or does this mean you're going to kill me?" Wolf wasn't sure he got it. He spoke with the man every day in the greenhouse. Standing meeting, told each other what was on the to do list for the day; must've said his name a thousand times in the last year.

"I'm doing my job Badger." There, shut him up.

"Don't you feel sick working for that fat bastard? He robs, cheats and steals from your people Jose." Badger's turn to drop names, not off limits.

"'Whoa amigo, no acceleres, don't get excited, we're just talking." Glanced over his shoulder, everyone going about their recreation. Beer, pool, darts, foos-ball, everyone with one eye on them.

Someone scored a goal on the foosball table, ca-thunk of wooden ball hitting the ball return, none of the players noticed.

"Oye Giovanni!" El Lobo beckoned to the young bartender. Light complexion with a smattering of freckles gave him a mottled look, exaggerated in the colored light and hazy smoke.

"Si Patron." Ready to help, wiped his hands on a white apron, clean and crisp, no sign of blood.

"Una ronda de cervezas para todos." He spoke loud enough for Giovanni hear, the Ranchero ballad too loud for the rest to hear. Giovanni had the beer flowing in seconds, draft, bottle, tequila, rum, whatever they wanted. El Lobo would explain to Isabella it was necessary to stave off the violence that bubbled in the cantina. Like a bad stomach after questionable enchiladas, sooner or later it was going to explode. He'd kill them all if they so much as twitched, nip it in the bud.

"Really Lobo, as a co-worker for ten years, can't you admit the man rapes our American dream, snatches it from our mouth, our of our beds, chews us up, uses us up, then discards us when he's done?"

"Yes Manuel, I can admit it." Slow sip, stare at the man's light brown eyes. Smoke in his eye, stare at the ceiling. El Lobo was sitting beneath a calavera, dressed in cowboy getup, Mexican style. Banderoleros looped over both shoulders, two holsters, two guns, big hat on is skull. Isabella was laughing somewhere.

"Si Manuel. My American Dream is long since dead. I'm dead inside too, like these calaveras, just not in the ground yet."

"Que hablas hombre? You and Isabella are rich." Stopped to lower his voice. " If any two people are proof of the Dream, you are it." Gestured with his bottle of beer, finished it, slammed the bottle on the bar, beckoned for Gino to bring another.

"At what price? Would you all become hollow shells, void of loyalty, love, hope and happiness. I haven't remembered my dreams in years." He wouldn't say he and Isabella were happy either.

"Sabes que Jose, we're all paying that price. Hollowed out, used up, shells of wasted potential, ten years to realize our only chance is to be the step, the hand up, the shoulders our children stand on. Maybe they can get up and out of this damn poverty." New beer, Manuel drank deep, he was on a tear. He had a handsome face beneath his three-day stubble and clear brown eyes, light brown like almonds in the sunlight. A gentle, honest man, work his ass off for you, get the job done, thank you for the opportunity type. Do it all over again tomorrow. Which was why El Lobo liked him.

"Don't you get it Lobo? That is the American dream. I might struggle, I may never get out, I will very likely die in this place but someone that comes behind me, one of my people, will. Hope for our family, hope for better, whether it ever comes or not, the struggle toward the light, the right to dream and hope, that is the American Dream." Fervent eyes, impassioned plea, spittle in the corner of his mouth.

"Jesus Maria, I was feeling sorry for myself but thanks to you I now feel positively suicidal." El Lobo smiled at the Badger Captain, take it any way he wanted. "You're gonna make me puke."

"I know, did you hear me? I sounded like a stupid gringo." Dry washed his face in his hands. Stared off into space. El Lobo looked up at the calavera hanging above his head. Manuel sounded like Ramon.

"Yes you did, doesn't make it less true. The passing on to our people part is out of the question for Isabella and I, the kids, maybe the dream too." Behind the bar, shadowy reflection of his darkness, he needed to leave. Too much scrambling his brain, like Katarina with a broken leg or wounded knee, naked in back, getting fucked. The story didn't seem plausible.

"Is she O.K." Glance at the storage room door in response to the man's quizzical look.

"Katerina? Si, esta bien. Lastimo su rodilla, fue al enfermeria, para chequear lo y para ver Ramon. Dicen que el esta mejor desde que ordenaste dialysis. She's wearing a knee brace, but she should be fine in a week or so, if she doesn't hurt it tonight. He mimicked fucking the air, bit his lip for effect.

Badger captain was happily married with two little girls, another fact EL Lobo liked about his right-hand man. Live vicariously through those soccer games, school pictures, children's artwork. Horrible artwork, ugly artwork, what is that supposed to be artwork, tacky, hanging over his desk in the greenhouse, but admirable none the less.

El Lobo finished his own beer, patted Bader Captain on the back, see you at work tomorrowed and left. The storage room door opened, boys in line cheered the fellow exiting the back room. They all shouted Ole! El Lobo resisted the urge to walk around back, down through the storm cellar and up into the storage room. Just barely.

He relented, gave in, succumbed, submitted and as soon as, she found a way to reappear, to enter as it were. Though unsure of her intent, the fact that she was so close ricocheted within his soul and echoed down the hallways of his mind, dragged hope and wonder along behind like a raggedy child's toy. Rubber ducky, you're the one, she'd make bath time so much fun. Mrs. Wolf didn't mention she'd be at the Cantina, in fact she didn't even mention it. How could fickle Wolf such as he understand the push-pull of the karmic flow? Or women for that matter? He and Katherine did pow-wow about Hood for an hour or so, Gloria included. What had been a torturous hour, kept his hands to himself and mind on task. Hood was still in the thick of it and not coming home soon, she thought Little Jon could keep him on the rig for another week or two at most before things got weird, they'd need to move him to the other rig. So she really did come about business, he might make up excuses to see her but could hardly imagine her doing the same. The ego rears its ugly head once again, shrivels like flaccid penis.

Submitted, relented, let jealousy seep from the body like infection oozing puss. The wound is cleared by irrigation with a saline solution of tears and the sour acid of bile in the back of the throat. Then she's gone.

***

It is said behind every great man lies a great woman, or stands, whatever the case may be. At times more than one, standing or lying, such is the nature of the feeble male ego, El Lobo included. Though there is much to be said on the subject, the case of El Lobo was such that Mrs. Wolf and Miss Hood had the dubious honor of standing for and lying with El Lobo. As a cub Isabella worked hard and was educated little. She lived a hard life full of beatings and violations, physical and otherwise. Being the youngest female in her father's pack she received unwanted attention of the adults and adolescents alike. Miss Hood had grown up under very different circumstances, protected from a hard day's work, the sun's rays and all of the ugly things in life by her father. Globe quickly learned no amount of bribing or cajoling could keep her galoshes out of the stable and away from the horses or the Barrio. Miss Katherine Hood asked if she could have El Lobo once, asked Isabella way back when she ran daycare for the Barrio out of her house, before she saved up, bought the bar.

"I want him." Ten years old and precocious, mother recently deceased, not yet shipped off to boarding school. She pointed to El Lobo working the backyard, chopping something, sweaty and muscled, grim and grizzled.

"I think he's too ugly and scary for you, he's a monster." She smiled at him across the yard, took the girl by the hand and walked toward her husband.

"I know, but his ugly monster face is the best, he's so scary even the other monsters are afraid of him." When the girl was right, she was right, even at that tender age. Isabella never shared that story with El Lobo.

***

The house was dark when he pulled up. Large willow in the backyard like a crouched old grandfather kept an eye on the place. Certainly felt eyes back there, nothing triggered alarm in his gut, just shadows that nibbled at the light. The usual he supposed, for his home life; wasn't sure whose ghosts haunted them most, his or hers. Candle-light flicker. Rays, protons, ejected from the room, collided with the floor of the hallway, bounced, twisted and tripped through window pane, to his eye, to his brain. The bedroom then. He slipped in, sat on the cushioned bench by the door, removed his boots. Wooden floor creaked his way to the bedroom.

She wasn't drunk, good. She was awake even and wearing her All Hallows Eve outfit. Beautifully embroidered black skirt, twining black roses, large thorns, black flowing blouse, no veil though. White Aster behind her ear, black slippers. She appeared to be waiting for him, lying in the middle of the bed, pillows piled behind her sat her up, legs out straight. Peek-a-boo brown skin, lovely. Her black hair brushed out behind her, framed her face and all its fine angles. She looked ready to drift off to sleep, except her nostrils flared like a horse ridden hard. Her eyes moved under her eyelids, left, right, up and down. She opened them when he sat on the bed.

"You're back."

"Yes Mi Amor, I'm back." Stroke her leg, kiss her, boring married peck.

"How did it go.? Loaded question? Hard to tell when she was like this, not picking a fight he hoped.

"I think you know Isabella, Katarina is in the Cantina fucking two dozen men, with a bad leg." His voice was grating, hard to say the words.

"Are you jealous of your lover? Worried about your baby?" Now she was picking a fight, he could tell she was picking up steam.

"Isabella please. You know I'm worried about the business and Hood's interests." Hated saying that name.

"Hah," She laughed, sat forward, leaned against his back, soft breasts pressed into him, wrapped her arms around, nibbled at his ear, "what a crock of shit. Did you go back and see her then?" Nibbled too hard on his ear.

"Ouch, no." Swat at her like a fly. "I didn't want to interrupt her, plus as scared as they all are I'd probably have been mobbed. I gave them free booze too keep them from lynching me."

"That's fine, they probably would've picked a fight with you otherwise my dear. She certainly was giving it away wasn't she? Remember when we were young and idealistic?" Mocking him or not, he couldn't tell. She didn't care about the alcohol apparently.

"No." Like yesterday.

"Of course you wouldn't, you're like a stone." Slapped him on the back, candle light collides with her cheeks, misses her eye holes, shadow in the hollows of her face, calavera.

"I'm going to sleep lover." She dragged out the word lover. "I have some things I need to take care of." Her dreaming skills were not a secret to him, but no one else in the Barrio knew of her dreaming. She said she'd always been able to do it, her mother showed her some tricks and practice made perfect.

"Like?" Usually as secretive about her work as he was, this was a rare occurrence.

"I'm going to fix Hood dear, he should be better tomorrow, at most a few days." She leaned forward, patted him on the cheek, and promptly threw all the pillows on the floor. Lay back, spread her hair, moved over, patted his spot.

"Come to bed Mi Amor, I want you in bed with me even if you are thinking about that little bitch." He acquiesced, puzzled as to why. Lay next to her softness, she kept the outfit on, except the slippers, even under the covers. Soft caress of candle flicker, fell through the candle-light to the edge of darkness, caught her words just before blackness. Felt her flower petals play across his forehead and cheeks.

"You stupid Wolf. She is giving the workers their back-pay, not her body. You should know better."

He cracked an eye, but she was asleep and breathing deep and even. Was that her? He should've known better

Nightmares woke the Wolf. Miss Hood in the arms of another, she paid the man, left the money on the night stand and tip-toed from the room. Let it be. Damn fool. She was not his to command, or touch. He dreamed of genie. A whisper here, a sentence there. Barely see her before Mrs. Wolf swooped in, shooed him away down the hallways of his mind. Saw Miss Hood happily hugging in the arms of another, who was he? The churn, the burn, how could one live so possessed with possessing? Meditate, OM, let her go Lobo. If only to see her for a moment. She was not a woman of dormant libido and the Wolf smelled another on her, she enjoyed the affections of another, howl at the moon. She lay money on another table and walked through another door. He woke in a cold sweat, screamed at the ceiling, thankfully Isabella didn't wake from her slumber, at least he hadn't disturbed her. Tried to sleep again.

Chapter 17

End of the Madness

He swam through money, an ocean of his money, green, fresh and cool. Boats everywhere, poor blacks and browns in dingy and skiff cast nets, hauled in his money. Swim and scream, money in his mouth, gagged and gasped. Snake from the depths, wrapped around him, pulled him down. Money in his mouth, snake down his throat. Claw away, claw for freedom, toward the hatred toward the dammed. Use the efforts of the righteous indignation, green flame of anger, backstroked through female legs. All naked, all brown, no arms, no torsos, an ocean of legs. Erection hurts. Swim for the modesty of money.

He clung to anger, hated them all, Little Jon's voice in his head, telling him blacks an browns were everywhere. So many of his capitalist brethren were ignorant or unwilling to accept the growing demographic shift toward blacks and browns. Their last stand, battle of the bulge, beaches at Normandy. Symbolic righteousness, like a cross at the tomb of the unknown soldier. Let their aging, white, shrinking, scared districts see how willing their congressmen were to stand up to the system, the establishment can go to hell. As a businessman Hood knew they were fools but misery loved company, make that illegal alien disguised as the first black president suffer as much as possible. Sometimes no was the only answer worth giving. Even if he did choke on it. Turned on his side, vomited on the floor, splatter and stink. Shadows and light. Smelled the air, felt the bed for the first time. Coming out of it maybe, out of what? Pretty nurse came with the Wolf, little Jon droned on. Been a week already? Hum and whir. Someone left the window open, heard the machine hum, a sound that soothed his mind.

Hood was unable to deny the truth, the inevitability, the crashing wave of clamoring voices, reaching arms, wretched refuse finding their collective voices. Maybe they could stop it yet. But for now the truth worked for him, picked strawberries, applied fertilizer and pesticide, cooked his meals, drove his trucks, made him millions.

He could not blindly stand on the hill and deny the changing face of the nation. First generation farm hands and store owners gave rise to second generation chefs, scientists, politicians and voters. Follow the money and there was money to be had in the Barrio, that was for sure. The Barrio wanted health care, spicy peppers, beans, rice, ox-tails and cow tongue tacos. As much as he wanted to stick his tongue out, thumb his nose at the liberals, he knew, as did the demonized moderate Republicans that their actions would not garner any favors come the next presidential election. Go group think. Sure the bastions of gun-toting, right to white life conservative enclaves in Colorado, Oklahoma, Iowa, Kentucky, Tennessee, Arkansas, Idaho, Nevada, the Dakotas etc. were safe for the next ten years. But even that was pushing it. He'd bet there were already enough blacks, browns and imports living in those places to seriously derail the conservative agenda. The trick was to keep them from the voting booths. Keep them uninformed, apathetic and unqualified. Thank God for voter ID laws. At least some-one was trying.

Snarky, sarcastic talking heads played word games with sound bites and misinformation, drool rabid foam. Make sure he gets his rabies shot after this, bark like a dog. Belittle the administration for pandering but quick remind us about the WWII vets. Fear monger me please, keep the immigrants and the money away from the entitlement programs, that's why we have the problems we do. Look how uppity they all are. Business was business after all, maybe strangle the taxed enough a little, if business suffered anyway. Loony toons weren't good for the bottom line, scare an investor asshole closed, sit on their money, keep the golden egg for themselves. Tooth sucking, mouth drying, cell screaming desire, counter with rage, em-braced the seething hatred.

Sucking vacuum of need, quicksand, pulled him down, slurp and gobble. Shanty town was where those whores be-longed, bring them he needed them. He was stuck in a quicksand trap, sand through the hourglass. Pulled him under, down to the hell of pigs and capitalists. Whips and chains, naked women all around, no dick to work with. Food piled high, mouth the size of a straw, his belly screaming for food, eternal hunger, eternal need. Scream until his lungs bleed. If only to die. The world was full of willing people, he was willing. Some were willing to work, others willing to let others work, was that Frost? Ah, the entitlement state, he could smell their filth even out in the ocean.

They were the people unwilling to work while they could rely on the social safety net. Anyone can achieve the American dream, just get in line and put out your hand. Hate them all. Anyone can achieve the American dream, as long as they're willing to sell their soul to the bank, or lease it for the next thirty years. Drug test them all, American work ethic long gone, undermined by hand-outs, Chinese workers, Mexican workers, Indian workers, NAFTA and stupid, smiling, hand-shaking politicians. Fine by him, cheaper that way. Blame the social safety nets for lassitude and uninspired forty-ounce drinking, stoop-sitting philosophers and neighborhood can collectors. Alcoholic anyway, probably better keeping them out of the workforce. Just don't send them his money. Liberals at the gates, infiltrating school board, town government, college campus. Brainwashing the youth, defecate on the American Dream, blame capitalism for everything. The main stream media was disgusting. If they didn't want him to burn coal they could go back to reading by candle light, the fools. What's a mountain top or two?

The girls were on the television. The Tweedles, naked, blew kisses, fondled and played with each other, moaned in pleasure. He screamed, chest bursting to explode, scratched his eyes until he saw blood. Screamed until the girls were gone. Television gone blank, he was truly mad. Mumble of voices in his head, pornography was out of the question, just had to wait. The Wolf and his brilliant idea...sweet smelling, white lab coat, green scrubs, leaned over him. His private doctor, or rather his Physician's Assistant back again, so soon? She wasn't afraid of the helicopter, unlike the doctor. Dab his brow, take his temperature, invade his body with drugs. Scream and vomit, pass out.

Waves in the ocean, tsunami, flooded river, cracked and parched earth. Cattle carcasses, sheep bodies, pigs cannibalizing each other. Political top-hat denied, dances a jig, bully pulpit and microphone, eyes closed, bound tight screaming the world is not changing, global climate is fine. Writhe and squirm, one issue he couldn't get on board with. Too many changes were obvious to the farmer, the rancher. The global system was changing, precipitation, harvest, plagues, fungal pathogens, all crazy as a mercury doused rabbit. Too much was changing.

Maybe get them to admit in private that something was changing, never admit man was to blame. Never admit any such thing in public, more coal, more mining, burn it all, but those that lived and worked the land knew things were very different than they used to be. Don't tell the libs and don't you dare admit it at the Republican fund raiser. Scream bloody murder, the injustice of it all, who was he to be punished so? Who were they to take his money? He'd give it to the girls willingly, impale them on his penis. Erection tightened, hurt, spasm of muscles. Legs stiffened, soaked the sheets, eyes rolled into the back of his head. Of course he knew the truth, even those in denial knew the truth, health care was an entitlement, like social security, Medicare, unemployment. Health care would be good for the little guy, the small fry and another entitlement the Republicans would swear to defund for the next fifty years. Just like welfare, the same hatred, galvanize it while they could, the real fire under the asses of the Republican party was the Marxist subversion of the free-market economy.

Talking heads on screen above his head, secretly pleased the government was shut down, gave them a sense of importance, almost hear the giggle in their voices. Scold the politicians too far to the left, blame them for intractable overspending, temper tantrum throwing overlords of the government. When our government has become too large, fire or furlough all unessential employees, then scream bloody murder about un-employment. It would work, he knew it would. The only essential government employee was that soldier. God-damn welfare state, hand-out, hand-out, give it all away.

Damn them, damn Roosevelt and his New Deal to Hell. Swirling, tumbling, falling, dry throat, burnt to a cinder more like it. Had to be careful or tea leaning loonies would cannibalize the party. Chew their legs off, escape the bear-trap. The piranhas were swarming, chum in the water. Sharks, piranhas, vultures, descend on the wounded flesh of the moderate who dared object. Mange, leprosy and rotting flesh. The coming age of change, increasing numbers of blacks and browns scared the shit out of sphincter-clenching white men and women. No compromise with that black bastard, he can go to Hell too. The millionaires and billionaires were the ones that really counted anyway, don't tell gun toting, tobacco chewing, moonshine making, trailer living red blooded American that.

Make sure to keep your head down when the believers come through, God save us all. Fundamental bible-thumping, Christ will return Christians. Make sure to visit church once in a while in case he really did. Fundamentals of negotiation, principles the tea toting loonies were ignorant of apparently. No leverage, no nothing, no way to bring the other side to the table. Dumb asses were standing on the side of the road with a pile of poop in their hands offering it to the American people. Hate them all, even the fools on his side, no patience for fools.

Better not pass immigration reform, he had no intention of paying a living wage, benefits or hiring more legal workers than necessary. Too expensive, too bold, too lazy, not scared enough, those were the problems with legal workers. He was chased down a dusty road, wolves nipped at his heels, blood dripped from snapping jaws. Farm road, uneven, rolled an ankle and go down in heap. Watch the Wolf disembowel him, slurp the intestines, tug on ribs, chew on organs. Woke screaming, pile of clothing on the floor next to the bed. Little Jon still slept on the couch when he went to investigate.

How long now? Was he still alive? Porcupine quills up his spine, pins and needles to the thousandth degree. Inflict pain on the most vulnerable people, would if he could. Scream. Balls in a vice grip, Isabella and Gloria and their million clones. Scream and howl for forgiveness.

Tears fell from his eyes, swelling, expanding, became a river winding over the edge of the platform and into the ocean. His mass carried with it over the edge, fall into infinity. Hit the water like a cement sidewalk, sucked downward, naked, blood leaked from his testicles, jellyfish swarmed his face. The socialist bastards were designing a country for the lowest common denominator. Hate them all, feel the heat of hatred course from his chest to his limbs, invigorates, elates, more power please. Life saver of hatred.

Molasses in his mouth, roll and tumble, thunder in the distance. Water became cotton sheet. Lightning forks, molasses seeps from his penis. Black stringy syrup, collected on the floor, coiled into black hissing serpent, smelled him with forked tongue. Scream in his mouth, melt into the floor, puddle of fat, sheet between his teeth. Isabella pays him a visit.

Standing above him, cigar in her mouth like El Lobo. Smoke wrapping her, buffeting him with nicotine caress. Raised her foot, stomped on his crotch, laughed the whole time. She bent over, cut off his prick, put it in a collection jar, dropped it in a boiling cauldron. Gloria and Katherine appeared at her side, all three cackled, stirred the black cauldron together. Large wooden spoon. A beaker of his blood, into the cauldron. Gloria at a table, chopped up the Tweedles, into the cauldron they went. No blood, they sliced like cake, skin and hair like frosting, nearly swallowed his tongue. Isabella held his head back, spooned in the liquid from the cauldron. The world was on fire, his crotch set the whole thing ablaze, practically molten, felt like lava.

Black snake dove back into his penis, halfway in before Isabella grabbed the tail, pulled, pulled, pulled, grim faced, flower in her hair gone black, black skirts swayed as she pulled. Hissing serpent went limp in her hands, fifty feet of coil at her feet, burst into flame, gone. Woke screaming, stink of his room. Feces and urine stained the bedspread, stained his skin. Dry heave, vomited on the floor. Fled to the bathroom. Hot as possible, wash it all away, put on new skin if he could get it.

Gentle tap at the door. Little Jon wanted to know if he was alright. Alright as can be expected, what day is it? Two and a half weeks on the rig. Damn immigrant whore. That conniving communist bitch would pay.

Chapter 18

Monkey Squad

Isabella hadn't been to see him in days. He'd seen Katherine a few days past, she'd hurt her knee, riding accident, those were rare for her. He wasn't on dialysis anymore and he felt surprisingly good. His chest was still sore, lungs still protested, a decade worth of particulate and contamination delivered in the span of an hour. Ramon was glad to be alive. The dialysis may have been what did it. The fog dissipated once they hooked him up, filtered his blood. The black shadows creeping in at the edge of everything fled, faces became clear, he could see again. A week after the dialysis started he was strong and safe from danger. Took him off, started feeding him real food. Dr. said Ramon would definitely never play soccer again, but they'd wait and see, he was still young, his body might recover more than they expected.

Autumn day. Red maple leaf pinned against infirmary window, the wind held it pressed until gust was blown out. The leaf remained against the pane, moist with rain the water held it to the window through adhesion or was it capillary action? Well his brain was almost right. Flicker of fluorescent bulbs, stale tan walls. Drab and dreary, white and beige inside the infirmary, gray dour September sky outside. Melancholy coating of his recovery. Would Hood screw him to the wall? Did the man even know? Rumor had it he'd been on the gas platform as long as Ramon had been out cold. One of the nurses told Ramon, said she was the one that went and that Hood had gone mad as shit, wallowing in it too. Maybe Katherine would end up in charge and Ramon too, sooner than everyone thought. See how the board of directors liked that.

The infirmary was for Hood employees only. Hood strongly discouraged its use, life events, birth, death and grave illness only. Oddly enough the workers only used it as such, they didn't abuse it, wanted to keep their jobs is what it came down to. Ramon had started using the bathroom again, glad to have the catheter out and no nurse checking his shriveled prick and wiping his ass. He fell on his face the first time out of bed. Legs too weak, head too loose, felt unattached, float away, until he hit the floor with a thud.

Pretty nurse helped him to go, knew her from the barrio, she grunted as much as he, kept saying "Aye Ramon!" in a way he liked. While Katherine was being treated for her wounded knee she caught him up on her plan. She arranged meetings with the movement members who were willing, she named the operation Sleeping With the Enemy. She was far too pleased with her own cleverness. He told her as much. She'd be meeting with all the men first, arrange need and appropriate legal counsel for each. Pay them what they were owed. A good faith gesture to show her sincerity and willingness to work with them. Ramon applauded her, showing her he could move his arms on his own again too. Little victories she said.

Dinner was some chicken and rice, a salad with lettuce and cherry tomatoes. Whistle in the hallway. He knew the sound, signature whistle. Monkey squad. One whistled a tune, the other sang the words.

> *Pick me a boomer, put em in a pie.*
> *Pick me a boomer, get me really high.*
> *Fuck a damn boomer, belong in a stye.*
> *They fuck us all over, then they wonder why.*

> *The shit is broke, 'cause it hit the fan.*
> *Get the dogs, sell the house as quickly as you can.*
> *Head for the hills, grab your guns, kids in the van.*
> *Forget the boomers, let them drown, heads in the sand.*

First verses to a theme song that didn't exist, made up one night while writing pamphlets and being idealistic, whiskey chaser. Monkey squad Lieutenant and his right hand. Computer geeks to be sure, good fun and good at what they did. Beep beep in the hall, from the nurse station, clatter of solid object hitting the ground. Ramon was happy to hear his people coming down the hall. Dark clothes, dark eyes, dark hair, multiple piercings, irreverence, Tommy was punk-rock, to Tania's librarian.

Pretty and slim, wire rimmed glasses, black hair cut shoulder length, nondescript in every way. Ramon's favorite squad and his favorite two members. High school friendships, original revolutionaries back in the day, more about double dates with Katherine than changing the world.

As with so many things, flotsam, jetsam, friends, family, they'd drifted. Tommy and Tania to college for degrees in IT and now they ran most of the IT for Hood's farm and some of his businesses beyond. Hardware, software, greenhouse lighting, irrigation, easy. They were perfect members for the movement, highly useful in the unseen, intangible, binary based world of digital technology. They'd arranged the shutdown of the warehouse cameras and security, planted some seeds in Hood's mainframe for later, surprise. He wondered if they were coming to visit or if they had a surprise in store. Stupid question.

"Surprise, surprise." Tommy vaudevilled his way into the room, brandished invisible top-hat and cane, high kick. Tania a few steps behind was less exuberant but a pleased smile split her face. Tommy was in black pants, black shirt, short hair in spiky points, hair product necessary. Tania decidedly less conspicuous was non-descript in her blue jeans and think gray sweater, wool. Cute horn-rimmed glasses and shoulder length brown hair framed her pale face. She pushed a wheel chair, Tommy pulled back the sheets, Ramon's legs looked pale and shrunken emerging from the blue gown.

"Up and at 'em Commander." Tommy saluted, embellishment not lost on Ramon.

"I'm not sure they'll let me out, El Lobo's orders." Ramon was sure the nurses, doctors and all the staff were ordered to keep him under lock and key until El Lobo decided what he wanted to do with Ramon or until Hood recovered. Somewhat fortuitous that, Hood's descent into lunacy timed well with Ramon's capture, he'd have to thank Isabella for that.

"Don't worry your pretty little confused head my friend, we've taken care of that." Motioned to Tania, she threw some sweat-pants they'd brought, didn't want his pale ass giving them away.

Ramon slipped them on, he no longer felt weak. Up to no good was their modus operandi, they were up to something, Ramon was sure of it. Something good he hoped. Pulled the blue hooded sweatshirt over his head, leaned on the two of them, leveraged his way into the wheelchair. Tania pushed. They escorted him right out, like they'd come in, no checking for nurses, no checking for guards. They were very obviously not worried. Ramon relaxed.

Returning strength, color in his cheeks, semblance of an appetite, all signs he was distancing himself from the precipice of death and the strangle-hold of toxins that nearly snuffed out his light. The distance allowed for other problems, trivial when confronted with the gravity of death's icy finger but resuming importance to the whole and hardy excommunicated commander. Anxiety, rock in his gut, barbed wire in his chest, waiting for El Lobo to turn up and turn him inside-out. He had no illusions. The Wolf would slaughter the goat.

"Why are you two so non-chalant, where is everyone?" By everyone he meant the handful of nurses and doctors that ran the clinic.

"The nurse is at the car dealership in the barrio, she got a message that she won their contest and she did, even though she never entered. That should take a while to straighten out or maybe she'll get a new car out of it. The Doctor is at his bank, appears some of his money managed to get into his wife's account and her lover's. He's not happy. The custodian is one of us." long stare, no words needed.

"The receptionist got an email that someone is trying to break into her apartment, so she went home, called her boyfriend first, then the security people, landlord etc. The rest had their schedules updated, tweaked by an hour here or there, enough so we shouldn't see a soul on our way out of here, except the custodian of course." And so it was. They'd managed to bamboozle the entire staff. Not a person except the shadowy back, gray jumpsuit, of custodian mopping down adjacent hall. He never turned around.

Automatic sliding glass doors, movement activated, whoosh on the way out.

"We left the surveillance video. Thought El Lobo would appreciate that." No doubt he would, though perhaps appreciate was the wrong verb to describe the man's interest in Ramon. Maybe he was too busy to come. Tania read his mind.

"He'll be too busy to care in a day or two honey, don't you think?" Tania asked, opened one of the doors of her four door sedan, late nineties, Japanese make, ran forever. They shoved Ramon in. Tommy, rambunctious, sugar-rushed, bounce off the walls to Tania's third-grade teacher, deep breath taking, sweet smiling, how does she do it, patient mother.

Tommy bounced up and down, kid on a pogo stick, ran around the car, got in the passenger seat.

"Oh yeah hermano. Oye, Ramon, Comandante, she won't let me drive, says I'm too excitable, too distracted, tell her I'm good man." Whining nasal third-grader, perfect.

"I'm inclined to agree with your level-headed, smarter than all of us, beautiful wife Tommy, you're ready to pop. What's going on?" Tommy sighed, shoulders slumped, deject-ed, battle lost. For about five seconds.

"You'll see. To the bat cave Mi Amor." He leaned over and kissed her cheek, stuck arm and shoulder out the window pointing the wrong way. Ramon knew the bat cave, another teenage hangout from years gone by. Where they drank beers, smoked cigarettes, nudie mags, burned stuff, broke stuff. On the edge of the barrio and the adjacent industrial park and trail-er park neighborhood. The ware-house was old and abandoned back then, most of the windows boarded up and broken. Perfect space for hard-wiring, keyboard punching, far away world hacking type of trouble the two excelled at. She peeled out of the empty parking lot, Tommy whooped it up.

Far side of the barrio, twenty minutes later. Asphalt landscape, forgotten fences, bent, rusted, cut an age ago when reason to invade and protect what lie within existed. Pitted, cracked, exposed soil. Upwelling of water, stagnant pools, grasses in the cracks and corners, salt tolerant rush, mulberry. Garage door opener on the sun visor, Tania pressed it once they pulled into the lot adjacent a big green and black warehouse, dirty windows, couple of forgotten dumpsters, fifty-gallon barrels. A few fluorescent bulbs visible through the first floor window. Lent to the facade, maybe something was being made in there.

Tania parked the sedan inside a garage with a door painted black like the rest of the warehouse wall, barely tell the difference. Garage door slid closed behind the car. They unloaded Ramon, pulled crutches out of the trunk. Tommy carried the folded wheelchair, helped him up the stairs onto the first floor, sat him back in the wheelchair. Tania pushed Ramon across the huge empty space toward a service elevator. Ramon guessed the space had once been a machine shop or some such industrial incarnation. Layers of dust, rust, grime, soil, rodent feces and uncountable variations of urban decay and entropy covered the cement slab of a floor. The area under the fluorescent lights seen from outside was an explosion of technological tinkering. Naked, exposed, mother-boards, wires of varied size and hue undulated across the table, monitors, speakers, divided and hollowed out. Four or five tables worth of workspace. Cabinets, shelves, drawers against the wall behind them. Disassemblage, tinker, return. Nice.

Wheels left tracks in the dust, her footprints between, trail in the dust behind them. Tommy's happy shuffle like dance steps through the grime. Ramon didn't see any footprints coming in with theirs, or anywhere nearby, plenty by the work space though. The floor was clear of dust in two thin lines running from the stairs next to the service elevator and from the elevator to the work area. Tania stopped him in front of the grated door of the service elevator. Tommy shot up the stairs, bats squeaked in the darkness, behind the elevator, or in the shaft. Tommy shouted that he'd be waiting.

Ramon wondered if he too could dash up the stairs. Highly doubtful. Even if his legs could support him, three steps into the trial his lungs would mutiny. Just thinking about it made him wheeze. Tania rubbed his back.

"It's OK Ramon, we're with you." Elevator up, second floor. "Idealist Insurrection and Information Technology Anarchists, everyone out." Mysterious Tania, her eyes twinkled above his head, Tommy's infectious energy seeped into both of them. Ramon's heart rate increased considerably. Tania wheeled Ramon down a long hallway once they reached the second floor, creak of the accordion gate. Multi-colored and festive the hall was a left or right choice, horse shoe shape, she went right. Pushed him down the hall, the wall to the left came to shoulder height, mustard yellow, Caribbean blue, tree frog green, past the shoulder glass blocks allowed light and shapes to creep into the hallway, kept it from being oppressive. Through the glass could see a central room with fireplace and social area. Black doors spaced fifty meters apart on his right. Large apartments in there if that's what they were. He counted four such doors on his right, perhaps four more on the other.

Black shapes rippled behind the glass blocks, underwater scenes of cosmopolitan hipster loft. Between the two long hallways was the social and common area for the Monkey squad, if this was in fact their base, as Ramon suspected. Each of the squads had their own, some better than others it seemed. The common area was elegant and unassuming in its simplicity. A circular fire place with circular chimney and flu, very metallic, very hip, beach chairs positioned around it. A pair of forgotten slippers, someone's feet were cold. A bookshelf along the terminal wall of the common area, opposite side of the same wall one saw when debarking the elevator. Loaded with literature and manuals, worse than stereo instructions. A techno-geek dream come true.

On the other side of the fireplace a few sofas faced each other with a coffee table between. A coffee bar against one glass wall, espresso machine, cups, mini-fridge, the works. Across from that, unseen by Ramon as he was passing behind it, was the cooking station. Stainless steel setup, extra burners, someone cooked a lot, wooden prep area, adjacent and connected.

Knives stuck to the wall on three magnetic strips, utensils and necessary flatware in an open cabinet with no doors. Beyond the cooking area toward the large threshold, also lacking doors, were two small circular tables, one large dining table, a pool table, ping-pong, couple of video games.

Ramon emerged from the hallway, Tania explained what was in the common room and when they used it. A utopian living space for the IT types who lived and worked there. As long as they had their computers they were happy. She pushed him into another large open space, he guessed they were above the workspace he'd seen below. This was set-up more like the trenches at a trading firm. No cubicles, but desks, file cabinets, multiple computers per individual and space for everyone. Tommy hovered or circled rather. Trotted around a desk and a computer console like an over-excited maniac, practically panting. Still jumping up and down. Tania sighed behind him, whispered to Ramon, "He hasn't been this excited since the first time I gave him some, he's more excited even." No need to ask what she gave him.

"What is it?" Ramon was getting excited himself.

"You'll see." She pushed on. Tommy danced his little dance around the largest setup. Presumably his, being the Lieutenant of the squad. High stepped, hopping up and down the man was barely contained. One moment a marching band leader the next a chorus girl. Tania chuckled above him, that was her man after all. Melodrama and hop, land with a stomp. Tommy stopped in front of a computer, code language on the screen in one pop-up window, he hit enter and a red light rotated on top of his desk. Undercover police detective type, think old dragnet, coiled cord and everything. A siren accompanied it, screaming in Spanish, echoing down the halls, rubber bouncy ball of sound.

"Venga, venga. Mami venga." Come, come, mami, come.

Doors opened along both hallways, half-naked members appeared, night shirts, underwear, bra and panties, it was bedtime. The Monkey squad was as tight nit as they came.

All the apartments had private bathrooms but there was a common bathroom and shower attached to the gym they'd built. Tommy said it was obviously once a shower and locker room for the workers of some forgotten industry, they reclaimed and rehabilitated. Now it was as common to see a naked woman as a naked man lathering up after a nice workout. There were stalls for the more modest.

Ramon hadn't realized it was so late, his circadian rhythms were all out of wack. Seemed like eight people remained including Tom and Tania. Monkey was a small squad anyway, but they'd lost a few members. Tommy held his arms up for silence, half the group yawned with fatigue. Four women, four men, right down the middle. He wouldn't have guessed it from an IT group but he knew them all by name.

"Silencio porfavor." No one was talking, still. Tania leaned over, tapped a button, the siren and light went out.

"Ramon, each of us here is loyal to the cause, whether because we're too young to be afraid, too connected to believe in happy endings or because we all had parents and family taken from us by Hood and ICE. We're all here and we're with you."

"Hood may not lose the farm, but we can damn well make sure he loses money, a lot of money." Faint applause, loud sneeze echoed. Tommy pressed the enter key on his keyboard.

"Ya esta." Genuine applause, hoots and hollars, heartfelt this time. A few minutes of back slapping for Tommy and close inspection of Ramon's health by the bra and panty wearing girl. Ramon was definitely not dead, stirring in his pants, waft of female sleep. Bit his tongue. He'd almost forgotten Tommy and Tania were there the morning after the ICE raid, forget the whole thing if he could. Problem was he couldn't.

***

Ramon stepped across the threshold, crunch of glass in his living room, echo of footsteps in his parent's hallway. Held breath against the impossible. Tommy and Tania come around the corner, they looked like scared kids holding each other like that, sniffle and shake. They were both crying. He must have looked like that when Katherine found him.

"Ramon!" Tommy ran over and shook him by the shoulders, "What happened to our parents? I thought they were all meeting here to talk." Tears in his eyes.

"They were, someone called ICE, someone tipped them off, they took all of our parents." Ramon scanned the ground, the shoe was still there.

"Where were you Ramon? How are you just getting here? Where have you been?" Tommy's tone was panic with a dash of accusation. Tania rubbed his back. Ramon pointed to the white bandage wrapped around his head.

"Katherine found me wandering around like a zombie, bleeding from the head. She took me to the hospital, then to her apartment. Kept an eye on me what with the concussion and all, didn't want me dying in the middle of the night. At least that's what she said." Heat in his cheeks, how old were they? Almost thirty and thinking about her in a state of undress still made him hot under the collar. Tania elbowed Tommy in the gut, tissue to her own red nose. She'd been crying too, still was a little.

"Told you Katherine came and got him." She pointed to the floor of the porch, dried blood next to the folding chair. "We knew you'd be out here and the viejos wouldn't let you participate, we guessed this was your blood. We were worried. Tommy's just angry at the world right now." She rubbed Tommy's chest, he reciprocated, squeezed her tight. All of their parents had been at the meeting.

"I'm angry at the world too, I think it's time to execute our first action, the one we talked about." Tommy nodded next to him, Ramon didn't notice. The wheels in his brain churning and turning, he'd give Hood some headaches, more than a few. Get the workers on his side, rise up, put an end to Hood and his heartless pursuit of dollars and profit. Accidents happen, media circus, string the man up by his own lust for money.

"Let's meet later Tommy, Tania. I need to see some people, check on some things, then the Movement of the American Dream is back."

***

Ramon watched the screen of Tommy's computer. Lines of code, too fast for him to read. Might as well have been cartoons. Traffic signal on the wall changes from green to flashing yellow. Warning something, stickers surround it repeated the message.

"What's this?" Ramon pointed, Tommy shrugged.

"Ever hear of stux net, a virus or worm that infiltrates company computer systems and can manipulate machinery and anything connected to the mainframe? Well we just sent a little packet out to Hood's rig in the Gulf, where he is currently hiding. The little bug should do the same, it should screw up the computer systems, the control systems for the equipment, alarm systems, bathrooms. It should be great, they'll need to get off the rig in a couple of days."

"Is that why your people clapped and then went back to bed?" Ramon gestured to the empty common area.

"Yes, this should take a few days, then we'll all vacate for a couple of weeks or months until the heat dies down, just in case."

"Or not." Tania from her console a few feet behind. Light flashed from yellow to red. Warning in big letters across Tommy's screen.

"Shit," long pause three minutes of Tommy typing and swearing, "this might yield results sooner than I expected. Honey please let everyone know, and tell them to have their rooms cleaned and go bags ready by tomorrow afternoon." Sweat on Tommy's brow.

"What's wrong Tommy?" Ramon didn't really need to ask.

"Pressure release valve, I thought the code needed some teeth so I added a few things; that may have been a mistake."

"So what are you telling me?" Ramon scratched the stubble on his chin, wished for coffee. The panty and bra wearing movement member appeared from somewhere, Sol was her name, smelled good, brought him a cup, perfect timing. Her white panties climbed up her right cheek, tried to hide folds of cotton in her smooth ass. Sipped his coffee, watched her walk away. A damsel in need of rescue if ever he saw one.

"I'm telling you the rig is going to go boom. Soon. Maybe twelve hours, maybe eight, maybe twenty." Ramon watched the smooth brown ass saunter out of the room. She looked over her shoulder at him, tossed her hair, pulled the cotton hem from her ass, disappeared down the hall. He heard a door shut, halfway down then. Kaboom was right. He shrugged to Tommy and wheeled his way after Sol. Time to see if his bits and pieces were still working. Not dead yet.

Chapter 19

Money Matters

Hood felt claustrophobic. Three weeks in confinement had him chewing on the edges of everything, bite the head off of. Spit it out. He'd since been relocated, cleaned, scrubbed, disinfected and debriefed on his lunacy and his businesses. Little Jon, Gloria and El Lobo worked with him, mostly Little Jon, the other two were up to their elbows running the farm. Gloria advised him that the USDA had finally sent a letter, they were planning on visiting in the next ninety days. No call first, just a random unannounced visit. She had it on a tip there would be ICE agents with the auditors, no surprise there and maybe some IRS people wanting to talk about, of all things, Chinese investors. No doubt he would end up forking over more money to the feckless, unaccountable, totalitarian, authoritarian monster that was the federal government. At least the visit was coming in the winter months. He had far fewer illegals to hide in the off-season.

He wanted to make his last day on the rig a short one if possible. Gulf breeze was nice, but he was ready to head north toward Autumn, hurricane season was too blustery on the rig. The sunrise that morning had been iridescent pink and orange, gold spilling over the Gulf waters with the new day. Hood visualized looking down through the water, through the earth to the gas deposits below, being sucked up into the rig, cha-ching. Damage control well under way; constant state of damage control for the last several months. Gloria and Little Jon were taking care of the scheduled USDA visit, the Chinese investors were still interested and the bad press they'd received as a result of the food contamination, greenhouse disaster, and warehouse fire had been limited to the local press, thankfully nothing had gone national yet. A very big yet. One local rag had a green-horned, snot-nosed, idealistic Mexican-American little

girl working the story. A local community issue she was apparently approaching the story from the angle of worker's rights
and the budding insurrection. The rich vs. the poor, the have-
nots rising up against their slave masters.

Hood groaned the day El Lobo plopped the paper down
on the bar in the suite. A picture of a red-faced Hood at the
Senate hearing, foaming at the mouth. He looked mad in the
photo, as in insane, a scared doe-eyed young field worker in the
next photo. Hood yelled at El Lobo but the man left before he
could vent his bile. Of course he was taking care of it but Hood
should read the article so he knew what was being said. El Lobo mentioned the girl had already been fired, that was in the
story too, must've had a second run. Hood drank his coffee,
splash some Irish cream for color. Little Jon at the computer
typing furiously, crafting Hood Industries official response to
the police department inquiry regarding attacks on workers. As
far as Hood was concerned and what Little Jon asserted was
that the uneducated, barely civilized immigrants, legal or otherwise brought cultural shortcomings with them. Through such
deficiencies, spousal abuse, molestation, rape, violence and
gang activity were a reality and a scourge. A stain on the once
pleasant, god-fearing farmers that were now inundated with
these denizens of the underbelly of society. In vetting his
workers he undoubtedly missed some of the unscrupulous,
questionable individuals who then partook in violent and illegal
behavior. He currently had his best men on the job to cull such
unseemly persons from the workforce and those deemed guilty
would be summarily dismissed and presented to the police
forthwith.

Complete drivel but effective. No going back to sleep
now. Not that he intended to anyway. Since the madness ended
he'd been afraid to sleep too much, Isabella might be waiting
for him. The dream-scape was her domain. Little Jon told Hood
they had a video conference with the bank, then they could go.
He settled in to wait. He'd never be able to prove his suspicions
to anyone, nor discuss them in the light of day without sounding like a lunatic. He was sure El Lobo knew something but
Isabella was an off-limits topic for them. Taboo. The balance
of power had shifted considerably since those days. If Hood

failed to tread lightly he might end up missing. Better to keep the man's attention on the movement members.

According to El Lobo the movement was quiet after the botched sabotage of the pesticide storage building. Though Hood was not pleased to learn he and his clinic had been financially responsible for patching up movement members. Men Hood thought were dead. He would ask El Lobo next chance he had. He wasn't paying the man to hurt people, he was paying him to solve problems.

The pending USDA visit had El Lobo occupied, clean house, hide the evidence. Send him out to the reporter's house later in the week. Bring her to her senses, show her sticking her nose places it was liable to get chopped off. Hood ambled to the wall behind the bar, pressed intercom button on the digital built-in control board, called the kitchen.

"Gentlemen, I will be needing someone to cook lunch for two, Jon and I will be staying through lunch, then we'll be out of your hair, but I'd like him to cook up here."

"Yes Mistah Hood, we'll send Javier up right away." Thick Caribbean accent, maybe Jamaican. Christ, did all the cooks of the world come from foreign lands?

"Lunch should be along shortly Jon. We'll eat and meet, then get out of here."

"Alright Globe, what's on the menu?" The man never stopped his typing.

"Oh, I don't know, some red meat I suppose, Javier can dig something up." And in fact he did. The young sous-chef showed up and the place was adrift in the volatile effervescence of garlic and onion oils five minutes later. Steaks sizzled on the stove-top and in the broiler. The smells were what Hood was really after. The sizzle and pop, fat and onion through the nose, open the appetite, salivate and wait.

Beeps and boops, raised voices in the office and control room beyond Hood's oak door and sound-proofed suite. Bangs, squeals, sounding alarms. Hood glanced at the computer terminal just inside the oak door. Display of colored bar-charts, gauges and color coded warnings.

Yellow to blinking orange, back to yellow. He opened the wooden door, shouted his question.

"We're controlling it sir, having some pressure control problems, gas pockets." Chief Officer speaks.

"Gas is good isn't it?"

"Well yes." Looked like he wanted to say more. Siren screamed behind him. "But not to worry sir, we've got it under control. I'll make a call for the helicopter to pick you up early just in case." Hood hoped so. Nodded, slammed the door. Just in case? That didn't comfort. He returned to the suite. He yelled at Little Jon, they would vacate the rig earlier than planned.

"It seems these gentlemen have work to do." Little Jon nodded in agreement.

"Video conference in one hour." Little Jon announced and finally left the computer, joined Hood at the bar, his own Bloody-Mary untouched or only just. They watched the young chef assemble their lunch. Maybe they'd eat twice, he was making enough. Peppercorns crushed, coated the meat, sizzled in the pan, spice up the nose. Forty minutes later medium rare peppercorn steak, black corns broken into the flesh, embedded in Hood's farm grown meat. Kale chips and half an acorn squash each. Lunch was served at 11:30. The large flat screen television beeped half an hour later. Time for the money meeting, because money mattered.

Chapter 20

Isabella's Box

Ramon was glad not to hear cicadas, just quiet music from the jukebox. He'd tried to feign interest in Sol's long legs and smooth brown skin but the sound of cicadas climbed into his skull and wouldn't leave him be. He fled the following morning, Tania gave him a ride to the cantina. Giovanni stocked beer behind the bar, nodded to Ramon when he limped in on crutches, panting with exertion. The place was dead, but why wouldn't it be? It wasn't even noon yet. Giovanni pointed with his thumb toward the back, the office and Isabella's "storage room". Ramon thanked him and wobbled his way into the back, stop and start to catch his breath. Isabella wasn't in her shrine room but her office. Regular workspace for the boss and owner of the small bar. Shelves lined with binders and books, cherry wood desk facing the door. Computer behind her on a smaller table. The room was utilitarian by all appearances, save the dimmed lights and Isabella in the louts position in her high-backed desk chair. Small porcelain Virgin Mary and a red prayer candle on her desk. She cracked one eye at his light knock and intruding head.

"Come in Ramon. I'm glad you're here." He obliged, sat in a deep leather chair in front of her desk. She closed her eyes again, was she asleep? He waited five minutes, or perhaps three. Spoke at her.

"I wanted to thank you for whatever you did to Hood. I'd have been done for if he'd been around while I was in the infirmary. Anyway, gracias Dona Isabella." She opened both her eyes, just barely, but enough to glitter in the candle light. So black.

"I wish I could say that was for your benefit Ramon but that plan was put into motion some time before I knew of your unfortunate mishap. Merely serendipitous or perhaps providential." She grew quiet again, deep even breaths, eyes still open. "Won't you stay for a little while Ramon, I would like to talk but I need to attend to one small matter, please keep an eye on me for a few minutes?"

"Of course." He didn't know why she needed a guard so she could take a cat-nap but he thought it better to agree. "What are you doing?" His curiosity was genuine.

"I have a package I need to unwrap for Hood. I gave it to him a little while ago, need to open it so he can enjoy it." Reached into the desk drawer in front of her, pulled out a small wooden cage, cricket chirped next to the candle. "For luck." She said, sat back, closed her eyes, deep breaths resumed.

Cricket rubbed its legs or wings or vibrated some part of its chitin-based exoskeleton. Vibrated wings, vibrated air molecules, vibrated Ramon. Hairs on the back of his neck stood on end, scared and excited all over again. Heart in his throat, climb out of his mouth if he didn't keep his mouth shut. Doggy paddle toward logical thought, no fear there. How did she reach Hood? What if Hood wasn't asleep? It was early still, would she sleep all day? Would she be upset if he left?

Her lips moved with silent words, Ramon strained to hear, nothing there. Her eyelids fluttered as her eyes moved back and forth beneath eyelids, nostrils flared. She laughed out loud, continued mouthing her silent prayer. The cricket started to chirp in earnest, louder and louder. Maybe, thought Ramon, just maybe he really would go mad, the cricket could take credit. He bit his tongue and tried not to scream.

Chapter 21

Blowout

Tail end of the meeting, the whole affair more than a little dry but money was dry, if you wanted to swim in it. Started
out well enough, technical difficulties threatened to scuttle their
money ship. Little Jon and the banker on the other end managed enough hardware prowess between the two of them to
muscle through the difficulties and eventually got down to
business. They pushed that ship around the table for some time
before Little Jon and the banker got into legal and financial
terminologies, both obscure and specific. Hood couldn't help it
and found himself dozing. Didn't worry about it much, Little
Jon was on top of it.

There she was. White orchid in her hair. She sat in the
blackness, arms and legs crossed, floating through the void.
She laughed when she saw him. Hood sat up with a start. Even
the banker thousands of miles away on the static laced video
feed noticed, stopped in mid-sentence to glance at Hood. Resumed talking to Little Jon. Beep, beep, beep. Swearing outside
the door, sirens screaming throughout the rig. Clanging of feet
filtered through the balcony door. Screaming of men's voices,
loud boom, rig shook. They both ignored the banker, looked
out the balcony door, smoke and fire, screaming men. The oak
door blasted open, panting Captain.

"Mr. Hood, you need to go now! The whole rig might go
at any minute, let's go!" Wall of fire, death by explosive erup-
tion. Hood didn't register anything but heat and orange flame in
his face, then the blackness of a pending concussion. Nearly
unconscious, fought through the shadows that pressed on him.
He felt the heat melt the hair from his arms, he rolled away.
Nowhere to go, he was pressed against a wall. And then the fire
was gone. Blink, blink, shadows and smoke cleared away. The
oak door to the outside office was gone, the office was gone,

geysers of fire spit upwards, outwards, everywhere. Crumpled steel, jagged edges, burnt furniture in the suite, burnt rug smelled like plastic, so did his smoking suit.

Globe's hands and clothes were covered in soot, collar burnt to ash, cuffs melted to his wrist. Little Jon on the floor behind the bar. Unhurt but stunned into stupidity. Hood grabbed the man by the collar, blessed be he, lacerations but none very deep, dragged Jon through the rubble, through the bedroom and into the private bath. Hood stomped his considerable mass on a section of the floor until he heard a loud click. He bent over and pulled up a three by three section of the tile on hinges. A rolled up ladder unfurled the forty feet to the platform below, which was still there thank goodness. Emergency escape route. Hood never imagined it would be necessary. He managed to goad Little Jon into action after a rough shake. Followed him down on legs quick with adrenaline and survival instinct.

Screams of dying men, tearing metal squeals in protest, puffing flame and poison smoke from fire breathing metallic nightmare, chaos and death. Tumble of human forms, at odd angles, hit the water hundreds of feet below. Two, three, four, screaming all the way. Blood in the water, hundreds of feet below, soon the sharks would swarm. Siren wailed, harsh staccato, automated emergency robotic voice told everyone to abandon ship. Hood ready to oblige. They finally made the platform below. Little Jon dazed, leaned against the railing, legs wobbling, rig moved beneath their feet, more and more violent. The rig lurched in the waves created by tumbling steel, jettisoned iron and metal, sacrifice of human progress to the flames and waves.

A hulking monster of a man materialized, running through a cloud of billowing steam, carried the biggest wrench Hood had ever seen. Hood was sure the man was going to crush him, use the escape boat for himself. The man stopped in front of Hood. Greasy work pants, greasy barrel chest under stretched t-shirt, faded logo of something. The man was seven feet tall and nearly as wide, his arms as thick as his legs, no neck to speak of, bald white head covered in soot.

"Mr. Hood, we need to get you out of here, there's a ladder and a few life rafts by the galley." Started to pull Hood back toward the steam bath.

"No man. NO!" Hood managed to pry is arm loose from the man's monster grip.

"Look here." A white box, size of shoe box, but longer and metal, Hood pulled out a key, the only other person who had one was the Captain and he was ash. He unlocked the box, flipped a much longer and more sturdy ladder over the edge, it trailed down to a crow's nest catwalk that circled one of the enormous pillars of the floating rig a mere ten meters from the water's surface.

Little Jon froze. This descent was more like one hundred feet, thirty-plus meters, maybe more. The broad expanse of open ocean beneath the pillars was daunting. The fifty foot diameter pylons disappeared beneath the surface of crashing waves. Hood could almost hear the waves sloshing against the metal hull. The ladder twisted in the wind, no amount of yelling was working. Fire burst, heat on the face. Mutter a prayer, looked over the edge. Wondered if he could survive the one-hundred fifty plus foot fall to the ocean below. Maybe when young and fit but not now, fat and soft. The hulk bent over Little Jon, who was not a short man, taller than Hood if not as thick.

"We need to go down this ladder Mr. Jon. If you need I can carry you." The man's voice was as husky as he was, oil, grease and metal shavings. Fitting. Little Jon looked up at him, looked like a scared old man. Positioned himself to go down, licked his lips.

"I can go down first sir and hold the ladder for both of you." Genuine concern, Hood promoted the man immediately.

"Why don't you son, that may be best." Little Jon motioned for the hulk, who obeyed quickly, scampering down the ladder even as it tried to twist in the wind.

"Is your boat big enough Hood? Is this monster going to exceed our weight limit? I can still cut this rope." A glittering knife sprang out of Jon's cane, Hood hadn't realized the man still had the thing. Fire and explosions, Hood almost wet himself.

"No Jon. This kid is a keeper. I'm gonna promote him to my new Wolf."

What remained of the office and Hood's suite screamed and ripped off the rig's skeleton, shriek of protesting metal, bend and fail, burst of flame and fire, zap of exposed wire.

"Alright. But you know El Lobo is not someone to be trifled with don't you?" Little Jon started down the ladder, held tight.

"We'll figure something out Jon." The suite tumbled into the ocean, detaching from the metal strands that held on for dear life with a loud sound of tearing metal, maybe the worst sound ever.

End over end the elongated box fell for seconds before hitting the water with a phenomenal crash. Rubble and geysers bid fond farewell to the luxurious suite as it was sucked below the surface.

Hood swallowed a scream and tightened his sphincter so as not to shit himself. Hoped El Lobo had already been notified or that the banker had called someone. Someone who should be on the way to pull him out of the drink. He climbed down the ladder with his heart thumping in his ears, panted all the way. His balls in his stomach, finally reached the catwalk. A foot-locker sized box on the catwalk, padlock on the catch. Hood pulled the key out again, hands shook, begged himself not to drop the key, performed the ritual, opened the box. Large inflatable raft, he threw it over the edge, it plopped on the waves, expanded with a whoosh, yellow with a canopy for protection from the sun. It was tethered to the box, waiting for them to claim it. Life-preservers, a backpack full of rations, Hood put it on. Little Jon was still catching his breath, the hulk motioning them down the metal ladder to the water's surface below. Hood knew gargantuan floating feet of the rig were submerged beneath the surface, probably between thirty and fifty feet and they were massive. The metal stairs descended into the blue waters of the Gulf and it looked bottomless there in the shade of the crumbling industrial giant.

Hurry and scramble, prayers to the gods. All of them, any that would listen. Whichever was paying heed or cared enough for his fat ass. Jon came up to him.

"We're not dead yet anyway." Rip and tear above them, the hulk screamed.

Hood looked up to see a section of the platform above engulfed in fire, sheet metal and rebar slough off like desiccated skin, fell toward Hood, off with his head. Hood grabbed Little Jon and dove for the water, kissed his ass goodbye. Say goodbye to Katherine, goodbye to Gloria, hello Lily. Water exploded in flame and white wash, blackness of metal pressing on him. Lights out.

Neither Katherine or Lily was waiting for him there. Instead it was Isabella. He knew it was her when he dozed at the meeting, all in black, white orchid behind her ear. She laughed at his arrival, throaty thing, sensual and threatening. A box in her hands. Small and square, black ribbon. She popped the top.

Chapter 22

Isabella's Cricket

Isabella's breathing changed and she was back, unfolded her legs slowly, stood and stretched her back, smile on her face.

"Got him." She sat back down, poured two shots of tequila from a bottle she pulled from somewhere, passed him one. Pulled a cigarette from a drawer, sat back, drank and smoked.

"Got whom?" Ramon knew who, she'd said it an hour ago but he wanted her to say it again.

"Have you seen Katherine Ramon?" She ignored his question.

"Yes." He had an inkling where this was going, better he went first.

"I know about the baby. I know it is mine, I'll be there for Katarina, even if she doesn't want me as a husband, I'll be a father." Ramon felt the heat in his chest, tears in his eyes.

"Do you? Will you? How very noble of you, Ramon. I mean it is the right thing to do after all, if it is your child." Long drag on her cigarette. She didn't elaborate. Eyed him with one eye, closed the other to keep the smoke out of her eye.

"Who else's could it be? I know Katarina isn't a saint but come on." Push away thoughts, he feared to hear the name. That damn cricket. He'd hoped it would stop once she returned.

"El Lobo, my husband. Katarina and Jose have shared something, I don't know what but something neither you or are I are privy to." Her usually thick accent was completely gone.

"I thought she was your student, aren't you teaching her? How do you know?" His brain was full of questions and denial, that was all he could get out.

"Of course I'm teaching her, when the student is ready the master teaches. As for how I know, a woman knows these things Ramon, this isn't hocus-pocus, dream walking or ju-ju stuff. This is a woman talking about her man." Cricket screamed, bounces around the room.

"Great. Great." Ramon shouted. "Can you turn off your cricket? It's driving me mad."

"The cricket is quiet Ramon, look." She pushed the cage at him, and there it was, still as could be in the center of the wooden cage, small miniature birdcage. She eyed him, her turn to look scared. Oh great. His phone rang. He silenced it, forward to voice mail, need to find out the why's and hows of her statement. The bar phone rang, Giovanni came in, told Isabella it was Tommy calling for Ramon.

"Oh yeah," she said as Giovanni brought him the hand unit, "the rig exploded, Hood's not dead yet, but may be soon. Congratulations or whatever, your friend should probably skeedadle, as in vamos nos."

"What?" Ramon asked the receiver. "Did the rig go? Did we get Hood?" He wasn't sure if he was happy or scared shitless.

"Yes the rig went, I don't know about Hood though. Let's hope for the best and plan for the worst. I'm not even going to ask how you know already." He didn't need to.

"So what is the worst Tommy and what is the best?"

"Worst case Hood is alive and angry, tracking us already, which means El Lobo, which means splat. I'm sending my people into hiding ASAP, I want you to come with Tania and I. I don't think you'll be safe anywhere else hermano." The man had a point, but Ramon needed to see Katherine.

"Do your thing hermano, I need to do something. I know how to reach you if I need to."

"Alright bro. Just one call and I'll be there." Tommy hung up. Isabella looked at him as if guessing his weight in her mind.

"Do you still hear the cricket Ramon?" Isabella exhaled smoke through her nose.

"No, they're quiet." He lied, the room sounded like it was full of them.

"That's strange because he's driving me crazy." She pulled the cloth off the top of the cage, the cricket was bounding and rebounding within the confines, singing for freedom and release. Ramon thought better of it and called Tommy for a ride, he wasn't doing as well as he thought.

Chapter 23

Hood's Nightmare

Globe Hood tumbled end over end, water invaded his nostrils, his throat, his lungs. Isabella's laughter rippled through the deep ocean. Light of flames above the surface glittered like crystalline jewels falling from the heavens. Their light distorted by the waves, refracted by the water. Orange red rubies tumbled through the water toward the darkness below. Flamed into the unseen depths, white hot, water and flame flow together. Isabella's visage surged up through the blackness, grabbed Hood by the neck, pulled him down into nothingness, into the blackness, floating void of his watery grave. Pin-prick of light, enlarged to a sucking vacuum of a whirlpool, pulled him in.

El Lobo in his truck bounced along farm roads, ventured to see Little Red. Seething desire to see her, to touch her, to devour her. How could it be that a flower, a breeze, the beating of his heart could remind him of her. Entered the Goat's shack a few days past, rather Ramon's container. So strongly he was thinking of her, he swore he smelled the scent of her must, her vaginal vapors painted all over the inside of the container. His face was surely distorted in a terrific snarl for the goat shook as if El Lobo were threatening his jugular. Damn she smelled good. He watched her walk hand in hand with some other fool, tried in vain to forget. Tended his crops, avoided the boss. Tackled the wrongs of Globe Hood, gave his workers a fair chance. But the truth couldn't be ignored. He loved her, hopelessly and forever. Flash, a memory of days gone by.

J.J. Martinez wiped the blood from his knife, sacrificial lamb and saprobes. Where would the world be without them? No one to blame and nothing to rot and degrade the corpses. The blame game piled high, corpses to the sky, the bodies of the forsaken. The teeming masses just like the statue of liberty says, longing to be free, the downtrodden, the refuse longing, aching. Underfoot and in the way. How dare they impede progress of the mighty. Evolutionary Darwinism yields to societal Darwinism. The weak are food for the strong... again and again.

The sacrificial lamb twitched a hind leg and the last gasp bubbled through slit throat. A tasty young lad, a newly arrived illegal he had been in the wrong place at the wrong time, quite literally. Hood caught the poor fool eavesdropping in the hay shed while he was wheeling and dealing with a local immigration enforcement officer, his pocket book and the Mayor. A bad spot to be caught in, hence the call came at two in the morning, animated El Lobo's telephone and assassinated his dreams. Sand and shovel, pick and hoe, the poor little bastard hadn't even seen it coming... just like that, a slit throat and a puddle of blood. Thrashing feet, sickly sweet. Blood and guts, wheels and ruts. Flash, another memory that belonged to the Wolf.

The Wolf found her, she played coy but not so much. Came to greet the rapacious man. Hood saw Little Red through El Lobo's eyes and didn't like what he saw. She pulled the man to her, opened her lips, pushed forward with her hips, kissed the man deeply. Pulled him, grabbed him by the hand, walked him to a bed that appeared from nowhere and the two were naked and intertwined in a flash, like a movie missing frames. Standing one moment, naked and coupled the next. El Lobo penetrated Little Red, she squirmed her pelvis into him flush with pleasure and orgasm, embraced her womanhood, embraced the orgasm. She squirmed beneath his red teeth, blood dripped from her neck and breast, she didn't notice, right above her heart. Hood screamed in vain, El Lobo howled over her writhing flesh, impaled as she was on his member, her ecstasy increased as he devoured her, thrusting harshly through her milky thighs. Blood streaked down her contracting, muscled legs, leaked from her baby maker. She was in ecstasy, pulled him into her, her nails gouged bloody marks on his ass. They exploded in screams, both howled at the moon.

Hood somersaulted through black nothingness, Isabella appeared, tracking his tumble. Waited him out. Once he stopped tumbling she spoke.

"Thought you might like to see what your little girl has been up to. I guess like mother like daughter."

"Fuck you, you bitch." He swiped at her, no use, floating in space as he was and she a non-corporeal entity.

"Oh just wait Globe, there's more." She disappeared.

Katherine was in the bathroom, plastic stick in her hand, purple cross on a small digital screen, positive, smiley face. She sighed and walked into the next room. Ramon lay sprawled on his back in her bed, naked. Sheet covered his intimacy and stomach, legs and chest bare in the morning sunshine, looked like they just woke up. She slipped into bed, naked as well, snuggled up to him, wrapped her hand around his flaccid penis and balls. She stroked them to life.

"Good morning sleepy head, time to go to work, but first." She slung a leg over him and sat on his erect member, more awake than the rest of him. She kissed his unbrushed mouth, tongued him until he wrapped his arms around her, pushed back with his pelvis. Hood watched her ride him over the clean white sheets that became tangled and twisted in their heaving forms, she stayed on top the whole time. She rode Ramon through imagined meadow, field and down the street of the barrio, he came loudly, screamed at the ceiling like she was tearing something from his flesh. She lay on his chest and he wrapped his arms around her, she wore the satisfied look a jockey pleased with her animal.

"I'm so glad you decided to join the movement." Ramon panted, kissing her hair.

"Me too Ramon, me too." She replied.

Hood sat up screaming, rolled on his side, vomit up the ocean. Black and green interior, Hood industries chopper? Bounce up and down, water against the hull, a boat then. The Hulk and Little Jon sat against the wall strapped in, by all appearances out cold. A paramedic checked Hood's vitals. Slipped toward darkness, he didn't want to sleep again but couldn't help it.

"It's OK Mr. Hood you're safe and well, on your way home." The medic soothed. Isabella was nowhere to be found, he had the blackness all to himself.

Chapter 24

Wound of Calamity

Disaster, calamity, catastrophe. Not that Hood didn't
have it coming. But if that fat bastard did, then El Lobo had it
coming too. Bridges to cross, crosses to bear. He'd sent a rescue team as soon as the emergency sirens sounded, directed
them toward the beacon in the life raft. Wet. The descriptor the
boat captain used to refer to Hood once El Lobo got him on the
radio. All four of them were wet. Four? Who was he counting?
Little Jon, Hood, a huge hulking mass of muscle and some chef
with a broken leg. Maybe they helped Hood escape the death-
trap of a burning rig. According to Little Jon the additions were
a mechanic that helped them escape and some kid Hood had
cook their meal that morning. Just dumb luck the kid or the
mechanic ended up with them but so was the nature of disaster.
Random and free of prejudice.

According to Little Jon the sous chef had seen the little
yellow raft bobbing up and down and jumped off the platform
some two-hundred plus feet above, live or die he supposed.
Little Jon tried to wave him off but by that time the kid was
already plummeting like a rock, nine point eight meters per
second per second. The kid kept his feet together, hands at his
sides, entered the water feet first. Graham, as they learned the
name of the mechanic, dove in after him, pulled a screaming
and gagging Javier to the surface. His ankle twisted at an un-
natural angle, no wonder he was screaming. Hood was unconscious, so was Javier when El Lobo got the Captain on the radio, owner and CEO fresh from the ocean like a hauled in tuna.

Pulled up to the helipad, bedraggled and rumpled Hood
gingerly slipped out of the cabin, Little Jon followed. Hood
turned, had a few words with the wall of muscle behind him,
the man nodded and stuck close to Hood, slid into the backseat
of the SUV with Little Jon. All three were damp, smell of salt

and ocean firmament. Tousled hair and red eyes spoke of pro-
longed submersion, salt water will do that.

They all wore clean sweat suits, he assumed provided by
the Hood industries captain that pulled them from the drink.
Shuttled them to the heli-port in Louisiana, put them on the
chopper, sent them home. El Lobo took them all to the main
office. Gloria's office and the bedroom upstairs she used were
dark. She was been working from home for once. El Lobo unlocked the front door and all four of them piled into Globe's
office. The portly, red-cheeked Hood ducked into the bathroom, shower coming to life. He shouted out to El Lobo.

"Wolf, could you please take Mr. Graham to the cabin
while I shower? Then I should be ready to deal with you."
Wave of his hand, dismiss. Little Jon didn't say a word, he was
nursing a brandy on Hood's love seat, laid out like he had no
intention of going anywhere.

"Graham, thank you for saving out lives, you're promoted. Come by tomorrow, we will work out the details." Slam of
bathroom door. Graham shrugged, followed El Lobo outside
into the dark.

Simple enough, Hood had two cabins on the property.
Luxuriant one or two room log cabins, typical design. Hood
installed them thinking agri-tourism would appeal to some of
his investors. Or perhaps the hippy-dippy upper-class privi-
leged types that wanted to put their fingers in some soil for the
weekend and say they tried farming and look at the goat cheese
they made. The reality was Hood's farm was a bit too industrial, a bit too large, a bit too mechanized and a bit too close to
the edge of legal. Too much attention from outsiders was not
always a good thing. Now he used them for investors that
wanted to come see, or new employees, the legal, professional,
upper level management types. The man Graham shook El Lobo's hand, let himself into the cabin, lights came on before El
Lobo pulled away.

He returned to the office, wondered how exactly Hood
meant to deal with him. Didn't have to wait to find out. Hood
started yelling at him as soon as the door opened.

"God damned Lobo de mierda, I'm sick of this shit. So I
come to find out after I emerge from my delirium that you nev-

er killed any of the movement members. In fact, you cut them up, then dumped them at my infirmary so I could foot the bill for the uninsured terrorists who have cost me millions!" El Lobo waited, watched the cresting wave, surely there was more to come. Diarrhea of the mouth was seldom just a squirt. Maybe a poke at the oozing sore of Hood's rage.

"I didn't think killing the same people that pick your food, prepare your meals, count your money, keep watch over you, would be the best idea you'd ever had. In fact I was concerned they'd harm you directly. Did you want the dead one's family members coming after you?"

"Yes! You god damned Wolf! I wanted them angry and afraid, I wanted them to do something stupid. If they came for me I have you to kill them! Little Jon sends them to jail, that's how this works!"

"I know those people Hood, intimately, especially the older ones, they come to my bar, Isabella raised their kids. You know that right Patron?"

"Don't condescend to me you piece of shit. Now you pretend to have a heart? Since when? Your best feature, the one I love most, the only one I like actually is your cold-blooded, heartlessness. Fuck. When I say kill them I mean dead, not just wounded, not maimed, I mean dead!"

"How about the cops Hood? Do you have that under control?" See how long he could keep Hood red in the face.

"Don't worry about the pig fuckers you bastard. I've got them paid off and under my thumb, again, thanks to Little Jon. You certainly hand nothing to do with it, Mr. run away and hide every time the cops are around. No cop is going to give a shit about a missing illegal. I don't care if they're buried under the soy beans or by the side of the road, no one cares! Instead you waste my time and resources, firing supervisors that rape the women and molest the children. Don't you see you immigrant bastard? I don't care." He made large sweeping gestures with his arms, like he was doing the backstroke.

"I don't give a damn if every one of those greasy immigrant whores gets raped by a toothless, AIDS infected supervisor. I just want the work done and my orders filled. Do you understand?"

"Yes Mr. Hood." No need to rub insubordination in the wound of calamity, would definitely prompt a heart-attack. Hood rubbed his eyes, threw some papers from his desk, they didn't go far, collected on the floor, futile.

"Enough, I'm tired and half drown, come by early tomorrow morning, we need to talk about the movement and Ramon." He poured himself a brandy, collapsed into the deep leather recliner.

Little Jon snored softly in the love seat. Tomorrow then.

Chapter 25

Fire on the water

Ramon watched the fire arc into the sky, black smoke billowed from burning plastic, metal, petroleum. Oil slick on the ocean surface, damn shame. Arcing white streams of water, water guns from coast guard ships, no visible effect. Ramon wasn't sure if this was the news or if Tommy was streaming the footage from some other source. It didn't matter, it was riveting.

Monkey squad headquarters was a beehive ready to move. All members were fully clothed and frantic. No more flirting with pretty girl or intimations of sex. People disappeared by the hour, didn't say goodbye, just told Tommy they knew how to reach him and vice-versa. See you later. Tania had duffel bags next to their computer stations, the large warehouse space was already powered down, empty of life and hipster techies crawling through the hallways. Dispersed on the wind like scattered poplar seeds, tufts and a wish. Float away, ride the wind, catch one for good luck. As was required by all Lieutenants and Captains every member of the movement had secondary and tertiary safe houses to which they retreated when necessary. This would be the first time they had to use said locations, some went home to parents, others to extended family.

Ramon, Tania and Tommy were the last to go. The three leaders had a few things arranged, though Ramon wasn't sure Tommy and Tania would appreciate his container hideout much. Ramon had his parents' house in the barrio, big enough for the three of them, rooms in the attic, tenants below. But he knew El Lobo and the authorities would check there first. Wring his neck or rip out his jugular. Tania's prediction had proven true, El Lobo's hands were full with the explosion on the rig and Hood's unknown whereabouts. He estimated they had about eight hours, maybe ten before the man came looking for them. They huddled around the screen, watching the rig burn. No new updates in the last hour.

"Oye, let's go to the bodega. I need to talk to Katherine." Katherine on his brain.

Tania nodded, poked Tommy on the temple to get his attention.

"Yeah, yeah. Let me put the computer in the car, infect the servers." Key strokes and alarm light.

Tommy insisted on infecting the monkey squad servers in preparation for the arrival of the FBI and other goons who would assign blame and point fingers. Ramon hoped no one died, except Hood, though it looked like that was too much to hope for. Piled into the sedan. Ramon was no good, he couldn't carry anything except his crutches across his lap and some bags Tania hung across the handles on the back of the wheelchair. They took the service elevator again, too much stuff to lug it all down the stairs. Around the other side the elevator shaft, several parked cars waited inside the warehouse, parked before a closed aluminum door. Tommy chose the thin European style delivery van. Dark blue with large passion flower painted on the side. The name Passionflower Plants in a flowing script like the artist painted the name with a flourish and a giant brush.

They piled in, another garage door opener on the visor, computer terminals, towers, hard-drives, wire guts wrapped around Ramon's ankles in the back. Most of the equipment stashed in elongated flower boxes. Barking dogs, frying foods, dirt roads characterized the barrio they grew up in. Pulled up in front of Katherine's market, the Bodega. Lights on inside, awnings rolled up, wooden shelves out front empty, doors and windows closed against the cold. Fluorescent overhead lights illuminated the corner store and the patrons inside with bright white light.

Nearly eight at night, only a few heads bobbed up and down the aisles of her corner grocery. Red hair behind the counter, moved back and forth, said Katherine was behind the counter ringing people up. A cluster of six black-haired, handkerchief wearing heads clustered around a table near the back. Display cases separated those perusing from the prepared foods. The most interesting and fastest growing section of her store. Katherine let Carmen's sisters and daughters sell hot food out of the back of the store. So popular she'd since blown out the back wall, put in two restrooms and sitting area.

She expanded the food display cases. In fact Katherine begged the women to stay, told them she'd turn the whole space into a restaurant in a couple of years if they wanted. They were all thinking about it. The store was a favorite for workers, those on their way to work, those on lunch, those on the way home.

You name it, they had it. Rice and beans, tamales, burritos, enchiladas, poblanos rellenos, pupusas, platano verde, platano maduro, arepas, empanadas, tortillas, chilies, smoked pork, just the tip of the display case. They made food to order too. Diversifying their menu, Caribbean rice and beans was hugely popular. The coconut smooth flavor a nice variation to the yellow rice. Needless to say Katherine was making a killing with the restaurant portion, though she kept only a small percentage, she only charged rent for the space, left the food receipts to the women that made the food. The women that cooked and served were the big draw and they deserved to be paid accordingly. Besides, more than half the patrons bought something from the grocery on the way in or the way out.

Stridulation is the term for the chirping of the cricket. The cricket rubs the top of one wing against ridged vein on the bottom of the other wing. Ramon considered the storefront.

"Maybe you two should wait here. I don't know how happy she'll be to see me, all of us together even worse." Ramon's jar of butterflies, open in his stomach, delicate, gauze winged beauties slammed into his stomach walls like driven golf balls. The two nodded but followed him inside anyway. They ducked down the first aisle, bee-lined for the back of the shop. They wanted enchiladas according to Tania. Ramon didn't argue, the cricket in his ear was distracting enough. Stridulation stimulation to insanity.

Katherine was very obviously displeased when he walked up to the counter. She had her head down, counting the till, making a drop; filling out some paperwork. She slammed a large three-ring binder on the table when he stopped in front of her.

"You are not someone I want to see right now Ramon. You have some nerve showing your face. I knew you and Tommy were behind this, that much is obvious. Computer malfunction my ass." She did throw something, an orange. It bounced off his head, he leaned on his crutches, didn't flinch. Where did she get an orange this time of year?

"I know Katherine, I'm sorry. It wasn't supposed to go bad so fast, it should have taken a few days, not a few hours. Is your father alright?" He pleaded, hands clasped in front of his face in supplication.

"You three are lucky I don't call the police, FBI or better yet El Lobo, turn you guys in and clean my hands of your nonsense." Her eyes were like hot irons, pierce his flesh, burn to the bone, no sympathy from Katherine. She sounded serious, chill up the spine, goosebumps from scalp to his toes. Sphincter constricted in panic.

"So you'd send us up the river, maybe forever. Never see us again, we've been friends for a long time, and now I'm the father of your baby." He tried not to put on his puppy dog eyes. Failed.

"Oh come off it Ramon, you killed people Ramon, first with the food poisoning and now this. The food poisoning alone was enough to get you sent away for most of your life. Even if that was a solo act, this was clearly not. You are effectively undermining your own movement, putting my efforts to negotiate with my father and the other members in jeopardy. The fact that I haven't reported you makes me complicit, teenage love affair or no, pregnancy or no pregnancy. Yes, my father survived, just barely, no thanks to you. Ten workers died, put that on your conscience, if you have one." She was so angry she could barely see straight, vein pulsed on her neck. Tears in her eyes.

"I'm so sorry Katherine, this wasn't supposed to go down this way." Tears in her eyes pulled on his heart strings, hot tears in his own eyes.

"Is that all you can say? You think you would've learned your lesson. Every action you've taken so far Ramon has blown up in your face in one way or another. Instead of down-trodden, exploited, victimized farm workers you've made us all look like terrorists Ramon! You're no Cesar Chavez, more like a want to be Che Guevarra. Grow up Ramon! Your remorse does nothing for me, does even less for my father, the workers and their families. My father will blame you for this, you know how he works." Pulsing vein in her neck, she had her father's temper, red-haired myth a truism in her case but the logical, cool, calm, collected analysis was all Lily. Her balled fists opened and closed like she was considering slapping him. He didn't deserve anything but.

"Can you help us, we need to lay low for a few days, set up our safe house..."

"Are you kidding me Ramon? You are murderers, all three of you, the whole Monkey squad is fucked. You tried to kill my father and you want me to hide you from him and El Lobo?" She did slap him then, ringing ears, numb jaw, she had heavy hands for a petite package, almost fell off his crutches. No mercy for the cripple apparently, especially murderous cripples. She sighed and rubbed her face, came around the cor-ner. She took him by the elbow, led him and his hobbling gait down the aisle. Her store was much more than a bodega. End caps were full of fresh fruits and vegetables, canned goods, real juice. She had plenty of crap in the first and second aisles. The usual junk in bags. Salt and chips, salt and crackers, high fruc-tose corn syrup everything. No ethnic food though, all of that was behind the glass windows of the deli counter at the back of the store, where Katherine led him.

Down the aisle to the back where Tia and Tommy had mouthfuls of rice and beans, enchilada cheesy goodness, real plate and silver ware. Ramon nodded to his cousins behind the counter. Tia Carmen's kids, he hadn't seen them in a while, they didn't wave back or say a word, just stared at him with angry eyes. They were probably angry with him for hurting Katherine. Everyone loved her. Katherine gathered Tania and Tommy with a gesture, swept all three of them in her wake into the back of the store. She escorted them through storage space, boxes here and there balanced on pallets. She made a left, opened a wash closet.

Utility sink a chair a mop, a bucket, cleaning supplies, an upside down bucket. She shoved the three of them into the closet.

"Wait here for now, hopefully I will have no unexpected visitors." Stared all three of them down, dared them to say anything. "I'll take you upstairs once I close the store, two hours, give or take. Then you can figure out where you're going because you are not staying here." She slammed the door, almost crushed Ramon's huddled knees. Stomping footsteps away, light went out under the door when she left the storage room.

Tania and Tommy brought their plates into the closet with them and resumed dinner, watched Ramon with full mouths and tortillas in their hands. They might as well have been on their couch watching a tele-novela for all their interest. The room smelled like baked cheese and beans in a matter of seconds. Ramon regretted not grabbing a plate, the intertwined smells of re-fried beans, jalapeno and salsa had his stomach snapping at the air. Either the butterflies dispersed or had been consumed by the snapping jaws of hunger. Cricket chirpped in the back of his head. Started singing anew, sound never stopped, stuck in the closet with them.

His nervousness dissipated once it was clear Little Red didn't intend to turn them in or deny them aid, even if only temporarily. He could handle angry, meant she was still willing to talk to him. He hadn't broached the most important subject, at least not in earnest, that subject being their approaching parentage. More anger would bubble to the surface during that conversation, he was sure. Waited in the closet. Sitting on an upturned bucket was cramped. They gave Tania the chair. The three of them hardly spoke. Once they finished eating Tania tried to console Ramon a little. Women were fiery creatures she said, right Tommy? Tommy nodded in agreement, chewed his fingernails, spit the chewed pieces across the room. Tania scolded him for being disgusting. He didn't stop chewing but did stop spitting his chewed nails.

True to her word a few hours later plus or minus Katherine opened the door, lead them through the dark storage room and up a back stairwell lit by a naked high compact fluorescent bulb. The stairwell let onto the second floor at the back of her apartment. The unfurnished section with the hardwood floor and long mirror she used for yoga and dance. Back corner, hidden behind a door and a Japanese screen painted with bamboo and cranes emerging from a riparian woodland. She didn't touch any lights until they were in the kitchen. She turned on the tea kettle, sat at the stool next to the island, rubbed her face. Tommy and Tania still carried their plates, sat at the small breakfast table between the kitchen and the cushioned, beanbag strewn lounge area. Katherine took their plates, put them in the sink, returned to her stool. She wasn't speaking to any of them. So Ramon went first.

"Tania, Tommy, make phone calls if you need to. I need to talk to Katherine." He stood at the center island, looked at her, she raised her head when he spoke. He made a pleading gesture, again, she exhaled loudly, walked into the back to her room. She sat at the end of her bed, he on the comfortable reading chair next to it. She waited, hands crossed in front of her, legs folded beneath her bottom, shoes slipped off when she sat. Ramon's turn to take a deep breath. Butterflies were back, maybe it was good he hadn't eaten, felt nausea gagging him.

"I know about the baby Katherine. I want to help, I want to be a father for the child. I know you're angry with me and you have every right, I deserve nothing less but I am a part of this baby."

He tried not to whine, or beg too much. She stared at him, twisted red strands of hair between her fingers. She looked pale, more than usual anyway, he wondered was it what he said or her condition?

"Look Ramon, I don't know how you found out but I will be the only parent this child ever knows."

"I heard you and Isabella talking in the infirmary." He interrupted.

"Even as addled as you were you heard that huh? Well no use fretting over spilled milk. Ramon you will most likely be in jail or on the run after I finish the negotiations with the workers, all of whom will finger you as the master mind behind the movement, and I'm afraid, Senor Commandante Cabra, (Mr. Goat Commander) I will encourage them to do so. Aren't you supposed to the scapegoat after all?"

"Sounds like you've already tried and convicted me Katherine." Ramon felt his own cool slipping, blood beginning to heat. Cricket on the brain, chirped again, lose his mind soon, if not lost already. She rubbed her head.

"What is that chirping? Do you have a cricket in your pocket or what?" She left the bed, hovered next to him, plucked something from his shoulder. A small black cricket. No shit, Isabella's cricket on his shoulder the whole time? No wonder he was losing his mind.

"Did Isabella give you this?" Though it was posed as a question it was more rhetorical than interrogatory.

"I guess so. I went to see her today and she was using that in one of her dream walking exercises. Said she had something she'd given to your father and needed to open it for him. Whatever that means." Ramon wasn't sure if his visit was a secret but Isabella hadn't suggested it was. "She was the one that told me your father was in the explosion, she wasn't sure he'd make it." Katherine sighed again, deep as the evening wind blows. Tsked loudly.

"I'm not surprised, Isabella wouldn't care if my father died a horrible death and he probably deserves both the death and her hatred. I'm ashamed to say so." Rubbed her face again, red splotches where she rubbed cheek, jowl and eyes.

"Let's stay on subject Ramon." She grabbed the cricket, walked to the window.

"Wait!" Ramon jumped up, ran to her, took the bug, crushed it between his fingers, flicked it out the window. Went to the bathroom, washed his hands.

"You didn't have to kill it Ramon." Sighed again. Must be heavy that load she was carrying.

"Now that I know I'm not insane, that cricket has been driving me batty for hours. What are you saying Katherine? I shouldn't concern myself with my child, you know I can't do that." He felt the flush in his face, the crack in his voice.

"Ramon look...listen, you have no legal, technical, or genetic responsibility to this child." Big brown eyes, wet and round. Drown in those tears, brown iris. Goat kick to the guts, so it was true, what he feared, what Isabella suggested, the child was not his.

"Who's is it? El Lobo or someone else?"

"I'm not sure." Made her sound like a whore. But her body told the lie for what it was. Same old body language she had when they were young. Braver than all the rest, she couldn't lie worth a damn. She looked into her lap, played with her fingers, wouldn't look up until the words were out.

"Don't lie to me Katarina, we may be over but for what we had, don't you think you could be frank with me?"

"I think I'll make us all a whole bunch of quesadillas because I'm hungry. After that, you guys can skeedadle. I won't kick you out, you can all crash in the cushion room but I'm going to see my father in the morning and I want all of you to leave when I do." She unfolded herself from the bed, paused in front of him like she was searching for words, he looked up into her face. She chewed on her bottom lip, tears dripped down her nose onto her pale green socks. He reached for her, she swept on into the kitchen to cook some quesadillas.

Chapter 26

Ship of Good Fortune

Purple blended morning sky, orange-gold, magenta and azure. Dew frozen on blades of Kentucky Blue, melt on tip of boots, brown leather, dark with age and use, water beads glittered, filled with the sun's ricochet. Rusty truck, old friend, creaked his way to the office. No office for Hood today. Chill in the air slipped under his shirt, shiver in the cabin of the truck. Gloria already in her office, no surprise there. An awful lot of spilled milk to clean up or oil rather. She was already frazzled, the phone wasn't even ringing yet. Just a matter of time.

"Hood is at home Wolf. I believe he's expecting you." Peered over her lenses.

"I know, wanted to check on you, check in."

"We'll be up to our eyeballs in the EPA, lawsuits and federal fines sooner than later, this is not looking good." As he suspected.

"Well, keep up the good work Gloria, I'll see you later." She didn't look up.

Rumbled to Hood's. Fat bastard was gonna pull something soon. Felt it in his gut, feel it in his bones. In the meantime, if he had to guess, Ramon was on the chopping block, probably monkey squad too. The IT geeks with their industrial warehouse. This was going to get ugly. Pulled up to Hood's digs. Large Plantation style. Broad and deep, columns out front, wings sprawling from each side, a greenhouse attached to the Western side. Large patio with a fountain, stairs climbed to Terra Cotta tiles and marble cherubs shooting water from mouth and penis, elegantly tactless, just like Hood.

Terra cotta tile to brick steps to Walnut door, stained almost black. Stained glass to the left and right, peak-a-boo. Wolf didn't bother with the brass clapper shaped like a small pineapple. The entryway foyer continued the red tile, benches to either side, seats that lifted to hide slippers and umbrellas. Hooks on the wall ran around the room at head height, a few lower, for the ladies. Three or four jackets hung from the hooks, duck boots in front of the bench like the owner is coming.

Like an outdoor catalog picture. Everything nice, everything for sale. Lobo hung his own, left his boots on, stepped up into the house. Light brown wood floor runs away, microscopic creases between the boards ran parallel away from the foyer. Lily's touch was evident from the first. She chose the light bamboo floor before bamboo was popular with the greenies. To the left a sunlit sitting room. Floral patterned fabric covered the chairs and love seat, light pattern with twining vines and trumpet flowers. He wondered if they'd been reupholstered since her death. A coffee table, Lion heads on the corners with rings through their noses, vase in the middle filled with flowers.

The flowers were wooden, different colors and shaped like tulips, they needed to be dusted. A cold fireplace, bricks blackened with use. The walls were a light rose color, wall paper strip wrapping around the room like a headband, bunches of grapes and Boston-ivy. Above the hearth a landscape painting of a palomino standing in waist high grass, staring out of frame. Muscles bunched for action, an oak tree and shade in the background. Beyond the sitting room and the hutch full of porcelain tea pots was a sun room and Lily's library, beyond that it opened into the conservatory. Lily's hideaway. He could hear the birds chirping from where he stood. Small surprise Hood never ventured into that side of the house, it was far too light and airy for his disposition. El Lobo hadn't realized how similar in shape Lily's conservatory was to his greenhouse office. Her bedroom was back there too, the one he'd found her in all those years ago. The day she named him.

Hood sent the new housekeeper to keep it up, Roslinda's niece, legally employed. She kept the pots dusted and the plants watered, missed the wooden Tulips though. Katherine used the greenhouse too, she had her own key and usually entered through the kitchen in the rear. The door Hood made sure the help used. Opposite side of the foyer was the dining room, a light yellow pastel on the walls, long yellow-wood table, sanded and beautiful. Treated and bossed to brilliance, just like Lily. Family portraits in the hallway, oil painting of sunflowers and blue bells on the wall. Room to seat eight.

Wolf was sure the dining room was seldom used, even in the good years. The main hall led straight back to the kitchen, stairs adjacent broad enough for three people abreast, led up to the bedrooms and study. Large commercial sized kitchen back there. Took Carmen some time to be able to work in her mother's kitchen without crying. Industrial stainless steel stove top, baker's racks, hood above the burners. Nestled within the white porcelain tile, blue hand painted designs scrawling from one tile to the next traced a blue line around the kitchen. Big window and white tile made the kitchen an open space, a favorite room of Katherine's when she was little. She had usually been found in the kitchen at the small chef's table eating something. Rosalinda made sure she was a chubby-cheeked toddler and a well-fed, smooth skinned teen.

El Lobo wondered how Katherine mourned for Rosalinda. Did she cry in her room all alone? Did she call her father and curse him out? She definitely lost someone near and dear to her. After Lily died Rosalinda assumed the duties of mother and confidant, with Gloria as backup. Between the two of them they raised Katherine from the flame-haired tomboy that beat Ramon at everything, to the self-confident beautiful defender of justice she was today.

The kitchen was wide. It ran the width of the entire house, a mud room on one side, a large walk in pantry on the other, stairs disappearing into the basement for more storage. Lily and Rosalinda loved that kitchen. Out back the manicured lawn stretched for two hundred meters, hedgerows of Privet, Honeysuckle, Japanese Yew, Rhododendron, Azalea and Hydrangea criss-crossed the lawn. Three gardeners were assigned just to Hood's mansion. El Lobo rotated the greenhouse workers through the assignment. It was a favorite and one could see why. Carmen cooked lunch for the gardeners, they had their own private carriage house converted to small office, locker room, break room with a kitchen, bathrooms and an apartment upstairs if they wanted to stay. Small wonder the greenhouse workers traded the assignment like a golden egg.

Wolf made his way up the wooden stairs, ran his hand up the smooth banister, smoothed by decades of palms, fingers, children's behinds sliding down. Top of the stairs, another hallway. Ahead to the library and sitting room with a fireplace large enough for him to stand in. To the left Katherine's childhood suite. Her own bedroom, play room complete with doll houses, tea sets, popcorn machine, private movie theater and then some. Beyond the playroom was her bedroom and her own little study and walk-in closet.

A private bath with a shower and bathtub, depending on her mood or how dirty she was deemed by Rosalinda. At the back of her walk-in closet a spiral staircase spun down through the floor, landing downstairs in what was Lily's hidden passageway. A hidden hallway that ran between Lily's library and bedroom, accessible through a revolving wall in an alcove with a bust of a howling wolf. Katherine frequently used the passageway to escape her father after Lily's death or to flee to Lily's bedroom when her mother lived. El Lobo was familiar with the hidden passageway. Hood had a similar one on his side of the house in his wing. With the exception that his led to the garage and drilled down another floor into the basement. Landed next to a storm door that could only be opened from the inside. The man was always cautious, or paranoid.

Katherine took to hiding in both during her troublesome adolescence, before Hood couldn't take it anymore and sent her off to boarding school. Many an afternoon El Lobo slipped silently down the absconded alleys trying to catch Little Miss Katherine. Not that she ever ran from him. She would stare at him defiantly, hands on her hips, dig in her heels. Façade would fail, tears would trickle down cheek and trembling lips. She almost always ended up crying on his chest and shoulder, lamenting the injustices of the world. The greatest injustice of all being Hood as her father when she really wanted to be the daughter of Jose and Isabella Martinez. Probably when he first started having a soft spot for the girl.

Twenty-something farm vet holding snot-nosed, lost and lonely little girl in dusty secret passageway. Seemed they two were meeting in secret even in the beginning. El Lobo turned right at the top of the stairs, walked down a short hallway to a dark oak door. Hood's suite, door closed but unlocked. He knocked once and walked in. He was no stranger to the Den, office and reading room; bedroom suite beyond. Funny name for a place that Hood never used, at least not for reading. The man never read anything he didn't have to, unless it had to do with money. Similar in many ways to his suites on the rigs, save more opulent, more luxurious, less stoic, stalwart and minimalist. Here Globe had the space and resources to spare and he spared none, space or expense.

Mounted heads on the walls, Deer, Elk, Bison, Wolf, Jaguar, Ram. The whole collection, in fact El Lobo marveled at the variety every time he entered the wooden sanctuary of Globe Hood. The man had been an avid hunter once. The busts on the wall were trophies of Hood's outings, each and every one of the specimens bagged by the fat bastard, eaten too. Wasn't as easy to hate Hood back then. The early days when the man still had a life, a wife and a semblance of a moral compass. Lost in the weed now, like the grouse that got away. Plush beautiful rugs covered the wooden floor, mahogany everything.

"There he is! El Lobo Maldito, son of a bitch in the flesh." Hood didn't rise from the leather recliner he sat in, feet up on the raised footer. A scantily clad girl daintily rubbed his shoulders, not kneading his hair covered shoulders nearly enough. She was pale skinned with blond hair, the roots just a little black.

"I'm eating out." Hood laughed, gestured to Graham who stood staring at them from his station in front of a large window. He didn't laugh. Hood laughed for him.

"He's a man of few words, doesn't laugh much. It appears all you tough types have that in common." El Lobo wasn't sure he was a tough, certainly hadn't started for Hood as one. He'd started as the man's Veterinarian way back when.

"Do you remember Lobo, back in the good old days, before we hated each other? Back when we had a slight disdain but could still stand one another? Not at all like the hatred we feel now." Sipped his coffee, Irish cream instead of milk to be sure.

"I remember those days Globe. You weren't so fat or full of yourself back then. You still cared about your Earth, your animals and your people. But I wouldn't say I hate you, perhaps strong distaste is a better way to put it." Pulled out a cigarette, this was going to be a smoky talk.

"Who's full of themselves now? You sure have changed from a bright-eyed twenty-five year old ready to please me, inoculate my livestock, cull my herds. Remember how you used to walk around with that six shooter on your hip? That was really bad-ass man. I'm sure that's where the nickname came from. Don't you think?" Hood pulled out a cigar of his own, started puffing once the big bosomed lass rested her breasts on his shoulder, lit his cigar with a lighter she pulled from goodness knew where. Graham had the presence of mind to crack a window.

"I carried that gun because your animals were overdosed on hormones, to the point of aggression. It only takes almost being gored once to learn that lesson. If you remember you had a problem with wild dogs, coyotes and rabid raccoons at the time. One uses the appropriate tool for the job." He wondered if Hood knew that is was Lily that named him.

"You know, Lily told me you were something else, even way back then, she always had a good eye for horse flesh." He stared at the ceiling, exhaled blue smoke to the heavens. "Speaking of appropriate tool for the job, Graham here will be filling your duties as bodyguard and 'problem solver' after the one last job I have for you." There was the first shoe, tip of the iceberg. Knowing Hood there was more to come, he liked for his plans to unfold in waves.

"I know this doesn't come as a surprise Wolf. Let's face it. I have you spread too thin as my Foreman, Veterinarian, strongman, problem solver, and on and on. It is a small miracle you've managed everything so well for so long. You are a competent man but there's only one of you. I know most of the harvest is in but we both know there is more to it than bringing in the crops." He gestured to Graham. "Now there's two. And I'll be frank Lobo, I've been disappointed with your problem solving of late. Your solutions have been less than complete, you've left loose strings untied, hospital beds full and illegals emboldened. You've cost me money and time, two things I never have enough of. So Graham here is going to take on your non-agricultural duties after you do this one last thing. How does that sound?" Hood crossed plump fingers over his belly, cigar puffed in the corner of his mouth.

"Sounds like a croc of shit." Not time to mince words, especially if they were getting sentimental.

"I know how you work Globe, first you divest, then you crush. Provide distance, then destroy. Is that what this is?" He could feel the hit being put on him like a binding hex mark.

"Come on over to the desk, I want you to see something." Globe rose from his recliner, blood red bathrobe untied and open.

Hello dolly, masseuse and nurse fondled his prick and balls, kissed him as he stood.

"No more tweedles Globe?" Wolf asked, genuinely curious, he knew where the girls were.

"No, No tweedles Lobo. They're in the fields, harvest season and all. We need all the help we can get, am I right or am I right? Like I said I'm eating out for a while." Patted twenty-something blond on bare ass cheek, thong left plenty of cheek free for fondling. Hood licked his fingers, wiped them on his robe. Sat behind the desk, turned the computer monitor to one side, stopped in mid motion.

"Oh yes, I always forget the new toys Little Jon has set up for me. Better yet look at the screen." He pointed to the huge flat screen one wall, it took up nearly the whole thing. Hood tapped keys on his computer. Black screen powered up, grainy low resolution image with a decidedly gray cast to it. Figures moved in and out of a glass door, after a few seconds of watching he realized it was Katherine's store. So Hood was connected to her camera system or was he watching on cameras he'd installed himself?

"OK, here it comes, watch this." Hood gestured at the big screen as if trying to poke the images. Hazy pixelated fellow on crutches hobbled through the door, followed by a man dressed all in black with a long black trench coat, spikey hair and a nondescript woman whom he would've ignored on any other day. Paired with the two in front she was guilty by association, Ramon, Tommy and Tania. He'd watched Isabella raise the three of them and send them off to elementary school. They all loved Isabella.

"Who are they Lobo?" Leading question. El Lobo answered without hesitation.

"They are Ramon, Goat Commander of the Animals, ex-head of the movement. Tommy and Tania, Monkey squad Lieutenant and his second in command, husband and wife."

"So you recognize them then. I thought those two were in the IT department. That explains a lot. What I see are three employees guilty of corporate sabotage and espionage, traitors to their country. What I see Lobo are three dead men but keep watching." The darkly dressed man and the nondescript woman walked down an aisle onto the screen of another camera, ordered food at a counter, sat down to eat.

The man on crutches stopped in front of the cash register. Talked to a white faced cutie behind it. Katherine. No audio was necessary to tell the two were having words. She threw something at him, slapped him a few minutes later. But then she took him by the elbow, collected the other two and walked them into the storage room and onto another camera's screen. She shoved them into a closet, Hood fast forwarded the recording two hours ahead. Katherine appeared again, guided them through the dark storage room, he could only just see the movement of shadows across the grainy image until the stairwell's light spilled into the storage space, four shadows entered the stairwell. Hood turned to face El Lobo.

"I'm assuming you know what this means?" Hood stared at him, no fooling, shit eating grin.

He grabbed the masseuse's hand, stopped the rubbing, asked her to bring him some caviar, cream cheese and crackers from the other room in the mini-fridge. Pat on the ass, sent her away. Graham didn't budge.

"It means your daughter was helping her childhood friends lay low and get out of dodge. You saw she yelled at Ramon, even slapped him." El Lobo wondered if Hood could stay calm through all of this.

"It means my daughter is working with the movement members, she has become one of them, betrayed me, her flesh and blood, cast her lot in with the god-damned immigrant scum." There it was, vein beginning to blossom in his neck. Explosion imminent.

"From what I've heard Ramon has been deposed as leader, the movement has broken up and your daughter is beginning negotiations with them, even giving some of them their back pay."

"Bull-shit, disbanded my ass. If she's paying them then she's part of the problem. Furthermore she's a liar, a cheater and has forsaken my sacrifices. All the things I've done for her for those damn wet-backed, sticky-fingered, whining illegals. I hear she's Ramon's lover and pregnant with his baby." Long pause. He stared at El Lobo, dropped his next bomb. "Or yours." This was all very interesting but the cresting wave of Hood's rage was imminent.

"Whoa, whoa, Globe. Where are you getting this?" Poker face while being tortured, not easy to pull off. He hoped Hood was as dense as usual today. He didn't have a gun on him.

"Isabella told me." Smug grin, like a secret he had on El Lobo. But Lobo knew better.

"Ahh. I see, one of her dreams." He waited for Hood to nod. Flicker of doubt in his eyes.

"The thing about the dream 'gifts' Isabella gives us Hood is that they tap into our own worst fears. She shows us shadows of those things we fear most. Such is the nature of the nightmare, we plant the seeds, she makes them grow. The truth, if a simplified, watered down version, but decidedly less hair-raising."

His hair was already on end. Wondered if it would happen then and there. Hood would die first.

"So that's your answer you god-damned Wolf bastard? The baby is not yours because what Isabella showed me was a product of my own mind, and you've not been fucking my daughter at all?" Red faced, about to burst, explosion of blood and guts imminent. Hood didn't look well.

"Precisely; or you can base the life of your only daughter on a dream you had. A dream planted in your skull by the one woman on this farm that hates you more than life itself. The one woman that would watch you die a slow death and laugh while doing it."

"I think I'll base my decision on this video." Hood pushed the screen on his desk so hard it fell off, shattered on the floor. Still Hood didn't erupt. Started to deflate, red to pink, back to white. Long exhale and drag on his cigar, sipped his scotch.

"I want them dead Lobo." Graham stirred, rearranged his crossed arms.

"Tommy, Tania and Ramon. Is that your test of loyalty Globe?"

"No, the test of loyalty will be Katherine, I know you have a soft spot for her." Dead pan, Globe's eyes gone beady.

"Your own daughter man? Are you mad? You lost it out there on the rig didn't you? Jeezus Globe…"

"I am NOT MAD! And you will kill them ALL!" Globe roared standing from his desk, hairy stomach and chest full of gray hairs standing erect with his decision. Scotch sloshed everywhere.

"Get this through your brain-pan genius, she is a liability and a traitor. She's been impregnated by one of you two Mexican-American assholes, which means she's been laying down with dogs. I'll not have you disgrace this family." He sat again, not at all winded.

"What if she isn't pregnant Globe? What if it is all a trick by Isabella so you will kill what is most dear to you? That would be her type of punishment for a man like you. Anguish and suffering for the rest of your days." It was true, Isabella would prefer to turn the knife and watch Hood die, no bullet from her.

"She's still a traitor and needs to be taken care of." Slammed a ham fist on the table.

"What if I make her disappear, tell you she's dead?"

"She dies Lobo, do you hear what I'm saying? Even if she is carrying your love child you sick bastard. She dies, I don't want her coming after the business when I'm gone. She gets nothing, much less her spic, greasy, Mexican-American mutt of a baby. I will not have some brown skinned, black haired imported kid running my billion dollar business. Her child will get nothing because she will die. Do you understand me? She dies Lobo." El Lobo nodded. It was all coming clear. The ship of good fortune that had been Hood Industries was going down, sinking beneath the waves, save yourselves. Hood was the mad captain cursing the storms that battered his ship against the shoals, going down with the ship, clueless to it all. He'd be surprised when he woke to find himself in Hell.

Chapter 27

Bloody Braille

Hood watched El Lobo's face. He felt like a blind man trying to read Braille on a stone tablet, he got nothing, just bloody fingers. Globe Hood nearly swallowed his tonsils trying to keep his anger in check. The insubordination and dishonor to the Hood name was inexcusable. If he could get the man to pull the trigger on monkey squad and Katherine then Globe would have Graham kill the Wolf. Tie up all the loose ends into a nice little bow. The busty nurse/ masseuse came around the corner, brought him his caviar and crackers, bottom lip ready for sucking. Hood patted her on the ass again, waved her back into the ante room.

"Graham, would you please attend to the little miss? Get her some breakfast or something. The intercom is on the wall next to the phone, just call the kitchen, tell them I'll have the usual, order for yourselves." Graham nodded, left his spot by the window, took the thong wearing little miss into the sitting area and sat her at the bar. Hood could hear them talking faintly and Graham ordering on the phone.

The problem with El Lobo, aside from being as dangerous as a viper in a shaken box, was that he and Globe knew each other too well. Which meant if Hood was thinking about killing El Lobo, then El Lobo was aware of it and maybe doing some plotting of his own. He'd always had the upper hand with his cool, calm, kill you as soon as look at you demeanor, compared to Hood's blood boiling, slam the table, vein popping on his neck, scream and shout intimidation. Which never worked on El Lobo anyway.

"This is all a bit much Hood. What would Lily say to us if she heard this conversation?" As if on command, the man pushed his buttons, blood boiled.

"How dare you mention my wife's name! You know that name is off limits for you Lobo!" Globe's voice sounded strained.

"Because you know she'd disagree with you and take my side or because of our past?" Wolf asked.

"You immigrant bastard, curse on my house! She is too fine, to high above you for her name to cross your dirty lips. She'd agree with me that you and Ramon have crossed the line by seducing our daughter, sullied her name, ruined the Hood legacy. If she found out Katherine was pregnant with your child she'd kill you herself and probably Katherine too. Do you hear me? She would do the same thing I am doing you bastard!" Spittle and rage, pound the table, throw a glass across the room. Hood's vice-like grip on his anger slipped, whipped free with violent force like a fire hose escaped from the hands of firemen. Rage grew like an out of control fire. Spit fire if he could, douse El Lobo, melt him with molten saliva, leave nothing but ash.

"It doesn't work like that Globe." El Lobo didn't seem fazed. Hood wouldn't admit it, but with Graham in the other room he didn't feel nearly so brazen."I'll tell you how it is. Even if you don't want to hear it, that's how it has always been. You swear at me because you are hot-tempered and short sighted enough to kill the messenger. Not because you are a fool but you are wasteful. The most tragic truth. Six-shooter on my hip or not you and I both know I deal with threats and messes. I make your messes go away Globe." Thinly veiled threat, El Lobo made up his mind, or perhaps not.

"I will tell you those things you don't want to hear Globe, as I have always done. You will fume and foam at the mouth but you will listen because you know I speak the truth and no one else will." He stubbed out a cigarette. Moved to the window Graham had opened, lit up another. Globe wanted to waste the man, pull out the pistol in his desk, end it there. Alas he could not, he needed the plan to run its course, assign blame to the corpse.

"We'll go to Hell Lobo de mierda." Hood's Spanish was good if square.

"I'm sure we will Globe." Sigh, rubbed his stubble. "Globe, this is it then. If you are hiring Graham as your enforcer I can discuss details later." The man put his cowboy hat back on, rested his hands on his hips. Globe was suddenly very grateful the man wasn't wearing a six-shooter.

"I'll clean up this mess, this will all look like a series of tragic accidents. We'll talk in a week or two. And keep Graham away from me Globe. I have a hair trigger and fits of paranoia. I don't want him to suffer an accident as well." Tip of the brim, walk out of the room, left the door open.

Globe wanted to scream after him but Graham came around from behind the bar and closed it. Hood considered El Lobo. The wily bastard knew something was up or he wouldn't have threatened Graham. No matter, the game was too far played by now. His mind was already made, this was the best opportunity to clean his hands and his books of one big mess. If he could blame employee sabotage and a disgruntled sociopath of a foreman as the root cause of his misfortune and malpractice everything would be perfect.

Of course the immigrants were to blame, their presence here was to blame, their suckling at his teat of good fortune, they had become spiteful and vindictive. They would provide the most opportune scapegoats for the innocent lives ruined. He almost laughed at the beauty of it, the elegant simplicity with which the pieces had aligned themselves. All the immigrants would pay. El Lobo and Ramon would be examples of what not to become. Fallen son that had flown too close to the sun, too close to Globe Hood and his bright light.

Katherine would be a great loss. He almost cracked when El Lobo mentioned Lily. All the more reason because he knew Lily would have never allowed such a thing, pregnant with a bastard Mexican or not. It was hard to keep Lily on her pedestal with her lover telling him what she would say. With Katherine gone there would be no one to refute his assertions, no one to protect the innocence of the movement members, no one to connect him to El Lobo's violence, no one to highlight worker abuse. She would be missed but he wasn't too old to make another. Gloria wouldn't take it well, he counted on that. He would offer her a severance package so loaded she'd never have to work again, with so much money she'd never be able to spend it all.

If she was smart, and she was, she'd take it and put the last fifteen years of her life down as an investment, a very lucrative investment yielding hundreds of millions of dollars. Not bad for a decade and a half of work. Which if she thought about it had been an excellent opportunity to learn and apprentice under the tutelage of a great business man like Globe Hood.

"Graham." He beckoned the seven-foot body guard over. "Have you eaten?"

"The kitchen just brought up her bacon and eggs. I'm having a bowl of fruit and yogurt. Your steak and eggs are ready too."

'Excellent, bring it over, I've worked up an appetite with that Maldito Lobo. Let's eat Graham, then send the little lady into my room and tell her to wait for me." Graham nodded, crossed the spacious room, footfalls quiet on the thick rugs positioned throughout the room. He returned with a large wooden tray, on it he carried Hood's steak and eggs, fresh coffee press and assorted condiments. He set it on the desk, Globe spoke to him as he did.

"After I'm done with the blond you and I need to talk about preventative measures and our course of action." He eyed the man. No signs of life behind those eyes.

"Yes Mr. Hood."

"That's all Graham, we'll talk after. Tell her to wait in my room after she finishes eating. And while I'm with her keep an eye out for my daughter she should be stopping by soon." Globe had a few questions for Katherine. Graham returned to the bar and his breakfast.

Globe broke his own fast, savory meat, textured and succulent, paired with his over easy eggs and potato rounds. For some reason he couldn't stop thinking about Lily and her horses. She'd loved breeding them, watching the aroused male stuff his oversized member down the mare's backside. She used to screw him mightily during breeding season. She would come home so turned on and hot to trot, literally. If he'd known how things would end up between them he wouldn't have protested so much. What kind of man complains about having to screw his wife, especially one as beautiful, cultured and funny as Lily? Globe Hood was that kind of man. Little Jon was not privy to Globe's new plan, Hood had only just come up with it during a night of very wonderful dreamless sleep. Exhausted and water-logged sleep came for him before Graham finished removing his shoes. Globe woke in the middle of the night asked Graham to procure the blonde, with whom he played for an hour before falling asleep on her large bosoms.

He woke to her naked backside pushed against his groin, spooning after all. There it was, sitting on the night stand, the idea that would solve all his problems. The idea that would assign blame for the sabotage, the oil rig disaster, worker abuse and poisoned food on the questionable character of El Lobo Maldito woke him like the buzzing of an alarm. He would blame every unconscionable act and malicious machination on that immigrant bastard. First he would get the man to do his job as usual and then turn him over to the authorities. Better yet Hood could 'catch' him in the act and defend himself. Shoot first, ask questions later. Lily would approve in hindsight, she was logical enough to see the benefits.

Chapter 28

Safe house

Tania was furious the following morning. Not at Katherine who made breakfast burritos for them but nothing more. She didn't even say goodbye when she walked them out, locked the door with her jangle of keys, walked around the corner to her car, drove away. Tania was not angry with Tommy who had a bad stomach due to nerves and kept making her stop so he could shit.

She was furious with Ramon for insisting she drop him in a forgotten corner of the farm. A large old farm field pressed up against a corner of Hood's property, Ramon's container on the far side of that field, his secondary safe house. She was furious they were on Hood's property seeing as it put them all at risk being wanted criminals and all. He apologized and offered to walk, which threw her into a whole other fit. She scolded him for trying to hide in an open, unheated space, may as well have been running around the fields naked as far as she was concerned. Wasn't beyond the realm of possibilities she reminded him. His brain was still a jumble.

He soothed her from the backseat while she navigated the back streets of the barrio onto a forgotten farm road that led as close to the container as she could get without going off road. He grabbed their shoulders from the back seat, tried to reassure them. He didn't look back once out of the car, shuffled his way into the trees, followed the tree-line to the container. No wheelchair here.

His container was in good order, no animal visitors, no nests. Good news, it was almost winter and he wanted to hole up there for the duration. He felt stronger than he had since the accident, almost back to normal. Strong enough to pull the burn barrel into the middle of the container and position it under a vent he cut out years ago, to watch the stars with Katherine.

The pile was only damp. What he'd piled in the container over the course of the summer was enough to get him through a few days, maybe a week then he'd have to forage.

If he really intended to stay there through the winter he'd have to come up with something more efficient than the burn barrel, more heat was a good thing, he was nearly numb before he got the thing lit. Smoke was his other worry.

It would only take is a few too many wisps of smoke to catch the wrong person's attention. And by wrong person he meant El Lobo. Ramon didn't expect anyone to divine that a fugitive of his importance, as he imagined he would soon be, would hide in such an obvious location as the same farm he'd sabotaged. Unfortunately he'd have to leave to acquire food but at least it would keep during the winter. He had a few extra burritos and some water Katherine had given them but other than that he had a running list in his head of things he'd need soon. It would be a nighttime foray, he would need to layer his clothes if it was too cold. The burritos were wrapped in aluminum foil on the table, he'd warm them over the burn barrel later if he wanted them hot. Worry about it later, now he felt like curling up in his sleeping bag, warm as it was and stare at the inside of his tent.

It felt cozy in there, the swaddle effect, wrapped in the sleeping bag, nested in the tent, tucked in the container. Like a Russian nesting doll. He just wanted to be wrapped and to feel safe. A false sense of security was at least warm and cozy. The creeping despair knew where to find him and would be along soon enough. Where there was a will there was a way. Guerrilla mantra, true to the end. As long as he could lay low long enough for the initial manhunt to wash over the area he should be able to move into the barrio, find an attic apartment or basement. Climb out of the hole he'd dug for himself. That baby should have been his, maybe it was. He could never tell with Katherine. She was an enigma inside a riddle or maybe he was blind and dumb.

***

A clear pond, cool and clear as crystal. Sunshine glittered on the surface, rays dove in. Illuminated little sunfish, tadpoles clustered around the Irises, yellow flowers fertile and beckoning, multiple partners, the more bees the better, beetles, whatever. Reeds gobbled the shallows at the far end, seem to have taken over. Sunlight failed to pierce the brown sediment holding the encroaching roots of the hollow stemmed reed. Small hummock on the far end, horse paddock and some Apple trees. Left the horse so he and Katherine could swim. Bathing suits at first. Lean and fit teenage bodies, alive with summer's flush.

Play some, talk some, lost the suits and played Marco Polo around the pool with his erection leading the way. He peaked a lot, she teased a lot. That was where it finally happened, where they took the virgin status of the other and dashed it against the grassy hammock. They stretched themselves on the back side of the knoll, checker pattern blanket, she allowed him to have his way with her, to make her his or to make him hers. She decided the when and where. He tried for months; romantic ballads, walks in the parks, ice cream and movies and on and on. He decorated the container with candles and roses, she didn't want any. He tried his house when everyone was away for All-saints day, no dice. He tried the same in her room before she got home, his Aunt let him in, still nothing.

As much as he tried and tried, hinted and hoped, ultimately it was she that determined the when, where and how. As it should be. Sunny summer day, naked and wet, throbbing and groaning, pushing and pulling, exploding and living. Days of happiness. No one to witness their act, only her horse and he wasn't impressed. Ramon chased her around the pond all day and she let him into her over and over that day. Golden days of summer. Cool off in the water, lean into soft mud, eat sandwiches, sword-fight with cat-tails, skewered him through the heart, slapped her on the ass. She played with him all day, never sure if she got her fill but suddenly the light was fading, colors becoming ethereal, one last scrum, it was her idea.

She won points for sexy, naked and panting, rode him into the sunset, frogs and toads croaked the evening arrival. Crickets in the woods. She would've worn the pants in their relationship, no question there. She also knew about the container but he doubted she'd think to look there or care enough to. If she really was with child and that child was El Lobo's the farm was going to blow up all over again. Once Hood found out heads would roll and more than likely someone was going to die. Ramon only hoped it wouldn't be him. Cricket in his brain. He hoped the damn bug didn't take up residence in his head again. Instead he listened to the winter breeze push on the container. Covered the burn barrel, crawled into the tent.

Death of the American Dream. His American Dream was gone, burned to ash in the fire, washed away in the flood, blown away in the storm, sunk to the bottom of the sea. His dream bobbed along the bottom of the ocean, congealed ball of petroleum, spewed from exploding oil rig of his hopes. Sunk to the bottom of the Sargasso, darkness and eels, mystery and crushing pressure. So still above, the ocean barely moved, not a breath of wind. But below, squirming in a slimy, writhing, breed ball of eels, thousands of balls, hundreds of thousands of eels writhing around the black ball of burned dreams. God bless the petroleum age.

The mechanized, industrialized blessed present was insidiously innocuous in its illusory belief that things would always be this way. The end of the oil age couldn't come soon enough. Societal disconnect and lack of community cohesion ham-strung a home, a street, a neighborhood. Corporate culture supplants that of our grandparents and great grandparents. The blink of an eye in geological time holds the rise and fall of the oil age. Holds the rise and fall of man. Ramon hoped that the old adage proved true. The adage that equated humans to cockroaches, the individual is weak, the colony is strong. Too bad humanity was too weak to acknowledge the necessity of our communal evolution. Share the work, share the risk.

Neo-capitalist, race you to the top, king of the mountain, cut-throat lust for money left little time for sharing, caring or family. No family, no community, no culture, no humanity and we all become machines. Man becomes brain dead, brainless machines. Struggle every day to put one foot in front of the other. Struggle to get by, struggle to acquire, struggle to keep, struggle to make ends meet. They were all victims of the mad chaos in the world. Drivers behind the wheel, teenage kids with the keys, didn't know where they were going or how to get there. Just followed the directions dad gave them. Perhaps the boomers were just the stupid kid to Uncle Korean War Vet. And trying so hard to please mom and dad who were frugal with their on and off love. Or maybe it was the world that had on and off love. Love for the wealthy, none for the poor. Weather was not malicious, famine was not vindictive but plagues and sufferings delivered by man upon man were.

Imagine being gifted a bag of wild African bees or maybe the keys to the vault. The lights were on and no one was home. We just found it like this. The world, the Earth, the seasons, the wind, the sky, the sun. They did not hate, they did not love, they just shone on the wicked, blew the hat from the head of the just and rained upon the righteous. Born to lead, born to breed, gone to seed. What of the introspection, the philosophical wonder, the probing inquisitiveness? Was it always this way? No! Scream the historians, No! Scream the scientists. Contemplate the station, the hierarchy of birth and death. Born to your station, born to your poverty. Was it at all possible to scrimp and save, claw his way to happiness? Claw his way to the American Dream, take it while he could get it or rather rip it from Hood's cold dead hands. That sounded better. Perhaps the colloquialism was correct. The haves were the takers, the have-nots were the chaff and chattel, the teeming refuse that simply failed to realize there was no prize for second place. If one wanted something, he had to take it with his own hands. Take whatever it was, from whomever had it, otherwise you got nothing.

The world turns, orbits the sun, rockets through the vacuum of space, spiral arm of the galaxy, back wood, out of the way blue rock. Thank the heavens humanity was still limited to the one planet. Spreading the cancerous form of civilization through the galaxy seemed self-centered. Have pity on the have-nots, were there celestial have-nots? Poor alien planets at the mercy of the takers. Would be if mankind ever made it off the planet. Rue the day.

He, Ramon Malquiades Mondragon as a resident of the third planet from the sun did then and there swear to dedicate what remained of his days to the enlightenment and education of the humans that resided there. He would put into perspective, the destructive, resource depleting, amoral, habitat destroying activities undertaken by man. Habitat destruction, not the Wolf habitat, not the coyote habitat but with ever increasing pressure placed on the planet, it was the human habitat that was in very real jeopardy. Denied by the naysayers, ignorant and illiterate, they couldn't read the writing on the wall.

Why? Throughout human evolution, the harbingers of doom, the prophets of human destiny have been ostracized, victimized, run out of town. Is the truth so very painful to hear? Realistically the haves don't want the drones to know. Ant in a hill, follow the orders they're given, do what they're told, for the good of the colony, for the good of the hive mind. The greatest percentage of heterotrophic biomass on the face of the planet was probably ants. More mass in ants than in humans, cockroaches, whales, birds, you name it. Hive mind must be working, they were doing something right.

Cosmic joke, evolutionary disconnect. Humanity had no hive mind, no tail to move, no pheromones to signal danger or food. No telepathy. Humans produced pheromones to communicate with each other but it was not so simple as all that. Unfortunately two thirds of the human experience could be summed up by the statement 'it's complicated'. For a species that worked best in groups, to survive, conquer, invent, and innovate. The human ego was the greatest weakness.

Maximize individual fitness through group fitness or rather the other way around. The more of us that survive the more of me that survives, genetic material anyway. Humanity is a species for which communal endeavor is a necessity for survival. Unfortunately the mental disconnect and lack of evolutionary device by which we could communicate instantaneously through gray matter of brain, chemical signals excreted by glands, required humanity to develop language. A more fraught, convoluted and erroneous method for conveyance of thought, desire and feeling has yet to evolve. Miss communication was fickle and mumbled when she spoke, made what she said hard to understand.

Boundaries defined, boundaries sublime. The boundaries of a system define it. He merely needed to determine the boundary of his American Dream. The limits of which were determined by his willingness to go out and take what he needed. That is what he'd been told, raised on, weaned with. There is no boundary other than the desire that burns within. Rules of the game, rules of the system. Each system presented a new set of rules, new set of requirements to maintain order, keep entropy at bay. Perhaps no amount of analytical iteration, systematic dismantling would reveal the answer.

The seed of truth, the yea or nay of the American Dream. Was it that only by clawing, pulling oneself, hand over hand, step on the shoulders of, trample those in the way, climb the tallest mountain of human bodies, could one hope to achieve the pinnacle, the acme, the apex of that ethereal utopian ideal that was the American Dream? Yes it was, and once there, bask in the light and glory of the realized dream. Only then will the light illuminate, only then can the masses see what true success is. They would succor at the sole of his travel worn boots, thank him for being the man he was, for the deeds he'd done, for the accomplishments he'd made, for stepping on their heads to reach the top. Ants working for the Queen because they were told to, for the good of the colony. Work for the Queen, the honor is yours. The good of the many over the good of the few.

Always looked good on paper. Goodbye to the Queen, goodbye to those he loved and lost, his fate was sealed. Gypsy wanderer, homeless box car companion. Shoot for the stars, be a winner, think positive, the cause was alive as long as he kept his hopes alive, kept himself alive. He was glad to be alive. Seldom were the little things, the moments between moments, lost and forgotten spaces of time, appreciated for their value. Such was the appreciation of the Greatest generation. Glad to be alive, the men took their women, women took their men to bed. A whole nation fornicating like sex starved rabbits. Hard to believe they were the same demographic group that made sleeping in separate beds so popular. Gestational bonanza, the streets must have been filled with the pregnant women of America. Obstetrics and Gynecology were probably invented to deal with the massive influx of semen filled women, milky goo absorbed, sucked into their wombs, fill 'er up boys.

And so they were born, the offspring destined to become the Baby Boomers, fruit of gyrating, thrusting, long-lost and found again loins of the Greatest Generation. Big shoes to fill. Smoke billows from smoke stacks, rivers on fire, hunger ravaged, innocents died. Key to the lock, skeleton key, the one that would open any door, every door. That's what he needed, a key to wealth, a key to Katherine's heart, a key to the masses. A key to a paradigm shift, ride the tide, what he needed was a Tsunami.

Fukushima, Chernobyl type disaster, scare the shit out of everyone, leave no room for maybe. Too much, too much death. Crickets on the brain. Hundreds of dead crickets. Grandma echoed in his brain. Cold sweat down his spine. Goosebumps across the skin, hair on the back of his neck has something to say. Rubbed his head and ran through the guerrilla routine, calm the nerves. Nothing to find but he checked anyway. No bugs, no listening devices, plenty of real bugs. Millipedes, centipedes, daddy long-legs, mites, mosquitoes, all hiding in a layer of leaf litter collected in the corner, cobwebs above. Crickets too. A black one with white stripes, hop away when he flipped the detritus.

Detritus of the Earth, detritus of the cosmos. Wandering rocks collide and burn, explosions of gas, burning mayhem. Molten rivers ripple across rock landscape. Cool and slow, box of rain, drench forever. Forty thousand years of rain. Oceans of boiling hydrogen bonded to oxygen, infected with bacterium. One hell of an infection, watch it grow. We are all the oozing, seeping pus of the infected Earth. Detritus, microcosm of the larger system. Repeat and behold, this side, that side, the middle. Hair sprouting on his arm, new hair, thick hair, strange electrons circle the atoms, proton and neutron, planet circles the sun. Round and round they spin, was it clockwise or counter-clockwise. Couldn't remember. Damn, according to his arm, he was becoming the Wolf man, counter clockwise.

Maybe if he sent everything he had home to Mexico. His parents' home, where his parents were. Resurrect the American Dream in Jalisco or Vera Cruz, Cancun or Oaxaca. Send his remittances home but how to empty his accounts, make sure they weren't frozen, it was probably already too late. He should've had Tommy do it before things went this badly awry. Instead he'd spend the winter freezing off his short hairs in an old shipping container while the rest of the masses were ensconced and comfortable in mansions, ranch house, trailer, cape cod, Victorian classic, cozy domiciles. Gas heater, oil heater, hot water heater in the basement, the attic, in the crawl space. Forced air tempers the bite in the air, protects the soft skin, coddles the cockles. Baby Boomers stormed the ramparts in their youth, cracked heads, burned bras, kiss don't tell, flower down the barrel of a gun. Sniff coke in their thirties, bad clothes, bad hair, chase the bull around the market, don't loan your savings.

Lulled and pacified in their forties and fifties, now complacent and dormant. Soft on the outside, softer in the middle, don't poke too hard, you'll pop them like a jelly doughnut all over your hands. Small wonder no one saw it coming or read the writing on the bathroom stall. Never mind the musicians, poets, writers, scholars, and artists screaming to any and all who would listen. Stormed the ramparts and went home bloodied and bruised, deadened, anesthetized and amnesiatic.

Forgotten were the ideals held so dearly, touted and brandished like a shield, like a badge, like a banner. Forgotten why they stormed in the first place. Sacrificial flag burning long forgotten they were dazed and confused, addled before the Alzheimer's had even been diagnosed. They'd burnt their own flag, the one with NO in large letters; the one with peace signs, the banners that proclaimed their rebellion in loud letters. The burning flag they planted on top of the mountain, claimed the land for the Boomers, no longer belongs to the Greatest, this is now ours. For the sake of the children, for the sake of the future.

Ever so quietly, little by little, one grain of sand at a time, day by day, baby steps but now they were everywhere. Big brother was everywhere, on your phone, in the airport, on the worldwide networks, on the street corner, on every screen you looked at every day of your life. Now they were all like sanatorium inmates, strapped to a bed, pumped full of drugs, not aware of what was being done to them. Every twitch measured, every tear counted, keystroke search term. Red flag words and phrases, keep an eye on us all. Crickets on the brain. Tired, Ramon was so tired, sleep didn't sound like a bad idea, he hadn't slept well at Katherine's, too much time staring at the ceiling. Crickets on the brain better than creeping up his spine.

He slept. Giant crickets nibbled on long gas cylinders, green metal bent and ripped, explosion of lime green gas enveloped Ramon and the world. He screamed for forgiveness. Opened box after box, ripped off the tops, clawed madly through cricket corpses for something. The crickets were fried and seasoned, crisp and crunchy. Nothing else though. Hood stood above him, gigantic, chortling, hands on hips, completely ablaze, face hidden in shadow, back-lit by orange flames.

He laughed, asked Ramon over and over if he found it. Every time Ramon opened a box Hood asked and every time the answer was no and Hood would laugh again. Ramon was digging, shovel in his hands, soil walls stretching upward around him. He stood in a hole, what appeared to be a grave, probably his own. El Lobo stood above, told him to keep digging, started dumping soil on top of Ramon. No laughter, only a fat cigar billowing smoke and blood red eyes. Soil fell atop Ramon, into his eyes, into his mouth, down his throat, choke him to death. Grave walls crumbled and collapsed on top of him.

Katherine and Isabella at his trial. He is dead and gone but still being tried for crimes committed during his reign of terror. The stands are filled with faceless bodies. A wolf pup in the arms of Katherine, she nurses the dark haired, razor-toothed monster with a smooth skinned breast. The wolf mews and yips when she removes the breast, she puts it back. The pup whines with contented bliss, mother coos to her babe. Isa and Kate take the stand, they both sell him up the river. The crowd in the stands roars, the judge bangs his gavel. El Lobo and Hood at the prosecutors table. Hood is laughing so hard he's crying, still aflame. El Lobo puffed his cigar contentedly as well, hands behind his head reclined in the chair with his feet up blowing smoke rings at the ceiling. Katherine and Isabella sat by his side after they testified.

A bitter cool breeze and his grave. A statue of a goat, chewing grass by the looks of it. The plaque read:

"Ramon Malquiades Mondragon. Gone but not forgotten. The path to Hell is paved with good intentions."

Crickets chirped him into darkness. Only place big brother couldn't watch. Yet.

Chapter 29

Witch's Broom

Big Bad submitted, yield to the will of the cosmic 10,000 things. Through submission hope springs eternal. Embraced the futility of his desire and the burning embers of lust in his loins. Replace them with concern for Katherine and the task at hand. Hood's madness was like a boulder rolling downhill, someone was going to get crushed, lose their head. Submit and accept, she may be his, one day, or not. Strength through submission. The fact that Hood wanted him to kill Katherine was preposterous and mad as hell. The police might overlook a half-dozen missing illegals but the heiress to a billion dollar fortune, sexy and involved in a sex triangle to boot, would have the local cops crawling all over the farm. They would be inundated with national media in a heartbeat and the feds would take an even closer look at Hood Industries. Unless Hood blamed El Lobo for everything. It was the best solution by far.

Figurative, symbolic, one must not deny the connection between submission, acceptance, transcendence, life, death and sex. Transcendence while riding the waves of spent sexual energy felt like heaven. Lobo took the reins of his burning desire, decapitated himself, exhaled, confronted placed obstacle, removed it, smash the boulder, human, blood, flesh, head. So Big Bad, El Lobo Maldito, sighed, a powerful, noisy thing that would've blown down any house made of straw, sticks or bricks. Winter in the air, the service roads across the Hood farm were all frozen ruts and mud this far into the freeze. Cold breeze pried at the tin roofs of the homes in the barrio, wear hat and gloves when visiting.

Tethered to hope Mr. Wolf floated down the stream of life, how to handle Hood and his mad request. The man would turn it around on El Lobo, all of it, everything, the rebellion and sabotage, he was certain. Rutted dirt road one day, forested path another, valley of death soon too. Though he did more ushering into that valley of death than guiding through. Book of the dead. Hope bobs along behind.

Slow stream runs and pools, meander and dawdle, safe in his wooden boat, work shoes or pawed feet. Life preserver of Hope, above then below the surface, ever present, not always visible. Relinquish the hand that would dare direct fate. Hope, like vibrations, rippled outwards from his boat, from his footstep, rippled the surface of the waters of life. Explosion of desire, explosion of flesh amongst fur and fern, nestled in a hollow. Ejaculated into fertile earth, fed fertility goddess with their gyrating bodies. Her severed head drips blood, red wine from the corner of their mouths. Nourished in delight, their lust brings life, feeds on death, decay. Interconnected oneness of yin and yang, he meets she, his semen, her egg, blood of the goddess. If Katherine was pregnant it could be his. Their encounter was some months past, she would be in the second trimester at least. Her propensity for baggy shirts and cloaks played in her favor.

Taste of her lips, sweet scented lips slowly fading from his memory. A fact that bothered El Lobo to no end. He wondered if Hood smelled the lie, noticed the change of subject, the dance around the question. It wasn't that he couldn't recall how firm her hips were or how good she tasted. Recall was one thing, touch and taste were another thing altogether. At first, after, he could still feel her lips against his whiskers, he could still taste the flowery bouquet of her sweet nectar. He had half a mind to kiss her again and again, to refresh the feeling of her lips against his.

Go with God as it were, submit to God's will, some would have said. El Lobo knew better, the push and pull of life's tide was not on a twelve hour cycle, as the ocean's. It was difficult to submit to a will other than his own. His own will would have him lay with Miss Hood again, that their loins might feed the beheaded fertility goddess with their sex, life and death. Harness the sexual delight and with it, transcend life, death and existence. Reborn again. He and she, they. Submit to the cosmic will, yield to the lord of obstacles. To place or remove whichever obstacle the elephant headed deity deemed necessary.

Submitted to his need for Miss Hood, transcendental stretch through his flesh into his psycho-spiritual dogma and joined him with the essence of the everything, the nothing. Relent, broken steed. Enlightened he was or rather longed to be. Black soil sticks to the sole of rubber rain boots. Red and pink trim with ladybug decals moving across the calf, shin and toes of her boots.

Isabella told him that morning, told him she knew he was fond of another woman and perhaps she should rip the young woman's throat out the next time they met at the cantina. Leave her jugular and blood sprayed across red and white checkered tablecloth. Fill in the white spaces with blood, make the color uniform across the table. He didn't like the image. Little did Isabella know that he would never let such thing happen. In fact he would defend Miss Hood with his own life if necessary, even from Isa. Black soil covers wooden table top, the murmur of morning voices as she packed seeds into germination trays, ready to grow skyward under fluorescent lights. Apical meristems to reach for the heavens. He was sure she was headed to see Hood that morning, his first morning back since his brush with death. Perhaps she was calming nerves, she liked having her hands in the dirt. She watched him walk through the greenhouse and into his office. He watched her watching him.

Oscillation between selfish and selfless; the plague, the infirmity of El Lobo's desire. Yesterday he wouldn't dare force himself on the beautiful Miss Hood, wouldn't risk destroying her life and all those surrounding them. Today however, he bit his tongue to keep from answering Isabella's assertion with an emphatic response in the affirmative. Fond was far too weak of a word for his affection for the damsel. His predator heart was singed, licked by the fiery tongue of passion's molten flame. Set ablaze by porcelain smooth, cream-colored skin, floral scented flesh spiced with cinnamon, oscillation to and fro. Black soil under nails, impossible to get all the dirt out. Like thoughts the grains of soil insert themselves into every nook, cranny and every in between space that was and wasn't.

Spades ply the soil, fingers release seeds, nestled within fertile blackness, provides sustenance. Fertile soil, fertile womb. Sowing seeds for the future. Workers, animal and human alike, preparing for the spring, on the far side of winter, not even winter solstice yet. In Spring the Earth will be waiting to precipitate, percolate, saturate and drink deeply all over again. Miss Hood's fertility was never in question, but perhaps a small bump did decorate her abdomen, stretching her tummy away from her hips. El Lobo wouldn't have noticed but out there with the workers packing seedling trays Senora Arias was practically been in tears with joy for the sweet young thing and making an enormous fuss.

El Lobo wondered if the paternity was contested between him, the Hunter lad and Ramon. He nearly bit the closest thing to him which was a young sheepish boy bringing his coffee who wouldn't have deserved the bloodshed visited upon him. Black soil indeed. Already beheaded El Lobo Maldito submitted. As much as he would rather rail, rage, scream shout and force himself into the young woman's life. That would be a horrible mistake. Let her go, see if she returns, maybe yes, maybe no, perhaps she'd fall in love with a better man than he. Isn't that the way it was supposed to work. Give her up, let her be free, afflict her not with his perversions and desires. Oscillations are troublesome. Held his head in his hands, El Lobo struggled to transcend such trivial concerns. The want, the need, the desire. Submit, transcend, obstruct, flow freely. To wish, to want, to be wise, to be a fool.

Drunken Monk once again, El Lobo fell head first into a bottle of wine, Cabernet Sauvignon, pulled from the cabinet. No work getting done today. Howl at the moon. Enlightened, transcended, on his way indeed. The fact that she had feelings for someone else was almost too much to bear. Who the Hell was so and so anyway. Certainly not the skinny pale-skinned Hunter boy by the looks of things. Maybe it was Ramon, her buddy who knew her the better than anyone. Give it up Wolf, your lot is chosen, no crying, no joy now. Or is there? See red, veins pulsed in time with crying heart,

He nearly said something to the young lass about her maternal glow but it was not his place, he seethed in silence.

As the rooster crows, she may have been the opaque one but he was the beheaded. He refused to think about it, in vain, let her go, held his head in his hands, ripped his heart out. At long last he understood. The beheaded one transcends life, death, desire, ignorance and all that traps us here in the circle of flesh and life. Beheaded such that he might be free of said weaknesses that wracked his soul. The paradox therein remained. His beheaded state carried him beyond desire, sustenance gained from copulation with Miss Hood seemed beyond his reach. Smelled the coming snow on the wind, taste it in the bitter bite of the cold. Voices and choices, back and forth, tickle the whispers. Chitter-chatter behind closed doors. This side, that side, the middle. True lesson of the beheaded not easy to live by. Lotus blossom, birth and death, fertilize and decay.

One day, one way, come and go, came and went. OM mani pae mae hung. Comes and goes, ebbs and flows, the power of the mind, throw himself off the precipice of desire. Absorb energy, strength leads to enlightenment, one would hope. He saw her again, wayward oasis for the fervent soul. Feed he on desire, feed he on need. Feed the Canis soul with howl at the moon. Please all of your women, not just the one you love. Om mani pae mae hung. Silence the soul of the wolf. The ebb and the flow and here we go. El Lobo ignored the pain in his heart, Chinnamunda, Ganesh and the Buddha blessings. They are he, he can see but for the tears in his heart. He was uncertain he could avert the destruction, dissolution, digestion of the marital bands that bound him like a madman in a strait jacket. Bleeding wounds leave red drops on wooden floor. Like a bitch in heat, sangria colored droplets leak from beast's chest. Wear Red and don't think of the girl for goodness sakes. Plant your seeds, turn the soil, smell the flowers. Damn those flowers.

Purgatory, the in between, neither here nor there, not really anywhere, not a where flesh and bone could understand anyway. Feels right, why? Why does the forbidden resonate through fiber, muscle and bone of being? Where had she gone? Transparent, opaque, let her be, lotus blossom, her scent on the breeze. Evening fell clear and cold, soothed the burning skin. Caressing breeze are his fingertips. Bothersome fly whispered his sweet nothings in her ear. El Lobo struggled to shed attachment, escape the predicament he'd put himself in. So she became the passing breeze, the phases of the moon to his rising tide. He could still visit her, locked in a secret corner of his psyche, sequester her in his heart. Bound and gagged like a hostage, he would allow no quarter, lest she should wriggle free and oh did he love it when she wriggled, naked rump pressed against his pelvis.

Thus he was free, free of wont, free of desire. A tepid, blond, tasteless existence, akin to eating unseasoned bean curd, day in and day out. Most difficult for a carnivore such as El Lobo Maldito but food was food. Sustenance for the flesh is not always sustenance for the heart. Soul of fire, spirit of the forest, howl at the moon. He couldn't begrudge her suitors, she was beautiful, so beautiful it hurt his eyes.

They were more age appropriate than El Lobo, nor were they crushed under the burdens of familial obligation or indebted to the patron Mr. Hood. The kind of heavy load that would crush her hopes and dreams before she had a chance to fly. Lost her, found her and lost her again. Away she wings from the now and here. Someday to alight anew on the perch of sublime scents and savors. Mind-body connection draws forth the power of mind over matter. Never mind her matter, he'd never touch it again anyway. Lick the freckle right off her face. So tasty, so lovely, so long love. See her when? Maybe never. So sad. Get to work you damn wolf, soil to till, people to kill, tasks to fulfill.

Isabella stalked his dreams, El Lobo struggled weakly to fight off unseen foe. Arms heavy, strikes weak, he moved slowly like through water. Unseen foe blocked, avoided and thrashed El Lobo soundly. Futile. Try as he might, strength failed him. Time as an idea, a construct of the mind. When the truth, the culmination of the past, present, and future. Everything you were, are and ever will be.

To be sure she is his already, soon will be, who is she? She straddles he, nurses he, her pink nipples erect, between teeth, enamel vs. flesh. Red hair tickles nose, chestnut eyes twinkle. Rough palm, phallus, push, pull and away we go. Two no longer, but one. She is his already, will be someday, already was. Roadblock created, roadblock imagined. Shuffle feet, scratch head, worry and fret, off the cuff, go,go,go. The power of an idea, power of the idea of ideas. Hammer and stone, boulder begone. Ebb and flow, rock dust in the current. Whether it be she or we, go or flow, paddle with the current, swim across the stream, take us here to there. The longest night of the year cometh, without her. Turn over new leaf.

Some of the workers suspected the nature of his dilemma. The dilemma he thought so carefully absconded, ensconced, behind teeth and visage. But some took note. The fawn and doe, the young buck too. All seemed to sense something was missing. A spring in his step, twinkle in his eye. Missing. They no longer feared. Winter would soon settle around the shoulders, frosty scarf of snow flake and icicle. Snow flake on the tongue tastes sweet. Sooner than later. Where did he lose the spring that belonged in his step?

He'd lost something, the sparkle, the shine, the bottomless well of possibility seemed shallow. Belay, lower he down into the murky darkness of her nether regions. Smell her must, her stink, nooks and crannies. Lick her ass, sphincter tight around tongue, red life savor, so sweet. She would be his. A certainty, a given, a fact, who, how, when, he couldn't say. It just was. Lost a step, lost a sparkle. What is the matter with you? Asked fair eyed doe, dark black eyes and hair as straight and smooth as could be. She was a gardener, sometimes transporter, not a coyote or a movement member.

Dream a little dream. Isabella stalked him for sure, he no longer cared. Little Red tip-toe into the ethereal gossamer of his dreams. Cotton rubs and grinds, straddled around his waist, her skin pressed against his. Tight bottom cupped in brown hands, pulled her to him, rubbed cottony veil against phallus. Pulse and throb, climb into her nether regions if he could. Kiss and grind against him she did. Moan in his mouth, mew against his cheek. Still felt the space between labia, cottony warmth, snatch moist and musty. Needs, needs. Kiss he, she. Her hands, back of his neck. Milky skin, made her his, soon, never.

Three days into the week he'd requested of Hood. Torturous, soul-searching meditative days and he decided it was time to pay a visit to the movement leader or ex-leader, and he knew right where Ramon was. Faded blue shipping container, almost gray after years of sun and rain. Late in the season, the twining vines that covered the opening gone skeletal and no longer much of a deterrent to the wind and prying eyes. He'd stopped by the monkey squad hideout. Nice digs, thoroughly abandoned, already fixed up nice. He thought he might buy the place from Hood Industries if it didn't become part of the investigation. Fat chance that. Hip, cosmopolitan apartments and contemporary design, he'd make a killing on the warehouse space and the added amenities.

He could probably buy it for a song considering neither Hood nor Gloria knew what had been done. No one there but the place was so nice he spent one of his long troubled nights in the place. Slept in someone's bed, still smelled female and sexy. Played some music, video games, drank espresso. He woke the next morning, went to Carmen's house. Ramon's Aunt. Her daughters agreed that they'd seen Ramon with Tommy and Tania a few nights past. They'd stayed at Katherine's for the night but were gone in the morning by the time everyone arrived for work. Katherine asked them to open the store as she was visiting her father. After that they hadn't heard anything. Rumor had it Tommy and Tania were out of town but that Ramon had been spotted in the barrio and skulking around the reconstructed warehouse. He wasn't using his crutches anymore but he still had crazy eyes and was talking to himself.

His cousins looked worried. They asked if Ramon was going to die. El Lobo gave his usual cryptic response to that type of question.

"We're all going to die someday..." Back to the truck.

Ramon wasn't in the barrio, not yet anyway. Single story craftsman style houses, scattered haphazardly between rutted dirt roads and sporadic patch of grass. Many lost dogs, matted fur, wandered in twos and threes. At least they weren't wandering in packs, mauling people. The residents of the barrio weren't skittish of the dogs, only outsiders were. Crumbling adobe walls, exposed brick, tin roof, garbage fills the roadside ditches, chicken crosses the road, rabbit hippity-hops, ducks waddle to dirty green pools, bathe themselves. The barrio was more like a third world country than some third world countries.

El Lobo had a few informants. Carmen's family turned on Ramon once they learned he was behind the food contamination issue. Seemed Katherine informed the members of the movement during her one on one meetings and they in turn disseminated the information to the barrio. Ramon would find a place to stay in someone's storage shed or empty room but he would find slim pickings for new recruits. The old movement members were keeping their heads down, thankful Katherine had the money to pay them. Globe Hood remained unwilling. They hoped and so did he, that Katherine could negotiate a deal with Globe and assist those that needed it with legal representation, limit the deportations and/or jail-time.

A few crotchety old-timers informed him of the goings-on in the barrio. Every neighborhood had one. The type of old man that hated the young and their attempt to change the world; hated the passion of youth and the rage at the machine that went along with it. Bitter old men felt things had always been a certain way and should continue to be that way, forever. Damn kids. Sour old bastards were good sources of information, the biggest gossips of all. Those men knew most of what went on in the barrio, who was in trouble, who was cheating on who, and with whom. The old men were bitter by age, circumstance, disposition, or a combination of the three. El Lobo used them often, but with a grain of salt. They required payment in booze, preferably liquor, the stronger the better.

Threatening said ancients with bodily harm proved ineffective as they were old enough that death did not frighten, in fact it offered relief. Sometimes the old codgers were sources of info but more often than not distaste and distemper colored perception, added bias to the recount of witnessed occurrence. Tainted any information with shades of Hell's spawn, fiery brimstone and eternal damnation. Not to mention sometimes the more alcoholic of them fabricated tales for free booze, a type of compensation so coveted by the old men.

Farm fields, rutted roads, worst management practices on this farm. No way Globe Hood would waste money on best management practices. Didn't matter if it saved Hood money in the long run, in the short run, in any run. Forget tax breaks and increased subsidies from the federal government. Didn't matter to Hood, it represented too much benevolence, too much admission that in some way his actions were negative. Too much like a bleeding heart, tree hugging environmentalist. Never mind it would increase operational efficiency, production and protect his resources.

Across the farm field, dead asters, milkweed, thistle. Brown to gray, stems blown over in the wind. Forty foot long shipping container, far back, had to walk five hundred meters just to see the thing. Scrub buckthorn, honeysuckle, holly pressed against metal sides. Pine, oak scrub behind, thicker and more dense. Ramon was acting the fool. Obviously doing little if anything to conceal his presence around the container. Seen from the air there was probably a spiral sunburst radiating from the container. Ramon must've trampled in every direction in search of firewood, wandering trails all over the meadow. El Lobo watched through binoculars, crouched in a thicket of honeysuckle, windbreak or a weed, it didn't matter. No sign of movement, make a move, he approached slowly, he hadn't decided whether he would kill this insolent fool yet, or just get rid of him, stuff him in the truck, take him to Mexico or somewhere far away.

Walked around the back side, someone had hollowed out a small hole in the ground, ashes and carbon covered grate suggested cooking. Peak past the skeletal vines and forgotten lattice into the container, burn barrel in the center, flames licked up and out. So Ramon was close and would be back shortly or so said the barrel. The sunlight managed to penetrate the first ten meters of the container. Sitting table and chairs, trash can, burn barrel were all clearly visible, beyond that a curtain of darkness, lifted by stepping into, irises dilate. Yellow tent in the back corner, faintly visible, rain fly catches the eye. A screened corner opposite, another burn barrel between, privacy curtain hung by Ramon. Probably the Jon. At least it was cold enough to freeze any waste.

A few milk crates, stuffed with non-perishables, canned everything. Several more grates hanging on the wall above. Aluminum foil on the table. Burn barrel positioned beneath a small square vent in the ceiling, hinges on it and a pole on a rope to open and close. Front vent was open, sunlight streamed through. Back vent was closed and only a thin sliver of sunlight passed through, thin line on the back wall. Seemed Ramon had begun stocking up, overwinter in the container perhaps. Lobo admitted it was not the worst hiding place, if done correctly. Sometimes hiding out in the open was the best place. Ramon was making a mess of it, so much for his guerrilla training, he seemed to have forgotten it all. Same thing happened to El Che. He didn't follow his own rules. Maybe Ramon hadn't been the brains behind the movement after all. Or like Che without Fidel, he was lost in the woods, stuck in a valley with enemy forces shooting down on him. Sold out by the locals.

Ramon would give himself away and end up captured even if El Lobo was not the one finding him. The paths that he left around the container were worn, he was using too many, and too obvious. He'd begun to pile scrub around the container in an effort to further conceal it. Another good idea, save for the fact that the container was already half concealed by shrubbery.

The additional piles looked odd, more like bushels for burning than for concealment. The piles called more attention to the container rather than less. It was he, El Lobo that placed the container there in the first place, a particularly horrific scene with a coyote piece of shit. The man showed up on the farm with the container full of illegals, forty six to be exact. They were all dead. Dead of asphyxiation, dehydration, panic and fear. Screaming for deliverance, cooked to death on the interstate in the hot summer sun. Oh the barbarity. El Lobo shot the man as soon as the Coyote opened the container. He always made the Coyotes open their own containers, he didn't trust what they would do behind his back. The stink was already rank when he opened the door. The miserable bastard didn't even have the decency to look guilty. El Lobo shot him in the face. Buried every last one of them in the field, sent letters to the families of the ones he could identify. Cleaned the container with industrial solvents, dropped it on the back corner, never used and mostly forgotten acreage of the Hood farm. He tucked it into the oak and pine, let it rust and corrode into the ground, tomb of the unknown immigrant. They'd never grown anything back there as long as he could remember and they wouldn't grow anything there as long as he was in charge.

Crunch of leaves, scrum of bramble and clatter of wood against wood outside the container. El Lobo made his way out, slow and steady. The fool was definitely not laying low during the daylight hours. Instead he was walking around the container, large witch's broom lit and smoking. Ramon waved the branch up and down, back and forth like a smudge stick of sage. He waved the thing like a mad man. Might as well send smoke signals to the barrio. El Lobo watched Ramon and his antics for a few minutes, peaked around the edge of the container, hid in the shadowy interior. Ramon hopped up and down, waved the witch's broom, a spruce branch, burning embers on the breeze, be lucky if he didn't set the whole field on fire. Good thing it was frozen. Plumes of smoke curled around Ramon's clothes and up around the container. He was speaking to himself. El Lobo exited the container, walked toward Ramon. Would the young lad scream and shout, or would he submit to death and darkness willingly. Hard to tell with a madman.

Hopes and dreams, ways and means, frozen fingers of the wind traced up his back. Wind across the old farm field, flattened plants evidence of gusty breeze, and Ramon's wander. Jackpot. Game over. He stopped a short distance away, called to Ramon.

"Oye,...orale, Ramon." The man continued his mumbling and chanting. El Lobo stepped close, grabbed Ramon by the shoulder, raised an arm to parry Ramon, wielded the burning branch with his madman stupor.

"Oh, it's you." Ramon was scruffy and a little bedraggled. He wore a brown poncho on top of his clothing, he needed it in the cold. Needed a shower. Would be a long winter for him if El Lobo didn't do the job.

"Yes, it's me." Let go of Ramon's arm.

"Help me secure this place from the bad spirits Don Lobo, I know a man of your stature and renown can understand the need to secure my stronghold from ill-intentioned, maladjusted attackers. I aim to fortify my base from prying eyes and worried intention, so that I might regroup, recover and regain my former glory." Ramon didn't take a breath the whole time, he may have already lost it.

"Are you pretending to be loco so I don't kill you Ramon?"

"I'm no more mad than you a killer." The statement didn't make sense, Ramon knew El Lobo was a killer. The boy was half-mad.

"What are you doing Ramon? If you're not turning yourself in, what are you doing?"

"I am fortifying my winter encampment from bad intention and evil doers." He waved the branch weakly, it was extinguished, needed to be re-lit. "There are evil spirits that wish to do me harm my good man and if you should have patience, your job will surely be done. They cannot confine me, but the darkness comes for me. It creeps through everything, from below, pulls me down." He high stepped in the tall weeds like the ground was tacky and sticking to his feet. Marching band leader.

"You're a fool Ramon and a dead man. I'm sorry but I'm done playing with you. This has to end, here and now."

"And it will my dear teacher, my mentor and finally, my enemy, it will end here. You have been bewitched my friend, lost to the darkness that leaks from this place. Your blossomed footsteps no longer sprout hyacinth and jasmine, lily of the valley or lotus. Skunk cabbage and sulfurous mud boil spew refuse in your wake now. You pervert the beautiful and lay waste to hope." Swung the branch, caught El Lobo on raised arms. Branches splintered and broke, Ramon stepped back but didn't retreat.

"Are you talking about Katherine Ramon?" The branch knocked the hat from his head and onto the ground, a piece of branch through the brim. El Lobo stepped forward to close the space between them but Ramon backpedaled, wouldn't let him get too close.

"Of course I speak of my beloved, the innocent damsel, queen of my heart and governess of my will. She that you have bewitched and defiled, soiled and discarded. But alas her beauty is so pure, her goodness so great that even your blackened mark slides from her grace. Radiance so bright she blinds you to her truth. You are not fit to be her mate, you are spoken for, you have a witch of your own."

"Boy Ramon, you sure lay it on thick. I'm beginning to believe your act, you may really be mad." He wanted a cigar to chew on, fished in his pocket, nothing. Left it in the truck.

"Not mad alas, but heartbroken, a poor dejected fool, that I do not deny. But victim and passenger on that ship named torrid affair, the ship of life. To every good there is a bad, to every light there is a dark." The kid was off the deep end, treading water, doing a backstroke in a soup of bat shit crazy and forget me-nots. Maybe he could knock the thoroughly disturbed man out and get him to a hospital, call the cops, have them take care of it.

He was so far gone any information he had on Hood would be disregarded as the ravings of a madman.

"And I am the darkness to her light, is that what you are saying?" He couldn't help but ask. "And why do you say this Ramon?"

"I say this because you have been chosen, she chooses instead to shine her light on you, gift of her garden to you so that you may picnic on the soft earth of her flesh, divine the source of her pleasure, breathe deep the scents of her womanhood. She has already decided to gift her fertile pasture and willing limbs to you. She chooses to wrap her luminance in the shroud, the black cloak of your soul. You are the beast that will devour her, that has devoured her and has claim to her heart. You black souled beast with eyes as black as your heart. I only hope her child does not possess your cruel nature and sharp fangs." Boom goes the dynamite. Gong in his head, blurred vision. Ramon bashed him in the head with what remained of the branch, brown poncho ducking around the corner and into the container. Hear his footfalls, clang of rubber soles against the metal hull. Maybe not completely mad.

El Lobo followed, couldn't quite see to the back, too much shadow. Seriously hoped Ramon didn't throw the shit bucket at him. Ruin everyone's day that would. Ramon rushed out of the darkness, chair held high, attempt to bash El Lobo's skull in. El Lobo put a foot in his chest and sent him flying the length of the container, felt bad immediately, caught the chair as it fell. Ramon was once wiry and strong, since his accident he hadn't recovered completely, looked like a pale frog that needed to eat something. His mother would've been scandalized to see the boy like that. He tumbled backwards, over and onto the other burn barrel, groan and moan.

"Stay back you red-eyed monster, beast of the nether regions! I know not if ever a heart beat in your breast, one of flesh and blood. I know not if your wickedness is more vile than Hood's but surely you are the hand of deliverance. The most unfaithful and turncoat in your affections toward those you purport to protect. Oh whence a score of years ago your soul was wed to the darkness was it your bones that oozed blackness into the earth and into us all or was it Hood that has drawn you into his blackness?" Ramon didn't try to get up but spoke from his back, sprawled on the floor, his legs over the barrel. Pathetic. Killing wouldn't serve any purpose if he was truly mad. One way to find out. Ramon was right, he was one with the darkness, a little trick of his own, like Isabella and her dreams. Pull the shadow around him, wonder if Katherine had a trick of her own. He suspected she did. Shadow as a cloak, space as thought, Ramon didn't realize the gun was to his head until he felt the cold metal. See how mad he really was.

"Do you have anything to say Ramon?"

"I do Don Lobo. How have you become so lost, so far from who you could have been, who you should have been? Perhaps it is better if you end my plight here on this desolate, heartless rock. If someday I too sacrifice my ideals and dreams, burn my beliefs to ash in the ovens of the capitalist machine, then I would rather die now, here in this hollow coffin of industrial disgrace. My tomb, my mausoleum. I would rather die here, strong in my struggle against those forces that wish to lash us to the yoke of servitude, the invisible evil that would suffocate us all. I would rather die here than succumb to it. I refuse to oxidize, to rust, to become brittle and frightened in my captive state. Kill me now Maldito Lobo." El Lobo watched Ramon, kept the gun where it was. "The child is yours. Katherine tells me it isn't mine. Says if I want a DNA test she'll oblige. Only other person is you." Punch in the gut. Not such a surprise anymore. The suggestion had been hanging in the air and if fell to the earth with a loud clang.

He removed the gun from Ramon's temple, holstered it. Ramon struggled like a flipped turtle. El Lobo helped him to the table, sat him in the chair, picked up the mess they'd made. Sat at the table. Sat with Ramon. That decided it, there was a bit of lucidity down deep in Ramon's brain somewhere. El Lobo knew he couldn't kill the kid and definitely not Kate. He'd never even really considered it if he was honest with himself. Time for a different conversation altogether.

"Stay in the container for the next couple of days Ramon, especially during the day. I repeat, do not come out during the day. If you have to go somewhere make it at night and don't go far. You are supposed to be dead. Given your current situation no one will ask questions if you disappear forever. Give me a few days to deal with Hood.

"Alas, could it be? That your stain, the blackness that fails to diminish the beauty, the radiance, the splendor of my beloved Katherine has in turn been illuminated, the bonds of hatred loosened, freed from malice? So the light of her shine illuminates the corners of your shadowy soul, reminding you of who you were and who she knows you can be." Hand to heart, tears in his eyes.

"Shut up Ramon. And stay inside." He set the fool up at the table with some crackers, sardines, a bottle of water, some instant coffee he heated up on the grill over the burn barrel and a grilled goat cheese sandwich. Told him to stay inside for the hundredth time. Didn't need tank, trucks or Graham finding Ramon and snapping his neck.

"Thank you redeemed soul, you have found a path back to the light. Perhaps it is Katherine's beacon that lights your way. Tread carefully and beware the shadow. It always follows you."

"Shut up Ramon."

Chapter 30

Isabella, Katherine and El Lobo

Isabella was angry. Ready to explode angry. Funny how the smallest thing set her off. Washing dishes, folding clothes, picking up dirty shoes. Sometimes that's just the way it was, why he thought storms should only be given female names. He wasn't sure what it was but it sounded bad. Maybe it was because he hadn't been home in three or maybe four days. He could hear her screaming and smashing something, heard his name among all the swears. Avoided the front door and the creaking faded planks of the front porch. Wooden four by four posts, badly in need of paint. Garage in the rear of the house. He ducked in, wait for the storm in the house to let up. He kept the garage free of clutter and well organized. Woodworking tools and table against the left wall. Miter saw, circular, table, all there. Hammers, tool belt, planes, levels, awl, hanging on a peg board. Drawers with partitions on the table. Red and silver vice attached to the edge.

Rear wall of the garage lined with wide and deep shelves for storage and another work bench and tool chest. Car and machine maintenance work area, a moveable office lamp attached to the edge of the table. Twenty years of titanic sized icebergs, sinking his ship, hole in the bottom of the boat. A man wondered if one day his boat might really sink. Would he swim for shore or go down with the ship. Who knew what madness crawled through the synapses of Isabella's brain. He'd avoided the big one so far but how long before they hit this shoal. He didn't think the little ship of their love would fare so well against those rocks in the coming storm. Maelstrom, gale, tidal wave, Hell of death by water.

Chrome plated, ten inches long by three inches wide, handle curved and sinuous for ergonomic grip, the head like the open beak of a hungry bird. Wrench. Wrench the heart and soul out of him to lose her. Yes, she was crazy, yes, she had anger, lots of anger. But so did he, so was he. They fit so well for so long, even damaged as they were. But the floor fell out, gone, fall through emptiness, wind whistles in the ears, air cold, rushing wind rips the heat from you. Wrench the heart from him.

Free fall of despair, curl into a ball, huddle for warmth. Could it be he and she were done healing? If so they hadn't done a very good job. If the bone knit they didn't set it right. Flash of light, pop of epiphany, no, just the light bulb popping in the lamp. Timely though, he was on to something.

Like a broken bone set in the field by an amateur, the bone had been set wrong, needed to be broken again and set correctly, then it could finally mend. To break a bone so thoroughly mended would require a terrible break, a violent impact of flesh against reality. A tooth jarring, gut wrenching, terminal velocity free fall, parachute doesn't work, hit the ground kind of impact. That was the kind of break needed if the bone were to ever be set correctly.

Hood's violation of Isabella broke the bone, broke the ankle of their newborn marriage. No first steps, no stumble and fall for their love. Broke the arms of their love, the arms that should have encircled, wrapped, caressed affectionately the body of the other, no long hugs for them. Broken the heart of their love, spilled like broken yolk on the kitchen floor.

Third wall of the garage was all gardening and landscaping implements. A table for potting plants, pots stacked neatly beneath the table, spade, fork, watering can hanging from another pegboard. Bags of soil he'd mixed in the greenhouses sat on the floor next to the table. Assorted containers of soil amendments lined another shelf. Bone meal, blood meal, bat guano, earth worm castings, perlite, etc. Fertile soil, fertile womb. Their wounded marriage suffered further by their inability to have children, especially after Hood's violation. Something shut down inside Isabella, in her eyes, in her laugh, in her womb. They'd been checked by doctors over and over, they should have had six or seven by now as hard as they tried. Whatever it was, it wasn't physical, sexual attraction was never a problem, they were barely able to keep their hands off one another, back in the day. They hadn't been very affectionate of late, an occasional morning ride or night time tuck in, but fewer and farther between.

Smooth bronzed breasts, broad areola, thick nipples, the nipple placed a hair above the equator of the fleshy mammary makes them point upward slightly. Goosepimples across the surface when he put them in his mouth. She liked to sigh and watch what he was doing, push his mouth onto her chest, play with his hair, giggle.

He theorized, surmised, hypothesized that Isabella was so spiritually charged, a conduit of so much spiritual energy that her human highway, her divination void, the hole through which she and all women summoned a living soul from the blackness of nothing to the light of life, was otherwise occupied. Like a phone that was constantly busy, he never get a call through. Emergency break through please operator. There was no zero on her phone, no operator to call. Her spark, her spirit, her light, was it too bright? Like a sun, and the approaching souls like comets, burned up on approach? Or like the claw game, her ethereal claw descends from uterus into the current of cosmic energy, pulls out nothing. A line of reincarnated and first time around souls, cued up at some ephemeral deli counter, waiting to dive in, pass her by, out of order sign hung on her upturned nipple, keep the line moving yells a voice in the back.

Soil through his fingers, push and pull it across his potting table with the hand rake, like a Japanese Zen rock garden. Push and pull the soil until it was a nice even layer. The potting table had walls about the edges, a box more than a table, a box of a table top. Furrows spread by metal tine, open, unfold, offer dark mysterious depths, pockets of mineral nutrition with which life was nurtured. Maybe El Lobo was the problem, El Lobo was everyone's problem. Long, strong fingers, groomed nails, dirty enough to tell he didn't have a desk job. Maybe the black cloud that followed him, the bleakness that plagued his life, the darkness of his words and deeds filtered through, poisoned her, sterilized her; static on her psychic link, bad connection, contamination in her soul soup was all his doing after all.

Or maybe it was Isa. Maybe after Hood violated her, the decision was made for her. Subconscious or otherwise, maybe she put the psycho-spiritual lock-down on her baby maker. Kabosh on the whole thing. She didn't want what El Lobo was selling, giving away or begging her to take. Red alert in her spiritual submarine every time he came near. Was bound to wear on her soul. They'd both been too far submerged for too long. Underwater in a world of distorted distances, bending edges and sunken ships. Brest stroke, side stroke, Australian crawl. Black soil in a pit, he'd transplanted a cutting, the body works while the mind wanders.

Not the time or the season for making cuttings, especially in the cold garage. Stiff gray stem, more of a twig, leafless, alternate buds on either side of leaf scars. Thin striated gray bark, no leaves left. He didn't even know what he'd pruned but bet his beard it was the Service berry. June bush, Shad bush. Sometimes autopilot wasn't the best way to run things, definitely not a marriage. Cold enough to see his breath, maybe it would make it if he took it to the greenhouse. Isabella walked in behind him, he could tell by the soundless leather slippers she wore, only scuffed her feet when she stopped. She had every right to hate him, despise him, want to give up. He'd been on autopilot for the last twenty years.

"We have company Jose. It's Katherine." She looked to have been crying.

"Good. I thought we should all talk." The worst part about this break, he couldn't anesthetize any of them. They all needed to be present for the pain, witness to it; feel the break in their hearts. Break the bone set it anew. Free fall to kersplat.

"Yes, we should." She turned and walked into the house. He followed. Forgot the cutting on the table.

Katherine sat in the living room. She stood when they entered, managed to look quite proud, if defiant. Isabella as well. She already looked to have eaten a mouthful of brass tacks, or so said her expression. Succinct if not eloquent descriptor of their predicament. He decided to chew on some brass tacks himself, bite the bullet man-up, etc.

"I've been to see Ramon Katherine. We spoke about you." She sat down when he motioned, they all did, there would be plenty of time for standing later.

"And how is he? Is he ok?" Hand wringing was genuine, as was the concern in her tired eyes.

"Not really. He's holed up in the old container, no one knows, only me." He reassured her. "He's half mad and half delusional. Either way he's not fit to be on the run. Turning himself in might get him into a mental health facility. He won't even have to fake it." He watched her mull it over. Isabella looked sad on the other end of the sofa, watched him like a hawk. Listened.

"Jiminy. You didn't call anyone did you?" She double checked.

"I told you, only I know." Period. Long exhale from her. Isabella kept watch; frightened cat or cornered fox he couldn't tell, claw his eyes out either way. Brass tacks.

"Ramon tells me I am the father of your child Katherine. I would like to know if this is true." No growl in his throat, good.

"I'm not sure." Quivering voice, she looked at the floor.

"Oh vamos Katarina! I raised you!" Isabella with something to say now. "That won't work on me, you're a terrible liar." Isabella's quivering rage.

"No really Isabella." Katherine had her hands up. "I slept with Jose and Ramon only a few days apart."

She didn't look down for that statement. Tingle in his chest, growl in his throat. Katherine's eyes hypnotized.

"You can play word games all you want Katherine but time will tell your lie." He stared into her brown eyes, tried to hypnotize her. Isabella screamed at him.

"Stop saying her name like that mierda," Finger in his chest, "might as well undress her you cheating bastard."

She stood and paced, he sensed pressure building, never knew when she would pop or what would come out of her mouth.

"Did you tell her about Lily? How close you and I were until you became her lover? While I became her nurse, I had to watch her die and sit next to that pig of her husband. I was the one that went with her to the clinic, then the hospice, she told me everything. She loved you, you bastard!! Did you tell her she was almost your daughter?" Katherine froze and Isabella sobbed with her revelation. They hadn't mentioned Lily's illness, how quickly she faded or how much they all missed her.

"Almost. Close but no cigar, thank you for that Isabella." Stepdaughter would have been the correct term.

"What is she talking about?" Those big brown eyes, so beautiful, her belly barely showing. Red hair framed her flushed cheeks and watering eyes. He wanted to kiss her right there in front of Isabella. Instead he explained.

"Your mother and I were..., involved once. For a short time. You were almost a teen. It was all very complicated." He did stroke her hair, she pulled away, angry eyes, he loved those eyes.

"Don't try that shit with me. I remember." She relaxed visibly. Whimsical fancy, light in her eyes.

"Well that explains why she was happy, I remember her singing. It was the only time she ever sang." She walked forward and grabbed him. Hugged him tight. Naughty look in her eye. Familiar that.

"Well I guess what mama loves the daughter loves as well." He swallowed hard, wanted to kiss her all over again. Isa wept so loudly she sounded like a wounded lioness. Katherine waited for her to quiet. "Would you tell me?"

"Yes Katherine, I will tell you. Sit down Isabella, you should hear this too." Surprisingly she complied. She'd never heard the whole story either. El Lobo told the two women he loved about the day he got his name from the woman they all loved.

"It was the same day your father raped Isabella. I went to your house after she told me what happened. I was mad with rage and intended to kill your father..."

***

J.J. Martinez stood in the doorway, Lily Hood smelled lovely, he could smell her even from the anteroom. She sat in a reading chair near large French doors that opened onto a private master patio. Her legs stretched onto the ottoman, silky smooth and perfectly curved calves caused his manhood to jump. Strawberry blond wisps attempted to obscure her smirking eyes, more strawberry than blond.

"Have you come here to kill my husband then?" Funny thing, she didn't even move.

Jose Jesus Martinez hadn't realized the he still held his hunting knife bare and glinting in his hand, other hand rested on the six-shooter he wore on his hip. The bedroom was bright, orange mauve light of sunset painted the clouds with the last rays of dying day. It all streamed through the French doors and Jose realized how revealing, exactly how sheer the teddy Mrs. Hood wore was. Her nipples were exquisite, he fancied he could even smell sweet female sweat on her neck. Her jugular pulsed with blood, he swallowed and answered.

"No Mrs. Hood, I am here to visit upon him that which he has visited upon me." Growled more than spoken, decision made on the spot, better not to open his mouth too much, he might start screaming.

"How very brazen." She still didn't move, only uncrossed her legs and lay the book on her chest. "How will you do it then, hold the knife to my throat the whole time? That could be fun for a while but it might prove..." she paused as if looking for a word, "more a handicap than an asset my dear."

He knew not where her familiarity was coming from, they had barely met thrice in his first year on the farm and here she was as comfortable with him as if she had known him his whole life. He didn't look and threw the knife at the headboard, it stuck with a loud thwack, vibrating like his barely contained rage.

"I don't think I will be needing it." He crossed the space between them in an instant and pulled her up by her wrists, she gasped, squeaked. He pulled her close, in the fading sunlight her hair blazed crimson. She panted against his chest and he could feel her legs and arms shaking, her aroma so intoxicating he felt light headed. She looked up into his face, blew an errant strand of hair from her face.

"No, I don't suppose you will." She stared up at him, he felt her body start to tense, like a coiled spring preparing to release. He couldn't. He let her wrists slip from his hands, washed his face with newly calloused palms and sat with a whimper on the empty chair. More Veterinarian than killer, still fresh and decent.

"I'm sorry Mrs. Hood, please forgive me?" Howl he should have.

"For what my dear, sweet boy? Your instincts are spot on, he took something important to you, so you should take something important to him. All is fair in love and war." She sat on the ottoman and took his hands in hers. "My poor little wolf, your instincts are perfect, you just haven't learned how to finish the kill." There were no more weapons in his hands but her eyes were daggers now. Anger gathered like a fist in his gut, no time to speak, her slap took the words from him. Spots danced, lights flashed, his neck wrenched, she hit like a man.

"If you want to cry, go home to her, I'm sure there are plenty of tears there. You two can cry together. I'm sure you will, sooner or later." She straddled his lap, diaphanous teddy more texture than covering. Her nipples and breasts pressed into his chest, she embraced him, felt her heat through his jeans.

"I don't think I can...." He couldn't finish. She snickered, he felt her quads tighten around his legs. Naughty eyes hers, smile more she couldn't.

"Let me see about that." She peeled the clothes from him, resumed her post on top of him, slapped him again. His manhood responded. He spent the next eight hours inside her. On the patio, in the bathroom, in the reading chair, on the carpeted floor, on the day bed.

Once or twice he became "distracted" and every time she slapped him back to the present or bit, or scratched. They rolled over and over, like Jack and Jill tumbling down a hill, so many times they changes places. First he on top, then she, they sat in the chair, she faced every direction of the compass, away from him, to the left, right, straddle. He lay on top of her, she flat on her belly, he had a breast in one hand and a fistful of hair in the other. Her bottom pushed up into his pelvis, groaning moaning pleasure flooded their brains, she held him tight, cupped his ass and pulled it into her. He pulled her hair and crushed the breast. Fucked hard, blood in his mouth, his or hers? Who knew, probably both.

After orgasm they lay panting. He still inside her, she flexing her muscles, either to milk him or reinvigorate, didn't matter, she accomplished both.

"You know Globe really is a son of a bitch, a real honest to goodness, dyed in the wool hijo de puta. My sexy Lobo." She was the first one to call him Lobo, even his mother called him Jose, "We are all just commodities to Globe. He was less selfish once, but that man is long gone and the one here now will fuck and kill all he wants." She devoured his lips and sent them both onto the rug. He tried to stab his member into her as hard as he could, imagined it making a hole in the small of her back, she rode him, galloped for the finish line. He flipped her over and did the same, ignored the rug burn and tried to punch a hole in her back with his member. Hard and deep as he could. Pelvis to pelvis, bruise the bone. Blood in his mouth.

She dismissed him when her daughter woke in the morning. Barely audible knock at the door and she was across the room, flash of naked white skin. She cracked the door and told her daughter she'd be right out, closed the door, stink of sex. She called Roaslinda on the phone and had her care for the girl. She mounted him, eyes hidden behind her hair.

"Last ride my Lobo Maldito, have to go be Mommy now." She pawed him into submission, climbed on top and drained his manhood of hot spunk after thirty minutes of hard-riding, pelvic grinding bliss.

He came deep inside her, muscles contracted as hard as the first lay, maybe the hardest of the night. His mouth in hers, she devoured him. She patted him on the ass and licked her lips while she watched him dress. She let him out through a portico hidden between greenhouse and ivy covered wall that separated her private patio from the outside. She nibbled his ear and grabbed his junk.

"More delicious than I allowed myself to imagine my Lobo Maldito. I will send for you." She sent him on his way, cheeks blushing. Stink of sex. He never knew how but the name stuck. She sent for him the next day and every day for a week until Hood returned from wherever. After that, never again.

Chapter 31

La Bruja

Both women were quiet, quiet as the grave, quiet as a cemetery. He grabbed a beer from the fridge, dry throat from so much confession. Isabella's rage bubbled free after five minutes. She stood up and slapped him, grabbed handfuls of his hair, tried to pull in two different directions at once. Got some hair for her efforts.

"You asshole! You son of a bitch, how could you?" Pry himself free, lose some more hair in the process. She slapped him on the face, on the neck, everywhere. Katherine squeezed between them, helped pry him free, got slapped for her efforts.

"Don't get involved you little bitch," another slap with some nails for Kate, the girl didn't go down but was pushed onto the couch, sprang right up, red lines on her cheek.

"She's already involved Isabella." El Lobo stated the obvious.

"And whose fault is that?" She leapt on him again, crying and punching, her eyes were closed, she pounded him. Finally he grabbed her wrists, sat her on the couch. She sobbed into her hands and lap.

"So my parents were in on it? I mean it sounds like my mother seduced you to give my father some cover." Something occurred to her. "I'm so sorry Isabella, I had no idea my father had done something so vile to you. I understand now why you hate him so much and want to see him suffer." She rubbed Isabella's back, stroked her hair.

"It's OK sweetheart, you had nothing to do with it." Sob and sniffle, patted Katherine's hand. Continued crying. Katherine rubbed her back. El Lobo decided then and there women were mad.

"That was very wrong of you Jose, I'm not saying you're completely to blame but it was a horrible thing you did."

"I know Katarina and it haunts me to this day." Ghosts of nightmares past.

"Haunts you because you were a bastard! She loved you and would've left Globe for you if she hadn't died." Isabella screamed.

'We don't know what she would've done Isa, she's dead." Finality in his tone.

"I have to agree Isabella, as much as my father is a horrible person, I don't think my mother would've left him. She always told him they were in it for the long haul, even if they hit some speed bumps and potholes along the way. That's what she always said to both of us, it was her mantra."

Isabella deflected, deflated, folded up on herself on the couch.

"I have no desire to destroy your marriage, I only want to be in your lives and you in the baby's" Katherine had trouble looking at them.

"I would also like you two in my life." Isabella hissed when she heard his reply. "It will be nice to finally have a family." He wanted the words back as soon as they were out. Isabella was a flash of movement, knocked a lamp over, crash on the floor, scream at the ceiling, top of her lungs. Katherine covered her ears, the scream had a deafening quality, hurt his ears.

"Isabella!" He yelled, shook her. "Stop! We can make this work. Like she said, she isn't trying to destroy our marriage, only share our family. We can do it, you, me, Katherine and the baby." Stranger things had happened.

"How convenient for you, hijo de la gran puta! You get a fresh twenty-something to fuck and your old washed up first wife can watch the kids while the two of you fornicate. A dream come true."

"Isa, you know that's not what I mean. You and I have a lot to work out between us. You and I need to figure out what we're going to do." True statement.

"Oh, so now you care! Now you want to fix this black hole of despair, the pig stye in which you've been wallowing for twenty years. I've been hanging on for dear life Jose, twenty years of a fingernail's purchase on a rock face. Twenty years of white knuckled panic that you wouldn't come home at all, that you'd leave me and never return. And now that you've got the younger, newer model you want to discuss what we're going to do? How about I use my powers of divination? You're going to leave me for Katherine and have a beautiful little family and live life in luxury far away from this place and all the tears and years of pain. How does that sound?" Isabella was picking up a head of steam. Her anger like inertia, a body in motion wants to stay in motion. He could see the monster rage stirring deep in her eyes, her hands flexed at her sides, open and closed, open and closed.

"That is not true Isabella, we could make this work, you and me, as long as we love each other there's hope. I'll probably end up alone, with neither of you. I'm no good for anyone." Also true. He deserved far worse.

"Don't you dare." She pointed a finger with threatened intention, close enough to poke out an eye. "You're not getting away from me or the reckoning. You've kept me holding on for dear life for twenty years, hoping, wishing, waiting for you to come back to me, to look at me with love again." Panting, nostrils flaring, not good. "And now you do, you turn up with love spilling from your cup, which runneth over, but none of it is for me. The hope, the heat in your voice, the love in your eyes is for her." Sobs wracked her body, Katherine slipped her hand into his, she must sense it too, recognized the signs in her teacher. The volcano would erupt, the storm would break, it was time for hell in a hand basket.

Isabella stood in the middle of the room, rigid, clapped her hands together in front of her chest, began chanting in her bastardized chicano-navajo. The whites of her eyes, iris and cornea rolled up into her skull, a breezed whipped through the room, stirred his hair, whipped Katherine's cloak back and forth. Lights dimmed, black veil dropped onto and over the whole room, cool air crept up from the floor, frosting breath, chilling the toes. Insects called from the ceiling, cicadas, crickets, bees.

"This is bad." El Lobo speaking to himself, but Katherine nodded in agreement, trying to squeeze his hand to pulp, "we need to leave." She nodded again.

"Oh no you don't."Other worldly voice came from Isabella like a thousand voices speaking as one.

The breeze increased, blew papers from the table, the sound of buzzing bees filled the room. Cold fingers of spirit wind chill to the bone.

"Let's go then, like now!" Katherine's turn to scream, he could barely hear her over the buzzing of bees.

Blackness everywhere, shadows skittered along the floor, clung to the wall, bubbled upward from the depths of hell. Black droplets, rising through the floorboards, supple and viscous, undulated and squeezed through millimeter wide gap between wooden floorboards.

Kerplunk and ripple, like scenes from astronauts eating in space. End over end, black balls spun and rose, collected on the ceiling, where they ran together, pooled into a black inky mass.

"We don't want to be here for this." Katherine's alarm, hair raising was her quiet collected tone. "This spell is called endless night and it will kill us if we stay here." She pulled him toward the door.

Isabella raised an arm, parallel with the floor, straight out from her body, black ball rose from the floor, settled in one hand, she repeats, settled in the other hand. Black ink sloughs off, leaving small white ball in each hand, like paper mache. El Lobo' s turn to panic, tightened his grip on her hand, backed them out of the room. He wasn't Isabella's apprentice and he didn't know what the spell Endless Night did but he knew what those paper mache balls were. Inside each ball was equipped with a little CO_2 charge that popped when the ball hit something. Puffer fish for tetrodotoxin, Jimsonweed for atropine, toad pituitary gland, dried newt, for bufotoxin, powdered tobacco for the nicotine, and opium poppy for the opiate. Tetrodotoxin in the fish paralyzed, atropine in the jimsonweed accelerated the heart and induced hallucinations, bufotoxin too, tobacco for the quickening and spirit, poppy to knock you out. If she managed to hit them with those powder balls they'd be awake for another ten to fifteen minutes, crazy as a fox-like, then they'd pass out wherever they stood, maybe never wake again. Or it could be the other type. The other type was just as nasty if not worse.

Contained a decidedly more lethal mixture, no coming back from that one. Death cap mushroom meant the long good night, poison ivy meant excruciating pain. Nasty things those. He knew she had them, he'd watched her make them, wondered if he'd get to use them on someone. Isabella raised her right arm, ready to throw, screamed at the ceiling, giant black pool released with a splash onto the floor, he felt the moisture blow through the room, watched the water pool around his boots. Katherine was the first to start running, pulled him after her. They crossed the threshold at a dead run, bursting through the door, the water crossed too, disappeared as it crossed the invisible divide separating indoors from out. A powdery ball exploded on the sill of the door, mili-second behind his head.

He pushed Katherine harder, didn't want to take a chance with those powdery balls of mayhem and death. Black liquid stopped at the door but the sound of the buzzing bees followed. They high-tailed it across the front yard and around the back, jumped the dry ravine, ducked past the willow, roots tried to trip them up, slow their escape. He swatted at bees trying to land on his head.

"Don't do that." Katherine scolded him as they ran. Another powder ball exploded on the willow trunk, Isabella in hot pursuit then. Pick up the pace, nearly picked Katherine off the ground. Dodge and swerved, zig-zagged through the woods behind the house. Ran blindly, panic crept up the back of his throat. He couldn't hear for the infernal buzzing, no bites yet. He ran and ran. Finally Katherine stopped them, panting they doubled over in a dark corner of the woods. The darkest corner they could find.

Katherine spoke, he couldn't make out her words, only saw her lips move. He curled into a ball, moss and fern, the hollow where they'd lain together, he hadn't realized. Covered his head, hoped the bees did not bite her. She straddled his back, or very nearly, wrapped her cloak and arms around him, whispered something in his ear.

"…the light envelopes you, feel the warmth of my light, my hope, my love. Think of our love…the only way to emerge from the endless night. The darker and more desperate your thoughts the more it will settle around you. You must calm down." She looked to be screaming, he saw the veins popping on her neck but she sounded miles away. Yelling from a ridge top to he, trapped in the valley of death. No bees swarmed her, none really swarmed him either, though his body and mind said otherwise, bites rose on his body, swollen red welts, the sound thick in his ears, he felt them crawling through his hair, over his skin. But if he relaxed and focused on her face there were no bees to be seen.

Focused on her voice, focused on her beauty, felt her body pressed against his. Somehow he'd rolled onto his back, she still straddled him, his face in her hands, her legs opened to him. Not the first time he'd felt the heat radiating from her body into his. First time he felt the peach sized bump on her abdomen, first time he felt it pressed up against him, the growing offspring he'd planted in her loins in the exact spot where she now held him, whispered sweet nothings that only lovers understand. She hugged him and whispered to stave off the madness.

"Thank you Katherine. I'm OK now. The darkness is gone, thank you." And so it had, with it the hive of invisible stinging bees, the encroaching blackness and suffocating panic. Wave of relief crashed onto his shore, left exhaustion in the tidal pools of his cove. She didn't move; she caressed him for some five minutes, never leaving her perch. Finally she kissed him and pulled him to his feet. She rubbed his back, checked his face again. He could feel the bee stings hot with venom and histamine reaction. Good thing Isabella hadn't summoned snakes, he knew she could. He felt hot, cold, weak and drained, a fever was coming.

"You are going to be in bad shape real soon, can you walk?" She recognized his swelling for what it was. A problem.

"Yes, get me to the road then leave me, someone will take me to the infirmary."

Who he wasn't exactly sure, he'd walk if he had to.

"Yeah right, the father of my child, the man I love, finally got my hands on you and you think I'm going to leave you on the side of the road to swell up and die. Fat chance." Pulled him out of their love hollow.

"I need to tell you something Katarina." He leaned on her, only a little, more to feel her than for support. His eyes began to swell shut, he'd need her to guide him in a few minutes.

"Tell me while we walk, if I know Isabella, she's stomping through the forest after us and I for one don't relish being caught." She tugged him along though the foggy world, growing darker and more constricted by the second. He agreed.

"Oh yeah, she's definitely coming. We're just lucky she's never spent as much time in the woods as we have. We'll hear her coming. I hope. I didn't know her magic was so...scary, I only thought she dream walked, minor divination, herbs and remedies." Kate squeezed his hand.

"Step over the log here baby." She bit down on the baby, making it sound clipped and curt, but the words were out, pitter patter in his chest. Squeeze her hand back.

"There will be time for us to have a long overdue talk, one I'm sure we're both anxious for. But now is not that time, soon, but not yet. Katherine, your father sent me to kill you, Ramon, Tommy and Tania. When I said I went to see Ramon I meant I went to kill him." He let the information sink in. She didn't speak for a while, crunch of leaves intermittent, she knew how to guide them through the forest making as little noise as possible.

"I'd like to be surprised but I'm not. If I am honest with myself and give up the hope that one day he'll hug me and hold me, tell me I'm the most important thing in his life, then of course I'm not surprised. I am heartbroken." Tremble in her voice, sniffle in her nose.

"I'm sorry Katherine." He was.

"Well, times they are a changing. I lost Ramon to extremism and madness, I lost my father years ago, that is if I ever really had him. But now I have a new man in our son." He stopped short, forcing her to stop as well. She guessed his question. "I don't know it's a boy but I'd bet on it Jose. He feels like you, a little rambunctious you." Jose's turn to sniffle, would've wiped his eyes if they weren't swollen shut. At least she couldn't see his tears. "And if I can ever get Isabella to forgive me, I may have the teacher and friend I always wanted too. I'd say I traded up. Of course change is tough but change is never easy."

If he hadn't already been in love with Katarina Hood, her philosophical analysis of the situation would've sealed the deal. Better to deal with the pressing issue at hand, leave the sappy, feel-good, touchy-feely stuff for later, if they survived.

"Well as per your earlier statement, Isabella can do much more than dream walk Jose. Not quite necromancy, she doesn't raise the dead, she calls spirits, casts illusion and enchantment spells. Love, confusion, obsession, see things that aren't there and the like. Endless night is a combination of the three. Spirits for the shadows that wrap you and bind you, which didn't work on you for some reason, the bees are illusionary and the enchantment is the madness. Nasty stuff. She's got a few more as bad. Let's hope we don't see them." He had to agree, feet on compacted earth, farm road.

"We're on the road now, I'm going to walk us to the barrio, take you to my apartment, get you fixed up." Sounded good.

"Are you sure you want to do this Katherine?"

"Well, you need to recover, the swelling should go down tonight, I'll give you an antihistamine, that should help. I know Isa's mad but I doubt she'll come to the barrio and make a scene in the store, we both know that's not her style."

"I don't mean that Katherine. I was telling the truth when I said I'm not good for either of you. I'm damaged goods, a sinkhole of despair. We all have baggage Katherine but you've seen mine, a few moving vans worth. You're young and beautiful with your whole life in front of you. I don't want to burden you with a middle-aged man with broken dreams and no hope. You deserve better." He may have been getting a little ahead of himself. His dammed eyes would have leaked in a most uncharacteristic manner were they not swollen shut.

"Oh no you don't't, I agree with Isa on this one Jose, you're not getting away from me. Don't get all noble on me. I'm in this, whether as your woman and mother of your child or some supporting role. I know you still love Isabella but I also know you love me. I'm staying, I have a vested interest and I want to see how this all pans out." Almost see the hands on her hips, except she was still leading him. She pushed him into some bushes, lay on top of him. Breathed into his mouth for thirty seconds.

"Isabella just went by in your truck looking for us." She was panting with nervous anticipation. So was he. If Isa found them he was toast.

"Who's being stoic now? And unrealistic." She squeezed his hand, kept walking. He continued. "So you're going to pine away for me as a single mother, hoping and waiting I'll be yours in some way? That is going to get old quick. A beauty like you will be able to have any man you like, even with a kid."

"Well Jose, we'll just have to see. I have needs, itches to scratch as it were. But I think I'll be busy for a while. Too bad for all those suitors." He snorted, blind as a new-born babe.

"Katherine this isn't a fairy tale, no happy endings for us immigrants."

"Isn't it Jose? I know who I am. Capucha Roja, Red Riding Hood, I know what the workers call me.

I know who you are, the Big Bad Wolf, El Lobo Maldito. Whether you want it or nor not, we are connected. You devoured me and I invited it. I only hope you remember that when the time comes."

Dirt road to asphalt, dogs and cars. They were entering the barrio. Wondered what she had planned.

"What sharp teeth you have Mr. Wolf." Tinkle of her laugh, smile in her voice.

"The better to eat you with my dear." Laughter catches in his throat, almost becomes a sob. The twist, the turn, the up-side-down of life. Stranger than fiction, she patted his arm again. She was doing an awful lot of comforting.

"We're here Jose. We're going up some stairs now." Gentle tug. He couldn't help but try to wonder who was whom in their fairy-tale, and who would rescue the damsel in distress.

Chris Travis

Chapter 32

Hungry Enough

Globe Hood was certain El Lobo was responsible for the
seduction of Katherine. She'd been half in love with the damn
Wolf since she was young. That would make Globe's second
woman that loved the man and slept with him too. Of all the
injustices, the greatest was losing his women to that immigrant
bastard. He'd given Lily anything and everything she desired,
helped to increase her family's wealth along with his own. The
same for Katherine, there was never an item she declared she
wanted that she did not receive before the day was done. To
think she'd allowed such a horrible crime to be committed
against her person, to think she'd invited it, longed for it. He
had himself to blame for Lily's disgrace. She bedded El Lobo
in order to place the collar around his neck. She let him violate
her so she could attach him to them forever, tame the savage
beast.

While Globe had not been pleased with the idea of another man fucking his wife, filling her with a pleasure of a different sort, he selfishly covered his own ass. Used her seduction as leverage against the man. Both Jose and Isabella were
legal citizens and they could press charges against Hood if they
so desired. Lily performed beautifully, she let El Lobo come
close and she collared him, bound him to Globe Hood for life,
even after she lost her own. She left the Wolf his teeth and
gave him his name, so was born the enforcer and man of many
skills known as El Lobo Maldito, much more than a veterinarian.

To Globe it felt more like he'd sold his soul for one of
the hounds of Hell, Cerebrus on a leash. Had been a pleasant
walk so far but now the animal needed to be put down. Even
more so if he'd defiled Katherine the way he'd defiled Lily.
Whatever mojo, sexual ju-ju he was playing at, Lily was under

his spell until the day she died, he could only imagine how enchanted Katherine was. Isabella and El Lobo had a magical mystery to them, decidedly different forms of magic, but undeniably something fantastical.

Four decades he'd toiled, let blood, sweat bullets and cried a river of tears for those two. He was entitled to his luxuries, he'd earned them, he pushed and fought his way to the top and no one would tell him otherwise. If he wanted something he took it, that is what had gotten him this far. He'd pry the spoils of war from their cold dead hands, from El Lobo's cold dead hands. Globe liked the idea more and more, turned the where and how over and over in his mind. The what, why and who already determined.

The caveat of his fantasy being Isabella. He fancied taking her for his own, even if he had to lock her away in his mansion, the idea of possessing her fine flesh fascinated. Payback is a bitch and that bitch was gonna pay. He'd let Graham scare her, then Globe would work on her for as long as it took. Days, weeks, months, years, until she submitted and then he would defile her most efficaciously. Many times, over and over. Who knew, if she cooperated maybe he'd let her be his mistress. Live in latina lover. Suck on her skin, make her his.

It would be the fulfillment of Hood's wildest dreams to have that immigrant whore chained to a bed. Convince her he could be trusted, she would have nothing to fear. Hot meals, a warm bed and a roof over her head. He'd provide her with everything she needed. As he had done for years, he would provide the sustenance they required, provide the work and pay with which they fed their families. All he asked was hard work, competent employees and willingness to do one's best. If his workers gave their best, he gave them everything they deserved. A decent wage, a satisfactory work environment and safety from immigration. So they inhaled the occasional cloud of pyrethium, the happenstance mouthful of organophosphate. A little self-sacrifice did wonders for the character and his bottom line.

He was a perfect example, a shining example of industrial capitalism at its best. Proud to be an American. He allowed his wealth and prosperity to trickle down to his people.

Let the wealth rain down upon them, sprayed from his hose of economic resource, let the children frolic in the rain. Hood controlled the hose, turned it on and off as necessary. Trickle-down economics worked for him, so nice, so elegant, so self-serving. It would be nice to bring his misbegotten, life altering relationship with Isabella full circle. Make peace with their past, maybe make do with each other. It was nice to dream. Hood laughed outright at his own absurdity.

She'd most likely end up taking a year or two to even look at him. Breaking the horse was more fun than breeding; that was what he always told Lily. The breaking was the true measure of the animal, he would break Isabella. Nearly a week since he'd given the order, he knew the job wasn't done yet, Katherine had been by to check on him every day, her belly hidden in voluminous clothes. She kept her coat on, a dark brown trench coat or riding jacket from the look of it, she didn't come close enough for him to see if it was leather. Maybe she was hiding a baby under her coat. She came close to kiss him goodbye, but approached his chair from behind so he couldn't wrap his arms around her. She kissed his head, squeezed his shoulders and high-tailed it out of the room. He choked up and pushed her from his mind. No room for sentiment now.

If she really knew what he was capable of she would've already left. As his daughter she must know the reprisal for working with the illegals and movement members would be decisive. And still she did it anyway. Maybe she stopped by hoping he'd say something, maybe she just wanted to check on her father. He'd done the best he could by her, by any of them. Maybe he didn't help them the way they wanted to be helped but he offered a leg up. He'd employed tens of thousands of workers over the years. Allowed them a decent life, a taste of the American Dream and if they were hungry enough they could have their own.

Chapter 33

Bull by the horns

El Lobo knew what day it was as soon as he opened his eyes. No sooner had he exited Katherine's back door and he knew. He was the man after all, the man designated, the man assigned, the man tapped for the job, tasked in the past. Crisp, cold, frozen air up his nose froze the hair. As if he were still the one in charge of Hood's 'dirty work', he knew today was the day Death came calling. To each his own. El Lobo knew nothing of Graham's background or past incarnations; only that the man saved Hood's ass on the rig and carried a giant wrench. Unseen eyes traced his steps, he doubled back through the barrio, criss-cross, jumped fences, invited himself in and through hovels, homes, tried to lose the man. Graham was out there somewhere, seemed Hood would wait no more and had sicked the new dog on the old dog for a good old fashioned dog fight.

Ears at attention he walked through the barrio, hustle and bustle not yet underway. Yawning shopkeepers lifted metal shutters, stray cats loitered at back doors of restaurants. Workers already on the job, or on the way, bleary eyed shuffle to work. Zig-zag his way through the barrio. Storefronts concentrated around the center, Katherine's being the largest. The many shops and offices offered a myriad of products, services, food, wire service, lawyers, shoe repair, knife sharpening and on and on. Peter out, phased into single story squarish homes. Aluminum roofing here and there. Unpainted, haphazard extensions protruded like budding abscesses from most houses.

Broken bottles, forgotten doll, wandering chickens, a rooster crowed behind a little blue house, the walls of which were definitely not plumb. The call was taken up by all the roosters of the neighborhood. Greeted the coming day, the untapped, the unwritten, the coming of the unknown. They welcomed the warm rays of the golden orb lighting the soon to come, banishing the darkness to shadowy confines. Young mothers, bleary eyed fathers, trundled to work, waved goodbye from the stoop. Quickie in the morning, send him off to work with a smile, she would smell him on her all day.

He'd slept with Katherine in her bed. Never in a million years would he have guessed where he'd be and who would be tending to his wounds.

She soaked his body in warm towels, rubbed him down, took him into the shower. A first for he. Her gentle hands lathered his body with patience, she scrubbed every inch of him. Ran her hands all over him, every nook and cranny. She tucked him in once she had him toweled off, powdered and lotioned. She cozied up, pushing her naked backside into his groin. Spook and fork. He fell asleep with his erection between her legs. Sex was not on the menu for they but something sublime about his member between the soft skin of her thighs.

He woke to the predawn sky, erection already awake, assumed the position, her ass wiggled closer. She pushed out her ass, tilted her pelvis, pushed his phallus on the doorbell of her flower. Blood rushed to his head, pound in his ears, tingle of excitement up his spine, tighten his ass. Pulsing pleasure in the head of his manhood, her moisture lubricated the tip, beckoned with sweet nectar. He denied himself the pleasure, kissed her first, long and deep, resisted the urge to push inside her, barely stopped himself, just the tip.

"I have something I need to take care of. I need to speak with your father, tie up some loose ends. Can I see you later?" It was a silly question, he already knew the answer.

"As if you had a choice my Big Bad Wolf. If you don't come find me, I'm going to come find you."

"Where will you be later? Once I'm done with your father I'd like to come work for you Miss Hood." He didn't need to explain, they both knew he'd no longer be Globe's enforcer. Those days were over.

"The movement and I are staging a protest today, out in front of the farm entrance by the boulevard where the trucks exit. You should come join us." Batted her pretty little eyes.

"Alright, meet you there. You and I need to talk to Isabella again. After the protest I'm going to speak with her since we didn't get to finish our conversation yesterday." He rubbed his hand over the invisible bites.

"No we didn't. Would you like me to come?" Her eyes asked so many questions.

"No, you being there will only upset her more. Her pride is wounded right now. Once she and I talk I'll call you."

"So you've decided then? What you're going to do, what we're going to do? What you're going to do with us?"

"I have." He slid out of bed and out of her apartment before the day managed to get started. He knew Graham lay in wait somewhere out there. That's what he would have done. Which was why he moved through the barrio with the zig-zag, lollygag, ears at attention, head on a swivel meander. He took note of the cars, trucks and pedestrians. Stop and start, stroll down an alley, cut through a basement, over a roof, no sign of Graham.

No use waiting around, better to grab the bull by the horns. He who arrives at the battlefield first will be rested and patient. Where their battlefield would be was a tossup. He doubted Graham would want to do anything near Hood's mansion, just in case. They would try to stay out of the fields, too public, even though they were fallow. First El Lobo needed to stop by the greenhouse and pick up his six-shooter. He wasn't sure if Graham would show up armed or just bring the over sized wrench, try to knock his block off. El Lobo considered taking Katherine's shotgun from her store when he left but deemed it unnecessary. In all reality he didn't need a gun to take Graham down, even if they ended up going punch for punch. El Lobo and his snapping jaws could still bring down a large bull, sharp teeth and Achilles tendons didn't mix, tasted the blood in his mouth.

The idea of blood caused his mouth to water. He crouched low on a tar covered roof, scanned the horizon. Smelled like baking bread. Someone was pulling golden loaves, brushing them with butter and honey. The kind of smell one missed when thinking of the barrio from far away. The smell of baking bread, brewing coffee, smelled like a good idea.

He crept down the stairwell, startled the bakers Don Julio and his wife. They were happy to give him a loaf and a cup of coffee. Sent him back up to the roof with Don Julio's folding chair to enjoy his breakfast. Café con leche, sweet buttered bread. A cigarette to wash it all down. Just in case. He had confidence that Graham would be the one dead at the end of the day but a moment to stop and savor the little things didn't hurt. He should have made love to Katherine. Just in case.

He prepared himself to meet the monster of Greed and his henchman. Cracked open the bread, warm interior spongy and soft, steamed into his face, crisp crust settled in his whiskers, on the front of his coat. Slurped bitter brew, smooth and silky thanks to the milk. The porcelain cup cooled quickly in the cold winter morning, the sky smelled like snow. Picketing in the snow would be better than in the rain. He'd love to see Hood's face when he saw Katherine at the head of the picket line. All they needed was to get Gloria on board and Hood would have a coronary.

One cup of coffee and it was time to go. Brushed off his coat, cleaned his whiskers, returned the mug and folding chair to the bakers. Thanked them, they looked more surprised than scared. Mrs. Julio came over and kissed his on the cheek and held his hand, told him to be a good boy, called him Jose. Take the bull by the horns, get down to the nitty-gritty, the devil is in the details. The devil is Globe Hood. The Devil is Jose Jesus Martinez.

Meander, worked his way around the edge of everything, stalked prey that he was. Wetland and dried phragmites. Brown and gray stems reached skyward. How he'd managed to wander his way to the pocket wetland was beyond him but it was as good a place as any. Sparrows flitted, flutter of wings, frolic in the sun warmed air. Winter Wren, Red-winged blackbird. Yellow Irises oh so pretty in the spring and summer hung their long broad leaves over the water. Phragmities invaded the pond as best it could, filled one corner of the pond with silt, soil and roots. Red winged sat atop reed, darted to cat-tail.

Damn the purple loosestryfe creeping around the edge, he hated the stuff, it was ever present and ever aggressive. He'd have to task himself with removing it in earnest if he survived this nonsense. If the farm was still here after all was said and done. The Phragmites autralis had to go too. Time to get the party started. He stopped on the edge of the wetland, surface of the pond so still it looked like a mirror reflecting the slate gray undersides of snow laden clouds. He looked past the fence that was the edge of the horse corral, apple tree was senescing, gradual die-off, bumper crop of apples because of.

"You may as well come out Graham, we can't get this over if we don't get it started first." Nothing for a ten count, then the hulk stepped from behind the apple tree. Graham may have been stealthy on the gas rig or winding his way down city streets but El Lobo doubted it. He wasn't the type used to lay-ing in wait or stalking, he was more the rip your arms off type. The man needed some tailing lessons ASAP. Graham started trailing El Lobo at the greenhouse, like a tick on a blade of grass. El Lobo stopped by, picked up the six shooter, slipped out without being seen. Except by Graham, who was lurking in the field next to the gray water storage tank.

"So you knew?" Stared at El Lobo.

"Yes Graham, I knew." El Lobo dry washed his face. Graham had no weapon other than the huge wrench. "And you should know Graham, you'll need to be more proactive when doing dirty deeds." He pulled the six shooter from the holster and aimed it at the sky. "I could kill you right now Graham, if I wanted to."

"Globe said as much Wolf, but I say you're not the type to shoot down an unarmed man, at least not me, not like this." The man stepped over the corral fence, didn't need to leap over, he just stepped over. Maybe Graham wasn't as dumb as he looked. El Lobo shrugged, threw his revolver into the pond with a loud kerplunck. Graham followed suit, tossed his wrench in after.

"Who says there's no honor among thieves?" Graham smirked.

"There isn't." Wolf answered, "but maybe there is be-tween cold-blood killers." Laughable farce. A cardinal flitted past, red-winged blackbird perched on a reed, cocked his head, waited for the show to start. Foolish humans in his pond. They stared at each other, count of sixty.

El Lobo charged, so did Graham. Two rams charging to destroy the brain pan of the other. As they met Graham's massive arm raised to clothes-line Lobo's neck, knock his head off. Lobo crouched low, slid across the frost covered grass and mud bank. He slid to a stop and executed a reverse heel strike, caught Graham on the shoulder with his muddy boot. He left a footprint on the man's sleeve. The power of the kick evoked a grunt from Graham. Lobo had his fingers in the mud. He dug in provide purchase and leverage for the heel strike. Graham twisted with the strike, using the momentum to pivot on his foot, spun to face El Lobo. El Lobo likewise continued his spin, planted his kicking foot and kicked out with the other, foot sweep of Graham's legs. Graham's attempted backhand would have knocked him silly if El Lobo stood up, but he didn't; he stayed crouched and the man's hamfist sliced through the air above El Lobo's head as El Lobo's right foot and shin took out the man's legs.

The lack of purchase on the bank facilitated the leg-sweep and Graham's feet were cut out from under him. The man fell with a grunt, feet and legs falling into the pond, ribs and torso crashing to the ground on the bank, mighty exhale of expelled breath. El Lobo considered letting the man get his hands on him, just to see how strong he was but immediately discarded that cinematic nonsense. If Graham got his hands on El Lobo he'd end up with some broken ribs at the very least.

Instead he walked his way around the wetland with its rushes and frozen frogs. He picked up a cobble sized stone, no smooth edge on it. It was limestone, jagged and cleaved, sharp enough to peel wood. He hefted the stone, tossed it up and down while Graham regained his senses. The big man rolled onto his stomach, onto all fours, wobbled to his feet. El Lobo tossed the rock. Pitching days of his youth, fast ball caught Graham in the side of the head, bounced off into the pond.

The big man went down in a heap, blood trickled from temple. Not unconscious, he held his head and swore at El Lobo. El Lobo took the opportunity and dove into the frigid water. Silt and loam soil particles disturbed by his movement through the fluid floated upward into the water column, increased the turbidity and decreased visibility. No matter, he scooped his gun from the soil, mud and soil stuck to the grip, the large wrench lay close by. El Lobo kicked, three strong strokes and he was in the culvert that connected this pond to three others around the area. Storm water management, irrigation ponds and swimming spot for the kids. He stopped in the mouth of the culvert, wedged himself in with arms and legs, backed himself into shadow. Loud splash followed by Graham's tree-trunk legs wading through the water, long muscled white arm snaked through the water and scooped up the wrench. Graham stuck his head underwater, scanned back and forth. The culvert would appear as a black hole to Graham, as long as the Wolf stayed put.

The man waded from the pond, El Lobo could hear him screaming. El Lobo shimmied down the pipe to the retention basin that was the junction for all the ponds. A storm drain with four pipes entering, one on each side. He stood in chest deep water and breathed deep. Submerged again and swam toward one of the other ponds, it was not a random choice. Stroke, stroke, hundred meters through bone chilling water. It hadn't bothered him for the first several minutes, what with the adrenaline firing through his veins, the cold seeped into his muscles, sapping him of what strength remained.

Stroke, stroke, emerged into another pocket wetland, the reeds not so thick as the last, but the water felt just as cold. Of all the luck, Graham had chosen the same pond. El Lobo heard the man thrashing and smashing his wrench against the surface of the pond, swearing at the top of his lungs. El Lobo waited, hoping he could hold his breath until the hulk of a man spent his anger. Just barely; as he started to panic for oxygen, come to grips with the truth that it was too late to swim back to the storm drain and he'd have to risk surfacing, Graham left.

El Lobo pulled himself up the far bank and lay there. He melted into the woods on silent feet and loped his way to the research dome. Stiff breeze tried to freeze all of his hair. So far so good. He hoped his plan continued to go so well, perhaps Graham didn't have much in the way of a brain after all. Roar in the distance. Ten minutes then, he had a ten minute lead on Graham.

He reached the dome and ducked into a utility building adjacent to the glass wall, rifled through a locker. Startled custodians and utility workers drinking their morning coffee. The men attended to the research dome, they were the invisible hands that unclogged toilets, mopped floors, disposed of trash. Cut from the same cloth as the rest. Four of the five men in the room wore their one piece custodian jumpsuits on their legs with the arms and chest hanging down their backs. Suits half on they watched El Lobo pushing through a random locker. He glared at them.

"Presta me lo?" (Let me borrow this?) He asked; not really a question. He was naked in a flash, no timidity here, no time to care about his hairy ass. They nodded as one.

He slipped on one of the blue jumpsuits, left his wet clothes and muddy gun in a pile on the floor. Someone slipped dry socks and work boots next to him.

"Gracias hombre." Stomped his feet into the boots and dashed through a door on the other side of the room. The whole farm would hear about this soon. Gossips everywhere. The door opened into a long hallway that led to the ground floor of the research dome. He stopped at the first bank of windows, scanned the fields and there he was. The lumbering hulk, red faced and running. Apparently he could track a little bit. It had taken Graham less time than anticipated but no worry, Graham would reach the dome in the next five minutes. Plenty of time for El Lobo to get where he needed to be. Ding of the elevator, he stepped inside, pulled out his key. Only two people with copies, roof access key, he'd have to leave it in here for Graham.

Elevator ding, opened door into a small machine room all metal cables, wires in conduits, pipe chases, colored lights. The top of the dome was a small cement footer on which stood the machine room and access panels for maintenance on elevators, HVAC systems, computer networks and all those technological necessities for a building like the dome. A row of lockers on wall, harnesses inside. El Lobo grabbed one and slipped it on, let himself outside. He took a step off the cement platform and hooked himself onto a spool of rope that was built into the side of the cement slab. Turn and wait. He had to give up smoking for Katherine and the baby. First he needed to survive this encounter with Graham, this part in particular.

The wind whipped around his ears and down his back. Cold as the Hell of the endless winter, horrible place for sure. And there he was. Graham stepped from the mechanical darkness of the utility room, chest rose and fell with heavy breaths. His mouth moved, rictus of a face, El Lobo couldn't hear a word. El Lobo tapped a finger to his own ear, shook his head and walked ten steps toward Graham. Graham did likewise stepping off the edge of the platform. If he eyed the glass panes beneath his feet nervously it was just for a second, a millisecond, he focused on El Lobo again.

Graham's skin was pink with the cold, exerted energy and anger. He dragged the giant wrench with him, scraped it across the cement platform, bashed it into the glass pane beneath his feet. He raised the giant wrench and bashed the pane again and again trying to turn the glass to dust. The glass panes were massive, specially designed for the dome. The glass had been designed to withstand hurricane winds, blowing debris and tree limbs flying at one-hundred miles an hour. The pane didn't notice the man's efforts, at least not the first ten times. But on the eleventh El Lobo saw a small chip fly off, the twelfth a spider webbing crack began to grow under Graham's feet. El Lobo walked backwards, putting his weight on the harness he had no fear of falling but he didn't want Graham grabbing him or his rope when he fell through the top of the dome.

He had a small remote in his hand that controlled the spool of rope that held him, he unwound the line to keep it loose while he backed up. He held the button down, he intended to unwind all the rope, it was long enough to reach the ground, though it unwound slowly.

"Oh no you don't you damn coward. I thought we'd have a good battle you and I, never knew you were just a punk." Graham bashed the pane one last time. It splintered and shattered just as he stepped off, impressive. Graham sprinted at El Lobo his face contorted in rage. Long strides, he reached El

Lobo in four, dove at him like a linebacker. El Lobo twisted, Graham flew by but managed to loop a hand through the harness. The resulting jolt snatched El Lobo off his feet and pulled them over the edge of the convex surface of the dome. Instinctively he clawed at the smooth glass to slow his descent, after consciously suppressing the urge he let them fall. Slipped over the surface, Graham swung the wrench with one hand trying to cudgel El Lobo into unconsciousness.

Their descent stopped with a jerk, they reached the limit of the rope already extended, they continued to descend slowly. El Lobo felt their combined weight straining the motor of the rope descent system. Chip, chop, choke and sputter, dropped them thirty feet in a second, then unwound slowly again. They were still a hundred feet above the ground, too far to jump yet. Twist, turn, the rope wrapped around his torso, twined around Graham's chest and ankles, bound them together.

They stopped with a jerk, again, almost bit his tongue off. Swore he heard a rib crack, they both moaned. Graham never stopped, swung his giant wrench every chance he had. El Lobo managed to keep his skull intact as they slid down the curved surface of the dome. He slid on back, head first, tried desperately to keep from being squashed like a bug.

Stop with a jerk, his chance, twisting spin, kicked out with a foot, devil's own luck, the rope uncoiled from Graham, El Lobo pried the man's hand from the harness, kicked him in the face once more for good measure, Graham slipped free and tumbled down the dome surface. At that distance from the center the dome the glass panes were nearly vertical and provided little purchase. Rope descent system choked and sputtered, gave up the ghost, stopped fighting gravity and dropped El Lobo toward the ground. He aimed toward Graham. Managed to get the man beneath him, ground rushed up to meet them. Graham first, no harness, too fast, back first. He hit the ground with a wicked thud, massive exhalation, definitely broken something. El Lobo landed on the man, feet first, on the man's stomach. Still had to roll with the fall, and knocked the wind out of him anyway. Hurriedly unbuckled the harness as fast as he could, limped off into the trees.

Any normal person would be dead, Graham was not, his chest rose and fell evenly, snarl still on his face, blood leaked from his nose and ears. He'd probably be up and after El Lobo in a minute or so. Not a bad pick by Hood, Graham was definitely not your average human being and would have made a great enforcer. El Lobo trundled away from the dome, limped for the first hundred meters before his legs stopped hurting. He switched back and forth through the wood lot, across a fallow farm field. A few workers were out, clover and sweet pea the off season cover crop carpeted the field. Nitrogen fixing plants reduced his need to fertilize in the spring and summer. The workers stopped to watch him dash across the farm field still dressed in the blue custodian jump suit. He had blood on his arms, wasn't sure if it was his or Graham's.

The plan was still working, providing Graham wasn't dead. Giant bellow behind, not dead then. El Lobo picked up the pace, time to finish this up. El Lobo knew how he was going to finish with Graham but he needed to put on a show for Hood first. Loped toward the mansion. He stopped in front of the house, next to a cherub pissing into the fountain. Huff, and puff and blow Hood's house down. Bellow behind him again, like an angry bull. Hood walked out onto the balcony wrapped tight in his bathrobe, smoked his cigar and billowed smoke like a chimney. He'd come to watch the show. That was the point, give the man what he wanted.

El lobo could make out the smug grin on Hood's face, even from this distance. Watched it fade when Graham came up the stairs five minutes later. Blood smeared the giant's face, dripped from his arm. No broken leg then but he limped with pained, teeth-grinding strides, wrench still clenched in his fist. He bellowed at El Lobo, Round three had begun. Time to give the fat bastard what he wanted. As near death Graham should have been El Lobo recognized the man was more dangerous now than ever. Wounded animal backed into a corner would skewer and trample him with adrenaline flushed muscle, ten times the strength. It would be a painful death at the hands of a mad beast that would snort and stomp on his corpse. Such was the nature of the mad frightened animal. El Lobo waited next to the fountain. Watched Graham struggle up the flight of stairs, skewer El Lobo with his eyes. The spirit was willing, but his flesh was broken and battered.

"Why don't you take a minute." El Lobo gestured to the fountain's edge, marble wall carved with irreverent cherubs. He was sincere, no sense fighting if the man couldn't stand.

"Fuck you spic coward. Why don't you stand and fight me like a man, stop all this running like a frightened little bunny." Huff and puff, his ear oozed blood, eye too.

"You're the fool Graham. There's no honor working for Hood and there is no honor in killing illegals. You should accustom yourself to having no honor, only dirty hands."

"Shut your mouth you fucking runt, I'm gonna grind you to do dust and shit on your corpse beaner fuck." Unleashed overhead smash, wrench through the air like lighting. El Lobo side-stepped, the marble edge of the fountain exploded into dust, huh, he wasn't kidding. Water from the fountain escaped onto the terra cotta tiles, running toward the stairs, stained the fired clay.

Backhand swing of the wrench, Lobo ducked, jeans and ass wet for the effort. Marble cherub atop the fountain, flaccid premature penis arcing perfect stream up and over bare breasted maidens exploded into a hundred thousand pieces. El Lobo dove from the satisfying smash, shielded his eyes to keep the dust out.

Time to give Hood the show he ordered, deep breath. He fell to the ground, raised a hand to his face, covered one eye like dust blinded him. Graham smashed a figure of Aphrodite nursing one of the cherubs, more dust. Aphrodite's head and shoulders, yaw through the air, tumbled. El Lobo dove in the direction of the bust, rolled so it looked to catch him on the shoulder, went down in a heap, dramatic flair from the soccer pitch.

Graham seized the moment, raised the wrench to strike, to crush the skull of. El Lobo rolled left, whoosh of the wrench past his ear, raised a booted foot and kicked Graham in the small of the back with the toe of his boot. Cry of pain from the hulk, Graham threw him away. He flew through the air, tumbled to a stop. Graham straightened to his full height, holding his back and grimacing, bloody portrait that, someone take a picture, he looked over his shoulder and asked.

"Are you getting this Hood?" Winked at the fat man. The fat man that was banging on the railing like he was at a sporting event and his team was losing. Madman Ramon from nowhere, danced and pranced around the fountain. Shit. The kid really was mad. In a flash he was perched on top of what remained of the fountain arms outstretched. He launched onto Graham's back, scratched and clawed at the man's head, rained blows on his ears. Graham flipped the fool to the ground, wrench ready to crush his skull.

El Lobo acted, tensed muscles, fired neurotransmitter, faster than light, before thought, message received. Dove in front of Ramon, the wrench connected with his shoulder and upper arm, felt the bone break. Hood hooted with joy from above, fat ugly bird shitting in a tree. El Lobo grunted with pain and rolled over the tiles, arm cradled. Ramon scampered off into the woods, hoot and holler of his own, mad as shit. Hood applauded from above, wiped the tears from his eyes.

Graham grimaced, leaned on the fountain, squinted at El Lobo. Well the plan wasn't ruined, he was still mobile, time to bring the thing to an end. He cradled his arm, ducked and rolled under Graham's next attack and ran in the opposite direction of Ramon. Every step sent pain up his arm. Shock dulled the pain and for that he was grateful, added urgency to his steps. His arm didn't feel attached correctly. Ground his teeth, ran as fast as he could. Heard Hood bellowing at Graham to get moving. El Lobo focused on his own labored steps, his own labored breaths. Broken and battered though he was, the plan was coming to the convoluted and circuitous end. Mud ruts, gritted teeth.

Bones rubbed jagged broken ends, nerves screamed, dulled brain muffled. Brain screams. Barn doors in front, brown and unpainted for years, back end of forgotten paddock. El Lobo's first office so to speak. The first four months in Hood's employ, when he was still just a vet this had been his office. He opened the door just a bit, slid through the crack and into the darkness. He didn't need to see, had the place memorized. This was the where, the reason why he started wearing a six-shooter. Once inside he jogged left, opened the gate and waited. Listened to hear the snort and clod hooves pass by. Slipped through the gate and closed it behind, the bull was loose. He exited through a side door and crouched behind an empty troth, just in time to see Graham slipping through the barn doors.

El Lobo limped to the barn doors and lowered the wooden beam across the outside, used his shoulder and good arm, hurt like hell. Then he heard it. The bellow of the bull. The snort, foot stomp, hurried human footsteps. He heard the insult to the bull, the bull that smelled female estrus and had come to find a human in his paddock. EL Lobo waited, listened. Graham screamed, swore at the bull, damned the beast to hell. Roar from Graham, bellow from the bull; sound of galloping hooves. Horns punctured the wooden barn door in an explosion of wooden splinters and dying scream. Horns slowly retracted, blood pooled under the door. Bellow of the bull. His name was Jack, Jack the Giant Killer. He was a good bull. Crack of bone, Graham screamed, the goring continued. The dark Hell of being skewered alive. No mercy for the wicked.

El Lobo peeked through a knot hole, nothing to see but darkness. Sound of Jack snorting, paw the earth, movement in the darkness, crunch of bone, snort of bull. Horned heard pressed against Graham's sternum, crushed his chest, skewered lungs. El Lobo didn't need to see, it sounded right. The giant was dead. Time to settle up with Hood, once and for all.

Chapter 34

Everyone's everything

He hobbled, dragged, limped his way back to Hood's, same way he'd come, little less round about. His arm was broken, felt clean enough. Better than smashed into a million pieces. No broken skin either. Damn Goliath Graham was crossing the river Styx now, thank goodness. He slung his arm across his chest with some cloth he pulled from the barn. Thank heaven for shock. Better to get things finished before the shock wore off, the pain would handicap him once it kicked in. Slid through the hedgerow of privet onto the grounds, down the drive. So cliché it was comical. Hood started taking pot shots at him as soon as he walked up the marble steps on the front lawn.

Frolicking cherubs were destroyed and dust, bullet rang off shoulder of already shattered and headless child-like figure. Rough day for the stone sculptures at Hood's house. It didn't seem like Hood was aiming, he stood at the railing, at least the man had clothes on, squeezed off rounds. Hood fumbled the pistol, dropped it over the edge, ran inside, started firing what sounded like a rifle inside the house. Jose wasn't even all the way up the steps yet. Rifle shot, closer, whizzed by his ear. Whew, a feint then, Hood was going for the kill after all. Maybe the man wasn't completely mad.

El Lobo shuffled and ducked under the portico, still heard shots inside the house. He crouched and picked up Hood's fallen pistol, resisted the urge to look around for the camera crew, resisted the urge to belly laugh and shake his head. Too cliché for words. Three shots left in the .38. He'd only need one. Hood behaved like a mad man but El Lobo knew better. The man was not to be trusted, ever, under any circumstance. The pistol would have to do.

He made his way inside to the sound of Hood's ricochet madness. Snaked his way through the house lower floor, stayed away from the stairs and random bullet. Into the garage when the man finally reloaded, ascended the iron spiral staircase that led into Hood's bedroom closet. Slow and steady as he could, no sound managed; not that the madman could hear a damn thing up there, firing his gun everywhere. Reached the top. Poked his head through. The closet was empty but the door was wide open. He paused for a five count, she walked by on three. Naughty nurse with an Uzi equip. Yikes.

Firm ass and black heels, black thong disappeared into the imagination. Yum. She saw him from the corner of her eye and spun, already firing. Rapid staccato incomplete sentence of fired Uzi nearly blew his head off.

El Lobo dropped from his perch, fell onto his back, painfully. Fired a shot of his own. Only one, he didn't have many. Tears welled in his eyes, broken bones rubbed in his arm. He'd fired through the ceiling, sent one bullet through the floor of Hood's closet. Lay on his back, caught his breath. Back up the stairs. Slower the second time. No sounds above. He pushed the hatch open, dumb move, if someone was waiting he'd end up with a bullet between his eyes. There she lay in pool of blood on the floor of Hood's closet. Open eyes stared at his entrance, dead and slumped next to the hatch, bullet hole in her head, so cliché it was absurd. He left her on her stomach, oversized breasts pressed into the shiny shoes in the closet. Poor thing. Knelt on one knee, peaked around the corner. Nearly lost his head, again.

Shots exploded the sheet rock and wood wall, ripped out a large chunk, ejected dust and destruction in a violent contraction of focused kinetic energy. More shots exploded the bathroom beyond the closet entrance, end of the hall, sound of broken glass on tile floor.

"I see you you bastard!" More shots, Hood was shooting blind. El Lobo grabbed the fallen Uzi, aimed it around the corner, fired in the direction of Hood, rapid fire, three bursts. He released the trigger, walked through the haze of exploded upholstery, atomized wall board and shredded wood into the room. Eviscerated leather couches, armchair, windows, mold-ing, bar stools. He didn't seem to have hit Hood, who was huddled on the floor in a ball. Hood opened his eyes and looked up when he heard glass crunch under El Lobo's boot.

Pot shot whizzed by El Lobo's head, he side stepped deftly, pistol whipped the man in the temple and took his gun. On his knees and sniveling. Bloodied and beaten at last they would end the affair.

Jose Jesus Martinez held the pistol to Globe's head.

"I fucked your wife and daughter Globe. And they both love me." He choked on the last words, tears rising to his eyes, he couldn't believe the heat in his words, heat in his chest. Globe laughed, as if advantage had shifted. Never mind the pistol to his head.

"Yeah, well I fucked your wife too, but you know that. I guess that's what happens when two people like us know each other long enough, eventually you fuck everyone's everything, eh? That is why I always win, you sot. That heart you think you killed is still thinking for you. Not even your prick would be as dumb, your heart, give me a break. They may both love you but what is a woman's love worth? At what cost? What ruin have you made of your life for the love of two cowardly women? Neither will come to your aide. One is dead and the other waits your rescue instead. Don't forget you spic bastard, I Fucked Isa..." He choked on the last, barrel in his mouth. El Lobo shot him in the head. Brain and skull, pool of blood.

Chapter 35

The Protest

Jose Jesus Martinez became to be known as El Lobo Maldito, the Damn Wolf. Damned he was, damned he had been, damned he would be forever. However he had come to be known, he felt blessed when he left Hood's mansion behind. He hobbled through brush and bramble, a wounded and broken animal. Reached the edge of the property and the protest. He heard the rhythmic chants and the honking of cars before too long.

She was there, wearing her read cloak, really playing the part. She separated from the marching throng and the infinite conga line that circled back on itself to forever. She ran to him, he stumbled into her chest, almost ready to be done. He didn't have it in him to take another step. He'd have to be carried out.

"It's okay baby, oh my god. We need to get you to the hospital." She sounded calm.

"Your father is dead Katherine. I killed him. I'm sorry." She stared at him with tears in her eyes, buried her head in his chest, wept. He stroked her hair with his good arm, pushed her away softly. Pointed. Blue unmarked four door sedan, behind that black, green, white ones, behind that the cops, DEA, ICE and the cavalry had arrived at last. They'd be pulling the place apart for weeks. It would be a terrible mess. Well they chose the right day to show up.

Scream from the crowd, scream of rage, scream of desperation, Isabella's scream. He watched Katherine's eyes, grown wide, mouth open to shout, time slowed. Widening of her eyes, contracting face muscles to fear and terror. She reached smooth delicate arm toward him, her red cloak cinched at the elbows. Isabella pierced his back with the machete, blood splattered across his chin and lips, she pulled it back out. Fat droplets stained Katherine's face, soaked into her hood. El Lobo Maldito. If Isabella couldn't have him no one would. The bastard. He fell to his knees, the pretty young thing screamed, cupped his blood covered face and glazed eyes. Rattle and cough, blood streamed from his eyes, he slumped forward onto Katherine. And now he would belong to none. Isabella fell to the ground and the two women wept, surrounded by protesters, blood and mud.

Just like in the story, the Wolf had been cut open after all. Blood on the concrete, blood in the grass. Tear the heart out of them. Stop and stare, silence of the dead, in awe of the phenomenal. He bled after all, the stone that bleeds, perhaps one could get blood from a stone. Katherine grabbed him in her arms, his head on her lap, weeping moans bubbling up from her chest, like the bloody bubbles covering his mouth. Isabella collapsed next to them, screaming and pulling at her hair. El Lobo stroked Katherine's face, bloody streak down her cheek, matched her cloak and hood, she'd worn the red one for the protest, playing her part as she'd said. El Lobo pulled her head to his mouth, whispered something in her ear. Her salty tears drizzled onto his face, she wailed louder, screamed as loud as she could, over and over. She stroked his face, kissed his lips. With his other hand he found Isabella's knee, found her hand, held it, pulled her to him, put the hand on his chest, stroked her face too, bloody smear, gurgle. He exhaled his last breath. The two women howled at the moon. He was gone.

The protest stopped. Picketing workers, illegal and legal gathered in an ever widening circle around the fallen mythical figure, one of them, embodiment of light and dark, good and bad, a living legend was dead. The best and worst of the American Dream, the American experience, bought and sold to the highest bidder, stab your brother in the back for profit, spit in the eye of the storm, capitalist bastards sent to hell. Redemption is painful, like giving birth, like molting, breaking out of a chrysalis, out of a shell. Turn over a new leaf sounded too easy, failed to capture the tithe of blood, the pound of flesh payment, the inevitable tears and the constant, ubiquitous sweat. Resolution, mantra, decision made, strip you naked and flay you. Rawhide bull whip on naked flesh, peel it off, re-dig the well, put the flesh back on. Doesn't always fit quite right after, no matter how hard you shove it in.

There were no heroes in the hell of being skinned alive. No stoicism, only suffering, scream and writhe, sweat on the brow, disemboweled while alive. Check the intestines, shove them back in, any which way will do. Sacrificial chicken in one of Isabella's rites, squirting blood and running legs. Free at last, free at last. Do as I say, not as I do. Vibrations of the universe, ride the tide, hang ten on the cosmic wave, neither created or destroyed.

Dark energy, dark matter, pass through, exists within, on top, overlapping with it all. Build on top of build. Soil deposits on top of soil, trapped critters become fossils, plankton becomes oil, becomes coal, becomes. Change is constant, human time, geological time, cosmic time. Eye blink of the cosmic watchers. Happens so fast you could miss it. Maybe the cosmic entity, deity, powers that be, blinked. He/She/It/They/We missed the rise of man from monkey, monkey to monster. Spin through the cosmos, Milky Way galaxy, dust bunny under the cosmic coffee table, lost and forgotten, can't get the broom under there, life of its own. Good thing the cosmic cleaners don't do a very good job, end up in a vacuum bag with the rest of the dust. Something grand, something great, something bigger than man, more knowing, more powerful, more creationary. Maybe. Or maybe a cosmic careening, crash and smash. Fender bender, star crash, molten rock, vacuum of space, wonder of wonders. Must be a cosmic rock star behind it all, God of Gods, alpha and omega, beginning and the end.

Had a nice ring to it, cosmic rock star; made all the sense in the universe of celestial bodies. Rocks and stars, stars and rocks, infinity to the end of the universe and nothing beyond. Dark matter, dark energy, whirling pool of chaos. Chain of glittering stars, twinkle-twinkle, burn hotter than the mind can comprehend. Beautiful from far, deadly up close. Systems large and small, solar system and atom. So alike, so different, atomic blast and super nova. Gamma-ray blast to nothingness. Dark matter, dark energy, like spirits, they're everywhere. Perhaps they're one and the same.

Dark and light, white and black, good and bad, heads and tails, one and zero, is and is not. Perhaps neither is true. Neither good nor bad but an oscillation through visible and invisible, tangible and ephemeral, dark energy and light energy. Can't see it to believe it, have to believe it to see it. Put that in your pipe and smoke it. Roll it in a cigar and puff on it, tastier than the tastiest Cuban.

With change, with shifting reality we confront the third state, the transitory state, the shade of gray, the forgotten space, the middle path, neither this nor that but both. Not heads or tails, not zero or one, not plus or minus, not black or white, not positive or negative, not dark or light, but something in-between. What lies between? Do not forget the in-between. The nice becomes the naughty, and the wicked becomes the righteous. Topsy-turvy, world on its head, blow your mind. Grand Finale, death spiral of the American Dream. It was a horrific crash, many casualties, only few survivors. ICU, respirator, IV, EKG, American Dream on life support. Stabbed through the back by a nameless attacker, couldn't see his face, only his nice suit and expensive shoes. Lying and dying, blood and mud. Farm field, back alley of Wall St., CPR, mouth to mouth, triage until the ICU. A rift in the chest of, a chasm of widening want, open mouths and clamoring voices of those that need. Alms for the poor, seems there are so many these days, a tale of three Americas, this side, that side, the middle.

Like El Lobo, stabbed through the back by a woman he loved, the American Dream suffocated on bloody gurgle, bloody bubbles, death throes, rushed nowhere. Bleed out onto the American heartland, fertilized the fields of fly over farms, enriched with blood meal, amendments ground and squeezed from the American people. Blood from a stone fertilized the Earth, may the fruits of prosperity and wealth tower to the sky and rain profits on us all, Amen. We the people are that stone, the people are the soil, the people are the tree, squeezed the blood from us. Till the soil until the bloody amendment is thoroughly mixed. Ground, blended American Dream planted in loam soil rich with blood yields prosperity for some and equality for none. God Bless America.

Blood from a stone. The stone, the foundation, the footer on which the whole United States experiment was built, complete with towering skyscrapers and interstate highways. Built on the limestone, granite bedrock and fragipan of the American immigrant. Every last one of them gave something to this place. The navigating Norse, the slave holding Brits, the fleeing Christians, the damn Spanish, all the chained Africans, the exiled Irish, the fleet footed first people. The stone footer of our pressed flesh leached contaminants into the psychic reservoir of our American experience. Leached out our hope, filled us with ferrous frustration, suffocated us under the sediment of sorrow. Forced to accept our crushed American Dream. Tainted is the aquifer of our collective conscious. Rest in peace, buried in a stone tomb. Do not put it in the ground or they will put something on top of the body. Strip mall and parking lot, car wash or fast food joint.

Glittering shiny metal and glass built atop our entombed American Dream. The ignorant worship sacrilegious monuments to the power of progress, the sacrifice of the many for the good of the few. Ghosts of the crushed immigrant haunt the outlet malls, boutiques, corporate board room. Too bad no one is listening. Choose your side or it will be assigned for you, as all things important the choice is never easy. This side, that side, the middle.

www.ingramcontent.com/pod-product-compliance
Lightning Source LLC
Chambersburg PA
CBHW070053030726
47506CB00002B/456